A Colin McD[illegible]

When a war ends, the killing doesn't always stop

Ridley's War

Jim Napier

From Britain, America, Canada, and Australia comes Praise for the Colin McDermott series

"A riveting procedural...Napier layers his story with subplots and suspense."

Kirkus Reviews

"A richly detailed and multi-layered mystery that keeps the reader guessing until the very last page."

Montreal Review of Books

"Mystery fans will not be disappointed. Legacy is up there with the best."

Quebec Chronicle-Telegraph

"A classic British whodunit, reminiscent of the Golden Age. Napier depicts the bitter rivalry of academia, and writes with dry wit and crisp dialogue."

Cath Staincliffe, award-winning and bestselling author of the *Sal Kilkenny, Janine Lewis,* and the *Scott and Bailey* series

"Napier writes a sharp narrative with a clear, crisp style, drawing readers straight into the intrigue."

Peter James, Cartier Diamond-Dagger winning author of the bestselling *Superintendent Roy Grace* novels

"A carefully crafted police procedural, with characters whose voices stay in the memory."

Michael Rose, author of *Interpol Confidential*

"A hint of Colin Dexter in the air. Napier writes unique characters in a vivid setting. His sly humor makes Inspector McDermott a very warm and likeable protagonist."

Phyllis Smallman, multiple award-winning author of the *Sherry Travis* and the *Singer Brown* mystery series

"If you like Dalgleish, you'll love Inspector Colin McDermott, an unflappable, stoic Brit with a warm heart and a professional's eye. Napier's London is 21st-century cosmopolitan, while his St. Gregory's College is an amiable throwback to the cloistered world of eccentric—and perhaps deadly—academics. Rich, textured, atmospheric writing with sensitively-rendered three-dimensional characters that keep you turning the pages. The writing is first rate."

Eric Brown, author of the Arthur Ellis Award finalist *Almost Criminal*

"Very well written, the English setting and the characters utterly believable. Colin McDermott is a most attractive character, the kind of man you always want to know."

Maureen Jennings, award-winning and bestselling author of the *Detective Murdoch* series, filmed for television as the *Murdoch Mysteries,* and the *DI Tom Tyler* series

"Addictive reading. The story draws you in and keeps you hooked till the ending you never saw coming. Set in the dysfunctional halls of British academia, Napier nails it with a great story [and] wonderfully compelling characters that stay with you long after the book is finished."

Peter Kirby, winner of the Arthur Ellis Award for Best Novel for 2016 for *Open Season*

Advance Praise for Ridley's War

"From the battlefields of Italy to a regimental reunion in Yorkshire, Napier weaves an intricate tale of murder, theft, [and] betrayal."

Ottawa Review of Books

"*Ridley's War* reminds us that death so often has deep roots. It's another fast-moving case for that likeable cop Colin McDermott, whose enquiry into a suspicious death takes him to Italy, and [to] events of the past which have a chilling impact on the present."

Martin Edwards, author of *Gallows Court,* and winner of the Edgar, Agatha, and Macavity Awards and the Margery Allingham Prize

"An intricately plotted, propulsive story that pulls the reader along to an unexpected conclusion."

David C. Taylor, author of *Night Life,* nominated for the Edgar Allan Poe Award for Best Novel of 2016

"Stepping into the past, *Ridley's War* investigates how events from the Second World War could be linked to a brutal attack on a decorated veteran decades later. The story is intriguing, the writing adroit, and Napier has created a vivid universe that spans Yorkshire, Italy, and London. Napier has written another classic puzzler."

Ann Shortell, multiple award-winning author of *Celtic Knot* and finalist for the Crime Writers of Canada's Unhanged Arthur Award for 2017

"Napier's clear-eyed exploration of the depths of human greed and the power of a son's love for his aging father is rendered with tenderness and great beauty."

Gail Bowen, award-winning author of the *Joanne Kilbourn Shreve* mystery series

"From the opening page, *Ridley's War* invites you into a world so well drawn and believable that you want to stay there and hang out with the characters. The sense of time and place is impeccable [and] as an ex-pat Brit I found the dialect totally authentic. Highly recommended!"

Maureen Jennings, award-winning and bestselling author of the Detective Murdoch series, filmed for television as the *Murdoch Mysteries*

"Tightly written and gripping from the very first page, Napier has created distinctive and engaging characters who capture our interest immediately...Napier leaves us with a cliffhanger; readers will be eager for Colin McDermott's next adventure."

Anne Emery, creator of the *Collins and Burke* mystery series, and twice winner of the Arthur Ellis Award for Best Crime Novel of the Year

A Colin McDermott Mystery

WHEN A WAR ENDS THE KILLING DOESN'T ALWAYS STOP

Ridley's War

JIM NAPIER

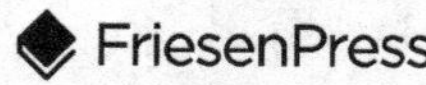

Suite 300 - 990 Fort St
Victoria, **BC, V8V 3K2**
Canada

www.friesenpress.com

First Edition — 2020

This is a work of fiction. All names, characters, places and incidents are the product of the author's imagination, or are used fictitiously. Any resemblance to actual persons, characters, organisations or event is entirely coincidental.

ISBN
978-1-5255-5309-7 (Hardcover)
978-1-5255-5310-3 (Paperback)
978-1-5255-5311-0 (eBook)

1. FICTION / MYSTERY & DETECTIVE / TRADITIONAL

Distributed to the trade by The Ingram Book Company

Dedication

To the memory of the many men and women who went off to defend their country and their way of life during World War II, and especially to the memory of those who did not return; and to Whisky, who made us laugh and enriched our lives.

Out of evil some good may come.

Prologue

Southern Italy, 1943

*The **platoon moved steadily** up the mountain road in two columns, alert for any sounds apart from the incessant drumming of the rain. But they heard nothing except their own footsteps in the mud and the rustling of their rubber rain gear.*

Rounding a bend in the road, they reached a broad expanse of gravelled drive with an imposing villa at the end. It looked to be at least two centuries old, but it might have been much older. An elaborately-carved wooden door was flanked on either side by tall windows that were enclosed by faded lavender shutters that complemented the pale-yellow plaster walls of the large house. Above the entrance, shallow wrought-iron balconies graced the windows of the upper floor, capped by a gently-sloped, terracotta-tiled roof, ubiquitous to Italy.

The officer at the head of the group paused and turned to the other men, using hand signals to gesture silently. One column of men took up defensive positions in the undergrowth on the far side of the road. The other remained on the near side, crouched at the base of a low wall, out of sight of anyone who might be watching from the villa.

He held up two fingers, then motioned forward, and the two men closest to him fell in behind as he moved cautiously up the drive toward the front door. As they reached the shallow steps he signalled the men to the side and listened for any signs of life within. He motioned for them to drop their rain gear, then he slowly turned the ornate iron ring, and using the barrel of his Sten gun, pushed the door ajar. Though heavy, it moved silently on its hinges, and swung open easily. Although it was mid-morning, the interior was shrouded in darkness, the shutters cutting off most of the light, heavy draperies completing the job.

The officer waited for his eyes to adjust to the gloom, then entered the hall noiselessly, indicating that the two soldiers should follow him. Once inside they moved into a large salon, at least thirty feet in length and nearly as wide. Although the furniture was obscured by large dust covers they could make out some shapes, including two large sofas, several overstuffed chairs, what appeared to be a library table, and a concert grand piano in a far corner. As their eyes adjusted to the light they were startled momentarily by a human form. They trained their guns on it, then realised it was a large sculpture, nearly life-size. The officer's gaze swept the room. There were pieces of expensive antique furniture and valuable artworks everywhere. Clearly this was a family of some importance.

The salon was flanked by more rooms on the left side and at the rear, and in the entrance hall an ornate staircase on the right led to the upper floors. The officer motioned to the two men to check out the ground-floor rooms as he ascended the steps.

As he reached the landing the officer stared down the darkened hallway, aware that he was very much on his own. If anyone were here they would have a definite advantage. At the end of the hallway a window had been left unshuttered, and the glare from the light that poured in made it all the more difficult to make out details nearer him. He could see a small table halfway down the hall, with a large vase on it, bereft of flowers, and another hallway leading off to the right. On both sides of the corridor large oil paintings hung in elaborate gilt frames, dark and apparently very old. He checked the door nearest him. It was unlocked, and he pushed on it. The door opened silently and he peered inside. A large four-poster bed was flanked by a dressing table with a mirror on the wall above, and on the other side a wardrobe, and a chair placed near the window.

The officer closed the door and moved to the next room. That door, too, was closed. When he pushed on it, the hinges squeaked, and he stiffened involuntarily, listening intently. Nothing. He pushed the door further with the barrel of his gun and stepped inside, his eyes adjusting once more to the gloom. He was perspiring now, his breathing heavy and his nerves raw.

He was about to leave when he caught the slightest suggestion of movement out of the corner of his eye. His reaction was immediate: he turned his Sten gun in that direction and fired, one long burst, then two shorter ones. One figure dropped immediately, the other cried out, then dropped as well. After that, there were no sounds. The smell of spent ammunition and smoke filled the room.

Shouting from below, then a racket on the stairs told him that his men were coming on the double. He crossed the room and pushed open the drapes to see what he had done. On the floor near the wardrobe, two people lay dead. A man and a woman, both elderly, but well dressed. The owners of the villa, very likely.

For the second time in as many minutes the officer's blood ran cold. He had panicked and killed two civilians, people of substance at that. There would have to be an enquiry. He had no witnesses to the dark, to his fear, to his many months of fighting an enemy that was unambiguously trying to kill him. None of that would matter now.

ONE

Outside Manchester, 2004

The large lorry inched its way along the M62, the driver tapping his fingers impatiently on the wheel. The rain was pelting down, making visibility difficult. He glanced at his watch: twenty minutes behind schedule already, and at least another forty minutes to go. The boss wouldn't be happy. He reached in his pocket for his mobile, then stopped himself; best to have some good news before he phoned.

The line of traffic began to move a little more quickly—still far too slowly for his liking. In the distance he could make out flashing coloured lights and a tangle of cars and trucks. Several minutes later a uniformed officer in a hi-viz jacket directed him into a single lane that had been cleared, and he saw the cause of the problem. A car had missed the slip road and tried to back up. Big mistake. The driver following him apparently had been inattentive, and had swerved to avoid him. A large lorry in the overtaking lane hadn't been able to slow down in time. At least half a dozen cars and trucks had been caught up in the resulting turmoil. Most had been lucky; some hadn't. One car was a smouldering mass of tangled metal, the ambulance just leaving with its grim cargo. Flashers off. No need to hurry.

Once past the accident scene the pace picked up. The van merged onto the M60, the ring road that skirted Manchester. Again, the driver glanced at his watch: half an hour late now, he reckoned. Ignoring the lesson of the scene he'd just passed, he put his foot down.

Before long the van reached the Parkway and headed for the Trafford Park Road. The driver was pleased: he'd made better time than he'd expected. He frowned as the mobile in the pocket of his coveralls rang.

'Aye?' he answered. 'No. Some bloody git's gone and killed hisself on the ring road north o' city. Stopped traffic for miles.' He paused. 'Aye. 'Bout another ten minutes, I reckon. Right, then.' He rang off.

The light was fading as the driver pulled his lorry onto the aging industrial estate and noticed a police traffic unit parked near the entrance. He eased up on the pedal. Best not to attract attention. He passed a small import-export business and a builder's yard housing some heavy equipment, and drove up to a large grey brick building with grimy windows at the top and a small office to one side. He sounded the horn and after a moment a man in blue coveralls appeared and walked over to his door, wiping his hands on an oily rag. Stitched on the breast of his coveralls was the name *Gary*. 'Where the hell have you been? We've been expecting you for best part of an hour!'

'You think I'm happy 'bout it?' the driver growled. 'Can't do nowt about friggin' road accidents, can I? Stupid git won't be causing any more, though, that's for sure. Now open the door so we can get done and go home, eh?'

The man on the ground scowled, but didn't budge. 'Here, you ain't the regular bloke. Who are you, then, and what's happened to Tony?'

The driver looked down at the man, none too pleased. 'Name's George. Tony came down sick yesterday, sudden-like. Spewed his guts all over the floor. His wife's cookin' I don't doubt. Woman's a menace. Spent all night in the bog, he did. Asked me to fill in for 'im. We're mates; used to work together 'afore he got sent down. Now are we going to stand here playing silly buggers all night, or get on with it?'

Gary looked him over carefully. Black hair with more than a few traces of grey, combed straight back, and in need of a cut. Large, greasy hands, with dirty nails. The man's coveralls were stained with oil, and he needed a bath and a shave as well. Deciding the man passed muster, he motioned to someone standing at a grimy office window above. A large overhead door began to rise. The driver put his truck into gear and lurched forward.

As he entered the shop floor he passed several cars being worked on by perhaps a dozen men. Some were being disassembled, others being readied for repainting. He found an empty bay toward the back and pulled into it, coming to a stop mere inches from a set of stairs leading up to the office overlooking the shop floor. Checking that his mobile was still in his pocket he got down from the cab and made his way to the back of the van.

'You want to be careful with this one,' the driver said. 'It's a nice motor, that is.'

The man motioned to two workers, who dropped what they were doing and wheeled a steel ramp over to the rear of the lorry. Gary swung open the doors. Inside was a sleek, black Lamborghini Gallardo, elegant and pristine. Or almost. The front cowl contained a large scrape where it had brushed against the wall of the truck during loading.

'What's this, then?' He looked at the driver accusingly.

'Nowt to do with me. You know the drill. I just drive the truck. It's chained down, innit? That way when I picked up the truck.'

Gary glared at him, then he turned to the others. 'All right, get it out of there. Nothing we can't deal with.'

The driver breathed a silent sigh of relief, then felt for hisphone in his jacket pocket. He found the button in the upper right corner and pressed it.

A few moments later all hell broke loose.

TWO

The chaos on the shop floor was drowned out by the deafening grate of metal against metal as a large front-end loader crashed through the overhead door and skidded to a stop, narrowly missing a youth who flung himself across the bonnet of the car he'd been working on. A dozen members of an Armed Response Team wearing black stab vests and helmets poured through the opening, guns drawn, closely followed by even more uniformed officers, also armed. There was pandemonium as the workers scattered in all directions, yelling and throwing anything to hand at their pursuers. A young female officer singled out Gary and ran toward him with her baton. He picked up a large spanner from a nearby tool chest and raised his arm, only to find himself in George's iron grip. 'Easy now, mate. Don't want to do summat silly, do we?' The man known as Gary simply glared at him, pure hatred pouring from his eyes.

Thirty minutes later Gary and the rest of the gang had been led away in custody and loaded into two police vans. A forensics team moved in and set to work recording everything on video recorders and fingerprinting the cars and tools. Other officers were busy seizing a computer and mobile phones collected from the gang members and sifting through the waste bins, logging and bagging various bits of evidence. A man in plainclothes came up to the driver. 'Well done, George. I've been talking to the brief from the Home Office, and he says it appears the rest of the raids went off without a hitch. We've got all we need to shut down this bunch. A good day's work.'

"THIS BUNCH" WAS AN INTERNATIONAL GANG OF CAR THIEVES who had been operating throughout the EU for the past three years. They had established a lucrative business stealing luxury cars and high-end off-road vehicles and disposing of them as parts, or to buyers abroad who didn't ask too many questions. What made this operation unique was their method of laundering the cars intact. They would locate other, similar vehicles on the street or at dealers, and photograph the manufacturer's number plate just behind the windscreen, then reproduce a copy that they installed in the stolen vehicle. If the car was stopped by the police the manufacturer's number would not appear on a list of stolen vehicles. They even stole to order: if someone wanted a car that was especially difficult to find, they would send a well-dressed potential customer to ask a dealer for a test drive, take an imprint of the key whilst it was in their possession, and steal the car from the dealer a few days later. After generating supporting paperwork the gang could confidently pass their cars through customs to buyers in Russia and the oil-rich Middle East.

The operation had gone better than expected. Police in the UK and on the continent and elsewhere had coordinated their raids and managed to catch the big boys napping. Soon their legal counsel would no doubt be throwing up all the obstacles at their command, but so far it looked as though the evidence would satisfy any jury. A good day's work, though it had been many months in the planning.

As they made their way back to London George said, 'Ah can't wait to get out o' these clothes. Right full o' grease, they are, and fragrant with it.'

'A shame,' McDermott chided him. 'They suit you. You could have been born a lorry driver.'

'Very funny, guv.' He gave his boss a withering look. 'Next time you try it, and Ah'll take the jammy role.'

McDermott laughed. 'Was that a pun?'

Ridley sat in silence for the rest of the trip.

When they arrived at the Charing Cross Police Station in London George Ridley made directly for his locker and a change of clothes, then disappeared into a shower room. Thirty minutes later he emerged showered and clean-shaven, hands washed and hair combed, in an undistinguished business suit, the only trace of his former appearance being a small grease smudge on his hastily-knotted tie. He headed for his desk in the CID suite and a coffee-maker perched on a nearby table. 'Now then,' he said, after filling his cup and taking a long drink, 'Ah'd best get to the paperwork on this.'

McDermott eyed his colleague and looked out the window at the gathering gloom. 'It's getting late. It can wait until Monday. You've made a good job of it. Why don't we call it a day?'

Ridley cast him a scornful glance. 'Meybe for some folk. But some of us 'ave other fish t' fry. Ah'm headed to Yorkshire Sunday for my dad's regiment's reunion, as you well know.'

McDermott looked at the duty board. 'Of course. Sorry, George. What with wrapping up this bust I'd totally forgotten.' He looked at the small mountain of paperwork before him. 'Yes, I'm afraid your evidence will be important to the prosecution. You know the faces, and can connect the transporter with the receiver. Best to get it done tonight. The Crown Prosecution Service will want to get started on the court case whilst you're away.' Noticing his colleague's dismay, he added, 'I have to pop upstairs to see Galbraith for a moment, but when I return I'll give you a hand.'

Ridley, who disliked computers and hated writing reports even more, rewarded him with a grin.

McDermott walked to the end of the corridor to the office of DCI Derek Galbraith. As he expected, even though it was late on a Friday afternoon, he was still at his desk going through staffing reports. A substantial man with wavy brown hair and matching brown eyes, he had been McDermott's immediate senior officer since he'd arrived at Charing Cross as a fast-tracked Detective Sergeant seven years earlier.

The door was open, and McDermott paused before entering the room. 'Afternoon, Colin. You look rather pleased with yourself. So how did Operation Mandy go?' He motioned for McDermott to take a chair.

McDermott winced as he sat down. The code names for major police operations were, he knew, generated randomly by a computer, and the investigation had been assigned the incongruous name Mandy. To McDermott it sounded more like a vice operation in Soho.

'Went like clockwork, sir,' McDermott replied, bringing himself back to the moment. 'We caught our lot red-handed, with the goods on the premises. We also seized a laptop and several mobile phones that the lads in forensics are having a field day with. The CPS solicitor said it was a good bust, and should hold up well in court. George did himself proud. He stopped a young PC from getting her head bashed in with a spanner. I should think there's a commendation in there somewhere.'

Galbraith looked up, pleased. He knew that Ridley had taken McDermott under his wing when the younger officer had arrived fresh from Police College. 'Put the details in your report and I'll look into it. Well done, Colin. The Chief Super will be pleased. These Joint Force Operations can be tricky.'

'Any news on the other raids, sir?'

'Early days yet, but the word is that things went well in Liverpool, Marseilles, and Dubai, not so well in Prague. Not surprising, really. Lots of Russian money greasing the wheels there. I expect you'll learn more at Interpol next week.'

McDermott stared at him. 'Excuse me?'

Galbraith smiled. 'You had a key role in setting this up—at least the regional operation involving Leeds and Manchester. Good opportunity for you to get your feet wet in the deep end of the pool, learn how things work at the planning stages, and make a few friends along the way.'

McDermott was still processing the information. 'But surely that's a task for a more senior officer. Shouldn't you be going yourself?'

'Part of your on-the-job training, Colin.' He sat back in his desk chair. 'Comes with being fast-tracked. You're earmarked for bigger things.' He handed McDermott a folder of A4 sheets. 'Here's the agenda for the Interpol meetings. You'll need to assess what we learned for future such operations: who are the strong players around the table that we can count on, and who we might want to avoid the next time around. You can look it over on your flight. Your airline and hotel reservations for Lyon are at the back. You leave Sunday afternoon, and the sessions begin Monday morning, whilst events are still fresh in peoples' minds. I'm told that Lyon is the gastronomic mecca of France. Good chance for you to check it out. I'm sure someone there can recommend a suitable restaurant.' Noticing McDermott's expression, he said, 'Don't look so shocked. You've earned it.'

McDermott had mixed feelings. After working the car-theft ring all hours for the past three months he'd been hoping to spend some time at home with his wife Anna and their daughter.

THREE

George Ridley was not a happy man. First he'd had to rummage through a dozen boxes in the gloom of his attic, each one laden with the accumulated dust of decades. When at last he had found what he'd been looking for, he'd pulled the box from amongst a stack of others, spilling their contents over the attic floor, prompting a query from his wife Dora, one floor below, whether he'd broken anything. In fact he had, and she would not be pleased: a framed photograph of their wedding, taken over thirty years ago, lay on the floor, its glass shattered as Ridley had trod on it whilst trying unsuccessfully to prevent other boxes from tumbling down. Nothing that couldn't be fixed, though.

Ridley opened the box and peered inside. The contents gave off the fragrance, if that was the word, of musty wool and camphor. He pulled a khaki-coloured field jacket from the cardboard carton and spread it out on the top of a larger box, examining it for signs that the moths had got at it. But apparently the mothballs had done their work: the jacket seemed intact. The campaign ribbons and medals, too, seemed little affected by the years. The ribbons were perhaps a bit faded and the medals slightly tarnished, but with a toothbrush and some Brasso they would clean up fine.

Ridley stripped off the cardigan he was wearing and unbuttoned the jacket, slipping first one arm in, and then the other. The problem came when he attempted to do up the buttons. The jacket might have remained unchanged over the years, but the same couldn't be said for George. He strained to bring the two sides together, but it wasn't going to happen. When at last he'd managed to fasten one button, the cotton thread broke under the strain, and the button shot across the room, coming to rest in the darkness.

Uttering an oath, he sought out the errant button. Perhaps Dora could do something with it. He checked the trousers and found the situation was even more bleak. There was no way he was going to squeeze his bulk into those trousers. Ridley sighed. He would have to attend the reunion in civvies.

Truth be told, Ridley generally avoided military reunions. Too much talk of the "good old days," which to George's mind had often been anything but good. But this one was different: his dad's regimental reunion, marking the sixtieth anniversary of D-Day—and likely the last such event for many of the men who had served in World War II. Almost all survivors were in their mid-eighties or nineties now, their numbers getting smaller every year. George had missed the big one, the fiftieth anniversary of D-Day in 1994, when a spate of murders in London meant he'd been unable to get leave, and he knew that it meant a lot to his dad to get together with his chums. It also meant a lot to both of them that George had served in the same regiment nearly thirty years later. So not going this time around was not an option.

After ruminating on his dilemma Ridley removed the campaign ribbons and medals from his jacket. At least he could pin them to his suit jacket and wear them for the Adjutant's Parade. Uniform or not, the regiment always liked its veterans to show off their medals.

When he came downstairs, Dora was just pouring him a cup of tea. 'Your breakfast is ready, love,' she said, motioning to the table. 'Did you find what you were looking for?'

'Ah reckon,' Ridley grunted, holding up the trousers. 'But they need your hand.'

'Oh, dear,' she smiled, not quite suppressing a smile. 'It's been a good long while since you've had those on.' She took them and looked at the seams. 'Not enough material to let them out, I'm afraid. What are you going to do?'

'Ah'll just 'ave t' go in civvies' he replied, showing her the medals. 'Reckon you could give these a polish?'

BY LATE MONDAY MORNING Colin McDermott found himself at Interpol headquarters in Lyon, seated in a large conference room with mid- and senior-level officers from most of the EU member states, plus a sprinkling of representatives from countries in South and Central America, Asia and the Middle East. Interpol had grown, and not always with happy results. The diversity of nations—Interpol counted 131 member states at the moment—meant that certain governments were less than willing to share their information with others, a fact that often frustrated efforts to coordinate activities across national borders. But progress was being made, and the working groups dealing with organized crime and stolen motor vehicles, combined with Interpol's recently-expanded database for sharing information, had helped McDermott and his counterparts successfully bring down the car-theft ring.

As his turn came and he summarised the results of the recent British raids, McDermott glanced around the room. There were a few familiar faces, but most were new to him. As Galbraith had said, face-to-face contact was always important: making new contacts and renewing established connections, informally sharing concerns and laying the groundwork for future operational liaisons. So he casually surveyed his colleagues around the table, trying to put names to faces, and was surprised to notice one man intently studying him. The man didn't seem familiar, and although he tried, McDermott couldn't place him.

So at noon, as McDermott collected his lunch tray and sat down in the dining room, he was not surprised to find that a moment later the man sat down opposite him.

'A fine presentation, Inspector McDermott,' the man said, smiling. 'I don't believe we have met, at least in person. I am Frans Decker, of the Belgian Federal Police. You may recall that a few years ago your Art and Antiques Squad cooperated on the disappearance of several paintings from a gallery in Bruges. You were instrumental in locating a stolen van de Velde for us, *Engelswache*—I believe you say *Angel's Wake*. Painted in 1882 if my memory does not deceive me. Somehow it had found its way into a private collection in your country.'

The light dawned. 'Of course. I recall the case: a British internet tycoon with more money than scruples. He walked, claiming ignorance, but at least the painting was recovered. Forgive me, is it still Inspecteur Decker? It's been a long time.' He extended his hand, which the other man shook briefly.

'Actually, it's *Hoofdinspecteur* now; I think you would say Chief Inspector. I see you have moved on to other pastures. Art theft to car theft on an international level. Quite a change!'

McDermott smiled ruefully. 'Budget cuts, I'm afraid. A few months after the case you speak of the Art Squad had its funding slashed by more than half, and my consultancy work at the Courtauld dried up. I applied to the Met, and they sent me to Bramshill. Once I graduated I was promoted to Detective Sergeant and posted to the CID in London, where I was assigned to SOC, Serious and Organised Crime.' He paused to sip his coffee. 'And you? Still with the Belgian art squad?'

Decker spread his hands on the table. 'Unfortunately, yes. I regret to say the theft of art works has not declined in my country. But our human resources are very limited. I am at present the only senior officer in the National Police working full-time on this dossier. In fact, I am here primarily to strengthen our connections with my counterparts in other forces. I attended your session this morning because I recognized your name on the program. Very well done, I thought—the talk, as well as the operation itself.'

'Thanks,' McDermott answered, 'but I'm only the messenger. A great many people were involved in our success.'

Suddenly Decker frowned and put his hand in his jacket pocket, retrieving his mobile phone. He put it to his ear. 'Decker. Yes? No, not really.' He sighed. 'Very well, just a moment.' He turned to McDermott. 'It seems I am in demand, even when I am out of the country. Perhaps we can get together before the conference ends. It is not right, you know. There are so few of us passionate about art. You should not allow your training to go unused.' They shook hands again and Decker put his mobile back to his ear, then turned and walked away.

McDermott stared after the man, ignoring his lunch for the moment. Decker was right, of course: he had strayed from his first love, which was art. But since his transfer to the CID his successes meant that he'd been increasingly assigned cases unrelated to his expertise. Decker's words reminded him that he had neglected an important aspect of his life.

McDermott glanced at his watch: soon the afternoon sessions would begin. He returned to his lunch, but found that his appetite had gone.

FOUR

While McDermott was in Lyon, reviewing his notes for his next meeting, Albert Ridley preened in front of the wardrobe mirror in his room at the Blue Bull. 'Ow about it, son? The old togs still fit! Right smart, if Ah do say so meself.'

George Ridley scowled good-naturedly. He had to admit his father's physique had changed little over the years. His arms and hands were scarred from burns sustained in the war, and he still walked with a slight limp from a farm accident he'd suffered decades back. A few more wrinkles that couldn't be denied, and his hair was a bit thinner, but Bert Ridley had retained the lean, wiry frame that he'd had for as long as his son could remember. Probably because until recently he'd worked the farm that they'd both grown up on, whereas George had spent the better part of the past two decades in London, doing work his father would regard as sedentary. It was not a pleasant thought. 'Aye, Dad, Ah 'ave t'admit you look grand.' He pulled on his suit jacket and they headed downstairs to the bar.

The Blue Bull—or simply the Bull, as it was known to locals—was located at the western end of the village of Kirk Warham. It was one of only two public houses that served the small local population; the other, the more upmarket Grouse and Claret, lay just outside the village to the east, at the junction of a major road. The Bull was presided over by Ben Richards and his wife Shirl. Richards was an ex-Londoner, a middle-aged, taciturn man with a short temper, unsuited by nature for the job of pub landlord. His attractive wife made up for his shortcomings, chatting up the punters, flirting when it was harmless, and pouring oil on the waters when things threatened to get out of hand.

When father and son entered the main bar they found the festivities in full swing. The pub was packed with villagers and ex-servicemen. The locals ranged from their twenties to mid-sixties, in contrast to the older veterans. Most were in uniform but some were not. Ridley supposed they'd had the same problem fitting into their mothballed uniforms that he'd had, and they were laughing and shouting over their pints. A few heads turned when George and his father came into the room, and a silver-haired man at a table in one corner beckoned them over. 'Oi, 'Ere's Bert! Pull up a chair, you old git. It's been donkey's years!'

They claimed a couple of chairs nearby and pulled them closer to the table. George beckoned to the barmaid, motioning for two pints, then took a chair himself. His father was already getting into the swing of things, he noticed happily. 'Ow are you, then, Dickey?' he asked of a tallish, thin man with a full head of white hair. 'Ere, this 'ere's my son, George.'

The men greeted him cheerily, as if they'd been chums for years. 'Name's John,' the white-haired man said, nodding. 'John Dickerson. But my friends—if you can call this lot my friends—call me Dickey. You can do same.' He extended his hand, knocking over a glass and spilling its contents over the table.

'Crikey, you always were a clumsy sod,' the man next to him said, moving smartly to keep the stream of beer from spilling onto his lap. He was stout and broad-faced, and had a florid complexion. He looked at George. 'Ah'm Sid Black. You don't look much like your da, if you don't mind me sayin' so. 'E's a little runt of a man compared t' you,' he joked.

Ridley was offended. 'Aye, well, that's 'cause 'e fed me proper when Ah were a lad. Looks like you 'aven't missed too many meals yourself.'

The others at the table gave out a roar of laughter, and one of them slapped George on the back. 'Good work, son. You want to keep Sid 'ere in 'is place, else he'll walk all over you.' He looked at Bert. 'Looks like you did ok, Bert. Chip off the old block.'

The elder Ridley preened for the second time. 'E's a good lad, and no mistake.' George felt a moment of intense pride. His father's opinion was important to him, but neither man was given to expressing his feelings.

Another man at the table weighed in. 'My name's Bert, too. Bert Busby—like the hat. Good to meet you, George. 'Ere, now, you're not a teetotaler, are you?' Busby was bald and heavy set, and was perspiring profusely. Just then the barmaid arrived with their drinks. 'Those are mine, love,' he said, handing her a couple of bank notes.

George passed a glass to his father, and raised the other to his lips. 'Cheers. Next shout's mine.'

A large man made his way to the table, tucking in his shirttails. He had a full head of wavy hair. Ridley could see that it had been ginger, though it was now turning lighter. He reclaimed the last vacant chair, but not before sticking out his hand. 'Who's this, then? You don't look old enough to have fought with this lot.'

George took his hand, and was surprised by the man's grip. He might have the advantage of youth on the man, but he wouldn't want to wrestle him for drinks. 'Name's George. Bert Ridley there is my dad.'

The man's eyebrows shot up. 'You don't say! Good on you, Bert.' He turned back to the younger man. 'My name's Tommy Riggins. I had the misfortune to be stuck with this lot durin' the war. They didn't know squat about engines and such, but a few o' them knew one end of a rifle from t'other, including your dad.'

Sid Black bristled at his words. 'What 'e didn't tell you was that they gave 'im a lorry and a set o' tools 'cause he couldn't hit the backside o' the fat lady at the fair wi' a rifle, 'e were that useless.'

The group roared, and Ridley watched closely to see whether things were getting out of hand. But it was evident that the others took everything Black said with a grain of salt. Riggins just laughed along with the others and drained his pint.

The last man at the table had been quiet, and seemed a bit older than the rest. Perhaps it was just the ravages of time. He turned his attention toward George's father. 'Good to see you again, Bert. You look none the worse for wear. What's it been, now—sixteen years at least?'

Ridley sat back in his chair and contemplated matters. 'All of that, Ah'd say. Missed you at the big one in '94, Frank.'

'I were feelin' poorly then. Had a hip replacement and triple bypass. All new plumbin'. Feel a sight better now, though,' he grinned.

'Glad to hear it,' George's father replied. He turned to his son. 'Frank Allenby 'ere were a Lance Corporal in charge o' machine-gun unit. Saved our hides more than once. Say, anyone know why reunion's been shifted from regimental HQ?'

Sid Black leaned in knowlingly. 'Kitchen fire, Ah hear. Made a proper mess o' things. Not fit for man nor beast. The Cap'n—that is, Brigadier, now—offered use of 'is place, not far from here. Regiment is layin' on lorries to bring us back an' forth from 'ere. Just like old times, that.'

Bert Ridley made a face. 'Meybe for you, mate. Ah'd rather ride in comfort than in back o' lorry on a bench. Did enough o' that during war. Where is his lordship's place, anyway?'

'It's called Coniston Hall,' Frank Allenby harrumphed. 'Just up road. In old days I reckon we could 'a walked. Nowadays…' His voice trailed off.

Allenby's choice of terms triggered memories among the group. Dickey Dickenson felt the urge to put in his two pence worth. 'In old days. Those were the days, weren't they? Bit o' water under the bridge since then.'

'Aye, an' no mistake. Good to see you sods, but Ah wouldn't go back an' do it again,' Black said. 'Lost a lot o' good men, good mates, too.' There was a general murmur of agreement, followed by an uneasy silence.

After a moment George said, 'It's all well and good to sit 'ere and 'ave a chinwag, but Ah'm fair peckish. 'Ow's the food 'ere, anyhow?'

His question got lost as one or two men looked up at the menu on a chalkboard nearby, and most of the others reached into their pockets and extracted various small containers filled with pills. Evidently growing old was not all smiles and chuckles.

FIVE

By nine the next morning Albert Ridley and his mates had finished breakfast and set out for Coniston Hall in three official cars. Apparently the powers that be had realised at the last moment that being jostled about in the back of a lorry was not the best option for a group of men in their eighties and nineties.

It was a brief trip, however, as Coniston Hall was located less than two miles from the Blue Bull. As they passed through the main gate they noticed a Victorian gatehouse, prompting Sid Black to comment, 'Is that the place? Bit small isn't it? Won't fit us all in there, then.'

George Ridley grinned, but his father was not amused. 'Always thought hisself a bit of a wag, our Sid.' The man looked aggrieved, and sat back in his seat.

The small column of cars made its way up a long avenue flanked by horse chestnut trees, which opened out at last to a deep gravelled forecourt. There was a large white marquee erected on the lawn to one side. The manor house lay at the rear, with more lawns and woods to the right.

Coniston Hall was a grey stone affair, Georgian in style, with tall mullioned windows at regular intervals and a portico flanked by white columns at the entrance. The centre block protruded forward on both sides and extended upwards for two floors. The building was topped by multiple chimneys at each end of the slate roof, and was surrounded by a granite parapet with balustrades at each corner. To the left of the house a high stone wall divided by an arch led to what appeared to be a block of stables and garages, and a Victorian glass conservatory to the right overlooked a terraced lawn with woods beyond.

Sid Black couldn't resist offering his opinion. 'Now that's what Ah call a proper 'ouse, that is.'

Again it fell to Bert Ridley to put him in his place. 'See that tent over yonder, Sid? The one with the folding tables and the blokes in uniform all milling about? That's for the likes o' you and me.'

The cars pulled up next to an olive-green army lorry where several men in fatigues were unloading a small field kitchen and foodstuffs. George and his father climbed out of the rear seat of the lead car, and Frank Allenby and others piled out of a second, while several men, unfamiliar to them, emerged from the final car. They made their way toward the marquee where they saw John Dickerson from the previous night, as well as a number of other men, some younger, who were also unfamiliar.

'Bout time you slackers showed up, then,' said Bert Busby, wiping his brow. 'You can help set out them chairs.' He pointed to a large stack of folding chairs that were being moved to the lawn beyond. 'That's to be the Parade Ground,' he added.

'Bloody 'ell,' Sid Black said. 'Didn't know Ah'd be put t' work. Thought we were invited to be honoured, not as bit o' cheap labour.'

Ridley couldn't resist. 'What's the matter, Sid? Too long in the tooth to shift a couple o' chairs, then?' The other men grinned, and Black made a point of picking up two of the chairs, one under each arm, and headed for the lawn, glowering at Bert as he passed by.

EVERYTHING WAS IN PLACE by noon, and lunch was being served in the marquee to the veterans, whose numbers had swelled since Bert had arrived. They were of all ages, Ridley observed: some would have served when he did, though he didn't recognize anyone. Others were younger; they might have seen action in Iraq or Afghanistan, or perhaps not have seen battlefield duty at all. They all tucked into their meals whilst a military band rehearsed quietly off to one side, and a number of enlisted men and NCOs in dress uniforms milled about aimlessly nearby. Some of them were sneaking fags, others simply looked bored. George noted that a podium had been erected opposite the rows of folding chairs that Bert Ridley and his mates had helped put in place that morning. Several officers were huddled in a group, consulting their notes and reviewing the arrangements. So that was to be the drill: an address to the troops and dress parade, complete with marching band. He hoped the ceremonies and speeches would be brief and by mid-afternoon they could adjourn to the pub, where they would swap war stories over a few pints.

Ridley's hope turned out to be wishful thinking. First the band marched passed the marquee, summoning soldiers in dress uniforms to the parade ground. A pair of corporals guided the guests to their seats facing the podium. After perhaps ten minutes virtually every seat was filled, and Ridley estimated that over three hundred veterans and soldiers on active service made up the audience. There were women present as well. Some were in uniform, others were clearly spouses of some of the veterans and, he supposed, of the men on active service. Belatedly he wondered whether he should have asked Dora to come along.

When the crowd had ceased milling around and people found their seats, the current Regimental Commander formally welcomed everyone to the event. The band was called upon a second time whilst the troops on active service paraded by and halted in front of the podium for a full dress inspection. After they marched off, the Commanding Officer called on an elderly man in a wheelchair to speak to the assembly. George Ridley hadn't seen him before, but looking at his father and his mates, he realised the man was familiar to them. His father caught his eye and nodded toward the man in the wheelchair. 'That's Baker-Simms. Brigadier now. 'E was nobbut Captain when Ah first knew 'im.'

The man maneuvered his electric wheelchair skillfully to the lectern, and, with the help of two canes, stood up. After a moment spent looking at his notes he tapped the microphone a few times, asked, 'Is this thing on, then?' and began to speak with only the vaguest trace of a Yorkshire accent.

'As your CO just told you, my name is Reginald Baker-Simms, Brigadier, retired.' He looked at the men facing him. 'Most of you won't know me, seeing as I retired some thirty years ago,' he said. 'But before I was made Brigadier I was Lieutenant Colonel of this regiment, like my father and grandfather before me. And before that I served in World War II with some of the men who are here today. We fought Rommel in North Africa, and then took part in the invasion of Sicily, and later, Italy. After that we fought our way through Austria and France, and joined up with the chaps from Normandy to take the battle to Hitler's own back yard. We had some grand help from all over the Commonwealth—the Aussies, the New Zealanders, the Indians and the Canadians. Had some help from the Americans, too, though it weren't always that grand.'

Several men in the audience laughed, and after shuffling his notes he went on. 'Not many of us left, now. Fewer each year. That's why I was glad to hear that the regiment decided to honour once again those of us who'd served in the Second World War, and why I offered the use of the grounds here at Coniston Hall when the Regimental Mess became unavailable. Those were hard times for all of us. I was a Captain then, wet behind my ears but proud of my men, and I am still proud of them sixty years on.' After a brief coughing fit he continued. 'Enjoy your time here, and you younger men never forget the debt that you owe these chaps. They maintained a tradition of service that goes back two hundred and fifty years. Over the years—no, centuries—our boys have earned nearly a dozen Victoria Crosses, along with scores of other battle honours. We fought bravely, and set the standard for those who followed us. It is only right that these men are acknowledged here today. And it is only right that we spare a moment to remember those brave lads who didn't return with us, who gave their lives for king and country, and who lie in foreign fields.'

George could have been wrong, but he thought he saw a tear forming in the corner of the elderly officer's eye.

It was an impressive speech, well delivered, and there was an outburst of applause and cheers as Baker-Simms returned to his wheelchair and resumed his place on the podium. The current Regimental Commander made a few concluding remarks, adding his own thanks to the soldiers, and following yet another pass by the marching band, he declared the opening ceremonies over. He pointed the crowd to a drinks tent nearby, where they wasted no time in forming into smaller groups. Ridley asked his father if he wanted a pint.

'Meybe in a bit, son. Right now Ah've got t'see a man about a horse.' He wandered off toward the main house.

Someone behind Ridley whispered, 'He's a grand old man, your dad.' He turned to see Frank Allenby holding two pints, one of which he thrust in George's direction.

'Aye, he is that,' Ridley replied. 'We've not talked a lot 'bout war over the years. But he thinks a lot o' his mates, and regiment, too, come t' that.' Ridley raised the glass to his lips and drained a third of it in one gulp.

BERT RIDLEY WAS A MAN ON A MISSION. At eighty-one his bladder wasn't what it used to be, and after sitting in the sun listening to the speeches, and looking forward to a pint, he went in search of a toilet. Passing through the main doorway at Coniston Hall he found himself in a panelled hallway with an imposing oak staircase to one side. He turned left and saw a large drawing room. Continuing into the room he noticed a finely-carved Adams chimneypiece, and his eye was drawn to the painting hanging above. It was dark and a bit grimy with age, but it held his attention. At first it wasn't so much the painting itself but the gilt frame that intrigued him. Surrounding the large work, the ornate frame had a golf-leaf rosette in each corner, and the frame was widened in both directions at the corners to accommodate this feature. One corner of the frame had been damaged; a piece had been broken off, and Ridley noticed the wood underneath had darkened with the years.

Ridley's eyes passed to the subject of the painting. The bulk of the composition was given over to a classic Roman temple in ruins. The sky was dramatically dark and shot through with storm clouds. A tree framed the left edge of the composition, the leaves on the branches turned over in anticipation of the approaching tempest. Several columns, already fallen, defined the foreground. Beyond them a woman sat on the steps of an abandoned temple, nursing her infant child while a maidservant stood nearby.

Something about the work intrigued him, though Ridley couldn't say what it was. Not normally a man who spent a lot of time in art galleries, he was puzzled.

His bladder reminded him of why he was there, and he was about to move on when a voice from behind startled him. 'Who are you, then? What do you want in here?'

Ridley turned and saw the Brigadier in his wheelchair, framed in the doorway. 'Nowt. That is, Ah were looking for loo.' He turned toward the painting he'd been admiring. 'Nice bit o' work. Seems familiar somehow.'

The man regarded him skeptically. 'Yes. Well, you won't find the loo in the drawing room, will you?' He took in Ridley's uniform with its campaign medals, and examined his face more closely. 'Do I know you?'

Ridley visibly relaxed. Here, after all, was his former CO. 'Like as not, sir. Ah were in War with you, forty-two to end of forty-three. Well, almost. Got myself shot up in Italy soon after we got there.'

'Did you?' Baker-Simms relaxed as well. 'I'm sorry, I don't recall the face. What's your name?'

'Ridley, sir. Bert Ridley. Trooper, C Company. Ah joined regiment in North Africa in forty-two. Farmer before that, on my dad's land, not far from 'ere. Couldn't bear to see all me mates goin' off, so Ah joined up soon as Ah were of age. Damned stupidest thing Ah ever did.' He looked sheepish.

The Brigadier smiled. 'I dare say. Think I have you now. Damned fine shot, as I recall. Not one for laying down a lot of fire. You bided your time and picked your man off with a single shot. Good move, that. Saved us a lot of ammunition and Jerry paid the price.'

Ridley smiled. 'By gum, nothing wrong wi' your memory, sir, an' no mistake.' Then he recalled why he was there. 'If you wouldn't mind tellin' me where loo is, Cap'n, I mean, sir.'

'Of course,' the Brigadier smiled again. 'As it happens the men have set up some portable loos just beyond the stables gate.' He turned his wheelchair and motored to the entrance, where he paused. 'Just around the corner to your right. Good to see you again, Ridley.' Before Bert could reply he turned and went back inside.

'And you an' all,' Ridley muttered, mildly annoyed at being given the boot. Then he went off to minister to the needs of his bladder.

SIX

That afternoon Bert Ridley and his mates returned to Kirk Warham. Several were lodging at B&Bs in the village, and others lived nearby. They agreed to meet later that evening at the Blue Bull and then went their separate ways. Since George and his father were staying at the Bull they hadn't far to go.

As they went upstairs to their room Bert told his son about his experience inside Coniston Hall. 'It were odd, Ah don't mind tellin' thee. At first 'e were right put out findin' me in 'ouse. Wasted no time in showin' me the door. But Ah'm sure Ah've seen picture before, just can't think where. It's not like Ah go t' picture galleries that often. Enough t' make a man believe in spirits an' such.'

George laughed. 'Don't be daft, Dad. Likely it just looks familiar. You saw summat like it somewhere, that's all.'

'Meybe you're right, son,' he said, unbuttoning his tunic. 'Glad t'get these togs off, though. Right itchy they are, and warm with it. Say, speakin' o' pictures, Ah brought along some old snaps from war. Thought they'd be good for a laugh or two.' He opened an old cigar box and produced a small packet of photographs that had curled and yellowed around the edges with age. He passed a few over to George, who squinted at them in the poor light. 'That there's Tommy Riggins.' He pointed to a stocky lad with a full head of hair. 'E were lorry driver, mostly 'cause he knew his way round a set o' tools. But despite what Sid said, he were right good shot, too, when it came down to it.'

Ridley recalled him from the pub the previous evening. 'Still 'as his hair, Ah see.' His own hair, he knew, was thinning with the march of time. He picked up another photo. 'Who's this, then?'

Now it was Bert's turn to squint. 'That'd be Dickie Dickenson. An' that's Sid Black, on right. Dickie were a trooper like me. Became a copper like you, after war.' He stopped, lost in thought. Then he rummaged through the box. 'See this?' he asked, producing a medallion. 'That's me medal for bravery, that is. Mentioned in dispatches, as they say. Got a Distinguished Conduct Medal as well.' He pointed with obvious pride to a silver disk with an image of King George VI on the face, and which was affixed to a red and blue-striped ribbon.

George examined the medal. He recalled seeing it only once before, as a young lad. It hadn't meant much to him at the time, but his father wasn't getting any younger; some day he wouldn't be around to talk about it. He asked his father how he came by it.

'Ah. Well now, there's a story,' the older man said, fingering the medal. 'Takes me back, that does.' He paused, lost in thought. 'It were in 1943, soon after we landed in Sicily. The Jerries were droppin' back fast as they could move, and we were right on their heels.' He stopped again, rooting amongst his memories, trying to put the events in order. 'We were first Allied troops on continent.' His pride evident. 'Nearly a year before Normandy. Folk don't remember that. The Eyeties might o' surrendered, but not the Jerries. They pulled back into mountains and up the coast, and we followed couple o' days after that. We landed at a place called San Giovanni, or summat like that, Ah recall. Right at toe o' Italy. Monty—he were headin' Eighth Army—he were all for movin' up coast toward Tarranto. But 'e didn't want t' be cut off, so 'e sent C Company – that were us—off to side, into mountains, t' keep eye out for any Jerries tryin' to outflank us.'

Ridley was impressed. His dad might have aged, but his powers of recollection were faultless. It was a story he hadn't shared before. 'What happened then?' he asked.

'We set up camp in a small village in mountains, not far from coast.' He rubbed the crown of his head and shifted in his chair. 'Can't remember name just now. Any road, a few days later Tommy Riggins an' me were ordered to take load o' gear back t' coast, to ship back 'ere to Regimental HQ. Stupid buggers in Supply sent us summer gear just when we were headed into winter! We was two lorries in a convoy. Weren't an hour out o' camp when Jerry scout plane spotted us and dived on us from behind. Never saw 'im comin.' He paused again, struggling to come to terms with old memories.

George waited for his father to continue, and when he didn't, said, 'Aye? 'Ow's that t' do with your medal?'

'Ah were just gettin' to that, son. Like Ah said, we was strafed, machine-gunned. Petrol tank in front lorry were hit and caught fire. Truck went off road, down side o' mountain. Rolled over an' over. Poor buggers never 'ad a chance. We was hit too, Tommy in his shoulder an' chest. Only 'e managed to pull us t' right. We climbed up side o' mountain and lorry tipped over, real slow-like. When it'd stopped, Ah could see Tommy were in bad way, bleedin' an' all, so Ah pulled off me shirt and made a bandage and wrapped it round 'is chest. Ah sat Tommy up next t' truck an' went down mountain t' check on other lorry, but it weren't no use. It were well on fire. Ah pulled the driver out, but it were too late. 'Other man 'ad been thrown out when lorry rolled. Ah could see 'e were dead, too, his head bent back all unnatural-like. Then Ah started to feel pain, and looked down an' saw me arms and hands were burnt. By time Ah got 'way from flames Ah were right sore. Reckoned Tommy an' me was both goners if we stayed there, so Ah walked back to village for 'elp. Must a taken more'n four hours 'afore I got there. Later, Cap'n reckoned Ah were hero. Put me in for medal, 'e did, for savin' Tommy and trying t' save others. It were second time Ah'd been wounded, countin' Africa, and Ah guess they reckoned this time Ah weren't fit for action, so after they patched me up they sent me 'ome. So glad t' be back 'ere that Ah forgot all about it, 'til one day got a letter sayin' Cap'n's recommendation 'ad gone through. Distinguished Conduct Medal, it were called.' He rubbed the silver image of the monarch between his thumb and forefinger.

George Ridley looked not at the medal, but at his father's face, and not for the first time, he felt immensely proud of his dad. 'How come you never told me 'bout that afore?'

His father smiled enigmatically. 'Can't remember everythin', can Ah? Any road, lots o' lads did more.'

'You should be wearin' this,' he said, looking at the other campaign ribbons and medals on his father's tunic.

'Pin's broke,' his father replied. 'Don't hardly ever wear me uniform. Didn't see point o' gettin' it mended.' He stuck it in his jacket pocket.

LATER THAT EVENING Bert and George were joined by the other veterans in the lounge. They were hashing over the day's events when the barmaid came around with drinks. Sid Black leered at her and tried to chat her up. 'Do you want to see a bit of magic, lass?' he asked.

She'd heard it all before. 'You mean you'll drink that up, then disappear?' The other men roared their approval, and Black quickly retreated into his drink.

'The Old Man was right, today,' Allenby said. 'Fewer of us each year. Likely won't be many more such get-togethers in future.'

Dickie Dickenson weighed in. 'Don't be such a poop, Frank. Don't know about you old farts, but I've got a few more miles in me yet.'

'Easy for you,' Black retorted. 'You were just a lad when you got called up, near end o' war. Some of us were already grown men, with jobs, and wives, and even little uns.' He coughed. 'All that fightin' for five shillin's a day. Not so many miles left on most of us.'

At a table nearby another, but clearly much younger, member of the regiment took the opportunity to goad the group. 'Made it through war, though, didn't you? And it could 'a been worse. A shame you chaps missed Normandy, bein' down south at time.'

His crack struck a nerve with George's father. 'Oh aye? An' where were you, then, lad? Suckin' at your ma's teat? Ah'll tell you summit for nowt: it were our invasion of Sicily that made Normandy possible! Brass learnt all sorts of things 'bout what goes wrong in a big landin' and 'ow t'fix it. We saved lot o' lives by goin' first, and paid a price, too.'

There was a chorus of support. Someone said, 'Oi, remember the song we used to sing 'bout that? 'Ow does it go, then?'

'Aye, it stayed with me all them years,' Tommy Riggins weighed in. He broke into song to the tune of Lily Marlene, and was soon joined by the others.

Oh, We're the D-Day Dodgers out in Italy,
Always on the vino, always on a spree.
Eighth Army scroungers and their tanks,
We live in Rome, among the Yanks,
For we're the D-Day Dodgers, out in Italy.

Naples and Cassino were takin' in our stride,
We didn't get to fight there, we went just for the ride.
Anzio and Sangro were just a farce,
We reached our goal, sat on our arse,
For we're the D-Day Dodgers, out in Italy.

By now most people in the pub had stopped talking to listen. The attention made the men warm to their cause, and they cranked up the volume.

On the way to Florence we had a lovely time,
We thumbed our way to Rimini
right through the Gothic Line.
Soon to Bologna we will go,
And after that, we'll cross the Po,
For we're the D-Day Dodgers, out in Italy.

Forgotten by the many, remembered by the few,
We had our armistice when an armistice was new.

One million Germans gave up to us,
We finished our war without much fuss,
For we're the D-Day Dodgers, out in Italy.

Now Lady Astor, get a load o' this,
Don't stand up on a platform and talk a load o' piss.
You're the nation's sweetheart, the nation's pride,
But we think your mouth's a damn sight wide,
For we're the D-Day Dodgers, out in Italy.

Then the singing slowed and the mood became more somber.

If you look around the mountains in the mud and rain,
You'll find the scattered crosses, some which bear no name.
Heartbreak and toil and sufferin' gone,
The lads beneath them slumber on,
Those are the D-Day Dodgers, who stayed in Italy

As they finished singing the room burst into applause. There wasn't a dry eye in the house. Some of the older men raised their fists in the air, earning them a dirty look from the landlord. 'Oi, you lot, mind you keep it down!'

Sid Black couldn't resist. 'Oh, shut your gob. Havin' us 'ere ain't hurt your sales none.'

'This 'ere's a proper pub,' the landlord replied, not used to having his authority questioned. 'None of your fruit machines here, no smoking, and I won't tolerate yobboes neither.'

The insult rallied the men. 'Ere, who you callin' a yobbo?' Bert Ridley asked. 'You forgettin' it's us you owe debt o' gratitude. Weren't for us you'd likely be speakin' German!'

Tommy Riggins joined the affray. 'Any road, proper pub, my eye. Beer's off and prices are 'nough to make a grown man weep. And service? A man could die o' thirst round here.'

That was too much for the landlord. 'That's it!' he said, 'You lot want barrin'?'

George Ridley had been at the bar collecting another round, and had watched the exchange with concern. The last thing he wanted was to be turfed out of the pub before the reunion had ended. He returned to the table balancing several pints between his hands, a knack he'd perfected over the years. 'Ere now, who's glass 'as a hole in it?' He set them down in the middle of the table. It was astonishing how quickly a group of old men could be distracted when a pint was involved.

As the group settled down, Bert Ridley studied his glass. 'Summat's been botherin' me.'

When he didn't elaborate after a moment, Frank Allenby looked at him. 'Well, are you goin' to share it with us, or do we have to work it out for ourselves?'

Bert picked up his glass, had another sip, and put it down again. 'Happens that after parade this mornin' Ah went t' big house, lookin' for loo.'

Sid Black couldn't help interrupting. 'Silly bugger. Didn' tha' see signs posted outside?'

Bert Ridley shot him a look that shut him up. He raised his glass, then put it down again, apparently thinking better of it. 'Well, as Ah say, Ah went into big house. Got as far as main drawin' room—leastways I think it must a been—when Ah saw a paintin' fair took me breath away.'

Several of the other men erupted in laughter. 'Ere now, Bert, are you tellin' us you're some sort o' art connie*sewer*?' Sid Black interjected. He drew the word out, emphasizing its absurdity.

This time George laid a large, beefy hand on Sid Black's arm. 'Let him tell it 'is own way, shall we?' There was no mistaking his tone. Sid shrunk back in his chair.

Bert Ridley took the uneasy silence that followed as leave to continue. 'Well, as Ah said, Ah stopped t' look at paintin'. Good size, it were. Must a been nearly four by six foot, Ah reckon. But what got me 'tention were frame. Real different. Ah'm sure Ah've seen it—or summat like it—afore. Just can't think where.'

Frank Allenby looked at him skeptically. 'That's it? Nowt to it but that? Have another sip, Bert. Maybe it'll come back to you.'

The others laughed, but George Ridley wasn't amused. His father wasn't going gaga; if he said something was curious, it was curious. It had been a long day, though, and George suddenly felt very tired. He pushed back his chair and rose from the table. 'Well, Ah'm turning in. Coming up, Dad?'

'In a bit, son.'

Allenby glanced at Bert's nearly empty glass. 'Top up?'

'No thanks,' He replied. He reached into his jacket pocket and pulled out a packet of cigarettes, and noticed the landlord glaring at him. 'Bugger. Don't want to give old misery guts there 'nother reason to grouse. Ah'm goin' outside to 'ave a ciggie before I come up.'

George scowled. 'All right. You want to watch it, though, Dad. Those things will kill you some day.'

His father looked up at him sharply. 'We all got t' go some way, lad.' He turned back to his pint, and George headed to their room.

SEVEN

I**t was the final session** of the conference at Interpol, and it had been a tedious morning. Colin McDermott stretched his legs underneath the conference table, then reached for his coffee, which had gone cold. Important as liaison work in policing was, it sometimes bored him to tears. He looked around the table; several of the others were surreptitiously checking their mobiles. It seemed they found the session equally compelling.

He was considering skiving off for the afternoon when his mobile, set to vibrate, rumbled in his jacket pocket. *The perfect excuse*, he thought to himself. He took it out and read the text message: *Contact Met ASAP. Marsh.* His face registered his surprise. To his knowledge nothing was going on back in London that required his personal attention. He held his phone up slightly and gestured his apologies, stepping into the hallway and punching in the numbers that connected him directly to his office.

After a pause, someone answered. 'CID. DC Marsh here.'

Colin smiled. 'Hello, Jack. McDermott here. I just got your text message. What's up?'

'That was fast. Thanks for calling, sir. Seems we got a message about Ridley this morning. Only found its way to us a few minutes ago. I checked with DCI Galbraith and he said to phone you directly.'

'And?'

'It seems George is lying unconscious in hospital in Wakefield.. No other details. Galbraith says you'd want to know.'

'What?' Colin shouted into his mobile, then gained control of himself. 'Too right. Got the name of the hospital?'

There was a pause and the shuffling of papers. 'Here it is, sir. Pinderfields. What shall I tell DCI Galbraith?'

'Tell him the conference here has almost wrapped up, and I'm on my way to Wakefield,' McDermott replied. 'I'll keep him posted. Has anyone contacted his wife, Dora?'

'Not that I know of, sir.' There was another pause. 'Do you want me to handle it?'

'No. I'll speak with her myself once I know more.' McDermott rang off. Rather him than some constable, or Galbraith, come to that. He considered his options: a trip by car across Lyon, followed by a plane to London, then somehow make his way to Yorkshire. It would take the best part of the day before he arrived. Not good enough. He walked toward the lift thinking, *I'll bet Interpol can do better.*

As it happened, McDermott was in luck. Two senior Interpol officers were headed for Glasgow to testify in court later that day about an international money-laundering operation; their chartered flight was leaving within the hour. They could modify their flight plan and drop him off at Doncaster, southeast of Wakefield.

He accepted gratefully, and after making his apologies to the conference head and hurriedly packing his things, he met them at the Saint-Exupéry Airport on the outskirts of Lyon.

He'd emailed ahead, and when he arrived at Doncaster two uniformed officers from Wakefield were waiting for him. The men introduced themselves, and after thanking the Interpol officers for the lift McDermott climbed into their car and they set out for the hospital.

WAKEFIELD PROVED TO BE A MAZE of traffic circles and one-way streets, and the experienced driver made a blue light run through the city centre, saving precious time. Pinderfields was a major medical facility serving all of West Yorkshire, and when they arrived they bypassed the car park, which sprawled over a large area, and headed directly for the Casualty wing. McDermott bounced from the car almost before it came to a complete stop, nearly forgetting his bag. He thanked the officers for their help and made for the main door.

Once inside, McDermott enquired at the reception desk, then headed to the third floor. At the nurses' station they directed him down the corridor and through a set of doors marked Cranial Trauma Unit. He was about to approach a midway down the hall when he saw a familiar figure seated in a waiting area.

'George! Marsh called me from London. I was told you were unconscious! What happened?'

'Daft bugger got the message wrong. It were me dad. Fell into a roadworks and hit 'is head, they reckon.' Ridley looked miserable.

McDermott took a chair next to him and turned it so that he faced his old friend. 'Bloody Hell. That's terrible! How—when—did it happen?'

'Last night, late. He were chewin' over old times wi' mates in pub, and stepped out for smoke before comin' t' bed. When he didn't show Ah went looking for him. Mates said he'd left 'alf an hour earlier. Ah went looking outside, and found 'im in 'ole, bleedin' from 'is head.' Even when it concerned him personally, George Ridley marshalled his facts logically and clearly.

McDermott studied his friend. Ridley's suit was rumpled, and his face showed the strain. 'You've been up all night, by the look of it.'

'Aye. Couple o' dad's mates drove me to 'ospital, but Ah sent 'em home. Won't know much right off, doctor said.'

McDermott was aware of someone approaching behind him. He turned and found a young, dark-skinned woman in her mid-thirties, wearing a white coat and stethoscope. 'Hello, I'm Doctor Sunita Chaudhari. I'm a neurologist on staff here in the trauma unit. Are you Mr. Ridley's son?' she asked, looking at George.

'Aye, right enough. 'Ow is 'e?'

'Resting comfortably at the moment. We've run certain tests and sedated him, and we're awaiting the results.' She turned to McDermott. 'Are you a member of the family as well?'

'No. George here is a colleague and friend. I came to see if I could be of some help,' he explained.

She smiled. 'Excellent! Well, you can.' She looked at her watch, then turned back to face the older man. 'It's going on three o'clock. That means you've been here for over fourteen hours, Mr Ridley. The best thing you can do right now is get some rest yourself. It will be some time before we have all the laboratory tests back. If you leave a number at the nurses' station I'll have someone contact you when we know more. Do you have any questions?'

'No, nowt,' Ridley replied, then, thinking better of it, added, 'Do you reckon 'e'll be awake by t'night, then?'

She smiled. 'I wish I could be that precise. Your father's had a serious blow to his head, and he's not a young man. We'll be running a CT scan to determine the extent of his trauma and whether any aspects of his brain might have been compromised. These things take time.'

Ridley was clearly exhausted, both physically and emotionally. 'Right. Reckon Ah should collect 'is things afore Ah leave.'

'Of course,' the doctor replied. 'They'll have them at the desk. Come this way.' She turned and walked down the corridor, with Ridley and McDermott following her. 'Had your father been in a fight, then?' she asked.

Ridley stopped and looked at her sharply. 'Don't know nowt about that. Why?'

'It's just that we found some minor bruises on his arms. They could have been defensive wounds.'

Ridley and McDermott exchanged glances. 'Excuse me, doctor, I should have mentioned that we're both police officers,' McDermott said. 'Are you quite certain about that?'

'As certain as I can be. I've been in Trauma for nearly six years, and I've seen my share of fights—well, the victims of fights, I should say. Perhaps you should speak with the ambulance attendants. They might have more information.'

When they got to the nurses' station Doctor Chaudhari had a word with the duty nurse, then turned and continued down the hall. The nurse went to a filing cabinet and extracted a large manila envelope. Despite its size, it was very thin. 'Not much here, I'm afraid,' she said, pouring its contents onto the counter. There was a pocket handkerchief and several coins, some house keys, the key to Bert's room at the pub, a book of matches and a pocket comb. There was also a rabbit's foot on a chain.

'That's it?' asked George, puzzled.

The nurse shook the envelope again and looked inside, and then consulted an inventory list on the cover. 'It seems so, sir. Were you expecting something else?'

Ridley looked at McDermott. 'No sign o' me dad's wallet.' Then he added, 'Nor 'is watch, neither. And 'e had a medal in 'is jacket pocket. Not right, that. 'E 'ad 'em last night, Ah'd swear to it.'

The nurse looked uncomfortable. 'Well, I only came on duty at seven this morning, but I can tell you our procedures are quite strict. When a patient is admitted we remove and inventory his personal effects, and seal them in an envelope like this one.' She held it up. 'Then we affix a label with the patient's name and ID number on it, and lock it away in a drawer,' she added, motioning to the filing cabinet against the wall.

'Things couldn't have gotten separated when the patient first arrived?' asked McDermott. 'Must have been a lot going on at that point.'

She looked concerned at the suggestion. 'Not really. The process is very clear cut. We have one nurse at the desk per shift whose responsibility includes removing and securing all patients' personal effects. The hospital administrator will be very upset if anything's gone missing.'

McDermott moved to calm her fears. 'Perhaps there was some confusion at the scene of the accident,' he suggested. 'Maybe one of his mates took charge of some of his belongings before the ambulance arrived.' He turned to George. 'The local police were called?'

'Aye. Took their sweet time, too. Area car were a good ten miles off. But I were there whole time, 'cept for steppin' into pub an' askin' them to phone for ambulance, and coverin' him w' blanket to keep him warm. No un else touched 'im until medics arrived.'

'Curiouser and curiouser,' McDermott said. 'Look, I should phone Galbraith, bring him up to speed. He'll be glad to know it's not you in that room. Then let's stop by the Wakefield HQ and see what's in their notes. I want to thank them for getting me here. We'll take a taxi into town.'

RIDLEY AGREED RELUCTANTLY, and thirty minutes later they were entering the regional headquarters of the West Yorkshire Police Constabulary. After identifying themselves at reception they were ushered upstairs to the office of the Detective Chief Superintendent.

The man at the desk was in his early fifties, with blond hair and dark blue eyes, tall and heavy set, and well dressed. He was studying a file when they entered, and didn't look up immediately. When he did, his face registered surprise. 'Colin? Well, I'll be damned! It's been donkey's years. How have you been?'

Ridley glanced at McDermott, who took a moment. Then he broke into a grin. 'Gareth Matthews. You old sod! Good to see you. You're right—it has been a long time. I see you've done well for yourself,' he added, looking pointedly at the nameplate on the desk, which indicated the officer's rank.

'You know what they say: the cream rises to the top. How about you?'

'Still at the Met. A DI now, but I haven't ascended to your lofty height,' he replied, grinning.

The senior officer waved his hand dismissively. 'More room for promotion in the rural ridings. Old wine in new bottles. Job hasn't changed, just a bit more pension—and the headaches to go with it.' He looked at George. 'Have a chair, both of you. Who's your friend, then?'

McDermott made a face. 'Sorry, Gareth. This is George Ridley. He's my DS in London, and a good friend,' he added. 'His father was attending a military reunion nearby, and was injured yesterday evening. He's in your local hospital right now, having tests. Thing is, some of his personal effects have gone missing, and I thought the overnight reports on the incident might shed some light on where they might have gone south.'

The DCS frowned. 'You're not suggesting that our boys had anything to do with it, are you?'

'Certainly not. Just trying to pin down when they went missing.'

Matthews visibly relaxed and turned to his computer. 'What is your father's name, George?'

'Bert Ridley. Albert Ridley, that is. We were stayin' at pub in local village. 'Appened last night, 'round midnight.'

The officer bent over the keyboard for a few moments, then he looked up, pleased with himself. 'Got it. Outside the Blue Bull, in Kirk Warham. Been there myself once or twice. Off the beaten path. Mind you, landlord's a bit of an old biddy. Now let's have a look at the Incident Report.' His fingers worked their magic again, then he smiled. 'Here we are. Two uniforms responded. Received call at 11:52, on the scene at 12:08.' He frowned. 'Not good, that. Not our best work, I'm afraid. Still, it is in the back of beyond.' He pressed a few more keys, and looked up. 'Report says the vic—sorry, George, your father—fell into a roadworks excavation in the dark. Hit his head on a drainage pipe under repair. That right?'

Ridley looked a bit put out. 'That's what we reckoned when Ah found 'im. But since then the doctor at 'ospital said looked like 'e'd been in ruckus, and some of 'is things 'ave gone missin.'

'Good enough for me.' Matthews reached for the phone. 'Is West in the building? Good. Tell her I'd like to see her, please. Well, Colin, it's been awhile.'

He hadn't exaggerated. Their friendship went back to police college, when Gareth Matthews had been a training officer, and a newly-minted PC named McDermott had found himself in a course on investigative procedures. They had hit it off from the outset, McDermott impressed by the instructor's ability to make the sometimes opaque techniques of the CID intelligible, and the senior officer equally taken by McDermott's obvious intelligence and personal commitment.

Gareth Matthews leaned back in his chair. 'Don't worry, George. We'll get to the bottom of this. Why don't I get us some coffee?' he added, reaching for the phone again.

By the time he'd hung up there was a knock at his door, and a woman's head peered around the corner. 'You wanted to see me, boss?'

'Come in, West.' He motioned to the men. 'These gentlemen are colleagues from the Met,' he said. 'DI McDermott and DS Ridley. This is DCI Philippa West. Best man in CID here,' he grinned. She seemed less than amused, but extended her hand to McDermott.

'A pleasure. What brings you up from London?'

A pro, McDermott thought. Tall, with shoulder-length brown hair and matching eyes. Well dressed in a beige pant-suit and crème-coloured blouse. But he noticed a nicotine-stain on her right middle finger, and her makeup didn't hide the crow's feet. McDermott put her down for a brittle fortyish.

'Actually, George and his father were both in the area for a regimental reunion.'

'Grand bunch, that. Leastways it was 'til Ministry merged 'em all together twenty years back,' Ridley added darkly.

'And you are a camp follower, then?' she asked McDermott, giving him a mischievous wink. Maybe he'd been wrong about the brittle part.

'Hardly. George's father was injured last night outside a pub in a local village. We thought it was an accident, but some of his effects are unaccounted for, and now it seems it might have been an assault gone bad.'

'Ah,' she replied, turning toward the desk. 'Then we want to look into it.'

'Too bloody right. If this was a case of robbery, then some vital clues might have already been lost. I want you to head a preliminary inquiry, Philippa. Talk to the uniforms and see if they noticed anything peculiar about the scene. Same with the ambulance blokes. And get a scene-of-crime team on site.' He looked out the window at the darkening storm clouds. 'It rained last night, and it looks as though it might open up again any time now. We need to get the scene covered with a tent. See to it right away, will you?' There was another knock at the door and a civilian entered with a tray. Matthews looked at the others. 'Now, who's for coffee? George, I want you to fill me in from the beginning.'

EIGHT

By the time George Ridley had finished his story his coffee had gone cold. In truth, there hadn't been much to tell. George had headed up to bed, expecting his father to finish his pint and go for a smoke, then follow him to their room. When he hadn't appeared some forty minutes later, Ridley put his trousers and a shirt on and went downstairs. His mates were still nursing their pints, and said Bert had called it a night and left for a smoke perhaps half an hour earlier. Although they didn't seem overly concerned, George decided to have a look around. His father had had several pints as well; perhaps he was in the Gent's.

Not finding him, Ridley had stepped outside. It was an unusually cold night, and it had been raining. He had been about to go back inside when something caught his eye. There was a roadworks excavation nearby, but it was badly lit. Something about it seemed not quite right. When George drew closer, he saw a man's boot. Ridley threw himself into the excavation, abandoning any thought for his personal safety. Fortunately it was only a few feet deep. His father lay face down in the mud, next to a large drainage pipe. He was damp and cold, and barely breathing.

Realising there was no time to be wasted Ridley climbed out of the hole and ran into the pub. One glance at his muddy clothes and stricken face told the woman behind the bar that something was seriously wrong. Ridley told her to phone for an ambulance; his look said *immediately*. Then he asked for a blanket and a torch.

Hearing the commotion the other veterans came out into the vestibule and asked what had happened. George gave a terse explanation, and snatching the blanket and torch from the woman's hands, rushed outside again.

The men followed and were shocked by what they saw. It looked as though Bert Ridley had not seen the excavation, and had tumbled into it in the darkness, striking his head on the partially uncovered drainage pipe. He was bleeding from a head wound, and was unconscious. George raised his head so it was well out of the water that had collected in the hole, and covered him with the blanket.

By this time other patrons had heard the commotion and had come outside. One or two suggested that George lift his father from the hole and offered to help take him inside, where it was warm. But Ridley realised his father might have hidden injuries, perhaps to his spine, and ignored their well-meaning suggestion.

Before long an ambulance appeared, followed soon afterwards by the police. The ambulance attendants quickly assessed the situation and determined that it would be safe to move Bert. After stabilizing his head with a neck brace and bandaging his head wound to prevent further bleeding, they brought a stretcher alongside the excavation and carefully lifted the unconscious man onto it. George wanted to ride with him to the hospital, but the attendant said it would be some time before they would know anything in Casualty. He suggested that Ridley change his muddy clothes and meet them at the hospital. Reluctantly, George had agreed.

And that, he explained to Matthews, was that. The uniformed officers at the scene had asked George how he was related to the victim, and what he knew of the incident. Annoyingly, they'd also asked whether his father had had too much to drink. Ridley was adamant that he hadn't. As George put it, he hadn't seen his father drunk in his lifetime. Bert's mates corroborated his story: he'd had perhaps three pints over the course of several hours, and they'd had supper just before that. George's father hadn't been drunk.

After looking at the roadworks site the officers were inclined to write it up as an accident. The night was extremely dark, the moonlight being almost nonexistent, and the excavation was not well marked or barricaded. An overhead lamp that was used to illuminate the side entrance to the pub had burnt out and not been replaced. All in all, as one of the officers explained, it seemed fairly straightforward: George's father had stepped out for a smoke and failed to spot the excavation, perhaps slipping in the mud and falling in. When he struck his head on the pipe he had passed out. A good thing Ridley had come along when he did, the officer had observed, or his father might have drowned.

'And after that, you went to Pinderfields?' asked Matthews.

'Aye,' George replied. 'Ah 'ad no idea the old man might a been robbed.' He looked furious with himself.

'No reason why you should have. Of course your first concern was your father.' He leaned back in his chair and made a steeple of his fingers, lost in thought. 'It's still not clear just when his personal belongings went missing. Let's begin by reviewing the

Incident Report. Then we'll have the uniforms in and go over it again. See whether they noticed anything unusual, in retrospect. That will give our lads in the paper suits a bit of time to examine the scene. By the end of the day we might have more to go on.' He put down his hands and leaned forward. 'Now, you two: I assume you still have a room at the pub. Is that right, George?'

'Aye, right. Biggest problem is gettin' there and back.'

'That's no problem. I'll arrange to have you taken back, and have an area car pick you up tomorrow.' He turned to McDermott. 'How about you, Colin? Made any arrangements?'

'I'm afraid I simply haven't had time, Gareth.'

'Then it's settled,' Matthews interjected. 'You can stay with Ellie and me. She'll be delighted to see you again.'

McDermott looked at his partner. Still wearing last night's clothes, and careworn as well. He made his choice. 'If it's all the same to you, Gareth, I think I'll stay in the village with George. We can double up on that ride, though, and have dinner another time, if that works for you.'

The senior officer shrugged. 'Of course. As for the ride, since there's the two of you, why don't I simply get you a car from the motor pool? It should only be for a few days, and we have several officers down sick, so we can spare the car. But Ellie will have my hide if I don't get you over for dinner. That extends to you, too, George,' he added. 'All brothers in blue, after all.'

Ridley looked uncomfortable. 'Thanks. Ah'd like to get back t' pub tonight and talk t' me dad's mates. They'll be wantin' to know how 'e is, and summun' might 'a seen me dad's things.'

'Of course. I'll sort out the car now. Meanwhile, I'll ring Ellie and give her a bit of notice. Shall we say tomorrow night for dinner? I'll give you directions.'

'That reminds me,' McDermott said. 'I'd better give Galbraith a heads-up in London. He'll be wondering about George.'

Superintendent Galbraith was out of his office. After leaving a detailed message on his voicemail McDermott rose and picked up his bag. 'We'd best be off, then.' He extended his hand. 'Thanks for your help, Gareth. I knew we could count on you.'

'Don't be silly,' Matthews replied. 'As I said, we're all brothers, aren't we? Brothers-in-law,' he added, not fully suppressing a grin.

IT WAS GOING ON DARK BY THE TIME MCDERMOTT AND RIDLEY pulled into the car park of the Blue Bull. When they entered the building, Ridley made directly for the bar and McDermott caught the eye of a woman at the desk and asked about a room. She told him that would ordinarily be no problem, only they were full up owing to the reunion. It was a small village, with limited accommodation, she explained, but she offered to call around. McDermott offered to share George's room, using Bert's bed, seeing as he was in the hospital. She could hardly refuse.

When McDermott joined Ridley in the bar he found George had been mobbed by the other veterans, anxious for word about his father. McDermott borrowed a chair from a nearby table and joined the group.

''Ere, now, who's this?' Sid Black asked. 'This 'ere's a private party, mate.'

'It's all right,' Ridley explained. 'He's one of us. My boss, in fact.'

'Colin McDermott,' he said genially, motioning to the lad behind the bar for a pint.

Black looked at him suspiciously. 'George's boss? That mean you're a copper?'

'No flies on you, then,' Tommy Riggins smirked. The others laughed heartily. Black was not amused.

'Does that mean there were summat queer 'bout accident last night?' he persisted.

McDermott's expression wasn't giving anything away. 'Not at all. George here is a mate. I knew he'd appreciate my being here.'

The group spent the next few minutes catching up on Bert's condition, during which Ridley and McDermott managed to get some supper just before the kitchen closed. There had been no mention of the missing wallet and watch. Intrigued, McDermott kept quiet about it until they reached their room.

'Why so mum, George? he asked, closing the door. 'Do you think one of your dad's mates might have taken his things?'

'Let's just say Ah gave them chance t' own up,' he muttered.

McDermott's eyebrows went up. 'Surely you father has known these men for years. Comrades in arms, and all that. You don't think one of them would stoop to petty theft, do you?'

'Ah don't know nowt,' Ridley replied. 'For years me dad's told me 'bout 'is mates, 'ow they fought next t' each other, shared their rations and looked out for each other's backs. But now I meet 'em, Ah'm not so sure. Take Sid Black. There's summat 'bout that man that don't go down well. A right weaselly bugger, Ah'd 'ave said.'

McDermott gave it some thought. 'Well, you're right, I suppose; people change over the years. Might as easily have been one of them as anyone else. But we'll need more than a hunch to go on.' He unzipped his bag and took out his toiletries kit. 'Meanwhile, let's have a wash and catch our breath. It's been a long day for both of us.'

NINE

The next day brought little in the way of new developments. McDermott and Ridley visited the hospital again, but Bert was still unconscious. They tracked down the neurologist they'd seen earlier and found her in her office, eating a sandwich from a vending machine and washing it down with a carbonated drink of some sort. *Physician, heal thyself*, McDermott thought.

Ridley came straight to the point. 'Any news, then, 'bout me da'?'

Doctor Chaudhari glanced at a file on her desk. 'I'm afraid not, Mr Ridley.' She motioned to several x-ray films clipped to a light box over her desk. 'The lab results came back, and they show several blood clots that concern us. We're looking at giving your father a thinning agent to dissolve them.'

It was all Greek to George. 'Aye? What's stoppin' you then?'

She sighed. 'I'm afraid it's not that simple. The medication itself could cause a clot to loosen and travel to your father's brain, or even to his heart, where the consequences could be serious.'

Ridley looked at her closely. 'So what's the plan, then?'

'For the moment, observation. We're still assessing his cognitive functions, and that will influence our decision to introduce a blood thinner.'

Ridley was clearly frustrated. This was getting him nowhere. 'So when will you know summat?'

She turned in her chair to face him. 'I'm afraid it's not an exact science, Mr Ridley. We're hoping to have more information later this afternoon. But it's only fair to tell you that it might be tomorrow, or even longer, before we have settled on a plan of action.'

By the time they left the building Ridley was struggling to contain himself. 'Bloody 'ell. All that schoolin' and 'quipment and they might as well be usin' a Ouija board!'

'I know what you mean, George. But for the moment, all we can do is wait and hope.' He thought back to his own father's final days in hospital, when they had tried everything at their disposal to defeat his cancer, and in the end simply had to let him go.

They returned to the Wakefield Police HQ to learn that the work there had been equally fruitless. The forensics team had so far found little in the way of evidence at the scene outside the pub, the rain and foot traffic having obliterated most of what had happened the night of Ridley's mishap. Nor had the ambulance team or the responding uniformed officers noticed anything unusual. No one recalled whether Bert Ridley had been wearing a watch when they attended him, and his pockets had not been searched as the priority was to get him medical attention.

The pair spent the afternoon in the CID suite going over the little information they had, and then joined Matthews and his wife for dinner. McDermott had enjoyed seeing Gareth and Ellie again, and the home-cooked meal had been a welcome change of pace. But not surprisingly, George had seemed preoccupied throughout the evening. The hospital had been no help: there was still no word on his father's condition.

BY THE TIME MCDERMOTT AND RIDLEY returned to the Blue Bull it was nearly midnight. They parked their car and locked it, and headed for the door. The forensics team had, after the fact, been thorough: they had erected a tent over the excavation and cordoned off the area with police tape. A uniformed officer was on hand to make sure no one entered the site. It was raining slightly, and growing colder, and he didn't look pleased.

When they went into the bar they were surprised to find a few of the veterans still there. McDermott was impressed. *These are not young men. Do they do this every night?* Yorkshire, he reflected, was not London; Dalesmen seemed to be of an altogether sturdier stock.

The men beckoned them over to their table and asked about Bert. When George said his condition was unchanged they expressed their concern and invited them to sit down for a drink. Ridley was tired, but he could hardly refuse. One of the men got the attention of the barman, a young man, and held up five fingers. He nodded, and delivered another round of drinks to the table a few minutes later. McDermott thought he looked familiar, and then glanced at the landlord, Ben Richards. Must be his son, he thought. He noticed a tattoo on the young man's neck, a stylized dragon's head. Body ink was becoming all the rage in London, he knew; even some young women were sporting tattoos now. But unusual, he'd have thought, for so far north.

McDermott brought himself back to the discussion at the table. 'It must call up a lot of memories, seeing each other again.'

'You'd not be wrong there, lad,' Herbert Busby said. 'As a heavy-goods driver I got around the country more than most, and when I was in the area I looked up some of our mates. Every year it seemed there was fewer of our lads about.'

'You ever see George Shea?' asked Dickie Dickenson. 'He's somewhere down south, I recall. Nice bloke. Pity he's not here this year.'

Busby took a pull on his pint. 'He's not been well. Last time I saw him his hip was giving him grief. Spends most of his time in wheelchair. Said he still has cold sweats at night, thinking about the war. Doubt we'll see him at one of these affairs again.' He looked at his glass, lost in thought.

'What about Arthur Ellsworth?' Dickenson persisted. 'He was always one for the ladies.'

'Arthur had a stroke some twelve—no, I tell a lie—must be fifteen months ago. He lives in nursing home in Southport. Saw him last June. He was sipping his lunch through a straw.'

Dickenson was relentless. 'Percy Tippit?'

'Oh, he died two year ago now,' someone said. 'Diabetes, I think.'

The silence was growing tangible. Sid Black said, 'Shame, that. Alf Beasley were always up for a drink. Must 'ave a lot o' time on 'is hands these days, bein' retired an' all. Ah'm surprised et ain't 'ere.'

'Alf's in Blackpool,' Busby replied. 'And he's not retired. He's a part-time short-order cook on the pier.'

Sid Black almost choked on his pint. 'You don't say! Still workin' at 'is age? Poor bugger.' The gloom was rapidly spreading around the table.

More to change the mood than anything else, George Ridley pushed back his chair. 'My dad brought along some of 'is snaps from the war. A couple o' you lads in there as well. He were plannin' to show 'em to you. Why don't Ah fetch 'em?'

The group jumped on the suggestion, eager to change the conversation. Moments later Ridley returned with a packet of his father's photos, held together by an elastic band. He passed the pictures around the table and each man examined them closely, reliving old times. As he'd expected, the discussion soon took on a happier tone.

'By gum, you 'aven't 'alf put on weight, Dickie,' Sid Black said. 'A fiver says you've added three stone, at least.' He grinned maliciously.

Frank Allenby came to Dickenson's defense. 'You're one to talk, Sid. Maybe it's 'cause he's got a good woman at home, cookin' for him. More than some people have!' The group laughed again at Sid's expense, and he retreated into his glass.

As the photographs made their way around the table Allenby picked one up. 'That's a good one of you, Tommy. Brings back memories.'

Tommy Riggins took the photo and examined it closely. 'Aye, look like it were taken in Italy. Must 'a been in late '43, then. What was the name o' that village? Santa Claus? Santa Cruz?'

'Santa Cristina something,' Dickenson recalled. 'Nice little village, it were. The Eyeties were right friendly. The women, too,' he winked.

Herbert Busby looked at the photo, then passed it along. 'That were taken up at that villa, I reckon.'

'You lost me, mate,' Dickenson said.

'You know the one. Where Cap'n Baker-Simms had his… unfortunate accident.'

The group looked puzzled for a moment, then Sid Black's face lit up. 'Oh, aye, where 'e shot them two Eyeties!'

McDermott had been lost in his own thoughts, but his ears pricked up at that. 'What do you mean?'

A couple of the men studied their pints, clearly reluctant to talk about the incident. But that didn't stop Sid Black. 'Aye, he did, right enough. 'Eck of a ruckus 'bout that. Had official inquiry at time. That's 'ow 'e got 'is name: "Butcher" Baker.'

'Here now, you don't want to go throwing stories 'round like that,' Allenby objected. 'He were cleared of any wrongdoing.'

Sidney Black laughed. 'Oh, aye? You mean by Company Adjutant? Right lot o' good that did, 'is father bein' Regimental CO an' all.'

'Hang on a minute,' McDermott interrupted. 'You lot are going too fast for me. Just what was it that happened?'

The others looked at Sidney Black. Since they were reluctant to talk, this was shaping up as his moment in the sun, and he wasn't about to let it go by. He took a long pull on his pint and sat back, ignoring the glares of the other men at the table. 'Plain enough,' he began. 'After landin' in Italy C company were ordered up into mountains, to keep tabs on Jerry. Rest o' regiment headed up the coast, an' we were t' join up later, once area were secure.'

McDermott glanced around the table. Some of the men were sullen, but no one challenged his account so far.

'Any road, we went to Santa-whatsit, just like Dickie said. We weren't there more'n a day when our CO, Cap'n Baker-Simms, led a recce up mountain road towards some national park. 'E reckoned there were enough woods for Jerries to 'ole up there an' be reinforced, and then hit us when we advanced. So we went along road from village to set up forward observation post.' Black stopped and took another long pull on his glass, draining it this time. He looked around expectantly, and when no one offered to get a refill, he continued his tale. 'It were rainin' real hard that day, and we couldn't 'ear nowt. We came round bend in road, and there were villa ahead of us, to one side o' road. A right grand thing it were, with wall in front and a big curved driveway and flower pots along front of 'ouse, and a tall double door, carved w' all sorts o' fancy designs. Shutters and balconies at every window. I recall 'cause I thought if Jerries were in there they 'ad a right good drop on us. So I stayed close t' wall.'

He paused again, and looked pointedly at his glass. George took the hint and headed for the bar.

'When we got t' front door, the Cap'n signalled for couple o' us to stand to each side, and follow 'im inside. We did as we were told, and once we got inside, 'e motioned 'e were goin' upstairs, and we were t' check out ground floor. I figured 'e took the easy job and left us the risky bit. We looked around real careful-like, 'cause everythin' was all covered up w' sheets like it were in storage. Made it hard t' tell what was what.'

Ridley returned with a pint, and for once Sidney Black seemed appreciative. 'Ta, George. Leastways there's some 'ere as knows 'ow t' treat a bloke.' He took a generous pull, and set the glass down, wiping the froth from his mouth.

'And?' McDermott was quickly tiring of the man's theatrics.

'Ah were just comin t' that,' Black said. 'Tommy Riggins an' me 'ad just about finished clearin' the ground floor when we 'eard Sten gun goin' off upstairs. You get t' recognize difference between guns after so long.' The other men around the table nodded in agreement. 'So we beat it upstairs, ready for God knew what. Reckoned the place were full o' Jerries after all.'

'When we got there we found Cap'n standing over two bodies, an old man and 'is wife. Leastways Ah reckoned she was. They was 'bout the same age. Both were civilians. They were in corner o' bedroom, next t' wardrobe. It were dark in there, but from all the blood Ah could see they were dead.' He paused for dramatic effect.

'And?' McDermott persisted.

Sidney Black gripped his pint, enjoying the attention. 'Cap'n Baker-Simms, 'e looked pale as a ghost. Claimed they'd been hidin' in corner when he came into room. Didn't call out an' say they were there. Said 'e fired when they moved. Any road, we went downstairs and found rest of platoon inside the main door, wonderin' what shootin' was all about. Cap'n gave orders to seal off 'ouse and not to let anyone in. When we returned t' village 'e reported shootin' to HQ straightaway. They said they'd be sendin' man down to 'vestigate things themselves.'

McDermott noticed the other men trading glances. 'Did any of you go into the room afterwards?' he asked.

'We were told it was off limits,' Riggins said. 'The Captain made it clear that it was important to preserve the scene just as it was.'

'So what was the outcome?' McDermott asked.

Frank Allenby put down his own glass and took up the story. 'Oh, there was an inquiry, all right. The Adjutant from HQ came and looked at the scene the next day, and interviewed every man in the platoon, including those who'd been outside. A gun was produced, all right: a Luger was lying under the edge of the bed. The old man must have dropped it there when he was shot.'

McDermott thought about what he'd heard. 'So it seems straightforward enough. The man in the villa must have been frightened when the Germans pulled back and your lot moved in. Likely he didn't know what to expect. If he saw your men coming up the road, it would have been the most natural thing in the world to have collected his wife, and perhaps taken a pistol to defend himself if necessary, and retreated upstairs. Not a wise course of action perhaps, but understandable under the circumstances.'

'Why not just 'ang a sheet out o' window?' someone asked. 'Ah recall seein' lots o' them in Sicily.'

'There were some as did,' Dickenson said. 'But remember it was early days. We'd been on the mainland less than a week. No one knew whether we were there to stay or might be pushed back by the Jerries a few days later. Lots o' Eyeties held off for a bit, seeing which way wind would blow. They didn't want the Jerries taking reprisals if they returned.'

'Makes sense, I suppose.' McDermott conceded. 'But why did the Captain get the name "Butcher" Baker?'

Sid Black snorted. 'Oh, aye? An old couple of civilians, and 'e machine-gunned 'em? And just 'ow did the owner of the villa come by pistol, do you reckon? Them things don't grow on trees.'

McDermott was thoughtful. 'Well, it's a fair question. You men were there. I wasn't. But it was dark, after all, and I'd have thought it wasn't that difficult to come by a pistol. The Germans had occupied the area for some time. Perhaps the villa had served as a command post, or the Germans billeted some of their men there, and when they pulled out…' He left the sentence unfinished.

Sidney Black felt the need to have one last word. ''E lost 'is bottle, if you ask me.'

'We didn't,' Frank Allenby said sourly.

TEN

McDermott awoke the next morning at half past seven. It would be a busy day, he knew, and he wanted an early start. He showered and shaved and then gave Ridley a push. 'Come on, old man. Time to stir your stumps. We'll start with the hospital. By now they should have some information on your father.'

That got George up in a hurry. They breakfasted quickly and headed toward the car park. The SOCOs were back on site, taking one last look before wrapping things up. The PC from the previous night had been replaced by a younger, drier, and more cheerful officer. McDermott gave him a nod as they passed; the man was nursing a coffee in a polystyrene cup, and smiled back.

Thirty minutes later they arrived at the hospital. McDermott parked near the Casualty wing and they made their way to the third floor. As they approached Bert Ridley's room a plump young woman emerged, nearly running into them. She carried a clipboard and had impossibly red and black-streaked hair and a cheerful disposition. 'Sorry about that,' she said, moving to one side. 'Are you here to see Mr Ridley?'

'Aye,' George answered. 'Does that mean he's better, then?'

'Well, he's awake,' she answered. 'I'll tell the doctor you're here. She can tell you more.' She turned and walked down the corridor.

Ridley pushed on the door and peered inside. The room was a double one, but the bed nearest the window was unoccupied. Bert Ridley was laying still, his eyes closed. He was pale, and although relaxed, the lines around his eyes were pronounced. There was a tube running from a bag on a moveable trolley to his right arm, and electric leads on his chest were connected to a monitor that recorded his vital signs and gave off beeping noises at regular intervals.

Concern clouded George's face, and he moved into the room, McDermott trailing him. 'Dad? You awake?'

The man's eyes opened, and he turned his head toward the sound. The blinds had been drawn, and the room was shrouded in gloom. He said, 'That you, son?'

The look of relief on Ridley's face was palpable as he moved closer to the bed. 'Aye. 'Ow you feelin' then? You don't look so bad.'

His father raised a hand to his head, grimacing as he touched it. The top and one side of his head had been bandaged, and he had several cuts and contusions as well. His expression showed his fatigue. 'Ah've felt better, Ah can tell you.' His speech was a little slurred. 'What 'appened? This lot won't tell me nowt.'

George visibly relaxed. 'You 'ad an accident, Dad. Leastways, that's way it seems. Ah found you in roadworks outside pub. Looks like you went for smoke an' fell in, hittin' your head.'

Bert Ridley looked thoughtful, wincing at even this small effort. 'News t' me, son. Ah don' recollect anythin' o' sort.' His gaze sharpened. ''Ow long 'ave Ah been 'ere, then?'

Ridley looked at his watch. 'Best part o' two days.'

'That long? Any o' lads been by, then?'

'Not yet,' George said. 'You were in bad way at first. Doctor told me it'll be awhile afore they know what's what. Ah'm sure they'll be in t'night, if doctors'll let 'em.'

He looked pleased. 'Aye, Ah'd like to see 'em. We've not 'ad much of a visit.'

Just then the door swung open and Doctor Chaudhari entered the room. 'Hello,' she smiled, ignoring the others and approaching the bed. 'How are we feeling today?'

Bert Ridley looked at her. 'Well, Ah don't know 'bout you, lass, but Ah could use a drink.'

She laughed and went to the bedside table and handed him a plastic cup with a straw.

'Nay, lass, that's not what Ah 'ad in mind.'

She laughed again. 'Good for you! Definitely on the mend, then. But I'm afraid that fruit juice and water are all you're allowed at the moment. I'll let the floor nurse know.'

She beckoned to George. 'Can we have a word, please?' She led them both into the corridor and turned to Ridley, lowering her voice. 'We've got the results back of the tests we ran yesterday. Your father has suffered a fractured skull and a slight concussion.'

''E seemed right enough just now,' George protested.

She smiled. 'Yes, he's alert and coherent. That counts for a lot, and as you just saw he's in good spirits. His scans look good as well. We are very hopeful at this point that he hasn't suffered any permanent damage.'

Something in her face told Ridley that she was holding something back. 'But?'

'But we want to be sure. He's suffered from exposure, lying out in the rain. Not the best thing for a man of his years. Are you aware of any family history for heart problems?'

George's eyes burrowed into her. 'No, nowt. His own dad died in France ' during Great War, and I never knew what killed Grandmum. Likely old age. Why'd you ask?'

'It's always good to have the family history. We're treating him to prevent clotting, and I've called in a specialist. We want to monitor him for a few more days, just to be sure we know what we're dealing with.'

Ridley took a moment to process the information. 'Well, you know best, Ah reckon.' Reaching into his jacket pocket, he found a scrap of paper and scribbled something on it, then handed it to the doctor. 'This is my mobile. You can reach me any time.' Then he turned to McDermott. 'By gum, what wi' everythin' Ah've not updated Dora since yesterday. She'll be beside 'erself. Best do it now.' He reached into his pocket and extracted his mobile while moving toward a nearby alcove.

'Will he be all right?' the doctor asked, looking at Ridley.

'Strong country stock,' McDermott assured her. 'I'll see to him. Thank you for your efforts, Doctor —'

'Chaudhari,' she reminded him. 'All part of the service. You're not from these parts, are you?'

'Is it that obvious? No, I'm from London. I think I mentioned yesterday that George and I are police officers. We're with the Metropolitan Police. CID.'

Her eyebrows rose fractionally. 'Really? Must be interesting work.'

'It has its moments. Not quite the same thing, of course, when it involves someone you know.'

'No, I suppose not.' Her mobile went off and she pulled it from her pocket and read the message. 'It seems I'm wanted elsewhere, Mr—I suppose I should call you —what?'

'Inspector McDermott. But Colin is fine.' He smiled. 'Thanks again, Doctor. I'm sure we'll be seeing you again over the next few days.'

She smiled. 'Yes, of course. Goodbye for now, then.' Her phone buzzed again and she turned and walked away.

Ridley returned, putting his mobile in his pocket as he did so. 'Dora were right upset. She an' Dad get on like a house afire. Said Ah'd call 'er again when we know more.'

'Right, George.' McDermott consulted his watch. 'Why don't you check in on your dad before we leave?'

Ridley grunted and returned to his father's room. When he pushed open the door, however, his father was fast asleep. He let it close again, and they walked toward the lift. 'If you don't mind, Ah'd like t' see if CID knows anythin' more 'bout me dad's case. It's not just the things as disappeared, you know. Ah want t' know if he's been attacked.'

WHEN THEY REACHED the West Yorks HQ it was mid-morning, and Gareth Matthews was already on his third cup of coffee. He smiled as they entered his office. 'Just in time for a fresh cuppa.' He pointed to a carafe on a table near the window.

He looked at George. 'How's your dad, then?'

''E seems t' be on the mend,' Ridley replied. 'They want t' keep 'im for few days, though.'

'Was he any help on what happened to him?' Matthews asked.

'Not a bit,' Ridley said sourly. 'Doesn't recall anything at this point.'

'Well, let me know when he's up to talking. I'll send someone over to take a statement.'

'Aye. Likely be glad o' company.

Ridley looked embarrassed. He stared at the floor for a moment, and then raised his eyes to meet the other man's. 'Ah'm not sure 'ow you feel 'bout this, but you reckon Ah could be part o' team lookin' into case?'

The DCS hadn't been expecting this, and looked to McDermott, who had been caught off guard as well. 'George is a good officer, Gareth, the best man I've got, in fact. I can promise you he'll not be in the way.'

'I don't know, Colin. You know the drill: if an officer is personally involved in an inquiry, or even might be seen as being involved—well, it might bugger a court case if it were to come to that.'

'It's not as if Ah'm some green PC,' Ridley pleaded. 'Got twenty-five years on wi' Met. Ah can 'elp your lads with routine work, record searches an' such. Free 'em for more 'portant things.'

Matthews considered the matter and then looked up. 'We're a bit thin on the ground, I don't mind admitting. Fully half our CID team is booked off sick with some bug going around. Tell you what: let's head down to the CID Suite and see what they've got.' His tone said that he'd play this one by ear.

When they walked into the CID area they found DCI Philippa West at her desk, engrossed in the contents of a file folder and tapping a biro against her teeth. At a desk nearby a balding man who seemed to be in his early fifties was hunched over a telephone. In the corner a younger and more dapper man was staring at a computer screen. They all looked up as Matthews, McDermott, and Ridley entered the room.

Matthews took in the room with a single glance. 'Morning, everyone. These gentlemen are DI Colin McDermott and DS George Ridley. They're with the Met. It was George's father who was injured—and possibly mugged—in the incident in Kirk Warham two nights ago,' he explained.

West put her folder down, and the man on the telephone muttered something into the mouthpiece and rang off. The younger man in the corner stopped typing on his keyboard and looked in their direction expectantly.

'George had a look around his father's room, and wasn't able to come up with his father's missing possessions. He thinks it might be a case of robbery with violence. Do we have anything that would suggest that?' he asked.

Philippa West drained her coffee cup. Apparently caffeine fuelled the work of the West Yorkshire Constabulary, just as it did in every cop shop in the country.

'Sorry, boss. Things are a bit backed up, what with the flu making its rounds. Three more of our lot are out since yesterday. Lose any more and we'll be hard pressed to issue traffic citations.'

'I know you've all been busy, and I might have an idea about that. Have the SOCOs had a chance to look over the scene?'

'I've just been on the phone with the lads, and they say it's a right mess,' she said. 'Nearly constant rain, and no shortage of tramping about by the ambulance team, not to mention the pub patrons who came out to help. Managed to get some shoe prints, but it's anybody's guess whether they'll be able to match any of them up.' She looked over at the young man on the computer. 'Dylan, any joy?'

He looked embarrassed. 'Not so far, mum. We checked the CCTV outside the pub, but it seems it wasn't functioning. In fact, according to the landlord—' he consulted his notes, —'a Mr Ben Richards, it hasn't worked for some weeks. He hadn't got round to having it put right,' he added, his face registering his opinion of the man.

She turned her gaze to the older man, sitting closer. 'Joe?'

'More of the same, I'm afraid. I went over the Incident Report filed by the uniforms, and talked to the ambulance boys as well. No one had anything to add. I haven't spoken to the pub patrons yet,' he admitted, 'but I will do this afternoon.'

Matthews turned to his DCI. 'So what do you have on your plate at the moment?'

Philippa West made a face. 'I just looked at the overnights. Two cases of Taking and Driving Away. Likely a couple of local toe rags with nothing better to do. A suspicious fire in a rubbish bin behind an off-license. Vandalism at a Chechen newsagent's on High Street, I'm guessing the result of a turf war. And a woman in hospital who looks all the world like the victim of a domestic, though we have no priors on her husband and she's not talking.'

Matthews paused for a moment, then made his decision. 'Well, I know you lot have been giving it your best, but as you know we're short-handed at the moment, and DS Ridley here would like to help. He's offered to pick up some of the routine work on his father's case, freeing you to pursue any leads that arise. Not standard procedure, of course, but he's an experienced man. I think he will be an asset.'

The expression on Philippa West's face suggested she didn't share his opinion. 'With respect, sir, I think we can handle this ourselves. It's not exactly the Great Train Robbery, is it?'

The DCS was prepared. 'Frankly, I'm surprised. You're always going on about not having enough staff to work a case properly, and what with more than half your team off sick I'd have thought that you'd welcome some additional resources.'

West saw the lay of the land, and knew better than to fight her battles in public. 'I'm sure he'll be an asset, sir,' she replied. Turning toward the other members of the team she added, 'In that event, George, you'll need to know the team.' She nodded toward a middle-aged man in rumpled trousers. 'This seedy-looking bloke is DS Joe Grimshaw, otherwise known as Giuseppi.' When he grimaced she added, 'He'll tell you what's funny later. The youngster in the far corner holding his desk down is DC Dylan Thomas. Trust me, no relation; I've read his reports. He's our resident expert on computer crime, would you believe it?'

She turned and motioned toward another, even younger man who had just entered the room. 'And this lad with the wet-behind-the-ears look and coffee stains on his shirt is DC Duncan Brookes. We call him Babbling Brookes, as he has a tendency to go on a bit,' she winked. 'We only put up with him because his father's a city councillor.' The young officer blushed. He was of medium height, with blue eyes and short blond hair, and was well dressed, except for the coffee stains West had just alluded to. McDermott imagined his boyish looks and innocent expression probably came in useful in the field.

Brookes interrupted her. 'Excuse me, ma'am, but if it might'a been a robbery, shouldn't we be running a trace on the victim's credit cards, see if there's any activity?'

Philippa West looked pleased. 'Occasionally he does earn his keep. Can you get that information for us, George?'

'Nowt to it,' Ridley said, moving to an unoccupied desk and pulling out his own wallet. 'Me dad don't believe in credit cards, but 'e does 'ave bank card for use at cashpoints. We use same bank.' He fished a card out. 'Ah'll get in touch and report stolen card.'

A few moments later he had the information and passed it along to DC Brookes, who was already busy on his computer. 'If it was a robbery, and chummy used the card at a cash-point, we'll have him on CCTV.'

'Chummy?' asked McDermott, smiling.

'Don't mind him. He's a fan of *The Sweeny*,' Philippa West replied. 'A case of arrested development,' she punned.

'You bein' funny, then, mum?' Brookes replied, straight-faced.

'Give me strength,' she said to no one in particular.

ELEVEN

By mid-afternoon the head of the SOCO team had phoned in their findings, which, as they'd expected, were bleak. The site was a mess, not least because it had rained almost continuously from the time of the incident until they'd managed to get a tent up. Add to that the contamination of the scene by all manner of people, including the ambulance attendants and casual onlookers, and there was little in the way of solid evidence. However, they'd managed to measure and photograph a section of drainage pipe that contained blood stains which doctors could compare with Bert Ridley's head wound, and they'd type the blood later; with any luck it might be traced to his assailant. Just the same, McDermott and Ridley left the building feeling that progress was minimal. After checking with the hospital and being told that there was nothing new to report they made their way back to Kirk Warham and the Blue Bull.

Returning to their room Ridley noticed the packet of photographs on the dresser where he'd left them. 'Reminds me,' he said, picking it up, 'Ah didn't finish showin' Dad's mates the pictures 'e brought along. Reckon Ah'll take 'em down wi' me, and give the lads an update on 'ow the old man's feelin.'

When they entered the lounge they found most of the same men that had been there the previous evening. Not surprisingly they were discussing the reunion.

Sid Black was holding forth on something or other, and the others looked less than captivated. They brightened at the sight of Ridley and McDermott.

''Ow's Bert doing, then?' asked Tommy Riggins, making a place for them at the table.

George took a chair. 'Better than Ah thought 'e might. 'E's awake and asked doctor for a proper drink.'

The men laughed. ''E's all right, then,' Dickie Dickenson said. 'Always was a jammy bugger.'

'Is he allowed visitors?' Frank Allenby asked.

'Doctors 'aven't said not,' George answered. 'But best t' phone first.'

The men nodded, and McDermott headed for the bar. It was still a bit early, and Ben Richards was staffing the place by himself.

Ridley reached into his jacket pocket. 'Ah brought rest o' snaps me dad brought with 'im. Thought you lads might want t' have a look.' He passed the packet to Albert Busby, who opened it with interest.

Busby held up a photo. 'Aye, that takes me back. Middle o' desert, just after El Alamein. See that tent? That's all we had to sleep in. Got bloody cold at night, I'll tell you.'

'And 'ot durin' day,' Sid Black piped in, not to be outdone. 'We could heat up our rations just by leaving 'em in sun.'

Dickie Dickenson looked at him, smiling at the others. 'We must o' been in different wars, then, Sid. Ah don't remember nowt like that.'

Sid Black gave him a dark look. 'You wouldn't remember your own name, Dickie, if it weren't sewed in your y-fronts!'

'Easy, boys,' Frank Allenby intervened. 'What's this, then?' he asked, looking at a tattered photo. He turned it over, but it was blank on the reverse.

Tommy Riggins squinted at it for a moment. 'That's near that bridge in Sicily—you know the one, Frank. Where all them Jerries died.'

Allenby peered at it more closely. 'Let's see, that would make it July, 1943, right?'

'That's right,' Riggins said. 'Primrose, Plimsole—summat like that.'

'Primasole,' Allenby corrected him. 'Now I remember. Middle of July it was. The Jerries fought like heck to prevent us crossing that bridge. It was on the main road north, along the eastern side of the island.' His face clouded. 'I remember an artillery shell hit a German lorry loaded with ammunition and petrol. When it went up it took a lot of their lads with it.' He paused, drawing up old memories and sifting through them. 'Some looting of the bodies, too, as I recall. Hard pressed to find a dead Jerry with a wristwatch.' He looked sharply at Sidney Black, who shifted uneasily in his chair.

Black seemed defensive. 'Lots o' lads did that. Makes sense. Need a watch t' do sentry duty.'

'What 'appened t' yours then, Sid?' Riggins asked.

'Got sand in it, Ah reckon. Couldn't say after all that time,' he replied, looking into his glass.

McDermott returned to the table, glasses in hand. He passed one to Ridley, then sat down as the photographs continued their journey around the table.

Riggins looked blank. 'My mind must be goin'. Ah don't remember this 'un.'

'Let me see,' Allenby said, taking the photograph. After a moment his expression brightened. 'Ah, right. That was taken in Italy proper, up in the hills, near the village we were billeted in. We talked about it last night, at this very table. Santa Cruz.'

'Santa Cristina,' Dickenson corrected him. 'Not much of a village. 'Bout like this un. Let's 'ave a look.' Allenby passed him the photograph, and he looked it over. 'Right enough. That were taken at villa where we loaded up pictures an' such, after Cap'n shot them two old people.'

That got McDermott's attention. 'Mind if I look at the photograph?' he asked.

Dickenson slid it across the table, narrowly avoiding a puddle of beer. McDermott looked at the photo closely. It had been taken in the hills of Italy on a rainy day. The road was rutted with mud, and a group of squaddies were loading various crates into one of several canvas-covered lorries that stood nearby. Bert Ridley was recognizable, helping another man—that was Riggins, in his younger days—ease a large painting into a packing crate. Other soldiers were mostly standing around, mugging for the camera.

Frank Allenby reached out for the photograph, and studied it. 'When the folk at the villa were killed we returned to company HQ in the village. It wasn't long before the locals heard about shootings. A few partisans came down out of the hills, where they'd been tracking Jerry, to tell us that the villa was full of art that needed protecting. Captain Baker-Simms, he took a platoon back to the house. You could tell he was upset about being there again, but he never told them he'd killed the old couple. They went through the house together and had a good look. Leastways that's the way it looked. When he came out he told Nobby Clarke—'

'Excuse me?' McDermott asked. He was having trouble keeping the names of the men straight.

Allenby looked apologetic. 'Of course. You won't have heard of him. Nobby was the Company Quartermaster Sergeant. Responsible for the logistics—the shipping of all the goods back and forth that an army on the move requires.'

'Ah remember 'im,' Sid Black interrupted. 'Bald as a badger's bum, he were. Fell off 'is perch in 1978. No, I tell a lie. It were a year later, in '79. I know because that's when that bint Margaret Thatcher 'came Prime Minister. Useless, she were. Made life a misery for Yorkshire miners, Ah'll tell you that.'

He was about to expound further when Frank Allenby took back the reins. 'Anyway, the Captain said there was a lot of important art in there, and the partisans were worried about it falling into the wrong hands or worse, being destroyed. So he ordered us to pack up most of it—the partisans told us which ones—and ship it to the rear for safekeeping.'

It made sense to McDermott. He recalled from his art history studies that when the invasion of the Italian mainland occurred the plans to protect cultural artifacts were not yet in place. Most of the Monuments Men—an Allied unit charged with preserving art works in conflict areas—had remained in North Africa, where the regional maps and lists of important works of art had been sent from the United States; a few of the men were already in

Sicily, preparing to come to the mainland, though at that point even their transportation had yet to be arranged. 'So what happened?' McDermott asked, his curiosity piqued.

Tommy Riggins leaned in. 'Jerry happened, that's what. There were two lorries, one with art from villa, t'other with company gear. Daft buggers sent us summer uniforms wi' short trousers to wear in Italy, durin' winter! We sent the lot back.'

George Ridley tried to put the pieces together. 'This were convoy attacked on the road back to rear?' he asked. 'My dad told me 'bout that t' other day. Got a medal outta that, 'e said.'

Tommy Riggins spoke up. 'That's right. I was one o' drivers, and Bert was my escort. Halfway there our convoy was spotted by Jerry plane. Must 'a been doin' recon, since there was only one of 'em. He strafed us, and both trucks were hit. Poor buggers in first truck went off the road and over cliff. Petrol tank caught fire and whole thing exploded. Both lads were killed outright.'

'And your truck?' George asked.

Riggins eyes brightened as his memories came back. 'Aye, that were my lorry with your dad in it. We was hit as well. I were shot in right leg and shoulder, but managed to keep on road. Pulled us up mountainside, where we tipped over onto side. Bert, he were a right 'ero. Pulled me out o' cab, and put bandage round me wounds, then he walked back to village t' get help.'

Ridley thought back to his last conversation with his father, in their room the night of his injury. 'So he got medal for that?' he asked.

'Aye, and not afore time,' Riggins replied emphatically. 'Even though he were wounded hisself he saved me bloody life!'

MCDERMOTT AND RIDLEY RETURNED to the hospital the next morning to find Bert sitting up in bed. The dressing on his head had been changed, and his colour had returned.

'You look a sight better, Dad,' George said.

'What?' His voice was slightly slurred.

George raised his voice a notch. 'Ah said you look like you're on the mend. That right?'

His father shot him a look. 'Well, Ah feel worse. Food 'ere is terrible. Ah've fed better swill to hogs! Mentioned it to the lass, but nowt came of it.' He began coughing, and some spittle formed on his chin. He seemed unaware of it, or perhaps unable to do anything about it, and George wiped it off with a tissue.

'You must be on the mend, then, if you're able to give them grief. Can I bring you summat next time I come by?'

'A decent joint a' beef wouldn't go amiss,' he smiled. 'Nor pint o' bitter, come to that.'

As they were removing their coats Doctor Chaudhari came into the room. She took Bert's pulse, checked his chart, and asked how he was feeling. Then she asked George if he would stop by her office before he left.

Twenty minutes later they appeared at her door. The doctor motioned them toward two chairs facing her desk.

'Your father's a lot stronger,' she said, smiling. 'Overall, we're really pleased by his recovery. However, our consultant is concerned about possible damage to his brain. Your father has suffered an intracerebral haemorrhage. Bleeding inside his skull has damaged some of his brain functions. Several of his senses, including his hearing and sense of taste, have been affected. As I mentioned the other day, your father is also experiencing some atrial fibrillation.'

Ridley gave her a blank look. 'Can you put that in plain English for the likes o' me?'

She looked chastened. 'Sorry about that. What I mean is, the system that regulates the beating of your father's heart is malfunctioning at the moment, causing the heart to speed up. This means that blood isn't being pumped efficiently to the rest of the body. Instead, it pools in the heart. This can result in varying symptoms, from relatively mild ones such as fatigue or cough, to more serious complications such as angina or stroke.'

'There's also still some swelling under the skin where he hit his head,' she continued. 'There's a danger that could increase. And even if it doesn't, a clot could form in one of the many blood vessels in that area, and travel to the brain itself, or to the heart. Either event would be very serious.'

Ridley was clearly concerned. 'An' what are you lot doin' 'bout it?'

'A fair question. At the moment we're giving him anticoagulants to prevent clots from forming, and other drugs to stabilize his cardiac—sorry, heart rhythms. We're also continuously monitoring his vital signs.'

'When do you 'spect to know summat for sure?'

The doctor permitted herself a small smile. 'It's not an exact science, Mr Ridley, despite what the television programmes would have one believe. But I expect the situation will be clearer in two to three days.'

Ridley digested this information. 'Aye, well, best he's here then, Ah reckon. You'll call me if there's owt change.' It was a statement, not a question.

'Of course.' She rose, extending her hand. 'Now, I'm afraid I have to have to get back to my patients. If you have any questions…'

'Not at moment. Ah 'preciate all you're doin' to help the old man.'

As they left, McDermott tried to buoy his friend's spirits. 'Your father seems to be in good hands.'

The worry lines on George's face stayed put. 'Ah suppose so,' he conceded, 'but me dad's never been in 'ospital, not since war. And at 'is age…' He left the thought unfinished.

WHEN MCDERMOTT AND RIDLEY ENTERED Wakefield CID they'd hoped for an update on the investigation into Bert's attack. But as DCI West checked her notes they braced themselves for a disappointment.

'Not a lot of progress, I'm afraid,' she said. 'There's been no activity on your father's bank card. And we've extended our look at CCTV coverage in the surrounding area. As we noted yesterday, it seems the camera directly outside the pub wasn't functioning. But there are two speed cams at either end of the village, one down the main road from the pub, the other near a school zone. Triggered by cars, of course, but we thought we might get lucky. We checked the footage for an hour on either side of the time of the assault. Nothing significant.'

Ridley took a chair at a nearby desk, looking dismayed. 'It's got t' be robbery, right enough. 'is wallet an' watch and medal are all missin.'

'It makes sense, George. But at the moment we have very little to go on.' She looked at him sympathetically.

'What about an 'ouse to 'ouse?' he suggested.

'It's a possibility, of course. But it's been several days now. The incident happened late at night and, as I understand it, it's a small village full of mostly elderly people. Likely they'd been in bed for hours. I'm not optimistic.'

The room fell silent. The frustration in Ridley's face was almost tangible. He took a deep breath and began laying out his thoughts, 'You know, t'other night my Dad and me talked 'afore we went downstairs in the pub, and summat interestin' came up. Seems 'e were lookin' for a pisser where the reunion was being held and went into the big 'ouse. He saw a paintin' in one of the rooms. He couldn't recall where he'd seen it, but he were sure it looked familiar. The owner of the 'ouse were a man named Baker-Simms, my Dad's company commander in Italy. 'E showed me Dad the door once 'e found 'im inside.'

The group looked at Ridley expectantly, and when he didn't add anything, Gareth Matthews said 'I'm sorry, George, I'm afraid you've lost me.'

Ridley shifted in his chair. 'It may be nowt, but my Dad's mates told us that after they landed in Italy they'd been ordered to set up camp in a village in the mountains near this here villa. It seems that after that, while they were on foot patrol they came on this villa. While they were 'vestigatin', the Cap'n in charge ran into this old couple upstairs and took 'em for Jerries, and killed 'em 'afore he reckoned who they were. Not long afterwards a bunch o' partisans came down out o' hills and asked their unit to move some o' valuables in the 'ouse to the rear for safekeepin'. Last night we saw an old war photo of a group of squaddies cratin' up some of the works. There were enough to fill a lorry.'

'And?' Matthews asked. Ridley could see that the others in the room thought that so far this was a bit of a rabbit-hunt. *In for a penny*, he thought, and continued his narrative.

'Well, that lorry were part of a convoy next day that were attacked by German scout plane on patrol. One truck were destroyed; t'other were damaged, but it made it to the rear more or less intact.'

Gareth Matthews pondered the problem for a moment. 'And you think the art works—or at least one of them—somehow made their way all the way back here, and ended up at this officer chap's home?'

Ridley spread his hands, palms up. 'I'm only saying it's possible. It would explain my Dad's comments to 'is mates 'bout entering the house and seeing summat familiar. Only 'e couldn't quite place it. Not surprising, given 'ow much time 'ad passed.'

'Let me get this straight,' Philippa West interrupted. 'You're saying this painting went south and ended up in Yorkshire, and your father recognized it what—some sixty years later—and was attacked to keep him quiet? That's a bit of a stretch, isn't it?'

'Not really,' McDermott intervened. 'According to Bert's mates he mentioned the painting to the Brigadier—that's the chap who as a Captain was in command of his unit in Italy, and who shot the couple at the villa. Apparently that's when he got stroppy with Bert and showed him the door. It was later that very evening that Bert was attacked.'

'So you're suggesting the assault on George's father was premeditated,' she said, raising her eyebrows.

'Yes, only the Brigadier couldn't have done it,' McDermott replied.

'Why not?'

'Because he's in his eighties and wheelchair-bound. At most he put someone else up to it.'

The silence in the room told McDermott that the others needed convincing. 'So what do you have in the way of evidence?' West asked.

McDermott looked sheepish. Even to him, it sounded thin. 'Bugger all, at this point. But I do have the photograph of Bert and his mates crating the artworks at the villa. I could visit the house and see whether anything looks familiar.'

'If only,' West snorted. 'All that stuff looks pretty much alike. And what do you have to go on? A tatty old photo taken before anyone in this room was born. I wouldn't put much on that.'

'Sorry,' Gareth Matthews interrupted. 'I hadn't mentioned McDermott's background. In your previous life you trained as an art historian, didn't you, Colin?'

'As a matter of fact I did. And I've been called in to work on several cases with the Arts and Antiques lads at the Met. But West is right: it's a long shot at best. The question is, do we have anything better at this point?' He looked around the room. They knew he was right.

'Ok, tell you what,' the DCS said, rising from the desk he'd been half sitting on. 'Go check out the place. But this is strictly unofficial, you understand: we haven't a prayer of getting a search warrant based on what you've told us. If you can talk your way in, have a crack at it. But if they keep stumpf and won't let you in, don't make an issue of it. The Baker-Simms are not unimportant people hereabouts. Gordon Baker-Simms is Secretary of the local golf club and well-respected. The family's been here forever, and they have a certain amount of clout. I don't want to be fielding any awkward queries from the Chief Constable.'

McDermott smiled. 'Fair enough. The reunion finishes up tomorrow. We'll just go pay our respects before they fold up their tents. Right, George?'

Ridley looked more like his own self, pleased that at least they had a plan. Philippa West looked dubious.

TWELVE

By the time McDermott and Ridley pulled into the forecourt at Coniston Hall it was mid-afternoon. Half a dozen men in military uniform were packing up their gear while others were busy taking down the main tent; in the background, other men, not in uniform, were grooming the lawn, trying to undo the damage caused by dozens of men in heavy boots trampling down the ground over several days. It looked as though the healing process would take some time.

As they exited their car McDermott discreetly bent down and let some air out of the right front tyre, then they wandered over to the sole remaining tent to chat with a few soldiers. Those who knew of the attack on Bert Ridley asked how he was. George fielded the questions as McDermott discreetly scanned the grounds. Finally he saw the person he was looking for standing off to the side. McDermott stood, looking at his car, seemingly perplexed, then wandered over to the man.

As he approached he saw the man was tanned and middle-aged, and dressed in expensive woolen trousers and a pale-yellow cashmere sweater and hand-crafted brogues. He summoned his best Oxbridge English. 'Excuse me. You wouldn't happen to know the owner of the house, would you? I'm not from around here. I'm afraid I've had a puncture, and I'd like to call for road service.'

The man looked him over carefully and extended his hand. 'I might be able to help.' His speech revealed an expensive public-school background. 'I'm Gordon Baker-Simms. This is my pile, for my sins. Come inside and we'll have you sorted in no time.'

'Very decent of you. I'm visiting the area, and I'm afraid I don't know whom to call. By the way, my name is McDermott. I'm here at the reunion with a friend.'

The man smiled. 'Yes, I didn't think you were a squaddie,' he replied, holding the front door for him. As they entered a large hall, Baker-Simms motioned toward a drawing room on the left. 'There's a phone in here,' he said, motioning McDermott through. 'We should be able to arrange something in short order.' He went over to a small drinks cabinet and opened it. 'Can I get you anything? Sun is well over the yardarm, as they say.' It seemed he enjoyed playing the squire.

'Thanks. I'll have a single malt, if it's going.'

'Highland Park? As it happens I have a rather nice Thirty-Year-Old. I think you'll find it's up to measure.'

'Sounds fine,' McDermott replied, 'but I don't want to put you to any trouble.'

'Nonsense,' Baker-Simms replied. He poured a generous measure of the amber liquid into two cut-glass tumblers, adding a single drop of water to each from a decanter nearby. 'A purist would insist that the water should come from the same stream.'

He smiled, swirled the glass, nosed it, and passed one glass to McDermott. 'Slainté.' He drained his glass and poured another.

McDermott nosed his own drink, paying careful attention to the fragrance, then took a substantial mouthful. It was a complex, heady mixture of heather, sherry, and spice, and it rolled around his palate effortlessly. He held his glass up to the light. 'I've had the Twenty-Five, of course, but this is really quite exceptional.'

'Indeed. Not like the local swill. But I expect I'm a shade more discerning than most,' he said smugly. 'You see, I own a brewery. Perhaps you've heard of it. The White Horse?'

McDermott had indeed heard of it, since he was staying at the Blue Bull, which was a tied house serving only White Horse ales. 'As a matter of fact, I have,' he replied. 'A very nice range of ales, if I may say so.'

Baker-Simms preened. *A man of some vanity,* McDermott's decided. His task would be easier than he had expected.

Baker-Simms set his glass down. 'Now, then, let's see if we can get you fixed up. Shall I phone the auto club?'

'I'm afraid it's not my motor. Borrowed from a friend. Where is the nearest garage?'

'Well, that rather depends on where you are staying,' Baker-Simms smiled.

'We're in a small village not far from here. Kirk Warham. Pub called the Blue Bull.'

Baker-Simms made a face. 'Know it well. Can't say the landlord is a favourite, though. The man lacks the basic social graces, if you take my meaning.' He scrolled through the directory on his mobile. 'Now let's see. Yes, just the ticket.' He punched in several numbers. 'Hello, Andrew? Gordon Baker-Simms here. Look, I've got a chap at the house here with a puncture. Can you come out and fix him up? Yes, I understand. How long? That will be fine. See you then.' He replaced the phone and turned to McDermott. 'He's all alone at his garage, so he can't leave straightaway. But he'll get his son to look after the pumps when he returns from school, which is any minute now. Says he should be here in half an hour or so. Damned nuisance really, but can't be helped. Still, as they say, a problem is merely an opportunity in disguise. Gives us time for another snifter, eh?'

McDermott allowed his gaze to wander to his surroundings. It was a large room, with tall windows that overlooked a broad expanse of lawn. The walls were hung with paintings, landscapes mostly, and the furnishings and carpets fairly screamed old money. *Time for an opening move.* 'You have a lovely home. I gather it's been in the family for some time?'

Baker-Simms was all too eager to show it off. 'Yes,' he said, 'although perhaps not by some standards. My great-grandfather started the brewery in 1882. He passed it onto my grandfather shortly after the Great War, who ran it until 1940. But Grandfather was the local Regimental Commander during Second World War, and he delegated the day-to-day running of the business to the board whilst he was away with the troops. Turned out to be a bad decision. The company was nearly run into the ground by the end of the war.'

McDermott contrived to look impressed by his surroundings. 'You seem to be doing all right now.'

'No thanks to the brainless bean-counters who were in charge—or to the banks, come to that.'

McDermott's ears pricked up. 'Gave you a hard time, did they?'

'Don't they always?' Baker-Simms snorted. 'No imagination. But I'm pleased to say we—that is, my father—sorted it all out some decades ago, and we have done rather well ever since.' He waved his arm expansively, as if to suggest the transformation was entirely his own doing.

McDermott decided it was time to move the topic of conversation. He had already gained some valuable information that he could parse later. Walking over to a Regency rosewood writing table set against the wall he ran his hand along its carved edges. 'A handsome piece. You don't often see quality like that.'

Baker-Simms smiled. 'Yes, we have managed to collect some rather nice pieces over the years.'

Their conversation was interrupted by the arrival of a stunningly attractive woman in her late thirties, with naturally red hair and piercing blue eyes. She was dressed casually but expensively in a flowered skirt and pale silk blouse over immaculately-polished brown riding boots. 'Oh, hello darling. I didn't realize we had company.' She extended her hand. 'I'm Fiona, Gordon's better half. I don't believe we've met.' She held him in her gaze, and her eyes suggested a more-than-casual interest.

'Colin McDermott,' he replied, taking her hand. He noticed that she held it just a fraction longer than necessary. 'I'm afraid I'm a bit of a nuisance. I've had a puncture. Your husband was good enough to phone the local garage.'

'So you're here for the soldiers' reunion, are you?' She looked surprised.

'In a manner of speaking. I've come with a friend.'

'Of course.' She noticed the glass in McDermott's hand, and turned to her husband. 'If you've got another one of those going, darling, I'll have one.' He turned back to the drinks cabinet. 'You're not from around here, I gather?'

'No,' McDermott replied. 'London, actually.'

'How exciting. One of my favourite cities. Gordon spends a lot of time there, don't you?' She looked at him sweetly.

Was it McDermott's imagination, or was her husband embarrassed by her remark? He returned with a glass, keeping his gaze on McDermott. 'My wife is referring to my recent absence. Only just back from a few days of meetings there. Necessary evil, I'm afraid. The City is still where the money is, right dear?' Again she smiled sweetly. *Too sweet by half*, McDermott decided. There was an underlying tension between the two, simmering just beneath the surface.

McDermott pointed his glass toward the table. 'I was just admiring your home,' he said. 'You have some lovely things. Been in the family for a long time, I expect.'

'How nice to find a man who appreciates such things.' Was it his imagination, or was there a sub-text again? She took his arm and guided him toward the drinks cabinet. She indicated a large, dark painting hanging on the wall above them. 'That's Gordon's grandfather. I expect he's told you about him already.'

McDermott lifted his glass and sipped the strong amber liquid. 'Briefly. Quite a man for his day, I imagine. So he built all this?' he asked.

'Not quite,' Gordon intervened. 'As I mentioned, my father took it over when he returned from the war. Had to modernize the production equipment and expand our marketing. In the mid-eighties I took the reins. It took years of hard graft, but eventually it paid off.'

'Well, you've certainly done well for yourselves. Your home is a real showpiece. You must be very proud.'

'Before my time, I'm afraid,' she smiled. 'Gordon and his first wife refurbished the house.'

'Once the brewery was on a solid footing we focused on renovating the house and improving the grounds.' Gordon's vanity was now in full bloom. 'My first wife died in 1986. Fiona and I met in London in 1992. We were married the following year. Made in heaven, wasn't it, dear?' He put his arm around her waist.

Trying too hard, McDermott judged. He decided to go for the brass ring. 'And your great-grandfather, did he collect all these lovely artifacts?'

'Oh no,' Baker-Simms replied. 'Most of them are from my father's day, or my own. Do you like them?' he asked, obviously chuffed.

McDermott smiled. 'You have some interesting pieces here, really quite striking.' He moved toward a marble bust on the writing table. 'Greek, isn't it? One of their gods?'

Baker-Simms couldn't resist a smirk. 'Actually, it's Roman. But you're right about the god. It's meant to be Priapus, the god of viniculture. Appropriate, don't you think?'

McDermott suppressed a smile. He'd known it was an Italian piece, and wanted to see whether Baker-Simms knew it—or would admit to it. As he moved along the wall he saw a large oil painting, dark with age, depicting a scene from Roman mythology from the Italian school. But it wasn't only the painting that caught his attention; the frame was also distinctive, and he took note of its features. A walnut bureau nearby was also Italian, if he was any judge. He did not linger, but focused instead on the gold-and-blue carpet beneath their feet. An Aubusson, he knew, and probably worth every bit of £20,000 if he was any judge. 'This goes very well with the room, doesn't it?'

'How very perceptive of you,' Fiona Baker-Simms said. 'You have a good eye. You aren't an interior designer by any chance, are you?'

McDermott realised he was sailing close to the wind. 'Not really,' he laughed. 'The result of being brought up in London, with all the galleries and antique shops. My parents were rather well off. I guess I just grew up surrounded by beautiful objects.'

Fiona's eye's sparkled. 'How interesting! And what do you do, there, if I may ask?'

'Nothing interesting,' he replied, seeking to avoid an outright lie if he could. 'I work in the civil service. Just another face in the crowd.'

'Not for Inland Revenue, I hope,' Gordon Baker-Simms laughed.

'Nothing so glamorous.' McDermott was spared the need to elaborate by the doorbell.

'That will be Andrew, I expect. And not before time. I'll just see you out.'

Baker-Simms headed for the front door, and McDermott set his glass down on the mantlepiece. 'It's been good meeting you, Mrs Baker-Simms. Thank you for your hospitality. I'm afraid I must be off.'

She took his hand. 'Please call me Fiona. And do drop in again.' She squeezed his hand just perceptibly and parted her lips. McDermott passed through the front door, wondering what might have happened if the garage mechanic hadn't appeared when he did, or if her husband had been away.

After making his goodbyes to Gordon Baker-Simms McDermott headed across the forecourt. When he reached his car George was standing alongside the mechanic, who was examining the tyre. 'It's more soft than flat.' The man stood up and brushed off his coveralls. 'No sign of a puncture. Do you want me to change it, or just add some air?'

'The latter, I think,' McDermott replied. 'We'll run it back to the village and see whether it needs more air by then. If it does we'll stop off at your garage for a proper look.' Ridley nodded sagaciously at the charade.

AFTER A LEISURELY SUPPER at the pub Ridley and McDermott settled in their room and went over things. McDermott dug out Bert's war pictures and was examining them. 'You know, I think your father was onto something, George,' he said, passing him a photo. 'You see that painting being crated? I'm almost certain it's the same one I saw in Baker-Simms' house this afternoon.'

Ridley examined the photograph, then handed it back. 'Ah dunno, guv. Pretty fuzzy.' More of a statement than a question.

'Yes, it isn't the best,' McDermott admitted. 'But a couple of things give it away. Did you notice the frame? You can just make out the presence of some of the details. It's really quite distinctive. The corners form enlarged squares, with what looks like a rosette in each one. Then there's the painting itself. The ruins of a temple. Lots of those around, of course, but the composition is rather odd, with the light coming from the left, the same side as the wind blowing the leaves. Throws the whole rather off balance. Unusual, I would have thought, given that the artist was technically quite skilled.'

George peered at the photo more closely, then handed it back. 'What do you make of it, then?'

McDermott pondered his question. 'Well, all I can say for certain at this point is that there's quite a bit of brass tied up in that house and its contents. I was only in the one room, but at a guess I'd put the value of the artworks in that one room alone at close to 100,000 quid. If that's anything to go by, then the entire house, together with its land and contents, must be worth several million at the very least.'

Ridley whistled. 'Guess the brewin' business must be doin' all right!'

'That's just it, George. Gordon Baker-Simms practically admitted the brewery was on its last legs when his father returned from the war. It must have taken vast amounts of cash to modernise it, and then he turned his attention to the house and grounds. So how did they come by all that brass?'

'The bank?'

McDermott smiled. 'Banks don't stay solvent by giving money away. Even if he had been able to put together some financing, he'd have had to reestablish his place in the market, and then expand. It would have taken decades. Yet he implied they'd improved the house and lands only a few years later.'

'So what do you reckon?' Ridley asked, looking skeptical. 'You think 'e copped a few of them pictures from house in Italy, and that paid for all that?'

McDermott studied the photo again. 'No, I don't think that's the way it happened, George, at least not exactly. For one thing, any painting worth enough to finance all the improvements to the brewery and estate would have been so valuable that it would be well known, far too well known to sell, at least on the open market.'

Ridley looked at him closely. 'So what d' you reckon, then?'

'I don't know, George,' McDermott admitted. 'But it's worth looking into. I'd like to discuss the painting with your father, get some more details from him.'

'Aye, we can talk to 'im in mornin',' Ridley agreed. He turned in, pleased that his dad was recovering nicely.

THIRTEEN

Following breakfast McDermott and Ridley made their way to the hospital. Arriving at the third floor they found Bert's room empty, the bed vacant but unmade. At the nurse's station a short, plump young woman with a pixie haircut in blue and green was busy at the desk.

Ridley wore his concern on his face, so McDermott spoke first. 'Excuse me. We were just in room 303, and it's empty. Has Mr Ridley been moved?'

'You're his son, then, sir?' she asked, turning to George.

'Aye. What's wrong?'

'I'm sorry. I'm afraid your father's had a turn for the worse.'

The colour drained from Ridley's face. ''Ow is 'e? Where is 'e? Why wasn' Ah called?'

The nurse looked sheepish. 'I'm afraid it all happened in the past few minutes. We haven't had time to contact you.'

'Well, Ah'm 'ere now,' George said. 'Where's 'e being looked after?'

Her expression was evasive. 'I'll just page the doctor. It won't be a minute.'

McDermott steered Ridley toward a small waiting area. 'Take it easy, George. I'm sure they're doing everything that they can. Why don't I get you a coffee?'

Ridley brushed his arm aside, then regretted it. 'Sorry, guv. Reckon Ah'll just wait for doctor.'

Within moments Dr Chaudhari came down the hallway, her face clouded with concern. 'Mr Ridley, I'm sorry you weren't contacted promptly. Things have happened rather quickly, and we've only just managed to stabilise your father.'

'What d' you mean?' Ridley asked.

She motioned them to a nearby doctor's lounge. It was a small room, with just enough space for two daybeds on adjacent walls, a table with a few magazines and two chairs. There was a stack of surgical gowns in one corner and a bin for used garments. She pointed them toward the chairs, and sat on the edge of one of the daybeds. 'I'm afraid your father has had a stroke, Mr Ridley. Quite a serious one. You recall that I did say it was a possibility.'

'Aye. You also said you had summun' on it,' Ridley replied darkly.

She looked sympathetic. 'And we do, Mr Ridley. Doctor Stephens is with your father as we speak, assessing his condition. As I believe I told you earlier, medicine is not an exact science. It appears that a blood clot travelled from your father's brain to his heart, precipitating a full cardiac arrest. When chest compressions were ineffective, we used a defibrillator and administered several medications, and were able to restart a regular rhythm. However, his brain was deprived of oxygen for several minutes.

Possibly enough to cause brain damage. We've put him on an EEG monitor to assess his brain activity.'

Ridley sat still for several moments, taking it in. 'And is 'e able to speak and move and such like?'

She smoothed her green surgical trousers. 'It's too early to say. Some of his functions may have been compromised, but we won't know exactly what the deficits, or their magnitude, are until later today.'

'That's what you said last time,' he replied, clearly exasperated. 'What *can* you tell me?'

The doctor leaned forward and took his hand, glancing at McDermott as she did so. 'I'm sorry, Mr Ridley. There is a strong possibility that your father is paralysed on his right side. At the moment he's also unable to speak, though I must stress that we don't know whether the damage is permanent.'

Ridley sat there, stunned. Finally he spoke. 'Can Ah see 'im?'

'I'm afraid not. He's in Intensive Care, and we've sedated him to minimise the stress on his heart. He's unlikely to regain consciousness during the next few hours. Perhaps it would be best if you got some rest and returned this evening.'

'Ah'll stay where Ah am, thanks. Ah want t' be 'ere when 'e wakes up.'

The doctor looked at McDermott for support. 'She's right, George. You're not doing any good here, and you'll need your rest as well. Why don't I drive you back to—'

'Nay,' Ridley interrupted. 'You go back to nick, see what you can suss out o' that lot. Ah'll stay 'ere. Any road, Ah'd only be in way there.'

McDermott sighed. He knew George was right. In his present state he'd be no help at Wakefield, and would in fact serve as a distraction. 'Let me know me if there's any change. I'll come by this afternoon at the latest.'

Ridley nodded, and sat back in his chair, staring out the window.

WHEN MCDERMOTT RETURNED TO WAKEFIELD he filled the others in on Bert's condition. Then he raised his trip to Coniston Hall.

'You didn't identify yourself as a copper?' Philippa West asked pointedly.

'Not a bit of it. I simply said I was a civil servant from London, taking in the reunion with a mate. They were far too wrapped up in showing off their home to focus on me.' He didn't mention Fiona Baker-Simms' obvious attentions.

'So what did you find out?'

'First, that they hadn't always been that well off. Gordon Baker-Simms, the present Managing Director of the Brewery, admitted they'd been in pretty dire straits after the war. Had to pour heaps of money into modernising and expanding the business. But interestingly, within a few years they were flush enough to renovate the house and grounds as well. It's a large Georgian pile, with a stable and extensive grounds. Inside doesn't look like a Sally Ann shop either.'

'Yes, I've been in the place,' Matthews admitted. 'Had a big do there for the previous Chief Constable when he retired.'

'Then you know what I mean. Inside looks like the V&A. Fine period furniture, quality rugs, paintings, sculpture, the lot. My question is, how did they come by it all, or manage to hold onto it, if they were nearly skint only a few years earlier?'

'We're getting ahead of ourselves,' Philippa West pointed out. 'It's not a crime to be successful in business. Any reason to think the Baker-Simms aren't on the up-and-up?'

McDermott took a photograph from his jacket pocket. 'Just this. The photo I mentioned yesterday shows George's father and his mates in Italy in 1943, loading a lorry with art objects from the villa to be evacuated to the rear for safekeeping. Do you see that painting in the foreground, the one being eased into a packing crate?'

Matthews looked at it, then passed it to Philippa West. 'Looks pretty ordinary to me. Not much to go on.'

'I agree it's not conclusive, but look at the frame. Do you see the way each of the corners are enlarged to form rectangles, with a tiny carved figure—a rosette—at the centre of each one? And did you notice the classical ruins, the columns, in the centre of the painting, with the light coming from the left side?'

Matthews took it back and looked at it again. 'Still pretty thin, Colin. Must be dozens, maybe hundreds, of paintings like that.'

'Perhaps. But what do you figure are the odds of there being another of the same subject, of similar dimensions, with a similar frame, in Baker-Simms' house today?'

Philippa West was clearly unconvinced. 'So running with your theory, you're suggesting that somehow the elderly Baker-Simms nicked that painting all those years ago, and George's father recognized it some sixty-odd years later, and then someone connected with the family attacked him the very same day to keep him quiet?' She looked frankly sceptical. 'Setting aside the improbabilities involved, who do you think it might be?'

'I'm not sure, to tell the truth. As I said earlier, it can't be the Brigadier; he's largely confined to a wheelchair. The most likely candidate is the son, Gordon; he's somewhere in his early sixties, I'd say, and certainly fit enough. He says he left for London the previous week, and only returned yesterday. Easy enough to check, of course, but if he was here Tuesday he's not off the hook. Then there's the wife. She's a piece of work. I can see her having the sang-froid to do whatever it takes to achieve her goal, but somehow I don't see her lying in wait outside a pub and then coshing an old man on the head.' He turned to Gareth Matthews. 'Any other members of the family who might have attacked George's father?'

The DCS rubbed his neck. 'There's a son, isn't there, Joe?' He turned to DS Grimshaw, who looked up from a file he'd been reading.

'What? Oh, yes. Sorry, sir. Gordon Baker-Simm's' son by his first wife. His name is Jeremy—no, Julian, I believe. He'd be in his late twenties, I suppose. Had a bit of form when he was younger, as I recall. Nothing serious. Bit of a hot-head. Underage drinking, a bar fight or two. His father had a good brief, and the charges were always dropped. Nothing since then, to my knowledge, but I'll check.' He turned to his keyboard and began typing. Within seconds he had his answer. 'A regular choir-boy, sir. Except for a few speeding tickets he's had a clean slate for the past six years.'

'Well, there you have it,' DCI West said. 'Not much to go on. Any suggestions, Colin?' It didn't escape his notice that she had used his given name. *Was a thaw in the offing?*

He was about to respond when he was interrupted by the phone. Grimshaw picked up and held up an index finger. 'Just a moment, please, I'll put him on.' He handed the phone to McDermott.

When McDermott put the handset to his ear there was a pause of several seconds, and he stiffened and went pale. 'I see. Please tell him I'll be there directly. And thank you for calling.'

Putting down the phone he looked at the others. 'That was the hospital. Bert Ridley has just died. I'm going there now to join George.'

As he left the room the DCS paused and said, 'Ok, you lot. From this point forward, and until we know better, this is a murder inquiry.'

FOURTEEN

Arriving at the hospital McDermott approached the room where they'd last seen Bert. The bed was empty, and a nurse was disconnecting the leads to a heart monitor and coiling them up. Ridley was standing at the window, looking out over the countryside. He was ashen. His eyes were red and his expression was grim. He heard McDermott enter the room and turned to face him. 'E should never 'ave come 'ere. Reunion, Ah mean. But 'is mates meant everythin' to 'im. Now look what's come of it.'

McDermott put his hand on Ridley's shoulder. 'You couldn't have known, George. No one could.'

Dr Chaudhari entered the room, and her expression reflected her distress. Ridley looked at the doctor. 'What 'appened, then?'

'It's what we feared,' she said. 'We've been medicating your father to prevent any blood clots from forming in his head wound. But as I told you earlier, one did, and broke off. It travelled to his heart where it lodged in one of the smaller arteries, causing an infarction. We thought we had him stabilized, but he suffered a heart attack. We tried to resuscitate him, of course, but there was simply too much damage. His body didn't respond.' She looked at George, who looked away. His entire body language said that he was gutted. His father was dead; that was all that mattered.

For the next hour McDermott and Ridley sat in a small consulting room the doctor found for them. Ridley refused all attempts to soften his grief. Despite their years together he had been a very private man, used to keeping things to himself. McDermott searched in vain for a way to lighten his friend's despair. The light outside was failing when McDermott finally rose from his chair. 'We should be getting back, George. You can't do anything more here.'

'Aye. Suppose so,' he said, looking up at his friend. 'Ah just want the bugger what did it. Any joy at Wakefield?'

'Not yet,' McDermott admitted. 'But we've been looking at several lines of inquiry.'

'Oh, aye?' Ridley said. 'That's what we allus say t' newspapers when we've got sweet f.a. You wouldn't kid a copper, would you?'

McDermott put his hand on his friend's shoulder. 'Don't worry, George. Now that your father's died, I'm sure Matthews will ramp up the investigation.'

'Been over three days, Guv. You an' Ah both know best results come in first few hours.'

'All the more reason to get on it,' McDermott replied. 'It's getting late. Let's get back to the pub and go over what we know. We'll make a fresh start in the morning. I'll let London know what happened, and see if we can stay on here for a few days.'

Ridley picked up his coat. 'Aye. Ah'll 'ave t' call Dora an' all.' He lumbered out of the small room.

Whilst Ridley telephoned his wife McDermott contacted DCI Galbraith at the Charing Cross Station. After learning that there was nothing pressing in London he suggested that since Bert's death was now a murder inquiry, they might be of use. Galbraith had agreed, realising that George would be of little or no use back at the Met. He had also asked where to send flowers.

IT WAS NEARLY DARK by the time McDermott and Ridley cleared the last traffic circle on the outskirts of Wakefield, and a few minutes later they turned off Doncaster Road. A narrow country lane flanked by large oaks gradually gave way to dry stone walls and hedgerows as they passed Coniston Hall. A mile further they were rounding a sharp curve when a vehicle seemed to come at them out of nowhere, its high beams on. McDermott was momentarily blinded by the intense light, and jerked the wheel hard left, narrowly missing the other vehicle, only to see a stone wall looming up in front of him. He yanked the wheel to the right and managed to miss the wall, but overcorrected and the car shot across the road. He hit the brakes as the car skidded off the tarmac and onto the verge, shuddering to a stop just inches from a large and very formidable hawthorn tree.

'Jesus wept,' he said. 'That was close. Bloody fool!' He looked to George, who was surprisingly calm, all things considered. 'You all right, then?'

'Ah reckon. It were a close one, right enough.'

McDermott climbed out and inspected the car. There was some fescue caught between the right front wheel and the wing, and some scratches on the undercarriage from a rock he'd passed over, but the tyres seemed okay and the damage seemed to be superficial. He climbed back in and reversed onto the road, then they continued on toward Kirk Warham.

As they approached the village McDermott said, 'You know, there was something funny about that truck, or whatever it was.'

'Oh, aye? Ah must 'ave missed the joke, then,' Ridley replied.

'Not funny ha, ha. Funny odd. Did you notice the headlamps?'

'Can't say as Ah did,' Ridley said sourly. 'Ah were too busy tryin' to duck.'

'Point taken, George. No, I could be wrong, but they seemed awfully close together.'

'Meanin? You think it were two blokes on motorcycles?'

McDermott laughed. It was good to see his friend's sense of humour returning. 'No, I wonder if it wasn't a Land Rover. You know, the older ones that had their headlamps inboard of the wings.'

'Right,' George said drily. 'Farmin' country. Must be a fair few o' those 'round 'ere, I expect.'

When they neared Kirk Warham McDermott pulled into the forecourt of the local garage. The sign said ANDREW WHEELER AND SON, MOTOR REPAIRS. AN appropriate name for someone in the garage business. It was dark, but he sounded his horn and a moment later a man in coveralls appeared in the doorway of the house next to the garage. It was the same man who had fixed McDermott's tyre the previous day.

'We're closed,' he said, then recognized McDermott. 'Oh, it's you, then. Tyre gone soft again?'

McDermott smiled. 'Not quite. A near miss, actually. Another vehicle forced us off the road just now. I wonder if you could check for any damage?'

The man looked back at the doorway, then seemed to resign himself to his fate. He unlocked the side door of the garage and stepped inside, emerging a moment later with a large torch. By this time a small boy had emerged from the house. 'Everythin' all right, Dad?' the boy called out. 'Your supper's getting cold.'

'Just be a moment, Trev. Don't bother yourself. I'll be right in.'

The boy was clearly consumed by curiosity, and joined his father. As the man slid underneath the car the boy looked up at McDermott. 'My name's Trevor,' he said.

McDermott smiled. 'And my name's Colin. This is George,' he added, motioning to Ridley, who said nothing.

Wheeler slid out from underneath the car. 'No serious damage. Some scratches, though,' he said, pointing to where the bodywork met the undercarriage. 'I'd have the alignment checked next time you have it serviced. Otherwise it seems sound enough.'

'I'm in your debt,' McDermott said, pulling a banknote from his wallet. 'I suppose this is a silly question, considering we're in the country,' he added, 'but are there many Land Rovers around here?'

The man laughed. 'Only several dozen, I reckon. Why? Is that the car you almost hit?'

'The car that almost hit me, actually. At least I think so. It was dark, and I only saw it for a moment, but the headlights were quite close together.'

'That'd be a Land Rover, then, like as not.'

'It was dark, blue or black, I think.'

'Ah, that's different,' Wheeler said, rubbing his jaw. 'Not a lot of them about. Most people favour tan or green. You know, ex-Army colours. Makes 'em feel all manly. A few grey ones about as well. Only dark one I can think of belongs to gent that owns the house where I fixed your tyre.'

McDermott's ears picked up. 'You mean Baker-Simms?'

'Aye, that's him. He uses it when he wants to play squire around here, which is most of the time.'

'Interesting. And you say it's the only dark Land Rover hereabouts?'

When he nodded, his son interrupted him. 'What about the gypsy that stopped by last week, Dad?'

'What are you getting at, Trev?'

'Don't you remember, Dad? The man who came in with a faulty alternator. Said he needed a replacement. He said it were for a Land Rover.'

Wheeler thought a moment. 'So he did. But he never mentioned the colour, as I recall.'

'Right,' said the boy. 'But he didn't say it *wasn't* dark.'

Wheeler laughed. 'Right enough, lad.'

'Don't suppose he left an address?' McDermott asked hopefully.

'A gypsy? Not much chance of that.' He rubbed his chin thoughtfully. 'Come to think of it, he mentioned he was camped in the field on t'other side o' river.'

'We're new to the area, as you'll have guessed. Where's that?'

'Nowt to it,' Wheeler replied. 'Take the turning just there,' he said, pointing to the road to Kirk Warham. 'There's a junction next to the pub. You'll cross a bridge, then the road bears right. There's a sign for pony trekking about a mile further on, then a gate to a field on the right. The camp will be at the bottom of the field, near the river. Handy for water.' He pulled an order book from his back pocket. 'Had to order his part. Man's name is Hearn. Noah Hearn.'

'Much obliged,' McDermott said, climbing back into his car. Ridley followed, and they set out for the pub.

'You want to nick that bloke for runnin' us off road?' Ridley asked.

'It might be nothing. Maybe he was just driving like a madman. On the other hand…' He left the thought unfinished. 'We'll save the gypsy for later,' McDermott said. 'Not a priority at the moment, and it's a slim thread at best.' McDermott concentrated on the road ahead. When they arrived at the Blue Bull they checked the lounge, but there were none of Bert's mates visible, only a few locals lingering over their pints. They had a light supper and McDermott elected to remain behind for a bit, observing the other patrons. Ridley decided to go to their room.

GEORGE RIDLEY BEGAN PACKING UP his dad's possessions. He had gathered the older man's clothing and shaving gear and hospital effects, and put them on the bed in what had been their room, *their* room, at the Blue Bull. He had paused to take stock, not only of his father's personal possessions, but also of himself. As a policeman he had seen his share of death in many forms, but this was different: this was his father. George was tough, but he was also grieving.

He reached into the wardrobe and pulled out Bert's valise. It was showing its age, the leather scuffed and the nickel-plated metal fittings tarnished with the years. He set it on the bed and opened it, and began to place his father's shoes inside when he noticed a small object at the bottom of the bag. He pulled it out and examined it. It was a journal, covered in calfskin, originally tan but darkened with age. The cover was tattered round the edges and grimy, and discoloured with what looked like water stains. When he opened it the pages were yellowed and dog-eared. He squinted at the contents and his brows went up when he realised it was written in his father's hand. On the first page was written *Property of Trooper Albert Ridley, King George's Yorkshire Light Infantry, Hill Farm, Croft Lane, East Ardsley, Wakefield, West Yorks, England. Please return if found. If I'm dead, see that it gets to my dad.*

Hill Farm. His father's land, and his father's before him. George had been born there, or as good as, in the village nursing home nearby. The smallholding had disappeared decades ago after his father retired, the land given over for a housing estate, the victim of what passed for progress. He turned to the second page, and there before him, in a careful cursive style of handwriting learned when he was a lad at school, was his father's account of his time during the war. Ridley put aside the shoes and began reading, and as he did he found himself transported back in time more than sixty years.

FIFTEEN

Bert Ridley's Journal

Near Liverpool, late August 1942

Well, I've gone too far to go back now. It was terrible hard leaving the farm and my dad. I know he's scared I won't come back, but I had to go. After my brother died on convoy duty off coast o' Canada I never felt right about staying on farm whilst others went off to war. Dad were that upset, I could see. Afraid o' losing his only remaining son. But I knew I'd never be able to look folk in the face if I stayed working the farm, never mind it's a reserved occupation. He'll be able to get help on the farm, land girls or even a prisoner of war, to help him tend the stock.

So here I am on a troop ship, headed for God knows where. Rumours have it we're bound for North Africa. It makes sense, since we've been playin' a game of see-saw with the Jerries, advancing and then retreating for months now. I hope it won't turn out to be a stalemate, like so many battles in the last war. A lot o' good men got left there.

I've never been on water before, except for rivers and such near our farm. The ocean is a whole other thing. I've only been on boat (ship they call it —get a bit stroppy about that!) for a few hours, but it already rolls a fair bit, and I can see it will be tough going if we hit rough weather. I'll eat light, just in case. Any road, the food isn't that good. We had it better at the farm, all the eggs and meat we could want, and cooked proper, not in big kettles for hours. The stuff they give us here has no taste, and the meat is grey. Tea's mostly ok, though, and as much as you want.

Somewhere off the coast of Portugal, 10 September 1942

The water came up rough yesterday. I spent the whole time trying to keep my dinner down. I went below, but that were worse, so I came back on deck and held onto rope (they call 'em lines on ship) near a ladder, and breathed in the cool air, which helped a bit. I tried small amount of tea, but no solid food. Those who ate big paid the price, leaning over the edge and giving it back to the sea. We had to make a wide swing away from Jerry submarine pens in France, which is making the trip longer. Sergeant said we'd another week, leastways if the Jerry subs didn't get us first. Thought of my brother. Will they get me, too?

North Africa, 18 September 1942

We finally arrived in Egypt. A grand city it is—summun said it's called Alexandria. You wouldn't believe how big the army camp here is! Tents for miles, and the docks full of lorries and field guns and barrels and jerrycans of petrol, and crates and crates of God knows what. I don't see how we can lose the war, what with so much equipment and men on our side! Everything is organized. After a bit of a wait they took us to a place called El Alamain. Leastways I think that's how it's spelled. By the time we arrived it were getting dark, and it was grand to meet my new mates.

30 September 1942

Been nearly two weeks now, and I'm just beginning to get the lay of the land. The food here is a sight better than on ship. There's a store, commissary they calls it, where you can buy ciggies and writing paper and chocolate and such, and just being on land with a proper bed, even if it is a cot in a tent, and not a bloody hammock, makes a world o' difference. Takes some getting used to, though. For one, even though the days are hotter than Hades, the nights are bloody cold, excuse my French. If you're outside on watch you want to dig your hands down into the sand to keep warm. But there's all sorts of nasty things down there, from insects to serpents, so you got to be careful! For another, the sand gets into everything, your boots and even your food if you ain't careful. When a storm comes up (I mean sand, not rain) you got to cover up right good and keep your mouth and nose covered and even your eyes shut when possible.

We wait for supplies to come, and the Big Brass use the time to give us more drills. The worst is the marching in formation. As if we didn't learn how to do that afore we came over! But a chance for us new lads to get to know the old hands. Seems a good lot. There's Alf Beasley (he's a cook, good man to know), Percy Tippit (farmer, now a medic), Frank Allenby (new to regiment, like me), and Arthur Ellsworth (don't rightly know what he's about yet). Then there's Albert Busby (a radioman) and Tommy Riggins (lorry driver), Dickey

Dickerson (trooper, like myself. Seems a good chap), and a few others whose names I forget.

I'm told it's been a bad time for us. Seems the Jerries attacked here in July but we held them off, and with the new supplies and men—me included—we're 'bout to make big push against Rommel. Looks like I got myself into summat. Still, the only sign of fighting I've seen so far are lights at night and sounds from their bombs in the distance. Our boys in Sunderlands and Spitfires and such head out that way every night and come back by first light to our airfield east of here. The older men say to expect the Jerries to give us tit for tat sometime soon.

21 October 1942

We been checking gear for days now, and word is we'll be seeing fighting afore week is out. Hope I got the grit to face down Jerry. Killed my share o' pigs and chickens, along with the occasional cow or horse, but never killed a man afore. Even the months of training has been just that, shooting at targets or bayoneting dummies. Still, it's them or me.

24 October 1942

Sure enough, after havin' our nose bloodied in July, just afore I got here, we're finally taking it to the Jerries. Saw my first battle last night. It were full moon, and after sun went down we—by which I mean biggest bunch of soldiers I'd ever seen on the move at one time—set out from base camp on coast road, headed west. We held up and regrouped in the desert until our field guns opened up. Idea was we'd soften 'em up with shelling, then infantry—that's us poor blokes—would move ahead, clearing the way for tanks. They reckon men on the ground are lighter than tanks, and wouldn't trip the mines the Jerries had planted. Nice for some! Any road, shelling started well afore midnight. We set out on foot, whilst artillery was still firing over our heads, and our tanks came behind us. Only all that shellin' stirred up dust and we didn't know which way were up! Lot of our lads didn't get through, and none of the tanks made it.

Today hasn't been much better. Our pilots attacked Jerries all day, but we didn't advance much, as minefields hadn't been cleared. Sure hope this ain't going to become a stalemate, like the trench warfare my dad told me about in the first war.

25 October 1942

Things are looking up. We got through the minefields and reached place called Miteirya Ridge. I were never so glad to sit down and rest, and have a bite, even if it were cold bully beef out a tin! By midnight 51st Division attacked Jerries and our night bombers dropped their loads on battlefield in front of us, and on German airfield behind their lines. A well-oiled machine, that's what we are—or at least I hope so.

27-30 October 1942

Busy days, and hotter than Perdition, pardon my French. Our sweat mixes with dust to cover our faces with mud. There were swarms o' flies on the bodies we passed, and a terrible smell I won't soon forget. At daybreak in the distance we could see black smoke from wrecked guns and tanks and lorries. Reckon this were as close to Hell as I'd ever seen. Explosions through night from Jerry lorries on fire. Word is we should be seein' the Yankssoon, pushin' from the West, but no sign so far. The old hands said not to get too excited, that the Yanks were always promisin' to come, but promises never came to nowt. Heard one of our Brigades was overrun by Jerry tanks and a bunch of our lads captured. Sure hope it isn't true.

02-04 November 1942

Big attack last couple o' days. Our lads bombed Rommel's lot and it were followed by shellin' I'd never seen the likes of afore. Went on for hours, it did, then after midnight us poor infantry blokes set off. But by next day I couldn't see it counted for much. Two days later our planes near covered sky, dropping bombs on enemy, and we set off to cross gap and bring it to the Jerries. Could hardly see for the dust we kicked up. Covered our faces but we were coughing and choaking all the same. Took our share o' Eyetie prisoners, who didn't have much fight left in 'em. The dead bodies in tanks, some o' which were on fire, made more than one of us sick.

07-11 November 1942

Got 'em on the run now! Officers all say the Egyptian border is secure, and the Yanks are finally closin' in from t'other side. Reckon the worst is over. At least I hope so. Know I shouldn't be writin' this, but where's the sense in it all? Most o' lads on both sides are just normal folk who are dyin' followin' orders. And who holds the land depends on which day you're talkin' about.

26 December 1942

Been that busy fightin' Jerries, this is first time I could sit down and catch up on things. Pushed Rommel back as far as place called Sirte, but had to stop for our own troops to catch up. Spent Christmas yesterday eatin' more bully beef from tins. Most men got parcels from home, and if they had biscuits and such they passed 'em round. I got piece o' shrapnel in my right arm three days ago. Nowt serious, but it won't clear up, so field hospital cleaned it out and bandaged it up again. Lot o' men are hurt worse, and some poor blokes won't be comin' home at all. No way to spend Christmas.

16 January 1943

Heck of a way to spend the new year. My arm is still givin' me trouble. Monty sent 51st Highlanders to rout Jerries yesterday, and Rommel beat it. Headed for Tunisia, Cap'n reckons. But the further he goes, the closer he is to his own supply lines, and the further we are from ours. I hope Monty knows what he's doin'.

24 February 1943

After some nasty fighting at place called Kasserine Pass Rommel finally turned tail. Dickey and Frank and Sid and me were on patrol when we got our first prisoners of war. A German tank crew that ran out o' petrol. They were sittin' next to their tank, a right sorry-lookin' bunch, just waiting for us. Knew they couldn't go nowhere. Four men, an officer—young bloke—and three others. They stood up and put their hands in the air, though officer were a bit surly about it. We took their sidearms and searched the tank for any maps or other papers that might be useful. They'd burned them all, though. Then our CO, Captain Baker-Simms, showed up and took 'em to rear to be questioned by our lads in Military Intelligence. Not likely to get much, though. Barely gave their names and ranks (which we could tell easily enough), and serial numbers. Still, one less lot o' enemy to worry about.

07 May 1943

Our armoured units entered Tunis today. Looks like the Jerries are done for. Word is the Yanks are on their flank to the west, givin' them what for as well. Too much to hope for?

20 May 1943

The Jerries give up! Thought I'd never see the day! So many prisoners that line reached back as far as eye could see. A few were still nasty 'bout losing, but you could tell others were just glad to have it over with. We put their guns in lorries and they marched back on side o' road, those that weren't too badly wounded. Ran out o' ambulances for them as weren't fit to march. They went in lorries with some of our lads. Must o' got some hard looks. Yesterday the high mucky-mucks held big parade in Tunis. General Alexander were there, along wi' Eisenhower for the Yanks, and some French bloke too. I weren't there to see it, as we were busy escortin' POWs back to rear, but the lads as was said it were a sight to behold. Still can't believe the war here is over.

03 June 1943

Finally got back to base camp near Alexandria. Never been so glad to stop marchin'! Rest and Recreation, they calls it, and more drills as we rebuild our forces. Monty says we control all o' North Africa now. Thought it might be over for us, but seems 'e has other plans. Don't know where we're headed next, but it's bound to be somewhere big, based on number o' men and gear bein' gathered up.

Sicily, 10 July-17 August 1943

Seems like we're vital to war effort. After months of trainin' and resupply they put us in ships last night and set off north. They wouldn't tell us nowt, but we all knew which way sun had set. Reckon it's Italy this time, leastways I hope so. From what I see the Eyeties' heart isn't in this war. Sometimes they fight hard enough, but when it's hopeless they put their hands in air. Not like the Jerries. Some will fight to the last man.

We landed afore dawn off coast of Sicily. Huge force, sent to beach in boats from troop ships. Nasty weather, and lots o' wind. Landing craft bobbed in water like corks, and the crew set some o' lads down too far from shore, which made getting' there a right chore. Still, there wasn't much fire from Eyeties at start, and most of us got to beach all right. Can't say same for paratroopers. Bunch o' their gliders crashed into sea, and a lot o' good men drowned. We were told the Yanks were coming in from other side of island. I hope so. If we meet up it'll be first time we see 'em.

No sand. Beach were right rocky. Reminded me o' Yorkshire. Got to work unloading stores onto beach. Traded our rifles for spades, but welcome all the same. A sight better than facing enemy bullets and shells. Other units moved ahead, and later we heard they came under fire from Jerry tanks. Our troops captured big port at place called Syracuse on first day, which made things a sight easier, though we only came along later.

A different war from Africa. No sand to slog through, no big tank units, leastways not here. We followed main coast road from one city to next. We got to place called Augusta a few days after Syracuse, and kept on headin' north. 51st Highlanders took our left flank, keepin' enemy busy and makin' sure we weren't cut off. The fightin' were different, though. No trenches or foxholes. We had t' pick our way through rubble in streets, keepin' eye out for snipers. Also had to watch for civilians, makin' sure we didn't shoot too quick and kill a kid, or a mother. The men we saw were all old. Expect the younger ones had gone off to fight long time ago. One o' men killed hisself today. Grenade landed in middle of us, and he threw himself on it. Saved three lads nearby. I'm not sure why he did it. Was he trying to be a hero, or had he just had enough of fightin'? He'd been in a funk for last several weeks. Said 'e'd had his fill o' war. Had a wife and all.

17 August 1943

Yanks got to Messina first, but only by hours, and were already shellin' mainland. The enemy were gone, crossed water into Italy proper. We marched into town in columns, like it were a fancy dress parade. Locals were mostly glad to see us. Waved white flags from windows and came out to line streets as our lorries and gun tractors came by. Some o' lads were kissed by girls and I could see they were pleased about that. Army handed out pamphlet to troops called Soldier's Guide to Sicily. *Not much help as we were about to leave island! Not much left, though. Railway yards were rubble, as were docks, and buildings in rest o' city.*

Italy, 03 September 1943

Crossed to Italy proper today, just two miles away, at place called San Giovanni. The Jerries were gone. Eyeties put up a bit o' fight, but not much, and surrendered afore day was out. Some of our units were ordered to head up east coast of Italy. The rest of us were sent north, up west coast a few miles, then our company got orders to go inland to make sure Jerries weren't waitin' in mountains to flank our troops. We're less than a hundred men now, and not many officers among us. Cap'n Baker-Simms took us as far as village in hills nearby. He reckoned it were a good base to recce from, as it were on a high ridge and not far from coast if we found ourselves outnumbered and had to fall back in a hurry. We set up HQ there and by evenin' the locals came out to see us. Not much fightin' there, seein' as it was up in the hills, away from the coast and on a small country road. Reminds me a bit o' Yorkshire Dales, though trees are different, with olives and lemons and grapes and such, and except for a few goats not much in the way o' livestock in sight.

04 September 1943

It were rainin' by daybreak, but Cap'n decided to move out. We needed to see just how close Jerry was, so as to report back to regiment. He formed a platoon and we set off on foot to recce area and create forward observation post. Rain were comin' down so heavy by then we could hardly hear owt, but that meant Jerries couldn't hear us and all.

After while we came round bend in road and saw a large house—villas they calls 'em here—with a stone wall in front. Cap'n ordered platoon to both sides 'o' road, and took two of us to front door. We waited a minute, but heard nowt, so we went in, real careful-like. It were darker 'n inside o' cow's belly at first, but we waited a bit until we could see proper. Cap'n sent us to check rooms on ground floor and 'e went upstairs. We were that scared, more used to street fightin' and battles in miles and miles o' sand. But we looked in all the rooms, and saw nowt. My mate and me were in kitchen when we heard Sten gun goin' off! We hurried upstairs fast as we could, but takin' time to be sure we weren't runnin' into summat. When we got there we found Cap'n standing over two bodies in bedroom. 'E said they had pistol, and ' 'e fired on ' 'em. I could see 'e were that upset. We went down to rest o' platoon, who'd heard the gunfire and were waitin' at bottom o' stairs. Cap'n ordered all of us out, and put two men on front door, with orders to let no un in. Then we returned to Company HQ in village. 'E radioed to Regimental HQ, who were up the coast, headed to Salerno. They said they'd send Company Adjutant, Major Strickland, back to look into things. Cap'n went back to villa to satisfy himself it were secure.

The Major arrived next mornin', and after lookin' things over decided the Cap'n had acted proper like. 'E took the pistol from 'ouse and wrote up report. Then 'e returned to regiment. Some o' men didn't like it. They thought Cap'n had been too quick to shoot. But they had to admit that in a dark place like that, when Jerry could be anywhere, they might a fired too.

08-11 September 1943

You never know when you're safe and when you're not. Few days back we had visit from civilians. Group of locals—partisans they called themselves—came to see about protectin' valuables in villa where shootin' took place. They were a mixed lot—commies and anarchists and God knows what all—and couldn't agree 'bout what to do with paintings and such in villa, but wanted them removed in case Jerries came back or house was bombed. Cap'n offered to take goods to rear where we'd landed, for safekeepin', and they agreed. This mornin' Cap'n took three lorries, one full o' men, me included, to villa to pack up things and move them to rear. One lorry were already full o' regimental gear we brought from Africa. No good to us. Summer uniforms and the like—and us goin' into winter in a few weeks! Took us best part o' three days, but by afternoon we finished packin' up all paintings and such, and truck with squaddies went back to village, and other two set out down road to San Giovanni, a driver and trooper in each, includin' yours truly.

The road were terrible twisty, and we hadn't been gone an hour afore a Jerry scout plane spotted us. Came at us from rear, so we had no idea until machine-gun bullets strafed both lorries and stirred up dirt on road in front of us. The lead truck were hit bad, and swerved off road and down mountainside, where it rolled over and over. My driver were Tommy Riggins, and 'e were hit in shoulder. But 'e managed to keep our lorry on road, and steered it up mountainside, where we tipped over on our side, all slow-like. When I untangled meself I could see Tommy were in bad way, so I pulled him out and used my jacket to tie off his wound and stop bleedin'. Then I went t'other side o' road, and saw the other truck in the brush below, which had caught fire. I scrambled down mountainside, but by time I got there I could see both lads 'ad bought it. One had been thrown clear, but he must a landed badly, 'cause his neck were broken. The driver were still inside, but covered in blood, and the fire was reachin' the cab. I pulled 'im out, but there were nothin' else I could do for him. I dragged him well away from fire and then saw burns had covered best part o' both my forearms. Then I made my way back up side o' mountain to Tommy. He were in no shape to stand up, let alone walk, so I leaned him up against truck and gave him my water, and set off on foot back t' village for help.

When I got there I reported to Cap'n, who ordered an ambulance and another lorry with half a dozen men. It were near dark when we returned and found Tommy. He lost a fair bit o' blood but were still alive. Medics bandaged him up proper and loaded him into ambulance, and me as well, and sent us off to field hospital in San Giovanni. The rest o' lads looked after the poor blokes who'd not been so lucky, and the trucks.

23 September 1943

Spent best part of two weeks in hospital afore the burns on my forearms and hands were startin' to heal. Tommy were worse off. His insides were right tore up, and he were ordered home for duration. Cap'n came to see us both, and told Tommy he were lucky to be alive. Said if I hadn't returned to camp that quickly he'd a bled to death. Then he said he were putting me in for medal for heroism! I didn't feel like no hero, what with two of my mates dead, and 'nother just hangin' on, and me the lucky un.

28 September 1943

'Nother week's gone by, and this mornin' the doc said I was too badly injured to be o' much use to army, so they're shippin' me home. Wasn't sure how I felt. On one hand I was that glad to see the last o' fightin', but I'm not best pleased leaving my mates behind. Great group o' lads. Some of 'em saved my own life more than once. Still, I reckon my dad will be happy to see me again, and all in one piece, more or less. And I reckon I done my bit.

05 October 1943

They put me on hospital ship today, headed back to Mother England. I'll be ever so glad to go down gangplank and stand on good British soil again! God bless His Majesty the King!

SIXTEEN

George put down his father's journal and sat back on the bed. For the first time he thought about how seldom he and his father had talked about the war, how little they had shared over the years. These few pages explained a lot, but the time for those conversations had passed forever. He sat there for several minutes before realising that McDermott needed to see his father's journal. He was just about to put it aside for the following day when McDermott entered the room. He noticed George's expression immediately. 'I'm sorry. I should have come up earlier. Must have been a very hard day for you.'

Ridley turned his direction. 'Aye, that's not far from the truth. But I ran across summat you might be interested in. It's me dad's 'count o' war, leastways his bit of it. He must a brought it from 'ome to share with his mates. You remember what they said 'bout shootin' at villa in Italy? Well, that's in here, and more, Ah reckon.'

He had McDermott's full attention. They spent the next two hours going over what Ridley had found and discussing what it all might mean. By the time they'd finished it was well after midnight, and they decided to turn in.

GARETH MATTHEWS HAD LAID ON A MEETING of the Incident Team early the next day to map out their plans for what had now become a homicide inquiry. The team had been formed immediately following Bert Ridley's death, and he was summarising the case for the benefit of several new members when McDermott and Ridley entered the CID Suite.

The DCS paused in his remarks. 'For those of you who don't already know these two gentlemen, the tall individual with the black hair is Detective Sergeant George Ridley of the Metropolitan Police. It was his father who was killed.' All eyes turned to George, who registered no emotion. 'The other, less-distinguished-looking bloke is DI McDermott, also from the Met.' Several of the officers smirked at the remark. Colin took it in stride; he knew that in every investigation of a violent crime there was a place for humour in order to lighten things up. Matthews turned to two unfamiliar plainclothes officers standing nearest the door. 'These are the newest additions to the Incident Team. The lass with the frizzy ginger hair is DC Emma Fox; she's just moved up from Uniform. People tell me she's right clever. The skinny lad to her left is DC Sammy—sorry, *Samir*—Singh. He's on loan from Leeds, seeing as we're short-staffed. If we like him we might just keep him.' Singh struggled to conceal a smile.

The DCS turned to address the group *en masse*. 'Following his father's death DS Ridley has asked to be more directly involved in the investigation, and I've agreed, subject to certain constraints.

He has personal knowledge of the movements of the deceased, and he's well experienced in our procedures. And as a member of the same regiment, and also as Bert's son, I think some people might speak more freely to George than to someone else.'

He looked at DCI West, who remained impassive, then back to McDermott and Ridley. 'I've just been going over the events of last Monday night, bringing the new members of our team up to speed.' He turned and addressed the group at large. 'Initially it looked to the responding officers like an accident, and as a result there was no attempt to secure the scene. An opportunity missed,' he said. Everyone in the room was thinking the same thing: *I wouldn't like to be in their shoes.*

'It had rained heavily that night,' the DCS continued. 'The ground had been thoroughly trampled by the casualty team and onlookers by the time we got to it the next day. The SOCOs couldn't come up with much.'

DC Fox spoke up. 'What about CCTV, sir?'

'No joy there either. DC Brookes checked into that earlier. The camera near the car park entrance of the pub wasn't working. And there are only three other cameras in the village. Speed-cams at either end, but only activated when a car passes exceeding the limit, and one at a cashpoint outside the only bank. We've checked. Nothing.' His expression registered his frustration.

'So what do we have, sir?' This from DC Singh.

'We know that the victim's pocket watch and wallet—and a war medal—are missing. We put an alert on his bank card. He had just the one. So far there's been no activity on it. That right, West?'

Philippa West had been sipping her coffee, and was caught in mid-swallow. She struggled to regain her composure. 'That's right, sir. We put out a description of the watch and medal to pawn shops in Wakefield, Leeds, Doncaster, Huddersfield, and Sheffield. No joy there either. A bit puzzling, that. If we assume the motive for the attack was robbery—'

'Never assume anything,' Matthews interrupted. 'It may be that the villain panicked when he saw what he'd done. Or perhaps he's waiting for things to die down a bit, or simply gone further afield to flog it.'

'Yes sir.' DCI West looked uncomfortable, not used to being called out in front of her team.

'So what's the next step, sir?' asked DC Fox.

Before the DCS could answer, Philippa West waded back in, anxious to reassert her control of the inquiry. 'We're going to go ahead with a house-to-house. Mostly OAPs, likely in bed by the time of the incident, but it's a small village where everyone knows everyone else. We might get lucky.'

Several of the CID team frowned. A house-to-house inquiry, they knew, was unlikely to yield results, especially after several days had passed. It was also dead boring. But then, much of police work was.

'Excuse me, sir,' DC Singh said. 'Do we know whether the victim hit his head on a drainage pipe, or was coshed?'

Matthews looked uneasily at George. 'The autopsy is scheduled for later today. But for now the injuries seem to match the drainage pipe pretty closely, and there are traces of blood and hair on the pipe.'

DCI West didn't miss the chance to reassume control of the discussion. 'The first thing is to establish a timeline of events leading up to Ridley's death. We need to begin twenty-four hours beforehand. Interview his mates—those that are still in the area, and get the names of anyone who's left the village since then. Also the bar staff at the pub, anyone else who might have had contact with him. Anything else?'

The room was silent. The DCS glanced at McDermott, who'd thought about raising the art issue, and the possible involvement of the Baker-Simms family. There was also the matter of the near miss on the road the previous day, but McDermott wanted to run his ideas by West and Matthews privately first. As the meeting broke up and the team members returned to their work stations he joined the two of them and said, 'A word in private, Gareth?'

'Sure. Come through to my office,' he said, holding the door open.

When they entered his office West took the nearest chair, leaving McDermott to walk around her to the sole remaining one. Matthews hadn't missed that, and took his own seat behind his desk. 'Something you wanted to talk about, Colin?'

McDermott said. 'A couple of things, actually. First, there's the art angle.' He summarized the events in Italy—the shootings at the villa, the removal of the artworks, and their apparent destruction in the attack by the German fighter plane on the way to the port at San Giovanni. It took some time, but Philippa West and Gareth Matthews listened attentively.

He ended by laying out his theory that the artworks might have made their way to England, where Baker-Simms—or someone in the family—might have disposed of them. 'I'd like to make myself useful, check in with Art and Antiques in London,' he said. 'A long shot, really, given the amount of time that's passed, but you never know. If Baker-Simms did bring back any artifacts from Italy he was unlikely to have sold them on himself; he wouldn't have the connections, and if they had been stolen he wouldn't want a trail leading back to him. But he might have disposed of them through one of the large dealers based in London. A query at some of the older auction houses might turn up records of sales dating from the late 1940s or '50s.'

West was openly skeptical, and Matthews' eyebrows shot up. 'You like fishing, do you? Bit of a stretch, that. If I was a betting man—'

McDermott had expected that response, and cut him off. 'I know, but at this point we've got bugger else to go on.'

Matthews acquiesced. 'Ok, it's your mates in London that will have to do the legwork. I'm all for sharing the load. You said there were a couple of things?'

'Yes. Last evening George and I were returning to Kirk Warham when we were forced off the road. Came out of nowhere. It was dark, but I'm certain the vehicle was a Land Rover.'

He had both officers' full attention now. 'Were you? And you think it was no accident?'

'I can't be sure. The driver must have seen us go off the road. But he—or she—didn't stop and see whether we were all right. And the owner of the garage in the village says that Baker-Simms owns a Land Rover of a similar colour.'

The DCS leaned back in his chair and interlaced his fingers, forming a steeple. 'A serious turn of events, if true. They'd have to be desperate, or very stupid, to try to kill a copper. And the Baker-Simms aren't stupid.'

'Maybe it wasn't meant to kill us, but to warn us off.'

'Just the same, a desperate act,' The DCS countered. 'A Land Rover, you say? Thick on the ground around these parts.'

'That's what the garage owner said. But not so many older models ones, which this was. You know, the ones with the headlamps set close together' After a moment he added, 'He did say that there might be one at a nearby gypsy encampment.'

The senior officer reflected on what he'd been told. 'That'd be the original Defender series. As it happens I used to have one in my younger days—well, near enough. It began production in 1948. Not many of those around, I'd wager, and they're worth a fair bit o' brass. Moved the headlamps outboard onto the front wings in 1969, due to safety regulations in export markets. So we'd be looking for a vehicle made within that twenty-year span.'

McDermott smiled. 'Didn't take you for a motorhead, Gareth.'

'I have uncharted depths, he replied. 'And a misspent youth. But for the incident to be intentional the driver would have had to have knowledge of where you'd been and where you were headed, and when. He—or she—would also have to have known which road you'd take, and be there before you. A lot of assumptions, that. Let's not rush our fences.'

McDermott was forced to concede the point. 'Put that way, you're right of course. Guess I was letting my imagination get ahead of me.'

Matthews threw his hands in the air. 'Well, there you go. Could have been anyone. Likely just some local on his way home. Lots of farmers round here drive as if they own the road. Failing any more information let's put it in the pending file, shall we?'

Philippa West intervened, 'Apart from interviewing his father's mates, what do we do with George?'

If she thought she was going to catch McDermott off guard, she was mistaken. 'I've been giving that some thought,' McDermott said. 'If Baker-Simms did manage to ship a lorry full of artworks back here, he'd have had to do it through regular military channels. There should be a shipping manifest and inventory records dated after the attack on the convoy. Even if they aren't specific, there should be something. George could look into that at regimental archives.'

DCI West blew out a puff of breath, suggesting that he'd have his work cut out for him. 'What can I say? You seem to have thought of everything. Let him have at it.' Her tone was acid.

Matthews moved to defuse the rivalry, real or imagined. 'As I see it, at this point the art aspect is only a peripheral line of inquiry,' he said, picking an imaginary bit of fluff from his tie. 'Bert Ridley's death is the focus of our investigation. So our main tasks at this point are the interviews, house-to-house queries and monitoring the victim's bank card. Oh, and the pawn shops as well. Should be quite enough for the immediate future. Any questions?' He looked at them both.

'It seems not,' West said, rising from her chair. She held the door open for McDermott. 'We should be getting on with things.'

McDermott saw an opening. 'Speaking of which, sir, George would like to know when the pathologist will be finished with his dad's body. He'd like to get on with the funeral arrangements.'

'Of course. I'll give him a call. I think it's safe to say that Ridley can schedule the funeral for Wednesday, or Thursday at the latest.' He exhaled heavily. Gareth Matthews seemed dejected, almost as if he felt that he bore some measure of responsibility for Bert's death.

SEVENTEEN

Bert Ridley's funeral took place on Thursday. He had not been a religious man, and in keeping with his wishes it was a simple graveside service. Dora Ridley had come up by train from London, and three of Bert's mates that McDermott recognized from the reunion were on hand, along with an elderly couple that had known him from his days on the farm. Matthews and the CID team also made an appearance. Although the sky was clear they all huddled against a biting wind that told of things to come. When it was over there were the usual perfunctory expressions of commiseration as the small group thinned out. There would be no gathering after the service.

McDermott stayed until the last of the mourners left. Ridley muttered that the turnout wasn't much to show for a man's life, and Dora tried to comfort him. McDermott couldn't bring himself to utter the usual platitudes, so he simply gripped George's arm and said nothing. By the time he had put Dora on the train back to London, Ridley had regained some of his composure, and he turned from dwelling on the past to the future. 'Ah'll get onto regiment,' he said. 'Tell 'em Ah'm tryin' to reconstruct me dad's service days. Ah'll see what Ah can find about attack on the lorries, and shipments from Italy to regiment right afterwards. If there's owt there, Ah'll find it.'

LATER THAT DAY MCDERMOTT CALLED LONDON. He had been away from the Art and Antiques Squad for nearly two years, and his sole remaining contact there was gone for the day. It was late Friday before he heard back. Not surprisingly his contact had come up dry: it seemed that many of the large London auction houses dating from the 1950s had merged or gone out of business in the intervening decades. Only two remained, and neither had records of any consignments or transactions involving anyone named Baker-Simms. If the works McDermott described had been stolen, there were no longer any records of them.

McDermott was stymied. Lacking a trail of evidence, he wasn't sure where to turn next. He wanted to touch base with Philippa West, but she was conspicuous by her absence; no one knew where she had gone, or when she'd be back. With no other options at the moment he snagged DS Grimshaw and asked him to join him in the canteen for a coffee.

There were few other people about. The dreaded flu going around had meant that most able-bodied officers were out on duty or at home catching up on much-needed sleep after putting in overtime hours. 'So,' McDermott said, easing into a chair, 'tell me about your given name. I can't imagine Giuseppi is all that common in the Dales.'

'Too bloody right,' Grimshaw replied, stirring his cup. 'And despite what DCI West said, everyone here calls me Joe. My old man was an opera buff. Big fan of Verdi. It's that simple. Suppose I should be grateful he didn't like German music.'

McDermott laughed. 'And you've been paying the price ever since, I suppose.'

'It's not too bad, really. Gets a bit tiresome when the group goes for a meal at an Italian restaurant. They ask me what's good, bein' from the Old Country, or they suggest that I order for them in Italian. That sort o' stuff.'

'You ever give it back?'

'Are you daft? And let them see they got to me? Never. No, mostly I just suggest that we eat Thai or go to a chippie.'

'Could be worse,' McDermott said, blowing the steam off his coffee. 'Ever been to Italy?'

Grimshaw made a face. 'You kidding? Never been further afield than Manchester, unless you count one visit to my sister's family in Slough.'

McDermott laughed. 'You really should go if you get the chance. Some incredible scenery there, and you'd like the food. Not at all the warmed-over spaghetti bolognese we mostly get here. The gelato's worth trying, too, if you've a sweet tooth.' An idea was forming in his mind, but it would need fleshing out before he'd raise it with anyone.

Grimshaw changed the subject. 'I don't know how you blokes in the big city do it, but we've got pretty well bugger all left to do here. DCI West has taken charge of the victim's bank card and pawnbroker queries, and the other lads are out doing the house-to-house interviews. I've been over the SOCO reports for the umpteenth time, and I can't see that they've missed anything. A few days back you mentioned a painting. Is that still on the table?'

McDermott weighed matters for a moment, then told him of his suspicions, and ended by telling him about the results—or lack of them—of the query through Arts and Antiques.

'Well, that seems to be it, then,' he sighed. 'Or do we have anything else?'

McDermott considered the question. 'We could go at things from the other end. Gordon mentioned that his grandfather had returned from the war to find the family brewery in dire straits, and turned it over to Reginald soon afterwards. Gordon was quite proud of the fact that his father had managed to keep it from going under, and had managed to modernise the works over the course of a few years. They did well enough that soon afterwards Gordon was able to plough some of the takings into upgrading the house and grounds. A substantial property, as the estate agents say. It raises the question, how did the family come by the cash needed for all these projects?'

Grimshaw was pensive. 'So it does. The thing about renovations and such is they all require permits. Let me get on to the planning department of the local council and see what they know. When did you say it was?'

'I can't be sure. If the brewery was already going under when he returned from the war he couldn't have waited too long. At a guess I'd say the brewery got a serious cash infusion sometime in the late 1940s, mid-fifties at the latest. According to Gordon the house renovations followed sometime after that, before his first wife died in 1986. Worth checking into.'

'We might also check with Inland Revenue. See how their income and expenses went during the years after the war. I'll run it by Her Nibs, see what I can do,' Grimshaw said, rising from his chair and looking considerably brighter.

'Brilliant! Let me know how you get on.'

'Mind if I suggest it was my idea? Might go down better.'

'It's all yours, my friend.'

BY THE TIME DC BROOKES ENTERED THE INCIDENT SUITE it was getting dark and had been raining for several hours. He dropped his damp jacket over the back of a chair, rubbing his hands to shake the chill off.

'Any joy in the house-to-house?' McDermott asked.

'Not so's you'd notice, sir. It was several days back, and the village is full of old wrinklies.' Seeing McDermott's scowl he said, 'Sorry sir. Most people were in bed well before midnight, and those who weren't were either watching telly or deaf as a post. One old gent said he *thought* he *might* have heard something, only he couldn't be sure it was same night.' Brookes' face said it all.

'That's another avenue closed, then, 'McDermott said. He stretched and rose from his chair, getting ready to return to Kirk Warham. Ridley had been working the phone, talking with some of his father's mates, and he, too, looked ready to pack it in for the day. Philippa West was still nowhere to be seen. He was startled by someone's hand on his shoulder, and turned to find Joe Grimshaw standing over him.

'You on your way out?'

'Just about. Why? Do you have something?' he asked hopefully.

'It's not complete, and not on paper, but I've been talking to a mate who works at city council, and it seems Baker-Simms must o' come into some serious brass soon after the war, just as you said.'

'How serious?' McDermott fought against getting his hopes up.

'In today's terms nearly three-quarters of a million pounds. A fair bit o' brass for a family that was struggling to make ends meet just before war. That's not all,' he smiled, parcelling out the information as if it were precious stones.

'You're enjoying this, aren't you?' McDermott said.

'It's not every day I get to impress an officer from the Met,' he said mischievously. 'Any road, when you told me they'd fixed up their estate, I had a thought. Yorkshire is like family. Everyone's related, and someun' always knows other folks' business.'

'And?'

'And thing is, my wife's family is in construction. Now, there's only a few builders round here that would take on a big job like that, with fancy stonework and plaster interiors and such. I asked my father-in-law, and he gave me the names of three firms that he said could o' handled that sort of job back in the day. Before his time, of course, but he said they'd been around for donkey's years.'

McDermott was torn between allowing Grimshaw his moment of enjoyment and wanting to get on with things. 'And?'

'Pratchett and Heard, big company hereabouts. No one in office could recall the job, but they looked through their files and turns out they'd done the work ages ago. Started in 1964, and finished—would you credit it?—in 1966. Two years, a dozen workmen full time, inside and out. Said the whole job came to nearly hundred thousand pounds!'

McDermott whistled. 'And that's in '66 dollars. Must be what—ten times that now?'

'Try again. In today's terms it comes to just over two and a half million. Not a bad return on a fourteen-thousand-quid investment in the brewery only a few years earlier. But that's only part of it.' Grimshaw positively smirked.

'Well, spit it out, then.'

'I tried to check into company earnings. Found out that it's privately held, by the family. So no financial statements in the public domain.'

'And that's supposed to be good news?' McDermott asked.

'Give me credit! I got onto Inland Revenue. They wouldn't fax me the records without a warrant, but I got the numbers, right enough. The net profits from the brewery during that time wouldn't have come close to covering all the renovations they did on the estate.'

'Brilliant!' McDermott said. 'We need to fill in DCI West when she returns.'

Grimshaw gave him a sly smile. 'Do we have to?'

THAT EVENING MCDERMOTT SHARED Grimshaw's information with George over supper. Ridley agreed they might be onto something.

'By 'eck,' he said, 'if Baker-Simms—the Cap'n, that is—nicked a pile o' art in Italy and 'ad it shipped back 'ere, 'e'd a been in a right tizzy if 'e thought my da had sussed what was goin' on. Motive for murder, right enough.'

'Easy, George,' McDermott cautioned. 'All we have at this point are questions, such as how did the family come by the pots of money needed to undertake major renovations to both the brewery and the house in a few short years? They may have floated a loan from the bank or a business partner, or someone in the family might have died and left them a pile. As a family-owned private venture they wouldn't have had to explain their actions to anyone.'

But Ridley was not about to let the matter drop. After apparently losing himself in thought for a few moments, he broke the silence. 'Ere, now, how'd 'e get all that art back 'ere to sell it on?'

'Early days yet. I have a theory, George. At the moment it's just that, but if I'm right it would explain a lot.'

For once Ridley was ahead of him. 'My dad were sent 'ome soon after 'e were wounded in that attack—the one 'e got medal for. His mates might remember when it was. Might help us track things down.' He paused. 'Most o' lads 'ave buggered off 'ome, but couple of 'em live nearby. Ah'll get their numbers from regiment and give 'em a bell. Meybe Ah can jog their memories.'

McDermott looked at his old friend, and felt his frustration. It wouldn't bring his father back, of course, but he was committed to finding the person responsible for Bert Ridley's death. He was coming around to the view that he had his man, but he was far from having a case, one that would stand up in court. 'Right. Let's look into it.'

EIGHTEEN

Ridley and McDermott entered the CID suite early the next morning to find Philippa West already at her desk and looking very businesslike. Apparently she'd decided—or been told—to put her temper on hold. She looked up from the file folders littering her desk. 'We seem to be no further ahead,' she admitted. 'Anything on your end?'

McDermott took a nearby chair, and Ridley leaned on an unoccupied desk. 'Actually, George and I tossed some ideas around last night over supper, and came up with a couple of possible leads. George, why don't you bring DCI West into the picture?'

Ridley was only too happy to do so. Over the next twenty minutes she listened intently, interrupting only occasionally to ask a question. When they finished, she said, 'You've done better than we have, I must admit. Where do you see taking it from here?'

McDermott was cautious. He didn't want to cause further tension between them and risk having Matthews pull the rug from under him. 'George is, I think, the logical person to check the shipping archives at regimental HQ. He served in the same regiment, and he can explain his interest as grounded in his father's service during the war.'

'Makes sense,' she agreed, levelling her gaze at McDermott. 'And what about you?'

'Ah, I was coming to that,' he said. 'Why don't we see if the DCS is free? I think we'll need to run this by him.'

As they were ushered into his office, Gareth Matthews looked up and sensed that there had been a rapprochement of sorts. He smiled. 'How are things progressing? Any breaks?'

'Not so much as a break, as a new line of inquiry,' Philippa West said. 'DI McDermott has raised some interesting questions and wants to follow them up.' She was carefully distancing herself from his proposals, he noted, which meant she was still free to support or criticize his ideas.

They both eased themselves into chairs facing their boss. McDermott admitted that his London queries had drawn a blank. Then he brought Matthews and West up to speed on the Baker-Simms family fortunes, noting that Grimshaw had looked into the extensive renovations as well as the finances of the Baker-Simms business and the family estate. By then Grimshaw had word back from Inland Revenue. A tax audit was not in the cards: in the absence of information about specific income or expenditures the department considered it merely a fishing expedition, leaving them open to a charge of invasion of privacy. It was simply not on.

Another dead end. Becoming used to those, McDermott turned to the logistical challenges of shipping a significant number of bulky artworks from southern Italy to Yorkshire during the war, and he described George's next task, to track down regimental records. When he was done, he put his cards on the table.

'I think I may need to go to Italy,' he said.

Matthews sat there for a moment, stunned, and wondering if he'd heard correctly. Philippa West was quick to jump in. 'Sir, I had no idea that DI McDermott was going to propose this. We haven't discussed it at all.'

The DCS recovered his composure and looked across the desk. 'For what purpose, Colin?'

A first name basis. That was a good sign. 'In a word, to see whether I can locate someone who was in the village at the time. Someone who knew the house, or at least was familiar with the artifacts, and who can confirm whether the painting in Bert Ridley's war photo was an artwork from the villa.'

'Is that all?' His skepticism was evident.

'No, actually,' McDermott replied. 'I'm hoping to find someone who can reconstruct at least a partial inventory of objects in the villa, detailed enough that I can compare it to some of the works at Coniston Hall.'

The other man leaned back in his desk chair and rubbed his jaw thoughtfully. 'It's been what, now? Sixty-plu years? That would mean that this person would likely be in their mid-eighties, at least. What do you think are the odds of finding such a person?'

'Not as long as one might think,' McDermott said. 'It's a rural village in an isolated region. Just as here, I'm betting that people there don't move around a lot, and they know one another very well. They also have long memories. Eighty-five isn't so long for someone to live these days. And the deaths of the couple at the villa and the loss of the artworks were not inconsequential events. Anyone around at that time would have remembered.'

There was a long silence. McDermott held Matthews in his gaze, emphasizing the seriousness of his scheme. Finally the senior officer leaned forward, his elbows on the desk, and clasped his hands together. 'I'm sorry, Colin. I can't authorise what amounts to a fishing expedition—a very expensive one at that—on the off chance that you'll discover the Holy Grail.'

'Hardly that,' McDermott rallied. 'It's the one link that will help us to build a case. Failing that, it's all supposition.'

'You're right about that,' Matthews replied. 'So far we have less than nothing to go on. Some unaccounted-for expenses by a family, more than five decades ago, and some car-boot relics that have gone missing even longer. I'm sorry, Colin. Maybe that's the way you do things in London, but my Chief Constable would have my—well, you get the idea.'

DS Grimshaw knocked and poked his head through the open doorway. 'Excuse me, sir. Ma'am, I wonder if I could see you for a moment. We might have made some progress on the cases of Taking and Driving Away. Might be time to act.' He waved a sheaf of papers at her.

Philippa West looked perturbed, but left the room with him. When she was gone Gareth Matthews adopted a more conciliatory tone. 'Look, Colin, I know you feel badly about George's father, and you want to help him in any way you can. But you're too close to this inquiry and it's clouding your judgment. Ask yourself if you would authorise such a trip if you were in my shoes.'

McDermott was not about to give up. 'You're right, of course. It does mean a lot to me. But I'm only looking at where the evidence is taking us. Suppose I go on my own? I have some airline miles, and some leave time banked. If I come up trumps you pay my costs. If not, I eat the expenses.'

'I'm afraid not, Colin.'

'Half, then.'

The DCS was firm. 'Not in the cards. You know what the budget cutbacks have been like. We're operating on spit and a hope around here, like everyone else.' Then he offered McDermott a bone. 'But you're on loan here. Why don't you run it by your betters in London? Who knows, you might get lucky.'

'Fair enough.' McDermott knew that it wasn't a done deal, not by any means. Galbraith was likely to give him the same answer.

'Right,' Matthews said. 'London wants to cover it, good on you. Nose around all you want, but keep Baker-Simms' name well clear of your inquiries. I don't want word getting around here, stirring things up with nought to show for it.'

McDermott sighed. He thought sadly that his friend, who had shown real initiative before he'd been promoted to the senior ranks, now only seemed interested in going by the book and protecting his pension. As he rose to leave he said, 'By the way, any word back on the cause of Bert's death?'

By now DCI West had returned. Matthews shuffled some papers on his desk. 'Yes, we only got the report this morning. It's conclusive. George's father died as the result of a stroke caused by injuries sustained in an attack on him outside the pub, which resulted in him hitting his head on a drainage pipe. Clear case of Constructive Manslaughter, assuming we find the bloke that did it.'

'I'll tell George.' McDermott left the room.

'A stubborn man,' West said.

Her boss shot her a stern look. 'Maybe so, but a good copper just the same. I wouldn't bet against him.'

IT DIDN'T TAKE MCDERMOTT LONG TO PACK, and by mid-afternoon he had arrived at Charing Cross HQ and immediately set out for DCI Galbraith's office. He knew that Galbraith regarded himself as McDermott's mentor and would support him if he could, but he also realised that he would have a job on his hands convincing him of his plan just the same. When he was ushered into Galbraith's office he was not surprised to see his boss seated at his desk, pouring over paperwork.

'Bloody thankless job, this,' Galbraith said, motioning to McDermott to take a chair. 'We could get a sight more policing done if we weren't tied up dealing with staffing reports and Parliamentary Questions and meetings with God-knows-how-many community groups and self-appointed defenders of the wrongly accused.' His expression changed from mild irritation to a small smile. 'Good to see you again, though, Colin. How's George holding up?'

'As you might expect. The funeral was yesterday,' he said. 'Grim affair, not a large turnout. But he's handling it well, I'd say. He's turned the corner from grief to focusing on the inquiry, trying to find a lead pointing to whoever did it.'

'Good. One thing about George, he's a copper through and through.'

'As you say. Actually, he's helped to map out a line of inquiry that looks fairly promising.'

'Has he, now?' Galbraith's surprise showed on his face. 'What's that, then?'

McDermott spent the next few minutes going over shootings at the villa and the strafing of the lorries, finishing with his theory that the artworks might have found their way into Baker-Simms' possession. He mentioned that Ridley would be checking out the wartime shipping records at the Regimental HQ. Then he sprang his surprise on Galbraith.

The senior officer played his cards close to his vest; during the whole time he gave no indication, one way or the other, whether he would support McDermott's plan or thought he was mad. No doubt such bland insouciance came in useful in meetings and interrogations, but McDermott decided he wouldn't want to play poker with the man.

When he was finished, McDermott sat back in his chair, waiting for Galbraith's reaction. After some moments of almost total silence, save drumming his fingers on the edge of his desk, Galbraith leaned forward slightly. 'What would you say to such a request, if you were in my place, Colin?'

The question didn't take McDermott by surprise, and he was prepared. 'I might question the wisdom of what admittedly is a long shot,' he said truthfully, 'but if I had confidence in the officer in question, I'd have to let him run with it. The only risk is returning empty-handed. The Met isn't even on the hook for the travel costs unless it pays off.'

'And what about your work here? You've been away for what?—nearly two weeks now—for what was supposed to be a few days at Interpol. Ridley as well. Am I supposed to run the division short-staffed?'

McDermott had done his homework. 'Actually, sir, I checked with DCI Robertson when I arrived. It seems there's not a lot on our plate at present. Whilst I am sure to be missed,' he grinned, 'the division seems to be coping embarrassingly well.' Then he added, almost as an afterthought, 'And of course, it's a case involving one of our own, isn't it, or as good as? We've got to go the extra mile on this. It wouldn't look good for the Met somewhere down the road if we'd let a killer off simply because we hadn't followed up on all leads.'

After what seemed like an eternity Galbraith smiled back. But it was the thinnest of smiles, not one that anyone could take a lot of confidence from. 'You always were a cheeky bugger. Very well. As you say, you've got some time coming. But it's down to you. If you return empty-handed, then all you've got to show for it is some vacation memories and a fistful of travel expenses that are yours alone. And a few days should do it. A week at most. Do I make myself clear?'

MCDERMOTT SPENT THE BALANCE OF THE DAY with Anna and Megan, packing and contacting Frans Decker at Interpol about contacts in the region where he was headed. Decker promised to look into things and get back to him.

By noon the next day McDermott found himself on a plane headed for Rome. He had a window seat on the port side, which spared him the direct sun. His seat companion was clearly a businessman returning home. He was a large man with a wrinkled suit and a fondness for garlic, and McDermott was hard pressed to maintain a measure of comfort. But after a while the man closed his laptop computer and tried to nap, and things got a bit easier. The cabin attendant came around and McDermott ordered a glass of still water with ice, to fight off the dehydration he always experienced on airline flights.

As he crossed the Alps and watched the Italian landscape unfold below McDermott thought back fondly to the last time he'd been in Italy. He and Anna had married in Tuscany, an impromptu affair witnessed by a few close friends, and they had honeymooned in Venice before returning home. Those were cherished memories, and he regretted that his job had often separated them as a family. As he settled back in his seat McDermott wondered whether Matthews and Galbraith had been right: maybe he was on a fool's errand. Sixty years on, to track down someone who was still alive, who had witnessed the events at the villa, and who would recall the details, and who wasn't gaga? Even if he was successful, how far could he take his case? McDermott wasn't even certain what the law was in these circumstances. Was there a statute of limitations? If so, it must have passed long ago. But he knew that he had to do whatever he could; George would expect no less, and he'd be right.

NINETEEN

After switching planes in Rome and a brief flight south McDermott arrived at the Aeroporto dello Stretto in Calabria in the afternoon. He collected his checked bag and set off for the main entrance, hoping to find a taxi. The airport showed the signs of being recently expanded, but although it was very contemporary, it remained comfortably modest and easy to navigate. McDermott had studied a travel guide on the plane and it seemed that regular public transport to the small village where Bert Ridley and his company had been stationed was almost nonexistent. It was located in the hills some distance from the airport, and although a bus connected several mountain villages, it ran only once daily in each direction, and even then it travelled a circuitous route along narrow roads, and took hours to cover the relatively short distances. A taxi would not be cheap but it would save precious time.

As he left the baggage claim area McDermott noticed a tall, well-dressed and clearly fit man wearing a dark suit and sunglasses standing near the exit. The man seemed to be studying the passengers, and when he saw McDermott he began to walk in his direction. McDermott's heart sank, but he put on a bland expression.

'*Ispettore* McDermott?' the man asked. Colin noticed an official-looking black car waiting in the No Parking area just beyond the main doors. He resigned himself to his fate. 'Yes,' he replied. 'You were expecting me?'

'But of course,' the man answered, making a small salute. 'Allow me to introduce myself. I am *Capitano* Cesare Russo, of the Carabinieri here in Reggio Calabria. *Ispettore* Decker of Interpol contacted us to say that you were coming. *Benvenuto*. It is a great pleasure to meet you.' He put his hand on McDermott's bag and steered him toward the door. 'Come. I have a car waiting.'

So Frans Decker had gone the extra mile. McDermott had hoped to keep a low profile during his trip, in part because it was an unofficial investigation and also because he wanted some latitude in dealing with the outcome, should he strike oil. The Italians, he knew, vigorously pursued cases involving stolen cultural artifacts; if they learned of the existence of works of Italian patrimony in England they would make vigorous efforts to repatriate them, which might jeopardize his own inquiries into Bert Ridley's death. There was ample time to bring the Italian authorities into the picture once his own investigation had turned something up.

As they approached the car the driver emerged and also saluted him. He was, McDermott noticed with dismay, in full uniform. *So much for keeping a low profile.* He handed his bag to the man, who stowed it in the boot, and entered the rear seat, where

Capitano Russo joined him. Turning to McDermott he said, 'It is too late to do much today. I have taken for you a room for the night. It is nearby and very reasonable. If you like I will take you there and you can, how do you English say, freshen up? Then we can have a drink, and afterwards, dinner. My office will pay for both. Over dinner you can perhaps fill me in, and in the morning we can make a start.'

To object, McDermott realised, would raise a red flag. 'An excellent plan, and very kind of you, *Capitano*. I would like to drop off my things, and then we can have that drink.'

When they arrived at a small hotel near the centre of the city Russo said he would wait in the lobby as McDermott unpacked his bag. When he came down Russo was on his mobile, obviously talking with his superior. '*Si, si, Commissario. Non lo so.* How would I know? *Bene. Grazie. Arrivederla.*' He put his mobile away and turned to smile at McDermott. 'How is your room? It is to your liking?'

'It's fine. Very comfortable. Thank you for arranging it. I'm afraid I'm putting you to a great deal of trouble unnecessarily.'

The officer waved away his concern. 'But no. It is a great pleasure to have someone from Scotland Yard visit our poor region. I have myself never been to your country, but I have heard great things about it. Come, we will have that drink, and you can tell me all about your visit.'

A few minutes later they were sitting on the sidewalk at a small café in a nearby piazza, enjoying the late afternoon sun. When their drinks arrived Russo raised his glass and said, '*Salute!* To the success of your trip. It is your first visit to Italy, Chief Inspector?'

The small talk gave McDermott a chance to divert attention from his trip. 'No. Actually, my wife and I were married in your country, several years ago.'

Russo's face broke into a broad grin. 'But no! It is a beautiful country for a wedding, is it not? Is your wife Italian?'

McDermott shrugged. 'No, English. We were on a holiday, staying with friends in Tuscany, and simply decided that there was no more beautiful setting to express our love for one another than here in Italy, in the company of those we cared for. So we were married in Siena.'

Russo raised his eyebrows. *'Che è romantico! Che è vero italiano!'* He lifted his glass in appreciation. 'And children? Do you have any yet?'

'A daughter, Megan. She is three years old.'

'Bellissima! Complimenti!' He raised his glass once again.

There was a long silence as they observed the passersby against the backdrop of the setting sun. The drinks carried into the early evening, and dinner involved several courses, so that by the time Capitano Russo finally turned the discussion to the purpose of McDermott's visit it was dark and the night air was growing comfortably cool.

'So tell me, how can we help you with your investigation, *Ispettore*?' It was delivered casually and with a smile, but it was clear that the man's curiosity would be put off no longer.

McDermott shifted in his chair and sipped his espresso before replying. 'Actually, I must apologise again for putting you to some trouble. The fact is, it's less a formal investigation than a personal inquiry. The father of a close friend—one of my officers, in fact—has been killed back in England. It might be a simple accident, the result of resisting a robbery. But it is also possible that it was not an accident, and that his death is related to events that happened whilst he was here in Italy during the war.'

Russo smiled. 'The war. Visitors to our country always speak as if there has been only one war. You see those ruins over there?' He pointed to some large columns lying at the base of an ancient temple near the sea. 'They are—how do you say—the remnants of war, too. But it was a war against the Lombards, almost fourteen centuries ago.'

McDermott laughed. 'Again, my apologies. Yes, I meant the Second World War.'

'And how is—*Mi scusi*—might this death be related to events here in Italy?' Although the tone of the question was still casual, McDermott knew he had Russo's full attention.

'That's not clear,' McDermott said. 'There might have been a…dispute…between two British soldiers that came to a head only recently. They had been attending a reunion of the regiment that served in this area.'

Russo's eyebrows rose fractionally. 'After so many years? It must have been a very serious dispute!'

'That's why I'm here. To see whether anyone in the area can recall what happened. Perhaps some local villagers knew of these events.' Even to McDermott's ears it sounded far-fetched.

'And what is the name of this village?'

'It's called Santa Cristina. I believe it is in the mountains not too far from here.'

'Ah. *Santa Cristina d'Aspromonte. Si*, I have been there many times. But it is a small village. Your officer must be a very good friend for you to travel all this way in search of so little.' There was the slightest edge to his voice, suggesting that he knew McDermott was being economical with the truth.

'What can I say? We have little else to go on. If I am wrong at least I will have spent a few days in your beautiful region.'

Russo smiled. 'Why not? As you say, it will not be a journey wasted.' He reached for the wine bottle and topped off their glasses.

It was close to midnight when Russo dropped McDermott off at his hotel. After arranging to meet in the morning McDermott showered and fell into bed. He hoped that Russo had swallowed his story, but somehow he doubted it.

SUNDAY, AFTER A LIGHT ITALIAN BREAKFAST of sweet rolls, cheese, and coffee, McDermott and Russo headed east into the mountains. The road was narrow and winding, and their progress was slow. 'There is a *superstrada* that runs north along the coast,' Russo said. 'It goes toward Napoli. But this road leads more directly to Santa Cristina.'

McDermott doubted that the route they were on led directly to anywhere, but he kept silent. The road clung to the mountain on one side, and dropped off sharply on the other. The curves were treacherous, and he recalled Bert's account of the German fighter plane that had strafed the convoy of lorries. It must have been easy pickings for the pilot: there was little room for his quarry to take evasive action. And even if the pilot did not succeed in killing the driver, a lorry was almost certain to hit the mountain and overturn, or else go off the road altogether, and over the cliff. What was the American expression? *Like shooting fish in a barrel.*

Their car hugged the winding road, climbing all the while, and they passed through several villages before reaching the top, where they emerged onto a road following the spine of a mountain range. The going here was easier, the road having been reworked in the not-too-distant past. They made their way past olive and lemon groves and vineyards, and McDermott was surprised to see a few small industrial plants as well.

It was late morning by the time they arrived in Santa Cristina, and McDermott's first impression was that, except for the cars and trucks, it had probably looked much the same during the war. Behind them the sea was just visible in the distance, and the road ahead of them led off toward yet another stretch of mountains dotted with houses and farms. The buildings became more numerous, and before long they came on a piazza, the heart of every Italian village. A religious statue and drinking fountain surrounded by several benches occupied the centre of the piazza, and beyond it a small hotel with, if he was any judge, a *ristorante,* adjacent to a string of small shops including a bar and a *panetteria* or bakery, and a *palazzo comunale* or municipal hall, which seemed to share its space with a post office. Directly across the piazza, a surprisingly large church dominated the scene. It was Sunday and Mass had just ended, and the villagers were streaming out into the midday sun. '*Santa Maria dei Miracoli,*' Russo said, noting McDermott's interest. 'Our people are very traditional, very religious, not like those in the North.' There was an element of pride in his voice. 'Every village here has a church. It is the soul of the village.'

McDermott had not failed to notice the condition of the building. The paint around the windows was peeling, and the roof was badly in need of repair. He wondered how many of the villagers shared the Capitano's religious passion.

The car pulled up in front of the small hotel. 'You will be comfortable here, I think, and it is the only *albergo* in town. We do not get so many tourists in this part of the region. I will go inside and make the arrangements. They will need your passport.'

McDermott handed him his documents, and before long Russo returned, smiling. 'You are, how do you say, in luck. They have a very nice room overlooking the piazza. I hope that is agreeable.'

'Just what I was hoping for,' McDermott replied. 'I noticed a bar just across the street. Can I buy you a coffee?'

The officer smiled. '*Mi dispiace.* I'm sorry. Unfortunately, I must return to my office.' His hand went to his breast pocket, and he produced a card. 'This is a small village, and there is no *Questura* here. But you can reach me at this number. When you have finished your work here call me and I will arrange for a car to, how do you say, collect you.'

So McDermott was being given a little space to conduct his inquiries. 'Again, thank you. You have been most kind. I hope I have not put you to too much trouble.'

'But no!' Russo protested. 'It is my pleasure to be of assistance. I look forward to seeing you again in a few days. *Addio.*' With that, he returned to his car.

TWENTY

The next morning McDermott rose late and took stock of his surroundings. The room was small, but clean. There was no elevator and the stairs were narrow, but that would not be a problem. The floor was tiled, and from the sounds coming from the room next to him the previous night he realised that the walls were thin. Whether that would be a problem remained to be seen. But as Russo had promised, the window overlooked the piazza and the mountains beyond, and the breeze it afforded swept gently through the room, promising to keep it cool during the day.

As he shaved McDermott considered the task before him. The war had been over for many years. No doubt many, if not most, of those who had participated in it had since died or moved away. It wasn't formal records he wanted, but local knowledge. It was well after nine by the time he made his way downstairs to the lobby and sought out the bar. It was one of the many anomalies of Italy, McDermott recalled, that establishments called bars served food and those called cafés served drinks. Confusing for first-time tourists, but there you were. The lone occupant was a young man whom he judged to be in his late twenties who was busy polishing glasses. Good, McDermott thought; that meant he had time to spare. He put on his tourist face. '*Un cappuccino, per favore*,' he said, deciding to work on his Italian.

'But of course, *signore*,' the young man replied in English. Apparently McDermott still had some work to do.

When his coffee arrived, McDermott tried to get a conversation going. 'It's a lovely little village you have here. I suppose it hasn't changed much over the years?'

'I couldn't say, *signore*. I am from Napoli. I am working here only for three months.'

McDermott concealed his dismay. He finished his coffee then ambled out of the hotel and took his bearings. In a nearby passageway a young boy was playing with a dog. Far too young to be of any use. Further along, a middle-aged couple were having their morning coffee at a sidewalk table. They seemed to be caught up in an animated conversation, and probably wouldn't welcome being interrupted by a stranger, an *Inglese* at that.

McDermott looked across the piazza. In the distance an elderly man was seated on a stone bench, reading a newspaper and shielding his eyes from the sun. He seemed in no particular hurry, and McDermott decided to try his luck.

As he approached the bench the man looked up briefly, then returned to his paper. Close up, McDermott saw that he was older than he'd seemed from across the road. At least seventy, he judged—perhaps older, looking at the lines in his face and the few wisps of hair on the top of his head. He sat down on the bench next to the man. '*Buongiorno*. Beautiful weather,' he said in English, not trusting his broken Italian. 'Is it always this mild around here?'

The man looked up from his paper. '*Che cosa? Non parlare Inglese*.' He returned to his reading, sparing a glare for the foreigner in his midst.

McDermott sighed. What did he expect? He noticed a woman in the doorway of a nearby bar, sweeping some debris toward the street. The faded sign on the wall indicated it was the Bar Versace. By the time he walked over there she had returned inside, and was putting away her broom and washing her hands.

'*Buongiorno*,' McDermott said, putting on his best face. He looked around. 'I would like a pastry or *panino*, please.' When she didn't answer him immediately he dusted off his rusty Italian. '*Che cosa è la specialità della casa*?'

She laughed. 'We have many good things here, *signore*. You can speak English if you wish.'

McDermott broke out in a grin. 'Thank God! I mean, it's been a long time since I've spoken any Italian, and I'm afraid I've lost most of it.'

The woman smiled, smoothing her hands on her apron. 'It's okay. We don't get many *Inglese* in our village. What would you like?'

McDermott was in a quandary. He wasn't that hungry, but he noticed a row of tables and chairs lining one wall. 'Something light—and sweet, I think.' It was still too early for a drink. 'You do coffee as well?'

'But of course.' She pointed toward an elaborate machine sitting behind the counter.

McDermott enjoyed his morning coffee as much as the next man, but he knew he couldn't keep this up all day. 'On second thought I'll have a mineral water and one of those fruit buns.' He pointed to a mound of freshly-baked pastries behind the glass.

She gestured toward a nearby table. 'Take a seat and I'll bring them over.'

McDermott sat down and observed her as she prepared his plate. Perhaps in her fifties, she would not have been alive to remember the war; at most a post-war baby, born to a soldier returning home. Still, recalling what he'd said to Gareth Matthews only a few days earlier, it was a small village, and memories were long. He decided to try the direct approach.

When the woman came over with his order a moment later he thanked her and tried again to get a conversation going. 'I see that your bar is called the Versace. Is that a reference to the famous family of the same name?'

'*Si,*' she replied. 'Donatella Versace was born in Calabria. We celebrate her here.'

McDermott smiled. 'You seem to be a local. How is it that you speak English so well?'

She laughed. 'My daughter is married to an American. They come over every summer to visit. Once in a while I go to visit them.' She seemed very proud.

'The world is shrinking,' McDermott said. 'It's good to be able to travel.'

the table. 'Do you have family here?'

Now it was McDermott's turn to laugh. 'I'm afraid not. Actually, I'm here as a favour to an old friend. His father was in the war, and served near here. I offered to look up anyone who might have known him.'

Her eyes widened. 'And you came all the way from England for that?'

'I was in Italy,' he shrugged, 'and had some time to spare.'

'Ah, *si*. Still, it is a long time ago.' Her expression suggested she thought McDermott had more money than sense.

'Yes. So far I've not had much luck. Still, as they say, early days.'

She was silent for a moment. 'You want to talk with *Il padre,* Father Moretti. He must be eighty-five at least. He's been at Santa Maria—the church—for many years. He might have been here during the war.'

'That's the church in the piazza?' McDermott asked.

Again, she smiled. 'Yes, we have just the one. It is a small village.'

McDermott thanked her and tucked into his bun. A priest. He would know everyone in the village, and probably many of their secrets as well. It was a promising start.

Before long the bar began to fill up with locals. One retrieved a worn deck of playing cards from behind the counter. Others focused on a small TV mounted high in one corner broadcasting the news. Most were simply gathering to talk, fueling their conversations with healthy cups of cappuccino or an espresso. They all seemed to know one another, not surprising for a village of this size. A few looked his way and then whispered to the woman behind the counter, and he had no doubt that by evening his story would be all over town.

McDermott finished his meal and left a few coins on the table, then made his way back out into the street. Despite the clear day it was noticeably cool, the wind cresting the nearby hills and making its way across the piazza. Still, people were determined to enjoy the sun, and sat on benches and at tables in front of the cafés, with scarves and jackets to warm themselves.

McDermott saw the church to his right, and began to walk toward it. As he drew closer he noticed that it was in a state of disrepair. Several slates on the roof were missing, and the church doors, made of wood, badly needed a coat of varnish. He saw some chipping on the stone walls and wondered if they could be remnants of the fighting so long ago. Surely that would have been repaired years ago, he thought. Then again, perhaps not.

He tested the main door and found it unlocked. Pulling the massive slab of ornately-carved wood open, he went inside. It was dark, and as nearly as he could tell, deserted. The altar was bathed in light from several large stained-glass windows, but there was no sign of life. He walked down the aisle, his footsteps echoing on the tile floor. When he reached the altar there was still no indication that anyone was there. Noticing a small door off to one side, he approached and knocked. After a moment the door opened. *'Si?'*

The man before him could not have been more than thirty. McDermott said, 'Excuse me, but I am looking for Father Moretti. I was told I might find him here.'

The priest regarded him with some interest. '*Si*, he is here,' he replied, opening the door wider. 'Not here exactly,' he added. 'He is *fuori*, outside. Does he know that you are coming?'

'No,' McDermott replied. 'I was told he might be able to help me about events that occurred here many years ago.'

'Before my time, then. I will take you to him.' The priest opened another door, and **suddenly** the small dark room was flooded with sunlight. '*Venga*. Come with me, please.'

They emerged into the churchyard and the priest led the way toward the rear of the building. Much of the land had been given over to the cemetery, but in a small plot near the far wall there was a small vegetable garden and some berry vines. There were,

McDermott noticed, even a few fruit trees beyond the garden, near a stone wall that surrounded the church.

There was a small pile of dead weeds smouldering nearby, and the earth had been freshly worked around several potato plants. An elderly man stood next to them, leaning on a hoe, resting from his labours.

'Padre, you have a visitor, *uno Inglese.*'

The old man turned and regarded him closely. His expression softened. 'Indeed? Then I can practice my English! Do you mind if we sit down?' he asked, moving toward a bench placed against the stone wall. 'It's just that I have been working hard, and I am not as young as I used to be.' The younger priest turned toward the doorway and they sat down. The priest leaned back against the wall, taking in the sun. 'Do you approve of *mio giardino*?'

McDermott took a guess. 'Your garden? Yes. It must take a lot of your time.' The man seemed very frail. McDermott wondered whether his mind was as clear as it had been.

The elderly priest laughed softly. 'Time is one thing I have much of. Ever since the Bishop sent Father Di Costa to help me, three years ago.' Then his expression changed. 'But I am not resentful. I cannot get out much anymore and visit my people. Father Di Costa does much of the work, and the young people, he understands them better.'

'I'm sure he's a great help,' McDermott replied. 'In fact, that's why I'm here. I'm seeking some information that goes back to the Second World War, and I'm told you might be able to help me.'

'The Second War, you say?' The priest rubbed his chin thoughtfully, his eyes staring into the distance at nothing in particular. 'A long time ago. So many things happened, so many people.

Most now dead, of course.' Several moments passed. 'What do you want to know?'

McDermott kept his tone of voice casual. 'A friend of mine, a very good friend, actually, has asked me to look into events that occurred when his father was stationed here, in late 1943. He was a British soldier, with the British Eighth Army.'

The priest was lost in thought again. 'Nineteen forty-three, you say? Ah yes, that is when the British and the Americans attacked Sicily, and then moved up the coast nearby. I remember. The Germans moved back into the hills. They never came back. After that, they moved further and further north, where the fighting was. Anzio, and Salerno, and then, of course, Rome. By then *Il Duce* was dead,' he said with some satisfaction.

The man's mind was still sharp, McDermott noted. Perhaps he could be of help after all. 'Yes, that's the period I'm interested in. Early September of '43, to be exact.'

'And what is it you wish to know?'

McDermott shifted on the bench so that he faced the man more directly. 'I would like to speak with some of the locals who might have lived here then, or even been involved in the events of that time.'

The priest's eyes narrowed. 'Italian soldiers, you mean? I'm afraid—'

'I'm sorry, I guess I'm not making myself clear. It's not soldiers that I'd like to speak with. It's civilians, especially those who might have been involved with helping the British after they arrived.'

The man paused and searched McDermott's face for any hidden meaning, then said, 'The *partigiani*, you mean? The partisans?'

McDermott leaned forward. 'Exactly. If that is possible.'

He had the elderly priest's full attention. 'For what purpose?'

McDermott knew he had to proceed carefully, even more so than when he'd spoken with Capitano Russo. He disliked deceiving the man, but to explain his real reason for being here would be to set in motion forces he couldn't control. 'My friend's father was billeted in this village in the early days of the liberation of Italy. Some of the villagers were very kind to him whilst he was here. My friend would like to make contact with them and express his gratitude.' He searched the man's eyes to see whether he would accept the story.

'Your friend's father, he has had many years to return to Santa Cristina, to seek out those who helped him. Why only now?'

'Because recently he attended a reunion of his regiment in England, and they relived what had happened during those days. Shortly after that he died. My friend only learned of those events a few weeks ago. It is his wish to contact the people who helped his father.'

The man sighed. 'It is the same with my people. Most are dead now. There are only a few left, and each year the number is smaller.' He paused to point to a nearby tree. 'You see that reddish and grey bird on the limb, near the trunk? It is a *tortora delle palme*—laughing dove, you call it in English. I know the nest. She is not young, that hen, and as you can see she has a damaged wing. Her mate is already dead, killed by our cat a few weeks ago, and she will live only a few months more, probably not through the winter. She has *bambini*, babies. They were born last spring. They will survive her, but they will know nothing of their past, their history. Perhaps we humans should be so lucky.'

'With respect, Padre, I disagree. Having a history and being able to sustain our relations with earlier generations is one of the things that makes us fully human.'

The priest considered what he had just heard. 'Perhaps you are right. You wish to speak with a former *partigiano*? Do you have a name?'

McDermott retrieved a piece of paper from the inside pocket of his jacket. 'It's nothing very reliable, I'm afraid. One of his fellow soldiers mentioned a young woman in the Resistance, the only woman partisan they saw. She would have been no more than eighteen or twenty at the time. That would make her close to ninety today. They thought her name was Irina or perhaps Isadora. Possibly her last name was Besso, or something like it.'

The priest thought for a bit. 'So many have died. Good people, too. You know, we had no collaborators here in the village. Not like in Rome.' He closed his eyes.

McDermott give the man time to rake over his memories. At length the priest opened his eyes again. 'I think I know the woman you mean. She was very beautiful. You must understand that I too was young at the time, about four years younger than her. I remember her well. Her name was Isabella. Isabella Brasso. She was a partisan. When the Germans came she and others fled into the hills. Our people made sure they had plenty of food,' he said with more than a trace of pride.

'Is she still alive?'

He shrugged. 'I do not know. It's been a long time. A lifetime. I do not get out much, and I have not seen her in many years. If she is alive, she does not come to Mass any more. But I will ask around. If I find her I will speak with her and see whether she wants to talk to you. It might take a day or two. You understand those memories are still very painful to us. She might not want to open up old wounds. I cannot do more.' He leaned on his hoe and rose from the bench with some difficulty.

McDermott thanked him for his efforts and gave him his name and said he would be staying at the local *albergo* for the next two or three days. He invited the priest to have dinner with him, thinking that a meal out might be a welcome treat, but the cleric declined. His stomach, he regretted, was not what it used to be, and he had to be very careful what he ate, which explained his garden.

WHEN HE LEFT THE CHURCH McDermott strolled down a nearby street. As he expected, the village was a veritable time capsule, with most of the buildings clearly dating from well before the war. Only a few houses on the hills above, a recently-constructed apartment block, the hotel where he was staying, and an industrial estate on the edge of the village showed signs of modernisation.

Something about the village began to play on McDermott's mind, but at first he couldn't put his finger on it. Then he realised what it was. Santa Cristina was unlike other towns and cities he'd visited on previous trips to Italy; he was virtually the only tourist in sight, and there were few cars, and no buses, to interrupt his thoughts. Thinking about it he began to understand why. This small mountain village had escaped the hordes of tourists precisely because of its remote location and lack of historical sites. It simply didn't have a leaning tower or a grand piazza or picturesque canals. It wasn't even on the way to somewhere else. In another hundred years it would still be a nondescript village, with little to bring it to the attention of travel agents and tourist guides. And he liked that about Santa Cristina; it was authentic rural Italy, uncompromising and unspoiled. McDermott had lost all sense of time, and dusk was already approaching when he returned to the hotel and had dinner.

TWENTY-ONE

When **McDermott arose the next morning** there was no message waiting for him. He decided not to rush the priest. He began the day by returning to the church and examining the gravestones in the cemetery, looking for villagers who had been victims of the war. His thinking was that he might locate the relatives of anyone who'd been alive, and possibly in the village, when the British Army had arrived. At length he tired of the exercise, realising it was very unlikely that these people could tell him anything of value.

Father Moretti had not put in an appearance in his garden, and McDermott hoped he had not suffered as a result of their conversation. By noontime he returned to the Bar Versace for lunch, and was not surprised to see it was nearly full. One or two of the customers nodded, having noticed him the previous day, and the woman behind the counter greeted him with a smile. 'So, come back, have you? I guess my food is not so bad!'

'Quite the contrary,' McDermott said. Looking at the handwritten menu on the wall behind the counter. 'I see you have *zuppa di pasta e fagioli,* I'll have a bowl of that, and a plain bun, please. And a glass of red wine.'

'Very good!' she laughed. 'We'll make *uno paesano* of you yet!'

When she brought the food to his table she put the bowl of steaming soup down in front of him and placed a small plate with a bun next to it, along with his wine. 'So, how did you get on with your search yesterday?'

McDermott smiled. 'I made a start. Thank you for suggesting the priest. I spoke with him and he was very hopeful.'

'Good.' She brushed some crumbs from the middle of the table. 'If anyone can help you, he can.'

After lunch McDermott settled his bill and emerged into the midday sun. For a small village there seemed to be a lot going on. Lorries were headed back and forth from the industrial estate he had seen yesterday, and shopkeepers were busy arranging their wares or clearing tables from the lunch crowd in preparation for the evening. Still, McDermott noticed, most of the people were middle-aged or older. He wondered whether the young people tended to abandon the village for the attractions of city life.

As he entered the hotel the owner caught his eye. *'Scusa, Signore* McDermott. There is a message for you,' he said, handing him a folded note.

McDermott opened the paper and glanced over its contents. It was from Father Moretti. He had found and contacted Isabella Brasso, and she had agreed to speak with McDermott that very afternoon. It gave an address which meant nothing to him. He asked the man how to get there.

He looked at the note briefly. 'Ah, but that is easy, *signore*. I will ask my son to take you there. Pippo!' he called out, '*Pippo, vieni*' A moment later a young boy appeared, the one McDermott had seen playing in the street the previous morning. 'Pippo, I want you to take the *signore* here to this address.' He handed him the paper. 'You know the way. It's just past Fabrizio the taxi driver's house, and across the street from that little girl you like so much. Michaela, isn't it?' McDermott was relieved to see that apparently the boy understood English.

The boy blushed and glared at his father. 'She is just a friend!'

His father was not about to let it go. 'Yes, Pippo, and pigs might fly! Please take the gentleman there now. He is expected shortly.'

They set off on foot, and McDermott struck up a conversation. 'How is it you understand English so well, Pippo? I don't imagine you get that many British tourists this far south.'

'It is true, *signore*. But it is changing. My father is very happy to have more business, so he speaks English to me at home. And French. And German. I am learning quickly!' he said proudly. Apparently many in the village were taking the same message on board. *One of the beneficial effects of the EU,* McDermott thought to himself, pleased.

After several minutes walking through various narrow lanes and up a long, winding hill they arrived at a nondescript one-story house painted white, with faded blue shutters and a small, sun-baked garden at the front. '*Bene*. Here we are, *signore*. You want I come back for you?' he asked dubiously.

'*Grazie*, Pippo. I think I can find my way back. If I'm not there by the morning, ask the Carabinieri to search for me.'

The boy scowled, not sure if he was being made fun of, but turned away and went back the way they had come, sparing a glance for the house across the narrow street as he did so.

McDermott watched the boy disappear down the hill, then moved to the door and knocked. After a few moments it was opened by a tall thin woman with white hair. Her face was lined but her eyes were bright, and she stood straight, he noticed, and seemed quite fit for her age. '*Scusami,*' he said, 'I am looking for Signora Brasso. I was told I might find her here.'

The woman smiled, as if at some private joke. 'You have been misinformed. There is no one here named Brasso.'

McDermott was confused. Perhaps the boy had mistaken the house. Before he could speak she broke into a grin and laughed. 'You must forgive me. I was having a little joke with you. I am the person you seek, but my name is Goldman, not Brasso. It hasn't been that for many years. Father Moretti telephoned me yesterday, and said you wanted to speak with me. Please come in.' She opened the door wide and he entered the small house.

Once inside, he saw an elderly man sitting in an armchair by the window. No doubt they had both seen him coming. 'This is my husband, Vittorio. He had a stroke two years ago and cannot speak very well, but he understands well enough, and his English is very good.'

'A pleasure, *signore*. I hope I am not disturbing you.'

The man shook his head. 'No,' he mumbled, and extended a trembling arm, indicating that McDermott should sit on a nearby sofa.

As he sat down Isabella Goldman remained standing. 'Would you like some tea? I think you English are very fond of tea.'

'That would be very nice, thank you, but please don't trouble yourself.'

'Oh, it is no trouble,' she said, moving toward the small kitchen. McDermott took a moment to glance around the room. It was clean, but modest. The carpet was worn, and the furniture was plain and bore the inevitable marks of many years of use. There was a hand-tinted print of Mary and Jesus on the far wall, and several framed black-and-white photographs on a side-table beneath it. The photos all seemed quite old, and there were, he noticed, no pictures of children or grandchildren.

Isabella Goldman returned from the kitchen and followed his gaze. 'We have no children,' she said matter-of-factly. 'But we have one another, don't we, Vittorio?'

The man coughed his agreement, and McDermott was left wondering how he would cope if he outlived her, though it seemed unlikely that he would do.

'So what brings you to our small village?' she asked. 'Father Moretti said you have questions about the past, the war.' Her tone was casual, but both of them were watching him carefully. He tried to keep his answer light.

'Nothing terribly important, I'm afraid, and I apologise for disturbing you. It's just that a close friend of mine knew that I would be traveling in Italy, and asked me to make some inquiries on his behalf.'

'He was in the war, then?' she asked.

'Not exactly,' McDermott replied. 'His father was with the British Eighth Army, and saw duty here briefly, when the Allies invaded Italy.'

'*Liberated* Italy, you mean.' Her expression indicated this was a distinction of no small importance to her.

McDermott coloured. 'Yes, of course. Anyway, my friend's father recently died, and George—my friend—asked if I could fill in some of the blanks concerning his father's time here. It seems they hadn't got round to discussing it much before he died.'

The old woman sighed. 'Yes, it is different for those of us who live here. We still remember the events clearly. We were all involved.'

McDermott thought he heard a tone of regret in her voice. 'It must have been a very difficult time for you.'

She pondered his words, and then said, 'Ah well, it was difficult for everyone, I suppose. A bullet hurts just as much if you are a foreign soldier or a villager caught up in the fighting. Still, the destruction, the suffering, remains with us years later. You know,' her tone becoming more matter-of-fact, 'here it is not like the rest of Italy. In the north there was money after the war to repair, to rebuild. But here there was very little money. It has always been like that. *Roma, Firenze, Venezia*—they get the money and the new factories. Here we make do.'

McDermott saw that the conversation was getting off course. 'You were involved in the war yourself, I believe.'

'Yes. Actually both Vittorio and I were involved in the Resistance movement. We were lovers then, you see, and being a Jew, Vitorrio had no choice: it was either fight the Germans or leave Italy. My mother and father were still alive then, and I did not want to abandon them, so we went underground.' A whistling sound came from the kitchen. 'That will be your tea. I will bring it. Do you take milk and sugar?'

Anticipating that the tea might be weak, McDermott said, 'Black is fine.' While she was busy in the kitchen he turned to her husband. 'So it must have been very difficult for you both. Did you have family here at the time?'

'Umm,' the man replied, shaking his head.

Isabella Goldman returned with a tray containing two cups of tea, and, McDermott noticed, a plate of biscotti. 'Vittorio does not drink tea,' she explained, passing him the plate. 'You must try these. I made them myself.'

McDermott thanked her, and dipped a biscotto into the steaming cup. It contained pistachio nuts, and reminded him of his previous visit to Italy, when he and his bride had discovered a cozy little ristorante tucked into a small side-street in Rome.

'Once the Allies reached Calabria,' she resumed, 'the Germans began pulling out. They moved from the coast into the mountains, and then into the National Forest just to the south of where we are now. We watched their movements and reported them to the Allies when we could. Everyone was afraid they would make a counterattack, which would have meant fighting right here. But they simply melted into the mountains and moved further north. Of course, we didn't know that at the time.'

McDermott edged closer to his topic. 'You mean there was no fighting, no violence, in this region?'

She smiled. 'Oh no, not to speak of. The Germans mined the mountain roads to delay the Allies, and blew up bridges wherever they could, but they did not stand their ground. The Master Race was too cowardly for that!'

'I'm somewhat confused,' McDermott admitted. 'My friend's father was wounded somewhere near here, we were told, in an attack by a German plane.'

She looked at him quizzically. 'Do you know when this happened, or where? My memory is usually very good.'

The room was cooling, and McDermott took another sip of his tea and put his hands around the cup for warmth. 'I only have the information third-hand, of course, but as I understand it he was part of a convoy, escorting two lorries from the village back to the port, when it was attacked by a German plane. One truck was destroyed, and its crew was killed. He was more fortunate. His truck was hit, and he was injured. The lorry crashed, but he was able to pull the driver out. Later he was evacuated to a field hospital near the coast, and ultimately sent home to England by hospital ship.'

She closed her eyes and was silent for a while. When she opened them she asked, 'What was the name of this man?'

McDermott tried to conceal his emotion. The next few minutes would reveal whether his hunch was right, or if he had travelled to Italy in vain. 'I'm sorry, I guess I'm not describing events very well. His name was Albert Ridley—Bert, his mates would have called him—and as I say, he was a trooper, a rifleman, with the British Eighth Army, a Yorkshire regiment. It was in 1943, around the first week of September, or perhaps a few days later. I understand they were stationed here in the village to monitor the Germans in case they tried to counterattack. Later they moved on, to rejoin the other units of the Eighth Army as they moved up the coast toward Salerno.'

She looked at McDermott for some moments, and the corners of her mouth tightened. When she spoke again she said 'Yes, I recall the events you mention. It was a very unhappy time for those of us in the village, even more so for me.'

McDermott saw the pain in her eyes. 'I'm sorry. I don't want to cause you any distress, but can you tell me why?'

Isabella Goldman put down her cup and leaned forward. 'The events you speak of involved the deaths of two good friends, *protettori*, I should say, from my youth. An officer in the unit you speak of shot and killed them. It was an accident, they said. He was searching their villa, in the hills near here, when he heard a noise. He thought they were Germans and opened fire. An inquiry by your army said they were armed, and let him off.' It was clear that she was not convinced by the account.

'I see. But my friend's father was not involved in this, was he?'

'Not directly, no,' she conceded. 'But these were, you understand, people of wealth, people of…culture. Their villa contained many artworks and other treasures that we wanted to preserve. There was always the chance that the Germans would return, or simply start shelling the area in a counterattack. A few days after the killings we approached the British officer in charge and asked him to remove many of the most valuable works in the villa and take them to San Giovanni for safekeeping.'

McDermott leaned forward. 'Again, I'm afraid you're losing me. How does this concern my friend's father?'

The woman shot a glance at her husband before resuming her story. 'Your man Ridley was one of the soldiers who helped to crate the art objects for evacuation. I know because I was there, helping them. The next day they loaded the boxes into a lorry for the trip to the coast. And that lorry was part of a convoy that was strafed by a German fighter plane on the way to San Giovanni.'

McDermott was close to connecting Baker-Simms to the missing artworks, but he needed more. 'So the artworks were all lost? That's terrible!'

'That's what we were told,' she replied. 'Here,' she said, moving to the table and opening a drawer. 'I might still have some photographs from that time.' She ruffled through the drawer and extracted a worn oversized envelope, yellowed with time and torn in one corner. She returned to her chair and opened it, sorting through the photographs slowly, pausing occasionally to examine one more closely. McDermott didn't try to hurry her.

Presently she muttered something and showed one of the photos to her husband. His hand trembled as he peered at it closely, squinting in the marginal light afforded by the small window next to him. He nodded as he returned the picture.

'Something of interest, then?' McDermott asked.

'It's a picture taken when I was a child, playing with the daughter of the owners of the villa, *il Conte* e *la Contessa*. My mother was housekeeper at the villa, you see. The two of us girls, we were the same age, or nearly so. When we were small my mother used to take me with her to the villa, and Gabriella and I would play together. *La signora* liked that, because there were few other children who would visit.'

McDermott let her tell her story at her own pace. He knew from experience that often some detail would emerge that didn't seem important to the speaker, but could be significant.

She caught him eyeing his empty cup. 'More tea?' she asked.

The first cup had been watery, and McDermott supposed the next would be the dregs, but he wanted to prolong their conversation. 'Why not?' he said, holding out his cup.

She returned a moment later with the teapot. As he suspected, the cup contained not only the dregs, it was also tepid. He took another biscotti from the plate, and dipped it in the pale liquid. Each enhanced the other, and he knew that was part of the tradition of serving the two together. 'So,' he said, returning his cup to the saucer beside him, 'you spent a lot of time at the villa, then.'

'Ah, *si*,' she replied. 'For a few years we were inseparable. Then, as we got older, I had to go to school in the village, and Gabriella was sent away to a convent to study. We did not see each other so much after that.' She seemed saddened by the fact.

'A shame,' McDermott commiserated. He was at a loss how to proceed when her gaze fell upon a small photo in a stack she had been leafing through.

'*È molto memorabile!* Here is a memory!' she exclaimed, sitting back in her chair and clearly savouring the moment. 'We were both about five years old then, certainly not more than six. One day we had been running around in the *sala da pranzo,* the dining room I think you say, even though we had been told not to. We were playing—what do you English say—hide-and-seek? Gabriella came into the room and I turned to run, only I forgot there was a small table behind me. I crashed into it, and it fell over. The table was not damaged, but it had a large silver tureen on it. It was very heavy, and I could tell it was very valuable, and now it had a dent in one side. I wanted to run away, but Gabriella would not hear of it. We pulled the table upright, and replaced the bowl on it, but with the dent on the side nearest the wall. Her father never said anything about it, but the next day her mother told us we must be much more careful in the future. Then she took our photograph. I think it was to remind us.' She passed the picture over to McDermott. 'After that, we mostly played outside whenever the weather was good.'

He took the photograph from her hand, and looked at it carefully. There could be no mistake: two young girls standing side by side, posing self-consciously in a dark, ornate dining room, surrounded by lovely furnishings. They were clearly ill at ease. On an ornate side table behind them was the same tureen he had seen in Baker-Simms' drawing room. The dent in one side was just visible, and confirmed the match.

McDermott was silent as he thought about his next step. To ask her for the photo would raise questions. After a moment he said, 'This photograph would be of interest to a friend of mine. He is a woodworker, a cabinet maker, you see. His specialty is making reproductions of Renaissance furniture. I think he would be very intrigued by the lines of the table in the background. The turned legs, the inlay, and the proportions are very distinctive. Would it be possible for me to borrow this from you long enough to make a copy? I promise I will return it to you intact.'

She looked at him closely, searching his face, he thought, for some indication that he was being less than truthful with her. Finally she said, 'Why not? You are a curious man, you English, always doing favours for your friends.'

'Yes, I suppose I am,' he replied, placing the photograph in his jacket pocket before she could rethink her kindness.

'But I have been doing all of the talking. What became of your friend's father? You said he has died? Age, I suppose. It takes us all in the end.'

'Actually, he was the victim of an assault,' McDermott replied. 'Most likely an attempted robbery. He fell and hit his head.'

'*Come terribile!*' she exclaimed. 'To think he went through the war with death all around him, and went back to his homeland safely, only to die at the hands of a *ladro,* a common thug. It is not fair.' Then her expression softened, and she looked at her husband. 'But life is not fair, is it? So at least he had many years after the war. He was happy?'

'I'm sure he was,' McDermott replied. 'I didn't know him well, but I saw him in the days leading up to his death, and shortly before that he was in good health, and surrounded by his friends. Yes, I'm sure he was happy.'

'*Va bene*. He was a good man, I think.'

McDermott glanced out the window, and saw the sun was fading fast. 'I want to thank you for seeing me,' he said to them both. 'It has been a great pleasure, but I have already taken up far too much of your time. I should be getting back to the hotel.'

She paused. 'I have an idea. You are in the village for how long?' she asked.

McDermott shrugged. 'I suppose I shall leave tomorrow, now that I have spoken with you. Why do you ask?'

'I have an idea.' She moved to the door. 'Something that might interest you. But you will need to stay for another day. First I must see if it is possible. I will not do it just now: it is almost supper time and the people I want to speak with will be preparing their supper. Give me a few hours. Can you give me the number where you are staying?'

McDermott told her the name of the hotel, and she promised to leave him a message.

'It was good to meet you,' she said, extending her hand. 'We do not have many visitors. Forgive me, but you will return my picture before you leave. It means much to me.'

McDermott reassured her and thanked them both, then stepped out into the evening air. The sun had finally disappeared, and it was already growing cool. As he made his way through the narrow streets it grew colder and darker still. One lane began to look much like another, and McDermott was beginning to wonder if he'd been wise to attempt the journey on his own when he turned a corner and found himself in the piazza. The hotel was brightly lit, and the windows of the dining room gave off a welcoming glow. He entered the lobby and saw the owner at the front desk, talking to the chambermaid. When he approached the man he said, '*Mille grazie* for your son's help earlier today. I couldn't have found my way without his help.'

'I will tell his mother,' the man replied. 'She will be pleased.'

McDermott reached in his pocket and pulled out a one-Euro coin. 'Would you pass this onto him?' he asked.

'Oh no, that is too much,' the man protested. He lowered his voice. 'Perhaps you can buy him a *dolci* when you see him tomorrow. But don't tell his mother!' he cautioned.

McDermott laughed and started for the dining room. His luck was holding out: the dinner menu described a wide array of regional dishes. He began with prosciutto and fresh figs, followed by a hearty *zuppa di pesce*, a seafood stew consisting of prawns, whitefish, mussels and clams, with rounds of toasted bread garnished with chopped fresh parsley. A leisurely hour later he finished his dinner with *zabaione*, an Italian custard made with orange zest and marsala wine, and an espresso. By the time he headed for his room, Colin McDermott was a man well satisfied, and not only with his meal.

TWENTY-TWO

The next morning there was a message waiting for him at the front desk. Signora Goldman would see him at two o'clock, if that was convenient. Then they would walk to their destination. McDermott was intrigued.

After a light lunch McDermott set out on foot for the Goldman's home. The sun was in full force, and in the daylight the streets seemed far less confusing. He arrived shortly before the appointed time, and was pleased to find she was ready. She took a thin shawl from a peg next to the door, and called out to her husband, saying they would be back by late afternoon. McDermott still had no idea what she had in store for him.

They set out at a brisk pace, taking McDermott somewhat by surprise. She might be elderly, he reflected, but she was certainly fit beyond her years. The gradient was low but constant, and he was glad when she stopped occasionally to point out some aspect of the landscape. After a few minutes they had left the village behind and were silently making their way up one of the numerous country lanes that bisected the mountain range.

The dwellings became fewer and, McDermott noted, larger, until they were mostly replaced by vineyards and groves of trees. They were nearing the crest of a ridge that afforded a view of the valleys to either side when Isabella Goldman halted. 'This is one of several roads leading into the *Parco Nazionale Dell'asppromonte*, the National Forest, where the Germans retreated,' she said. 'The difference is that this road is higher than the others, and gives a good view of several *stradine* below.' She pointed to winding tracks in the distance. 'So it was a natural place for—how do you say—an observation post. That is why your army came up here.'

They rounded a turn and McDermott saw an imposing villa in the distance. It overlooked both valleys below, and McDermott realised the old woman's goal in bringing him there.

'So that's the villa, is it? The one where the Count and Countess were killed?'

'*Si*,' she said grimly. 'I have arranged for you to meet the present owners.'

They turned into the gravel drive, and McDermott tried to imagine what it must have been like on that rainy day in September of '43. Certainly more foreboding, he decided: the soldiers had just come from fierce fighting in Sicily, and although the landing at San Giovanni had been largely uneventful—save for the Luftwaffe—the British soldiers would have had no idea what to expect here in the mountains.

As they approached the villa a woman who had been tending some plants stood to greet them. '*Buonasera*, Isabella.' She smiled at them both. She seemed to be in her early fifties, or perhaps older, and was deeply tanned from working in the sun.

'*Buonasera*, Sophia. It has been far too long.' Isabella Goldman introduced McDermott, who noticed that she described him only as a friend visiting from England. The woman took them inside and went to fetch her husband, and McDermott was able to get a brief glimpse of the rooms. The place was likely much brighter now than it had been during the war, he decided. The walls were a subdued shade of cream, and in the adjoining room, rose. The heavy draperies he had seen in Bert Ridley's wartime photos had been replaced by lighter curtains that diffused rather than blocked the sunlight, and the inlaid floors glistened with polish. There were fewer pieces of furniture in the room as well, although what remained was obviously of quality. After a few moments the woman returned with her husband. McDermott put his age at perhaps sixty, although he might have been a bit older. He was casually dressed in cream slacks and a dark blue silk shirt. His hair was brown and full, and was combed back over the tops of his ears. There was a hint of grey at the temples, and creases at the corners of his eyes, but he was tanned and clearly fit. He extended his hand to McDermott.

'*Piacere*, *signore*, it is a pleasure to meet you. My name is Giancarlo di Montefiori, and I think you have already met my wife Sophia.' He turned his attention to McDermott's companion. 'Isabella, it is so good to see you again. You have been a stranger!' he admonished her, smiling.

'The road is growing longer, and more steep, I fear. And I am not always able to leave Vittorio alone for so long.'

'But of course. *Venga*. Come. Join us on the terrace for a drink.' He guided them through a large drawing room and toward some tall glass doors.

When they were settled and enjoying their drinks Giancarlo turned his attention back to McDermott. 'It is the first time you are in our country, *signore*?'

Anxious not to deflect the conversation to himself, McDermott said simply, 'The first time in this area. It is unique. Visitors to the north would have little idea of the scenery here, and the food,' he added.

The man smiled. 'Just so. And some people would keep it that way, although most, I think, would be happy to see more *turiste* come with their money. How did you discover us?'

'The *signore* is here as a favour to a friend,' Isabella Goldman cut in. Clearly she too wanted to control how much they knew of his mission. 'His friend's father served with the British Army near here, many years ago. He died recently, and his son is anxious to learn more about his father's time during the war.'

'*Ho capito,* I understand.' The man's expression grew more solemn. 'I never knew my own parents. A wartime romance between my mother and a soldier, I understand. They both died during the war.'

'A pity. So much suffering during those days,' McDermott said.

'*Si.* Apparently my mother's parents also died during a bombing during the war. She was a girl at the time, and her grandparents were too old to look after her, so they sent her to a convent near Parma.' There was a slight catch in the man's voice. 'But it is of no importance to you,' he added, forcing a thin smile. 'When Isabella telephoned us yesterday she mentioned you have an interest in wine-making.'

McDermott put on an impassive face, wary of getting in over his head. Isabella Goldman moved to save the day. '*Si,* Giancarlo.

I served him a glass of your *Bivongi Rosso* last evening and he was—how do you say—very impressed.'

Giancarlo beamed. '*Assolutamente!* Perhaps you would like to see our vineyards.' He looked at the darkening sky. 'But the skies do not look good. Perhaps tomorrow?'

'*Mi dispiace*, Giancarlo. I am sorry. Unfortunately the *signore* cannot stay very long. He returns soon to England.'

'*Che peccato!* What a shame. Still, you can take a glass or two with us.' He reached for one of several bottles on the table, and half-filled a glass, passing it to McDermott. '*Salute*,' he said, lifting his own glass to examine the colour against the sky, then lowered it to his nose, savouring the aroma. When he lowered it further to his lips everyone joined him.

McDermott was anxious to establish his amateur status in matters of winemaking before Isabella got him in too deep. 'Forgive my ignorance, but I had no idea that this region produced such fine wines.'

Giancarlo spread his large hands on the table. '*Ah, si.* It has not always been so, at least for many years. Calabria has long been a poor region, ignored by the government and left to do for itself. After the war many of our people left for America and also for Argentina. It is only recently that we are known for anything but the red wines known as *Cirò Classico.* But in recent years a few of us have been working to develop some less tannic grapes. In *Bianco* we have succeeded in producing a sweet white wine, and here we are combining *Gaglioppo*, *Nocera*, *Calabrese* and other varieties to achieve what you English call red and rosé wines, mostly blends. But we also have some dry whites that, I think, will some day make a name for us.'

'It is a small winery,' he continued, clearly enthusiastic about his vocation. 'We have less than eighty hectares under cultivation, from which we produce about twenty-two hundred hectolitres per year. But each year we are getting better yields. I will prepare a small selection for you to take back with you to England.'

'That is very generous, *signore*, but—'

'Giancarlo. I insist. It is simply good business, *non?* You will tell your friends, and they will want more.' His gaze was disarming. The man was no fool.

McDermott raised his glass and smiled. 'In that case, *grazie*. *Molti grazie*.'

They all laughed, and their laughter was interrupted by a woman who emerged from the villa with two young girls, not yet in their teens, in tow. Sophia beckoned them to her side. 'This is our daughter, Adelina, and our granddaughters, Maria and Gabriella. You know signora Goldman,' she said. 'This is her friend, *signore* McDermott.'

The two girls smiled self-consciously. 'What have you been up to?' their father asked.

'*Niente*,' they protested. 'Would it be all right if we went to visit Bianca?' Maria asked.

Giancarlo made a face. 'Must you? We only see you for a few hours when you visit!' Then, seeing their expressions, he relented. 'Oh, very well. But be home for supper. No excuses!' The girls grinned and ran away.

'As you can see, they have Giancarlo around their little fingers,' their mother said, smiling.

'That is not so,' he protested. 'My wife thinks I am too soft with them, 'but it will rain tomorrow, and they need to get out.' Sophia rolled her eyes.

Isabella Goldman put down her glass. 'Giancarlo, I am afraid we will need to be going before the sun sets. But perhaps before we leave you could show *Signore* McDermott some of your wonderful villa. The main rooms?'

'But of course!' he replied. 'Just come with me.' They returned to the house and over the next twenty minutes Giancarlo and his wife led McDermott and Isabella through several rooms, pointing out the features of each room and the significance of a piece of furniture or a carpet, most of which had come down through the family over generations. 'There were many more pieces here during my grandparents' time,' Giancarlo explained, 'but most of them were lost during the war, before I was born.' McDermott shot Isabella a look, but her expression remained impassive.

'A great shame,' McDermott said. 'So many beautiful objects.'

'The fortunes of war, isn't that what they say? Still, there are many memories in these objects.'

'And much history,' Sophia interjected.

'And much history,' Giancarlo agreed.

After that, there seemed nothing more to say. McDermott and Isabella Goldman made their goodbyes, and Giancarlo said he would have a case of wine delivered to McDermott's hotel the next morning. He offered to drive them back, but Isabella demurred, noting that the sky now looked more promising than earlier, and their return trip would be mostly downhill.

AS THEY MADE THEIR WAY back to the village, McDermott looked at his companion sharply. 'You know, that was rather risky of you back there, suggesting I was knowledgeable about wines. I could have easily been found out!'

She laughed. 'Nonsense. Anyway, Englishman, you are a policeman, are you not? You must be used to fooling other people.'

The question took him aback. After a moment, he said, 'How did you know?'

She looked straight ahead, keeping her eyes on the road. 'It was not so difficult, really. Your questions were less about your friend's father than the events at the villa, and afterwards. And when you looked at the picture I showed you, I saw that you were more interested in the silver tureen than the table it sat on.'

Another moment passed, and McDermott smiled. 'You know, there's a job waiting for you back in England if you want it.'

'*Grazie,* but I don't think so,' she said brusquely. 'I don't really like deceiving people, you know. Does your presence here mean that you have tracked down some of the artworks from the villa?'

'Perhaps.' Seeing her annoyance he added, 'It certainly looks that way. But we have to be certain, don't we? Not only the ownership of the works but also people's reputations are at stake. To make an allegation that cannot be proved…' He let the thought go unfinished.

'The officer I spoke with all those years ago, the one who was in charge of the British soldiers here in Santa Cristina, he was involved?'

'It seems possible,' McDermott admitted. 'After the war he went on to become a senior officer in the regiment. All the more reason that I must proceed carefully.'

'*Si, copisco.*' Her expression was cynical. 'He is a man of much importance.'

McDermott waited, allowing her to speak in her own time. At length she said, 'The man you met today, Giancarlo, he is not merely the present owner of the villa. He is also the great-grandson of the couple that British officer shot.'

McDermott paused. 'I thought as much, when he mentioned losing the family's patrimony.'

She looked at him as though he was a particularly slow-witted child. 'And who do you imagine his own parents were?'

'Well, his mother must have been their daughter, the girl you were childhood friends with.'

'Exactly,' she interrupted. 'Gabriella, my friend. And when do you think she became Giancarlo's mother? Think about his age.'

McDermott was silent for a moment, then his expression changed. 'You mean that—'

She smiled sardonically. 'You begin to understand, Englishman.'

He stopped walking and gathered his thoughts. He had allowed himself to become preoccupied with the deaths of the couple at the villa and the missing art, ignoring the events that must have followed. But now he focused on what might have occurred in the following days and weeks. He saw a theory emerging, and although it seemed at first wildly improbable, it became more likely the longer he thought about it. 'Gabriella had been in a convent, you said, so she would have been what—no more than seventeen at the time?'

'*Si*. Go on.'

'So the officer who shot and killed her grandparents. Whether it was a genuine mistake or not is irrelevant. She must have been furious with him!'

They began walking again. 'You assume that she knew this, Englishman. I was there, remember? When Italy joined the Axis in 1940 she was sent away for her schooling and for her safety. She only returned when her grandparents were killed. And the only thing we were told was that a group of British soldiers had been searching the villa and encountered the Conte and the Contessa, who were armed. We didn't find it unusual that they should have a gun, almost everyone did. And the situation was... unsettled. Both sides had soldiers in the area. You didn't know who you would run into next. No one did. When we learned of the killings at the villa we were simply told that a British soldier searching the villa came upon them and fired in self-defense; we were never told who he was. Only later did we learn that a military inquiry had cleared the soldier of any wrongdoing.' She shrugged. 'In war there are accidents.'

'So how did Gabriella—?'

'Really! You English! Are you stupid, or just slow?' she admonished him. 'Gabriella was devastated to learn that her grandparents had been killed. When she returned from the convent she went to your officer for an explanation, and he tried to comfort her. Over the next few days they grew closer. Much closer. It was weeks after the unit had left that she discovered she was pregnant. By then she didn't know what to do. In those days to have a child out of marriage, especially for a member of the nobility, was unthinkable; it had to be concealed. I helped her find a hospital in Palmi, on the coast. The British had already passed through there, so we knew it was safe. She was an orphan, remember, and her grandparents were dead. No one here, other than me and a very few others, knew where she had gone. It was there she had the child.'

McDermott digested the information. 'But what happened to her?'

'Everything was fine until the end of the war. Gabriella moved back to the villa with her son and was putting her life back together.

There were rumours, of course, but people had their own lives to get on with. Then a *friend* of Gabriella's—I use the word wrongly—learned from her soldier boyfriend that it was your British officer who had killed her grandparents, and told her the truth. Just imagine: the same man who killed Gabriella's grandparents had made love to her, and she had borne him a son! She could not stand the thought, and hung—hanged—herself.' Isabella stopped walking and her expression grew steely cold. 'Dead before she was twenty. Such a waste. I remember…' Her voice trailed off.

'What?'

'Nothing. It's not important.'

They continued down the mountain road in silence for some minutes, then Isabella resumed her narrative. 'When Gabriella died, some of us in the village took her son in and made sure that he recovered what was left of his family home. Today no one except me is alive who knows the whole story, and for obvious reasons I never told him.'

He made a face. 'My God. It's like a scene out of a Greek tragedy, isn't it?'

'Or an Italian opera,' she replied. 'So you see the issue facing you, Englishman?'

'I'm not entirely stupid,' McDermott said, 'although I admit to being a little slow. The art works, if they still exist, belong to Giancarlo and his family. But the larger question remains: should he be told that his father is still alive?'

'And that his father killed his great-grandparents, and drove his mother to commit suicide? If you would assume such responsibility then you are more arrogant, and more stupid, than I think.' They stopped, and she looked at him closely. After a moment, she said, 'No, I don't think so.' They walked on.

When they reached her house Signora Goldman invited McDermott in and offered him a coffee. She left the room briefly and returned with some writing paper and a pencil. She sat down and began making notes, and when she was finished she dated and signed the document and shoved it across the table to McDermott.

'It is a list of what I remember was taken from the villa that day,' she sighed. 'I visited the house afterwards. It is not complete, of course, but some of the more important pieces, the valuable ones, are there.'

McDermott studied the list. Many of the articles listed were unfamiliar, but he recalled seeing three, perhaps four, pieces of furniture in Baker-Simms' home, along with a small vase and a painting that resembled a work on the list. He folded it and tucked it away in his jacket pocket. 'This should certainly help us in our inquiries. I'm very grateful to you for all your efforts.'

Again her tone was brusque. 'Don't thank me. Just do what you can to see that justice is done.' She rose, and extended her hand.

By the time he returned to the hotel it was getting on dark, and McDermott approached the front desk. A middle-aged woman was on duty, speaking with a chambermaid. Pippo's mother, he guessed.

'Is there a telephone I might use? I must place a call to Reggio Calabria.'

'Of course,' she replied, pointing to a small cubicle at the end of the desk. 'I will connect you, and add the charge to your room. That is ok?'

McDermott nodded and searched his jacket pocket. Removing a small card, he dialed the airport, and then he dialled another number and asked for Capitano Russo.

It was time to return to England.

TWENTY-THREE

When he came downstairs the next morning McDermott found Capitano Russo in full uniform, sitting in an armchair and reading a newspaper. The surprise must have shown on his face as Russo put down the paper and smiled.

'I thought you would simply send a car,' McDermott said. 'I'm afraid once again I've put you to a lot of trouble.'

Russo stood up. 'But no. We do not often see our colleagues—that is the word?—in this part of the country. It is a pleasure to be able to help.' He scooped up McDermott's bag before he could protest. 'Have you had breakfast?'

'Actually, no. I thought I would grab a snack at the airport.'

Russo made a face. 'Grab a snack? Perhaps that is the way you English take your meals, but here…' He let the words drop.

McDermott did the math. He had four hours before his plane left, and doubtless Russo could speed his way through Airport

Security. 'As you say. There's a nice little bar just across the piazza. But this time it's my treat. I insist!'

As they entered the Bar Versace the owner looked up. 'Ah, back for more, are you?' Then she spotted the Carabinieri officer. 'You have not done something bad, I hope, *signore*. Our prisons, they are like dungeons!' she teased.

McDermott laughed. 'No, this is a friend.' He stood aside so Russo could see the array of pastries, and let him order for the both of them. They took a table against the wall and waited for their food and drink. There were no other customers, McDermott noted gratefully.

Russo raise a single eyebrow. 'So, *Ispettore*, how did you get on? Did you find the answers to all of your questions?' His tone was light, but McDermott read the seriousness behind his words.

'I think I owe you an explanation, Capitano,' he said carefully. 'As I mentioned, I have been looking into events that occurred many years ago, during the war. There is a possibility that some Italian artifacts have gone missing and wound up in my country. I wanted to clarify some of the facts of the case before bothering you.'

Russo looked into McDermott's eyes before speaking, and McDermott was beginning to wish he'd been more forthcoming when he'd first arrived. 'Some artifacts, you say? Are they of significant value?'

'I believe they could be,' McDermott replied cautiously.

Russo's expression hardened. 'So, in fact, objects of national patrimony.'

The woman arrived with their food, and McDermott was glad for the interruption. As she left, Russo picked up his cup and sipped his coffee, his eyes never leaving McDermott's. 'You know, in Italy we take the theft of our art very seriously.'

'I am aware of that, *Capitano*. In fact, I was a member of the Met's Art Squad some years ago.'

'Yes, I know,' Russo interrupted. 'Your friend *Ispettore* Decker told me as much. He also said you were an honest man, a man who could be trusted.'

'And I hope he is right, *Capitano*. But you must understand that we had very little to go on, and there is also the matter of a man who was killed in England—'

'Because he knew of this theft?'

By now Russo was firmly in control of the discussion, and McDermott struggled to guide its direction. 'Possibly. We do not know that. During my trip here my colleague in England is pursuing other lines of inquiry. When I return we will compare notes.'

There was another pause. 'I see. And were you planning to tell me all this before you left today?'

'I don't know,' McDermott answered truthfully. 'Perhaps if you'd been a different man, or approached me differently, I might not have. But you strike me as an honest man, a "good copper" as we say in my country, and you have been more than patient. So I'm going to tell you everything I know so far.'

Over the next forty minutes McDermott shared his information with Russo, who asked surprisingly few questions. When he was finished Russo said, 'And what are your objectives in this case?'

McDermott spread his hands on the table. 'That, at least, is easy. First, to determine Albert Ridley's killer, and bring him to book. Then to examine such artworks as remain with the family in England, and if they prove to be stolen, to restore them to their rightful owners here in Italy. And finally, to compensate the family insofar as possible for works which cannot be located.'

'Most admirable,' Russo smiled fleetingly. Then his expression hardened again as he added, 'But you place me in a very difficult position, *Ispettore.* If I tell your story to my superiors in Rome they will insist on intervening. After all, our national heritage is at stake. If that were to happen, your investigation might be compromised, and a killer might walk free.' He paused and leaned forward very slightly, locking eyes with his McDermott. 'What would you do in my position?'

McDermott grasped his cup with both hands, then returned the man's gaze. 'It is not for me to say, *Capitano*. I cannot ask you to withhold information from your superiors, but we have an expression in my country: timing is everything.'

After a very long moment Russo gave the thinnest of smiles. 'Just so. So we did not have this conversation—yet. How long do you think you will need to conclude your inquiries at your end?'

'Perhaps a week,' McDermott said. 'Ten days at the most.'

'Very well. Contact me then by telephone and we will speak again. But you understand that at that point I may have to inform others, and it will be out of my hands.' He paused, then said, 'In my country we have an expression too: *non si discute la bellezza.* One cannot argue about beauty. The same applies to truth, for very different reasons.'

McDermott smiled. 'I understand perfectly, *Capitano* Russo.' And he raised his cup to the man.

ARRIVING AT GATWICK that afternoon McDermott found George Ridley waiting for him, having returned from Yorkshire several days earlier. He looked, McDermott thought, noticeably older than when he'd last seen him.

'How are you, George?' he asked as they headed for the exit. 'Made any progress?' On the journey back to London they exchanged information, so that by the time they arrived they'd mapped out a plan for their return to Yorkshire.

First, however, Derek Galbraith would have to be informed.

They entered the CID suite at Charing Cross early the next morning to find the DCI already at his desk. His civilian assistant had not yet appeared, and Galbraith motioned them in, gesturing toward the chairs facing his desk. He shifted a small mountain of paperwork to one side. 'So how did our globetrotting copper fare? More importantly, are you picking up the tab, or is the Met?'

McDermott managed a smile. 'The Met is, I think.'

He spent the next ten minutes outlining his findings, leaving any mention of his conversation with Capitano Russo for later. When he had finished, Galbraith leaned back in his chair and gazed at the ceiling for a moment. 'It certainly looks suspicious on the face of it,' he said, then turned to Ridley. 'I take it you've not been idle whilst our friend has been working his fingers to the bone.'

Ridley shifted to sit more upright. 'Not a bit of it, guv. Ah've been sortin' through records at regimental HQ in Yorkshire.'

'And you've found something interesting, no doubt, or you wouldn't be mentioning it.'

A flicker of irritation passed over Ridley's face. 'Nowt as much as Ah'd hoped. You'd expect records to be in apple-pie order. Normally the army don't do things by 'alf. Only, files were in a right state. They'd had a bad fire month or so back, when reunion were moved to Baker-Simms' estate. Seems fire started in the kitchen, but spread to storage room where records were kept. Lot o' what didn't get burnt up got soaked wi' water and 'ad to be thrown out. Ah talked wi' Quartermaster Sergeant—he's the bloke responsible for records, and 'e said boxes for last part o' war all way up through 1950s were binned. That included shippin' logs and inventory ledgers.'

Galbraith let out a breath. 'So no joy, then. A shame.' He turned to McDermott. 'Those records might have nailed it. As it stands, your evidence is entirely circumstantial. We seem to be at a dead end.' Grasping at straws he asked, 'I don't suppose we have anything suspicious about the fire?'

'Bit of a stretch, I'm afraid,' McDermott said. 'Our man does nothing about incriminating records for what—sixty years—then stages a fire to destroy the evidence shortly before the reunion? No, I doubt it happened that way. I think the fire was just what it seemed to be, an accident, albeit a fortuitous one for Baker-Simms.' He smiled ruefully. 'All the same, the fire was something of a two-edged sword,' he added.

Galbraith looked at him quizzically. 'How so?'

'Well, if it hadn't happened the reunion would have been held as scheduled at the regimental HQ, and Bert Ridley would never have seen the painting that set him thinking.'

There was a moment of silence as Galbraith pondered the situation. 'So what's your next move?'

'First, I'd like to track down the Monuments Men who were in the area.'

'And who are they when they're at home?'

McDermott smiled. 'That's what you pay me the big bucks for, sir: my knowledge of art history. The Monuments Men were a unit formed by the Allies during the war. The Allied Command Staff were anxious to prevent the Germans—or our own lads, come to that—from looting art from the occupied countries. They sent teams of experts into the battlefield once it was secured to meet with local museum officials and the like, and compile a list of important artifacts, and especially to identify any works that might have gone walkabout.'

'Ah. And you think they might have some information on the artworks from the villa?'

'It's just possible, sir. Certainly they will have records from the day. And they won't have disappeared in any kitchen fire,' he added wryly.

'And where are these records to be found?

'I'll get onto it later today. The Ministry of Defense will know. It took over when the War Office was disbanded in the mid-sixties.'

Galbraith mulled it over for a few moments. 'Very well, but don't let this drag on much longer. We need to get on with it. And hold off on submitting the chit for your jaunt to Italy. You haven't convinced me yet!'

TWENTY-FOUR

It took little time for McDermott to track down the whereabouts of the Monuments Men unit. A museum of sorts, containing the unit's archives, existed at Lancaster House, a stately home taken over decades earlier by the government, and located in St James Square.

The curator there, a Lieutenant Colonel Trueblood, was able to provide the information McDermott sought, but it wasn't good news. It seemed that a tiny contingent of Monuments Men, consisting of one lieutenant and a sergeant, had indeed crossed from Sicily to Italy in the days following the Allied invasion of the mainland. But their entire equipment consisted of one jeep, a camera, and an assortment of maps. The latter turned out to be useless as they focused on Naples and Rome, the other maps having been misfiled and left behind in Alexandria. By the time the missing maps had been located and sent to the men in the field a crucial three weeks had passed. The officer had searched the archives, but there was no mention of the villa near Santa Cristina, nor of any missing artworks in the vicinity.

McDermott was growing frustrated. It seemed that every time he explored a new source of information it turned out to be a dead end. Mere suspicions wouldn't earn him a conviction in court. What he needed was evidence, not conjecture.

But McDermott was not yet ready to give up. Something he had mentioned in his discussion with Galbraith had struck him as important. He put in a call to the MOD and was able to locate the file dealing with the review of the shootings at the villa. It had been a preliminary inquiry, not a court martial, of course; the information and the circumstances wouldn't support that—especially if the Regimental Commander was your father. But it did list the details of the inquiry. The company commander, Captain Reginald Baker-Simms, had testified under oath that when he entered the bed chamber at the villa the room was in near total darkness, the heavy curtains having been pulled across the window. He had been about to leave when he sensed a movement behind him and turned and fired two bursts from his Sten gun. Two people fell to the floor. When he approached the bodies he could see they were a man and a woman, both elderly. And on the floor, near the man's outstretched arm, he testified, was a German Luger pistol.

The report went on. Two squaddies from his platoon had entered the room a few moments later, their guns at the ready. Baker-Simms testified that he had shown them the scene, then said it would be important to preserve it intact. There would have to be a formal investigation, as they were civilians. He cautioned the men about touching anything and put one man on sentry duty outside the room, locking it himself and giving instructions that no one should be allowed inside. Then he did the same outside the main door of the villa, posting two men there and another two at the gate giving onto the road. He returned with the rest of the platoon to the company HQ in Santa Cristina, where he contacted the regimental field HQ by radio and explained what had happened. They were a hundred miles to the north, but indicated they would send a ranking officer to inspect the scene and take statements the following day.

The investigating officer, a Major Nigel Endicott, was Adjutant to the Regimental Commander. He arrived in the village by mid-morning, and Baker-Simms had assured him everything was in order. In fact, he had personally inspected the scene that morning to satisfy himself that the proper security was in place and that no one had been allowed to enter the building or the room in his absence. He had even drawn a diagram of the room, indicating the precise location of everything that was relevant. Escorted by two armed squaddies they travelled to the villa, and the Major walked through the scene with Baker-Simms, taking notes and asking a barrage of questions.

The formal inquiry was held later that day. By the time it had ended Captain Baker-Simms had been absolved of any personal responsibility for the couple's death, the Major describing the incident as 'just another of the terrible misfortunes of war.' There had been no recommendation for sanctions against the Captain.

McDermott pored over the report, searching for anything unusual. But the Major had been meticulous. His report even listed the serial number of the pistol found near the dead man's hand.

Then McDermott had an idea.

BY EARLY AFTERNOON MCDERMOTT HAD DISCUSSED HIS FINDINGS with Galbraith, and he and Ridley set out for Wakefield.

When they stepped off the train from London DCI West and DS Grimshaw were waiting for them. McDermott looked carefully at West for any sign of lingering resentment, but didn't see anything unusual. Grimshaw seemed at ease, so he took his cue from that.

Philippa West spoke first. 'So our wandering hero has returned!' She smiled ruefully and extended her hand. 'Sorry, I didn't mean to sound bitchy. Any luck, then?'

McDermott slung his bag into the waiting car. 'Yes, actually, we might have something to work with at last. What about your end? Any joy?'

'Depends on your definition of joy,' she said cryptically. As they made their way from the railway station to the Wakefield Police HQ she opened up. 'We confirmed that on the evening when George's father was attacked Gordon Baker-Simms spent the evening in London at his club. He had dinner from eight until about ten, then chatted with another member over drinks until close on eleven. Not even remotely possible for him to have returned in time to have assaulted Bert Ridley.' She cast an apologetic look at Ridley. 'Sorry.'

'No need,' he answered. 'Ah just want bugger what did 'im.'

'Of course. We all do. With him out of the running that leaves his son Julian. You recall he's got form. Nothing serious, really to date. Breach of the Peace, Taking and Driving Away a few years back, that sort of thing. Anyway, we looked into things, found out he'd spent part of that evening at the Grouse and Claret—bit of a twee pub at the other end of the village—with his girlfriend, Miranda Richards.'

'Richards?' McDermott interrupted. 'Isn't that the name of the landlord at the Blue Bull?'

'Yes, she's Ben Richard's daughter. Apparently Julian and her father don't get on, so the other pub is their local.'

'Having met Richards, I don't doubt it,' McDermott acknowledged. 'He's a surly bugger at the best of times.'

The car had threaded its way through most of the traffic, but was now tied up in a knot of cars as they neared the police station. 'Turn up anything interesting, then?' McDermott asked.

'Interesting, but not conclusive. Landlord at the Grouse recalled that Julian and Miranda arrived shortly after suppertime, and had a few rounds. Then a stranger came in, a Traveller looking for some trade. That would have been around 9pm.'

'Excuse me?' McDermott said. 'Remember, I'm not from these parts.'

She laughed. 'Sorry. A Roma, a gypsy man in his early thirties. He offered to sharpen the pub's kitchen knives. We get a lot of Travellers, around here. This one—did you get his name, Joe?'

'Noah Hearn,' Grimshaw replied. 'He's got form as well, only gyppos do, don't they?' He smiled mischievously.

Philippa West shot him a withering look and he lapsed into silence. 'Leaving aside the sergeant's biases, it seems the Hearn lad came onto Miranda in the pub, and Julian wasn't amused. They had words and he invited Hearn outside to discuss it. By this time they'd attracted a crowd, and the landlord wasn't having it. He gave the gypsy his walking papers, and Julian lit into Miranda for flirting. Apparently she gave as good as she got, and accused him of ignoring her. Shortly after that he left in a huff, leaving Miranda stranded there.'

'A real gentleman. How does that concern us?' McDermott asked.

'Well, he admits he rode off on his motorbike in the direction of the village. This would have been a good two hours before Bert Ridley was attacked. The Blue Bull, where Ridley was attacked, lies almost directly between the Grouse and Julian's home. Says he must have arrived around half ten, but he's no evidence for this. Went directly to his room, he said.'

By then they had pulled into the car park at Wakefield Police HQ, and McDermott emerged, pulling his bag from the seat next to him. 'It gives him opportunity, of course, and if he knew about Bert Ridley's visit to the house, and understood its significance, it would also give him motive. But not much to go on, all the same. And then there's the question of the missing two hours. Is it likely that he waited around for Ridley to emerge from the pub, assuming he even knew he was in there?'

'I agree there are some loose ends,' Philippa West agreed, swiping her key card at the rear door of the building. 'We wanted to put you in the picture before planning how best to question him.' She opened the door and held it for McDermott, who wondered what he'd done to get on her good side.

When they entered the CID Suite they found Gareth Matthews waiting for them. The desks were littered with coffee cups and takeaway orders, and the smell of curry, combined with fish and chips, gave the room a pungent air. It was getting dark, but despite the hour the change in atmosphere was evident, McDermott noticed, and things seemed to be going much more smoothly.

After he and Ridley had summarized their findings Matthews took over the discussion. 'We seem to have a mixed bag,' he said. 'On the one hand, we know that Reginald Baker-Simms killed the old couple in Italy. It seems entirely possible that he also used the opportunity provided by their deaths to steal some valuable artworks from their villa. We'll need expert testimony on that, of course, but with the list Colin brought back from Italy and his connections with the Art and Antiques Squad in London he's well placed to look into that. A shame about the lack of regimental records. On the other hand, his son Gordon seems to have an alibi for the attack on Bert Ridley, and we have bugger all to link Julian to his death.' He paused. 'Any thoughts?'

After a moment's silence Philippa West spoke up. 'There's a time and a place for everything, sir. In my view we've tiptoed around the family, afraid of offending the local gentry. At some point we need to confront them directly. I think that time has arrived. We should apply for a warrant to search their premises, and if necessary bring them in for an interview.'

All heads turned toward the DCS, who was taking notes. He put down his pen and looked at McDermott. 'What's your take on this, Colin?'

McDermott took his time, considering their options. 'I understand DCI West's concern. But a lot depends on our approach. As I see it, if we go in full dress, with a search warrant and officers to document and inventory the artifacts, the family will get their collective backs up and the press are likely to get wind of it as well, in which case it will be a circus. There's bound to be collateral damage. A lot of reputations might be ruined. Some people—many, I'd wager—will be outraged that we're raking all this up and impugning the reputation of one of our own soldiers, and a senior officer to boot. And of course, the entire thing happened half a century ago. We've already established that there's no paper trail of art works at the regiment, and witnesses to the packing-up of the artifacts in 1943 will be hard to find. Even if we are able to run them to ground, it's been a good long time. Memories will have become clouded. A conviction isn't at all certain. And stirring all this up with no hope of obtaining a conviction…' He left the rest of the sentence unfinished.

The room was silent. The group looked to Gareth Matthews, who turned to McDermott. 'Well, we've come this far. What do you propose?'

'As I said, I understand DCI West's frustration. But I suggest we begin by speaking with them informally, on their own turf. Start by raising the issue of Bert Ridley's death, centring on the lad's—what's his name? Julian's—alibi. They're bound to raise the question of motive, and that's when we confront them with what we know about the artworks in the house. Faced with the evidence, they might just be caught off guard, give us something to work on. If not, we've still got the physical evidence to go on: the partisan's list to compare to the art works still in their possession. If possible, I would avoid any mention of Baker-Simms being criminally responsible for the deaths at the villa. We've no evidence as yet, and it's bound to skew the discussion. We can save it for later, should we come into more information.'

There was a long pause. Finally Matthews said, 'Ok, it makes sense. In any case, it seems to be our only option at this point.' He looked at his watch. 'Going on eight. I'll run it by the Chief Constable tonight, and if he agrees we'll put it in place for tomorrow morning. I'll text you all to confirm matters.'

There was a real sense of relief as the members of the team rose and stretched and gathered their belongings. After weeks of work, finally some tangible action was set to take place. Philippa West intercepted her boss as he was leaving the room. 'So who's taking the lead on this, sir?'

Matthews stopped in his tracks. 'You are. You're the Senior Investigating Officer on this case. Take McDermott with you, of course. He's got all the art facts at his fingertips. And Joe, you go along to make a record of what's said. Remember, this is to be an informal inquiry: no caution is necessary unless or until someone is formally charged. It might also be wise to photograph the objects if they've no objection. If they're not guilty of anything, why should they object? Joe, you're handy with a camera; that's your remit. But no uniforms inside the house,' he added. Grimshaw, who had thought for a moment he was going to be left out of things, looked pleased.

'What about me?' George Ridley asked.

The DCS looked at him appraisingly. 'We have to be very careful here, George. We don't want anything going wrong because of a technicality. Some smart lawyer tracks onto your personal involvement he could tie us up in knots, even perhaps lose us the case.'

Ridley struggled to retain his composure. 'Think Ah don't know all that? Ah just want t' be there when you question 'em. Ah've got the details of the assault in me 'ead. Might spot a porkie that'd come in 'elpful.'

'Fair enough,' Matthews conceded. 'When we question them informally you can be present, but only as an observer. But as for being more centrally involved if and when we bring them in for a formal interview, I'm afraid that's not on. I'll have to run the plan by the Chief Constable, though.'

Ridley looked perturbed, but seeing the merit in Matthews' argument, nodded.

After laying out the next day's actions, Philippa West caught up with McDermott as he walked down the hallway toward the car park. 'At least we're finally moving forward.' Pausing to retrieve a cigarette and lighter from her bag, she said, 'Have any plans for the moment? I mean, fancy a drink?'

He was tired, but McDermott took her suggestion as a peace offering. Best not to pass it up. 'Why not? I'll just let George know that we'll be heading back to the village in an hour or so.'

She smiled. 'Might be simpler to just let him take his car. I can drop you off myself later. Not far out of my way.'

McDermott took that with a grain of salt. Still, the next day's operation required everyone's full cooperation. He nodded, and ten minutes later they were sitting in the snug of a nearby pub. McDermott had a single malt before him; West was nursing a Campari and soda.

She fingered a button on her blouse absentmindedly. 'I've been meaning to speak with you, Colin. I'm afraid we got off on rather the wrong foot when you first arrived. To be honest, I rather resented you being involved in the investigation.' She paused to sip her drink. 'Women CID officers are still a bit thin on the ground up here, especially in senior positions. We have to try that bit harder in order to get noticed. But I can see now that you were just lending us your expertise.'

McDermott took a pull on his drink and smiled. 'Not a problem. In your place I might well have done the same. Couple of London know-it-alls putting their size twelves in. The important thing is that we seem to be making headway. I know George, and if we don't solve his father's death, it will gnaw at him for a long time. I wouldn't like to see that. Not for any one.'

'Of course not.' Philippa West smiled, and shifted her lighter on the table from one spot to another. Evidently she was dying for a smoke. 'Tell me, doesn't your wife sometimes resent your work? I mean, the hours away? It can't be easy, trekking off to foreign shores for a week at a time.'

He looked at her more closely. Not an unattractive woman, save for the smoking habit and nervous tics—and her thin skin. He searched for the right words. 'You're not wrong there. My wife is an architect in London, and we have a young daughter. This is the longest I've ever been away since we've been together. Hopefully we can wind up things before too long. I'm looking forward to getting back to them both soon.'

Philippa turned scarlet red. 'Oh, I didn't mean to pry,' she said. 'I only meant—' Flustered, she knocked over her glass and the liquid crawled toward her lighter.

McDermott pushed a nearby napkin toward the mess. 'No need to apologise.' By their late twenties, or early thirties at most, most coppers were married; they welcomed the stability of domestic life to offset the chaos that sometimes overtook their working lives. That Philippa West was not wearing a wedding ring might have meant that she simply hadn't found the right person yet. Or it might mean that the pressures of the job had put paid to an otherwise promising relationship.

They chatted amiably for another few minutes, then set out for her car. West lit a cigarette as soon as they emerged from the pub, and not for the first time he noticed that her index finger was heavily stained. Pressures of work, or simply a long-standing addiction?

When she dropped McDermott off at the pub in Kirk Warham, she said, 'Nice to get away from the office, Colin. I hope for your sake we can wrap this up before too long.'

'So do I,' McDermott replied, leaving the ambiguity hanging in the air. He bent down before closing the door. 'Thanks for the drink. Best we get a good night's rest. See you tomorrow.'

As her car pulled away McDermott turned his attention back to the investigation. Something had been niggling him, and it wouldn't go away. From the start, he knew, the case had been weak. The evidence was still at best circumstantial, and any competent lawyer would make short work of it: sixty-year-old allegations with no eyewitnesses, against a decorated senior officer and veteran, now an elderly man in a wheelchair nearing the end of his life? He suspected most jurors would balk at this, and many would be sympathetic to Baker-Simms. McDermott knew he'd need something more, something linking the Brigadier inextricably to the events that took place at the villa. He had his suspicions, but then, suspicions didn't count.

And then he remembered what had caught his attention earlier. What was it George had said in Galbraith's office? *The army doesn't do things by half.* He hoped that was true.

Although it was well after hours, McDermott went to his room and sent an email to London. Now if only luck was on his side this time.

TWENTY-FIVE

It was a grey morning, but the news was good. The Chief Constable had reluctantly authorized a visit to Coniston Hall, and McDermott and Ridley joined DS Grimshaw and a severely-suited DCI West in the police car park, along with two uniformed drivers. After reviewing their tasks briefly they set out in two unmarked cars for Coniston Hall. As they entered the long avenue flanked by columns of mature trees, Philippa West looked at the imposing manor house in the distance and muttered to McDermott, 'I hope you know what you're doing, Colin, or it's both our pensions out the window.'

McDermott hoped so as well.

As they approached the house they noticed several cars parked on the gravel forecourt. McDermott, who was something of a motor enthusiast, recognized a two-year-old silver Bentley, a slightly older burgundy Jaguar XJ roadster, a newish Ducati motorcycle, an aging and rather battered Land Rover and, curiously, next to the front entrance, a black bicycle that looked so old it might have been made of iron. The Land Rover was dark, much like the one, McDermott reflected, that had driven Ridley and him off the road some weeks earlier. It looked as though they had caught everyone at home. McDermott allowed himself a small smile. That would make their job easier.

After asking the uniformed officers to wait by their cars, the CID team approached the imposing portico that sheltered the front door. Philippa West glanced at McDermott, took a deep breath, then pressed the polished brass button and waited for a response. After a moment they heard footsteps, and a middle-aged woman wearing a cotton dress under a flowered pinny opened the door. 'Yes?' she inquired, looking from one to the others.

'West Yorkshire Police. We're here to see the Baker-Simms, collectively.' West flashed her warrant card. 'I take it they're at home?'

The woman's eyes widened momentarily. 'Well, I'm sure I don't know. They're at breakfast.'

Philippa West cut her off. 'That's fine. Just point the way.' She brushed past the woman, with McDermott, Grimshaw, and Ridley following closely behind. 'They're down this way, I expect?' She indicated an open door at the end of the hall.

'That's right,' the woman said, resigned to losing the argument. 'Just let me tell them you're here.' She gave them a furtive look and led the way.

As they approached the breakfast room they could make out a murmur of voices. 'Who was that, Annie?' a male voice asked.

'It's the police, sir. They want to talk to you.' As they reached the open doorway she hurried off immediately, presumably toward the kitchen. West led the way into the room with the others following closely.

Seated around the table was everyone they had hoped to see, and more. At the head of the table at the far end, Gordon Baker-Simms was wearing grey trousers, a neatly-pressed striped dress shirt, and an expensive-looking silk tie. On his right the Brigadier was seated in his wheelchair in his pajamas and a rather old-fashioned dressing gown. Next to the Brigadier was a young man who looked to be in his late twenties. He had long, light brown hair, which was unkempt, and he was unshaven. He was wearing jeans, a jumper, and a surly expression. Next to him was a young woman in her mid-twenties. She was dressed in black, with eyeliner and lipstick to match. Julian's girlfriend, McDermott decided. On the other side of the table, next to her husband, McDermott saw Fiona Baker-Simms. She was wearing a lightweight summer dress in pastel hues, immaculately made up, with simple but clearly expensive gold earrings and matching bracelet. To her side, in clerical garb, was a pleasant-looking woman in her mid-thirties with sandy brown hair and an intelligent expression. McDermott had no idea what her connection to the family was, or why she was there.

West took charge. 'My apologies for disturbing your breakfast, sir. I'm DCI Philippa West, and this is DS Grimshaw, from the West Yorks CID. The other gentlemen are DI McDermott and DS Ridley. They're from London. We'd like a few minutes of your time. Perhaps you'd prefer to hold this discussion in private.' She looked pointedly at the vicar.

Gordon Baker-Simms blinked, and for a moment looked out of his depth. In an effort to establish control of the situation he said, 'Nonsense. Whatever this is about, we've nothing to hide. The vicar is here to arrange for the annual church fete next month, aren't you, Adrienne?'

'That's right. But I can return later if you'd prefer.'

'I think that might be best,' West said firmly. At this stage, the fewer outsiders who knew of the investigation the better. The vicar made her apologies and promised to give them a call later.

When she had gone, Gordon Baker-Simms looked at McDermott sharply. 'We've met before, right? I don't recall you mentioning that you were a policeman.'

'Quite right,' McDermott replied. 'But I did say I worked for the government. I was here in a personal capacity, attending the military reunion with a friend. You invited me inside to telephone about a puncture.'

'I remember now!' exclaimed Fiona Baker-Simms. 'Of course. We had a charming discussion about some of our paintings, as I recall. Nice to see you again. Will you join us for coffee?'

'Thanks,' West intervened, 'but I'm afraid we're here in an official capacity.'

'So what's all this about?' Gordon Baker-Simms asked. 'And why does it necessitate interrupting our breakfast?'

Philippa West made her opening move. 'Two weeks ago there was an assault on a man in the village of Kirk Warham,' she said. 'The victim, Albert Ridley, later died of his injuries. We understand that your son—Julian, is it?—may have been in the area at the time.'

The young man scoffed. 'Two weeks ago? And you're just gettin' around to it now?'

'This information has only recently come into our hands.' West hoped the story sounded more convincing to them than it did to her. 'You were at a pub, the Grouse and Claret, that night, and drove home through the village afterwards. Is that right, Julian?'

'What if I did? I didn't see anyone that night, and I didn't mug any old geezer either!'

West sensed she was on a roll. 'I didn't say it was an old geezer, Julian. Though in fact it was an elderly man. How did you know that?'

The young man flushed a bright red. 'Albert Ridley? Be serious! Ain't no one named that for the past hundred years! What'd he do, then, herd oxen?'

Before he could say more his father jumped in. 'See here! Are you suggesting that my son was somehow involved? Why would he stop on his way home to attack this man, anyway?'

'There were some valuables taken. A wallet, a silver pocket watch, and a war medal.'

Gordon Baker-Simms snorted. 'You're joking!' He waved his arm to encompass the room. 'Look around you. Do you think my son needs to mug some old age pensioner for a few quid?'

West kept her composure. 'Actually, sir, we don't think it was about pocket money. Earlier that day the victim had been in your home. He was, in fact, one of the veterans from the Second World War who was attending the regimental reunion on the grounds outside.'

'I remember him!' the Brigadier interjected. 'Found him in the front drawing-room. He said he was looking for the loo! Cheeky, he was. I sent him packing.'

West cocked an eyebrow. 'Yes. And later that very evening he was killed, just outside the Blue Bull.'

By now Gordon Baker-Simms was thoroughly confused. 'So I fail to understand why you have come to question us. The assault, you say, took place in the village, several miles from here?'

'That's quite true,' West admitted. 'But some of our inquiries have led us back here.' She turned to face the Brigadier directly. 'Generous of you to host the reunion, Brigadier. Not everyone would welcome a gaggle of old soldiers into their home.'

The Brigadier couldn't help preening. 'Nonsense. All part of the same family. The regiment, that is. Good to see them after so many years. Grand bunch of lads,' he said, apparently forgetting his earlier remark. 'Went through a lot together.'

The breakfast room contained a glass display case, topped by a large silver compote and war memorabilia arranged on shelves inside. McDermott wandered over to take a closer look. 'I gather your family has a long tradition of military service, sir.'

The Brigadier eyes glinted with interest and he turned his wheelchair slightly to face McDermott. 'Indeed. My father was Regimental Colonel, and his father before him. My father first saw action during the Great War at Le Cateau. Lost a lot of good men there.'

'And you, sir? A distinguished career, I've been told.'

The man straightened with pride. 'I like to think so, young man. I joined my father's regiment immediately after Sandhurst—1938 it was. Just in time for the hostilities. Served in North Africa, Sicily, and Italy, then we worked our way north to the Gothic Line, and later into the heart of the Boche. The regiment was posted to the Far East after that. Dare say we've seen our share of action over the years.' He looked into the distance, and for a moment seemed overtaken by his memories.

McDermott saw his opening. 'A dirty business, war. So much killing. So much of it unnecessary. I understand that during the time you were in Italy you were involved in an unfortunate incident. In 1943, I believe. An elderly couple at a villa near the village of Santa Cristina. They died tragically and unnecessarily, I hear.'

The Brigadier stiffened noticeably. 'Do you, now? Strange how baseless rumours persist, even after so many years. As I recall the couple was armed, you see. Still, it was all very regrettable.' He turned back to the breakfast table.

But McDermott pursued his quarry. 'Yes, peculiar, that. Actually I heard a rather different account.'

Baker-Simms glared at him. 'Then you were misinformed, young man. There was a full military review of the incident, and I was cleared of any wrongdoing.'

'So I gather. I suppose civilian deaths in wartime are inevitable. Still, not much of an inquiry, was it? Conducted by your company's adjutant, your father being the regimental CO.'

The Brigadier's expression hardened as he struggled to contain his temper. Their eyes locked, the older man's filled with—what? Not hatred, McDermott thought, nor fear. No, he saw contempt. When he began to speak his voice was strong, though his lips were barely moving. 'How old are you, young man? Forty? Forty-five? Never served in uniform, I'll wager. You've no idea what it's like to go to war, do you? They say that in the heat of battle there's no time for fear. Well, sometimes that's simply not true. Sometimes…' He turned to his son, his voice by now faltering. 'All this is quite unpleasant, Gordon. I don't feel well at all. I must go to my room. You can show Mr McDermott out.' He started for the doorway when West spoke up.

'Actually, sir, you may want to be present for this. It might save you a trip to Wakefield Police Headquarters later.'

The Brigadier glared at her. 'Such impertinence! Just who do you think you're talking to?'

'A person of interest in a wrongful death inquiry,' she said calmly, carefully avoiding the question of whether she was referring to Albert Ridley's death or that of the couple at the villa. 'And I believe DI McDermott also has some questions he'd like to put to you.'

'Really! I don't see why I should be bothered in my own home by some jumped-up stranger making outrageous allegations!'

But McDermott was not to be put off. 'It might save you some embarrassment, sir. That's why we're doing this here, Brigadier, and not down at police headquarters. I understand that following the shootings at the villa some important works of art were removed, and subsequently disappeared.'

This time the Brigadier swung his wheelchair around to face McDermott directly. His contempt had turned to outright anger and his energy seemed to have returned. 'You must be mad! Do you imagine that just because I'm getting on in years that I'm senile? My memory is perfect. Those works were removed at the request of the Italians. Later they were destroyed in an enemy attack on one of our convoys returning them to the rear. A number of our own boys were killed in the incident. It's all a matter of record. Nothing to do with me! Gordon?' He glared at his son.

Gordon Baker-Simms put down his linen napkin and stood up to confront McDermott. 'My father is quite right. What gives you the right to come in here and stir up the past, making hurtful and unwarranted accusations? I think you'd all better leave.'

Ignoring him, McDermott picked up the hand-tooled large silver compote from the top of the cabinet, turning it over in his hands. 'All in good time, Mr Baker-Simms. Did I mention I have a degree in art history? I was formerly with the Arts and Antiques Squad, in London. Your collection is really quite impressive. A number of fine works. This piece, for example. Must be two hundred years old, at the very least, and quite valuable. I had no idea that the brewing industry could be so financially rewarding. Perhaps you can tell me how you came to acquire it.'

Gordon Baker-Simms took the piece from McDermott's hands and placed it back on top of the display case. 'Certainly not! Before my time in any event, and none of your bloody business! Now please leave immediately, before I call the Chief Constable!'

McDermott decided it was time to strike. 'I'll come directly to the point, sir. I've reason to believe that several of the items in this house were removed from the villa in Italy—the same villa where your father shot and killed the elderly couple living there. I've looked into the matter in some detail and the shooting is hardly as clear cut as your father suggests. If Albert Ridley recognized one of those works in this house when he visited a few weeks ago, and realised where it came from, it would provide a compelling motive for his death.'

TWENTY-SIX

McDermott's bombshell had the expected result. Everyone at the table looked at him incredulously, unable to believe their ears—all except Julian, that is, whose expression seemed to lie somewhere between cunning and calculating.

Gordon Baker-Simms was clearly upset, and struggled to retain his composure. 'This is beyond belief. I think our discussion is at an end. I will contact our solicitor and you can put any questions you have to him. Now unless you have a warrant, I must insist that you leave immediately.'

But West was unflappable. 'As you wish. We can continue this discussion at a later date, and at the West Yorks HQ if you prefer. But if, as you claim, these charges are unfounded then you will have no objection if we photograph a few art objects in your possession. Purely for the purpose of elimination, you understand. It will only take a few minutes.'

Baker-Simms was caught off guard. 'Well, I don't know—'

Like a seasoned tennis player moving in for the kill Philippa West lost no time putting Baker-Simms off balance. 'As I said, if there's nothing to these claims then you can't reasonably object, can you? It can only help speed things up. Alternatively, I can come back with a warrant. But then it would be a matter of public record, and the press might hear of it.'

'Oh, very well.' Clearly Baker-Simms was anxious to be rid of them. 'But be quick about it!' McDermott risked a glance at the Brigadier, who was glowering. It seemed that not all members of the family were in agreement with his son's decision.

It took the best part of two hours for Grimshaw and McDermott to compare their inventory against the art works at Coniston Hall and take their photographs. In the end they had compiled a list of nearly a dozen artifacts of Italian origin in the house, and McDermott thought several items were of interest. The list included a number of paintings and pieces of silver, an ornately carved chest, a marble sculpture, and even a couple of tapestries. Gordon Baker-Simms objected that some of the pieces had been purchased during his lifetime, and offered to provide documentation to that effect, given time. DCI West told him he was free to do so, and warned him that any attempt to remove any of the works from the house in the meantime would constitute obstructing the course of justice.

As they returned to their cars West gave McDermott a wry smile. 'Well, if that didn't put the wind up them, I don't know what would! Was it wise, though, revealing so much at this stage?'

'Merely dotting my i's,' McDermott shrugged. 'First, I want to make sure that we've a photographic record of the artworks in their possession. It wouldn't help our case if anything went walkabout. Now they know we have a clear record of suspicious objects. Second, I want them on notice before we question them further. We don't want any fancy trial lawyer later on claiming that they weren't advised of their rights. This way the questioning itself will be on tape and a matter of record. The important thing now is to get our ducks in a row for the interviews that will surely come. That means following up on the list of objects the partisan gave me, comparing it to the photographs that Grimshaw just took, as well as looking into a point or two I have about the record of the shooting at the villa.'

West was intrigued. 'Yes, you mentioned that just now. What's your line of inquiry?'

'I'll have more for you once I receive a call I'm waiting on,' McDermott replied cryptically. The expression on West's face showed that she was intrigued.

WHEN THEY RETURNED to Wakefield HQ the team reviewed their progress and their next steps. There was general agreement that McDermott had struck a nerve with the Brigadier when he'd raised the issue of the deaths at the villa. And Julian Baker-Simms hadn't really accounted for his time during the attack outside the pub. Philippa West was anxious to follow up on that during their next interview. 'My feeling is that we should strike whilst the iron is hot. Let's set up an interview date for the family in a couple of days from now. We'll want to interview Gordon and his wife, their son, and the Brigadier.'

'Separate interviews with each of them? That might tax our resources,' McDermott said.

But West was not to be deterred. 'We can begin collectively, I think. I know it's not standard protocol, but they're already aware of our line of questioning, and will have already had ample opportunity to discuss matters and get their stories straight. And this way their lawyer can be present for the interviews. Saves time.'

Although he had misgivings, in the end McDermott agreed, and they each set about their respective tasks. West placed a phone call to Gordon Baker-Simms informing him of their decision and setting a meeting for two days' time. Although he was clearly unhappy with this turn of events, in the end Baker-Simms grudgingly agreed to inform his family solicitors, who were based in York.

As this was going on Joe Grimshaw set about downloading the photographs he'd taken of the artifacts at Coniston Hall, and forwarding them to McDermott's mobile. If anything looked suspicious McDermott could follow up with his contacts in London, and if necessary he could email the photos to Capitano Russo for a look by Isabella Goldman herself.

McDermott spent the rest of the day cataloguing the photos Grimshaw had taken, identifying the artifacts, and checking them against the partisan's list. But for the most part the list was so generic that he was unable to state definitively that any of the works on the list was a match for anything they had photographed at Coniston Hall.

He was just about to leave for the day when he got a message from London. They had put him onto the *Bundesarchive* – the military archive of the German Federal Records Office. They in turn directed him to the *Wehrmacht* – the organization overseeing the entire Nazi German military records for World War II. That led him to the *Fledzügge*, which held the records for specific campaigns during the war. At length he managed to speak with Sturmbannfuhrer Gerhard Müller, who, it turned out, was something of a walking encyclopedia for German military campaigns in North Africa. It didn't take him long to come up with the information McDermott sought. When he thanked the man and put down the phone, McDermott had a look of quiet confidence. He had the missing piece of the puzzle.

BY MONDAY THE TIME FOR THE INTERVIEWS had rolled around, and the CID team had put together their strategy for questioning the Baker-Simms. The family arrived in two cars, the elder in the Bentley, to accommodate his wheelchair. The family solicitor and Gordon had shared the car. Fiona and Julian, accompanied by Julian's girlfriend Miranda, had elected to take the Jag.

The team was prepared for them. The group and their solicitor were ushered into a large conference room. Not used for formal interviews in the normal course of events, it had been equipped with two video cameras and an audio recorder for the occasion. As a concession to the family there were even carafes of chilled water on the table, accompanied by genuine glasses. Miranda wasted no time in claiming one, pouring a glassful for herself, and slunk down in her chair. The Brigadier was wheeled in and placed in a central position, with the other family members flanking him on either side, and the CID team facing them across the table.

As the Senior Investigating Officer Philippa West led off the proceedings. She began on a conciliatory note. 'Thank you all for coming. For the benefit of the audio record, my name is DCI Philippa West. I am a senior officer in the CID unit of the West Yorkshire Constabulary. To my left is Detective Sergeant Joe Grimshaw, and to my right assisting us today are two CID officers of the London Metropolitan Police, DI Colin McDermott and Detective Sergeant George Ridley. We appreciate you coming here to help us with our inquiries, and I should tell you that although none of you is at the moment being charged with any crimes, your statements are being recorded.' She motioned to the cameras in the room. 'Any misinformation may be regarded as an attempt to obstruct the course of justice.'

Several members of the group seemed taken aback by this warning, and a silver-haired man in an elegant bespoke suit interrupted her. 'Excuse me, Chief Inspector. I am the family solicitor. My name is Alistair Summerfield. I am a senior partner in the firm of Gates, Summerfield, and Davies, based in York. As you can see, the family has been most cooperative in agreeing to respond to your questions. But frankly, we are somewhat perplexed. Can you explain why these *gentlemen*—'he looked toward McDermott and Ridley, making the word sound slightly suspect—'being from outside the immediate jurisdiction, are participating in this inquiry?'

'That will become clear in the fullness of time, Mr Summerfield. All I can say at present is that each has a specific reason for being here. As will become evident, due to the extraordinary nature of this inquiry our questions will transcend normal jurisdictional boundaries.'

Summerfield sat back in his chair, his expression indicating that he was not entirely satisfied with her explanation.

'If we may begin,' West said, opening a folder in front of her. 'I would like to address my first question to Brigadier Reginald Baker-Simms. Sir, for the record, it is your position that all of the paintings, sculptures, and other *objets d'art* in your home have been acquired legally, over the course of years?'

Baker-Simms faced her squarely and his voice was strong. 'Absolutely, to the best of my knowledge.'

West raised her eyebrows fractionally. 'To the best of your knowledge,' she repeated. 'Forgive me, but that sounds less than clear. Are they or aren't they?'

Summerfield wasted no time in coming to Baker-Simms' assistance. 'I'm afraid my client has given you the only possible answer to what is surely an ambiguous question. Coniston Hall and its possessions have been in the family for generations. No one in the family can be expected to be familiar with all of the furnishings that make up the property.' He sat back, managing to look both self-assured and censorious at the same time.

But West had confronted smug lawyers before. 'Of course, Mr Summerfield. But we're talking about a much more manageable list of perhaps a dozen objects.' She withdrew from her folder a list of objects, supplemented by photographs of each. 'Perhaps Brigadier Baker-Simms can comment more specifically on the provenance of these objects?' She slid the materials across the table.

The man peered at the photographs for several moments, then said, 'What do you want me to say? I recognize them, of course. I see them every day, more or less. But I couldn't possibly tell you how long they've been in the house, or just when they came into our possession. They are simply the background of my daily life, like the newspaper or scrambled eggs in the morning.' He sat back, clearly pleased with his answer.

West looked to McDermott, who picked up the discussion. 'Then I take it you would be quite surprised, sir, to learn that each of the items in the photographs just passed to you match objects on a list provided to me directly by an Italian woman who had been present many times at the villa where you shot and killed the owners. She alleges that these objects were taken from that house by your troops in the following days, and subsequently disappeared.'

'One moment, Inspector!' Summerfield took the list from the table and examined it cursorily. 'This is a very general list. There must be hundreds if not thousands of objects that fit these descriptions. The person whom you say gave you this list: if she had been alive during the war she must be, what—eighty or even older by now? She'll not have seen these objects for more than sixty years? You'll have to do better than that!' He looked at McDermott derisively.

McDermott was unperturbed. 'You see this *zuppiera*, or soup tureen? Quite beautiful, isn't it? An exceptional piece, hand-tooled, in solid silver.' He extracted a photograph that Grimshaw had taken at Coniston Hall from a folder, and shoved it across the table.

'And one of many such objects, I dare say.' Summerfield's patience was wearing thin.

'Indeed,' McDermott agreed. 'Except for this rather unfortunate damage on one side.'

'What of it,' the Brigadier said. 'Accidents happen. Unfortunate, but there it is.' He sat back smugly. But Summerfield was wary. He could see where McDermott was heading.

'Particularly unfortunate in this case, Brigadier.' McDermott opened a different folder and produced another photograph, a copy of the one that Isabella Goldman had given him in her home. 'Here is a photo taken many years ago, before the war began—and long before your unit was in Italy. As you can see, it shows a surprisingly similar tureen, right down to the damage on one side.' He passed the photograph over to the Brigadier, and noticed that Summerfield also looked at it closely.

'Cheap as chips,' the Brigadier intoned. 'Must be hundreds like it.'

Summerfield touched the sleeve of the Brigadier slightly, a cue to let the solicitor do his talking for him. 'Indeed, Inspector. Hardly conclusive. As my client says, there must be many similar objects in the world. Some, I suspect, might even have similar damage.'

'You're right,' McDermott admitted, reaching again into his folder. 'But taken together with other objects, including tapestries, which as you know are often quite original pieces, they add up to a sizable list of coincidences that might well persuade a jury that something more than mere chance was at work here.'

At the mention of a jury the Brigadier had taken on a stricken, almost pained, expression. He glared at McDermott and then looked to his solicitor for help. McDermott was reminded of the line attributed to Henry II: *Who will rid me of this meddlesome priest?*

Summerfield summoned all the indignation at his disposal. 'See here, Inspector. This is a most serious, and if I may say so, unfounded, allegation. You're relying on a few fuzzy photographs and an old woman's vague recollections in an effort to tear down the reputation of a decorated war hero. All in the service of what?'

McDermott spread his hands out, palms up, on the table. 'You're right, of course. I don't know whether your client has told you, but this evidence only came to light as part of an investigation into the death of another veteran and war hero,' he said. 'Trooper Albert Ridley paid a visit to Coniston Hall during a regimental reunion there a few weeks back. Whilst he was in the house he noticed a painting that seemed familiar. He shared that information with his mates that very evening. Then, in the early hours of the morning, outside the pub where they were staying, Albert Ridley was attacked and left for dead. And in fact, he did die, days later, in hospital, here in Wakefield.'

'Most unfortunate,' Summerfield replied. 'But just what does this have to do with my client?'

'Just this. The Brigadier here ran across Albert Ridley in the drawing room at Coniston Hall, where he'd entered the house in search of a loo. The Brigadier redirected him outside, but not before Ridley saw the painting. As I noted previously, if Ridley had noticed anything familiar about the work, and the Brigadier saw that, then he'd have had an excellent motive to silence Bert Ridley before he could plant any suspicions amongst his fellow soldiers.'

Summerfield was torn between being openly skeptical of McDermott's theory and showing respect for the murdered man. He decided on the former, although with just a trace of respect for Albert Ridley. 'So you're saying what? That my client, who is in his nineties, wheeled himself to this pub in the improbable chance that this Ridley fellow would put in an appearance, and then he managed somehow to kill him? Did I mention that Brigadier Baker-Simms does not drive? So at the very least he'd have had to have an accomplice.' Summerfield clasped his hands and stared at McDermott, waiting for a response.

McDermott was ready for him. 'Hardly, Mr Summerfield. Our working hypothesis is that someone did it for him. His son, Gordon, or even his grandson, Julian. Or perhaps the pair of them.'

Gordon Baker-Simms rose to object to McDermott's allegations. 'Now see here! I've already stated that I was away in London during the time that you mentioned. I can confirm that with several witnesses at my club. If necessary,' he added.

'And indeed we will be requiring that information. Thank you for volunteering it. DS Grimshaw will take the particulars from you before we're done here.' McDermott turned toward Gordon's son, Julian, and continued. 'But your son might have been involved. He has no alibi for the evening. According to his statement the other day, he was at a pub earlier, with Miss Richards here, but it seems they had a falling out and each went their separate way.'

'That's right,' Miranda Richards intervened. 'Jules had a barney with that gyppo who fancied me, and then me and 'im rowed afterwards. 'E left in a huff. But he didn't do nuffin'!' she sniffed.

'You see our problem,' McDermott said. 'It seems young Julian here cannot account for his activities after he left the pub, and during the time that Ridley was attacked.'

Fiona Baker-Simms had a smug expression on her face. 'But I can, Inspector. Jules was with me. We spent the entire evening in bed together, making love.'

TWENTY-SEVEN

There was pandemonium as the significance of what Fiona Baker-Simms said sunk in on everyone. Miranda Richards hurled a glass of water in her direction. 'You cow! You bloody cow!' Fiona deflected it neatly, and it splashed onto the floor, leaving a trail of water on her husband Gordon, the table, and the carpet below. Arthur Summerfield looked as though he'd just bitten into something disagreeable.

Brushing off his jacket, Gordon rose from his chair, open-mouthed. He looked daggers at his wife. 'I don't believe it! How could you do such a thing!'

Fiona merely looked at him, a trace of amusement on her face. 'Really, dear. And just what do you get up to on your frequent trips to London? Or are you the only one in the family permitted to have a little fun?'

'But your own stepson? That's'—he searched for words—'That's outrageous!'

She smiled sweetly. 'Why? It's not as if we're related by blood. And really, Gordon, you haven't been quite up to the mark for some time. All those extra puddings and lack of exercise, I expect.'

Her husband was still beside himself. 'Really, Fiona? Your behaviour is unforgiveable!'

She looked at him icily. 'I don't recall asking for your forgiveness.'

Utterly deflated, he glowered at her and sat down again. West took advantage of the moment to reassert some control. 'As interesting as that is, Mrs Baker-Simms, we have only your word for it. Under the circumstances, hardly an alibi. I don't suppose anyone can confirm it?'

Fiona Baker-Simms rubbed further salt in the wound. 'Oh, dear. Actually, the housekeeper happened on us in my bedroom that evening. It seems she had a question about the next day's lunch, though I can't imagine why it wouldn't have kept. We were—what's the phrase?—*in flagrante delectable*.' She did not look at all contrite, and Julian actually smirked.

West had a quiet word with DS Grimshaw, who stepped out of the room to telephone the housekeeper and ask her to confirm Fiona Baker-Simms' account. If she did, he was instructed to have her come to the station immediately and sign a statement to that effect. Meanwhile she suggested they take a short break. Fiona's husband looked as though something a great deal longer would be needed.

It didn't take long to establish that Fiona had been telling the truth. The housekeeper had finished her work late that evening, and before setting off for home had remembered the meal arrangements for the following day, when guests were expected. Gordon Baker-Simms had failed to return home on more than one occasion, but when he had, and found that the luncheon arrangements were not to his liking, he could, as she put it, be difficult. Hence the late-night visit to Fiona's bedchamber.

She had found Julian and his stepmother on the bed, quite naked, their clothing strewn about the room. Shocked, she had dropped her notes and muttered her apologies, then scooped up the papers and beat a hasty retreat. She hadn't mentioned it to a soul, least of all to them, and it seemed that both Fiona and Julian had thought the incident immensely amusing.

When they reconvened, McDermott focused on the Brigadier. The elderly man had lost none of his bravado, and Summerfield sat at his side, looking at McDermott pityingly, as though he was the lowest form of street life by calling into question the actions of a decorated war hero.

McDermott opened a folder in front of him. 'I've had an opportunity to review the records regarding the shooting deaths at the villa. It was your position that the couple were armed. The officer investigating the incident was a Major Endicott, I believe.'

'That's correct,' the Brigadier replied confidently. 'A good man, as I recall. Very thorough.'

'And, as Adjutant, close to your father, who was the Commanding Officer of the regiment, I gather.'

Baker-Simms' expression hardened. 'That's correct. His report completely exonerated me of any wrongdoing.' He sat back in his wheelchair, outwardly satisfied with the way things were going, but there was a glimmer of concern in the man's eyes. McDermott thought back to the events at the villa, and what it must have been like when the young officer had sensed the presence of others in the darkened room, and fear—raw, primal fear—had taken hold of the man and determined his actions in the following moments. Maybe the Brigadier had been right: *if you weren't there, you couldn't fully comprehend what it was like at that moment.*

Again Summerfield put his hand on his client's forearm and intervened. 'Look here, Inspector, what you're suggesting is quite outrageous. You're asking an elderly man to recall specific actions on specific dates well over half a century ago. You know, as well as I do, that events in wartime are frequently confused, and records, as well as recollections, cannot be trusted. This is most upsetting to my client. I demand that you halt this...*pernicious* line of questioning immediately.'

But McDermott was unmoved. 'Not going to happen, I'm afraid. Albert Ridley, the man who was killed outside the pub in Kirk Warham, just a few miles from here, was also present at the villa when the couple was killed. I'm afraid your client has some very significant questions to answer.'

The lawyer tried another tack. 'So what, precisely, do you hope to establish by this callous line of questioning? Are you building a case for a war crime? If so, I very much think you're exceeding your authority. In my understanding these matters are handled by the military, and then only with the explicit approval of the Home Office. I cannot recall a single instance of charges being laid against a member of the British military in the past forty years, and especially against a senior officer. Just what is your purpose here?'

'You're quite right, Mr Summerfield. It is not my intention to bring charges against the Brigadier for the events that happened that day at the villa. That is for the Home Office, or perhaps a military tribunal, to take up. But there is a connection between those events and the artworks we observed in Coniston Hall. As I have said, we have reason to believe that following the deaths, certain valuable *objets d'art* and other historical artifacts were removed from the villa and somehow found their way to England, and, indeed, to the Baker-Simms' home, where they remain today.'

Summerfield put on a brave face. 'We've already covered that. What else can I say?' He looked first to Gordon, and then to Gordon's father, for help.

Improbably, the Brigadier himself seemed to have caught his second wind and came to his rescue. 'Simple. Your claims are rubbish. The works to which you refer were removed from the house in Italy at the request of local partisans, who came to us concerned for their safety—the artworks, that is. They were fearful that the Jerries might counterattack and the area would become a battlefield, or that the Luftwaffe might send planes to bomb our troops, and the villa might be caught up in the crossfire. It was a legitimate concern. As a result I detailed a number of our troops to crate and remove the works so they could be shipped to the rear for safekeeping. I recall it quite clearly.' He sat back in his wheelchair, the very picture of confidence.

'I'm delighted to hear that, Brigadier. Then perhaps you can enlighten us as to the events immediately following the removal of the artworks from the villa.'

At this the Brigadier's expression became clouded. It wasn't clear whether his memory was failing him or he sensed a trap. 'Well, as I recall, after we finished crating the works we formed a convoy to take the goods to the rear.'

'Only it wasn't that simple, was it?' McDermott pressed. 'What happened on the way?'

By now the Brigadier was aware that McDermott knew more than he was letting on. 'Well, that's the way of war, isn't it? On the trip to the rear the convoy was attacked by a Jerry patrol plane. The driver of the lorry carrying the art works was hit, and the truck went off the road and down the mountainside, turning over and catching fire. The other lorry had been hit as well, but managed to stay on the road, more or less. The man accompanying the driver ran down the side of the mountain and tried to save the men in the first lorry, but they were both goners. Just the same, he pulled them out and away from the fire. Unfortunately the truck and its contents were destroyed.'

'And do you recall the name of the man who performed those heroic acts, Brigadier?'

Baker-Simms clouded for the second time in as many minutes. At length he said, 'Not really, not after all these years.'

McDermott pressed his point. 'I'm surprised at that. The man was subsequently awarded a medal for bravery on your recommendation. In fact, it was Albert Ridley, the very same man who died just outside the pub in Kirk Warham.'

The room went quiet. Alistair Summerfield saw all too clearly where McDermott was headed, and moved to shut down his line of questioning. 'See here, Inspector. You said you were moving on from allegations concerning this Ridley man's death, and yet here we are again. Is the point of this inquiry to clarify the circumstances of this man's death, or to go rabbit-hunting about the loss of some art objects as a result of a German air attack? My clients have better things to do, you know.'

McDermott was unfazed. 'I can understand your confusion, Mr Summerfield. I, too, was confused until I figured out what happened. I'm afraid that the Brigadier here has left out some rather important details.' He turned to the elderly man, who was growing increasingly apprehensive. 'You neglected to mention that the second truck in the convoy was not carrying artworks at all, but rather military provisions belonging to the regiment.'

'That's right,' he admitted. 'I remember now. Some damn fool in Supply had sent us summer gear right after we landed in Italy. Lightweight uniforms and such, totally useless, as we were heading into winter. Surplus to requirements. I had it returned for something more suitable.'

'Commendable, I'm sure,' McDermott replied laconically. 'So what happened to that gear?'

'It wasn't my job to follow up on that,' the Brigadier replied. 'I was operational, not supply and services. I expect it ended up at some supply depot, or back at Regimental HQ, where it belonged.'

'Except there's no record of that, either in the shipping manifests of the day nor in the inventory records of the regiment afterwards.'

Baker-Simms looked contemptuous. 'As I said, not my job.' He sat back, wary but satisfied that he'd answered McDermott's questions.

'May I tell you what I think happened, Brigadier? When you arrived on the scene of the ambush you found two lorries. One contained the artworks from the villa. It was more or less intact, lying on its side but still on the road. The other lorry had careened off the road and rolled down the mountainside, where it had caught fire. By the time you arrived, the contents of that lorry had been totally destroyed and the men in it were both dead. Then you had an idea. Albert Ridley and his driver had both been injured, and you sent them to a field hospital at the rear so they weren't around to observe what you did next. You switched the cargo manifests for the vehicles, indicating that the contents of the crates on the lorry still on the road were military gear to be returned to regimental HQ here in Yorkshire. The truck on the road was righted, and once it was checked out another driver was assigned to it and ordered to continue on to the port at San Giovanni, where it was offloaded and the crated contents eventually shipped here. A simple instruction on the cargo manifest to the effect that the packing crates were not to be opened except on the authority of the Regimental Commander—your father—would have sufficed. You sorted the paperwork with your father afterwards. And that's how the valuable artworks came to be in Yorkshire—and ultimately your home—these sixty-plus years later.'

The entire room was silent for what seemed forever, as the solicitor struggled to determine what options were open to him. At length Alistair Summerfield said quietly, and with more than a trace of condescension in his voice, 'I must say I'm rather disappointed, Inspector. I would have thought that as a man engaged in the enforcement of the law you would have put together a—how shall I put it?—a more rigorous case against my client. As matters stand these allegations amount to the flimsiest of speculations on your part, and are entirely unsubstantiated. Unless you can provide some evidence to corroborate your claims, I think we are done here.'

And with that, Summerfield rose from the table, his clients quickly following suit.

TWENTY-EIGHT

When he heard the news back at Wakefield, Gareth Matthews was beside himself. 'Christ on a bike! That was a bloody waste of effort! As I understand it, at best we have the old man for the art theft decades ago. But,' he added, 'if the housekeeper is to be believed, we can't implicate Gordon or Julian Baker-Simms in Bert Ridley's death, as each has a compelling alibi. We look like a bunch of blind men stumbling about in a dark room, looking for a black cat that isn't there!' The DCS glared at everyone in the room as they each contrived to look elsewhere.

'That's about it,' McDermott agreed. His body language, and that of everyone else present, expressed their frustration.

'So where do we go from here?' Matthews asked. 'It seems to me we're no further ahead in identifying a person of interest in the murder of George's father. You might be interested in missing art, but I have a murder to solve!' From the expression on Ridley's face it was clear that he, too, was far from satisfied.

McDermott searched for options. 'You're right, of course. We need to look in other directions. One thing's been bothering me, though. Wherever we go we keep running into this gypsy. What's his name, Joe?'

DS Grimshaw shuffled though his notes. 'Hearn. Noah Hearn.'

'That's it', McDermott continued. 'First there's the matter of the Land Rover that ran us off the road. The garageman's son said a gypsy owned one like it and lived nearby. Then there's the run-in between Julian Baker-Simms and this Hearn fellow at the other end of the village. The man left soon afterwards on foot, presumably headed back to his camp, which as the garage mechanic indicated was on the other end of the village, not far from where Bert Ridley was attacked later that night. If this Hearn fellow had been involved in Bert's death he had plenty of time to do the deed and return to camp.'

Philippa West intervened. 'His motive?'

'Maybe there's no connection to the events in Italy at all. Perhaps a cigar is just a cigar,' McDermott replied. 'Maybe it was just a robbery gone wrong. But I don't like coincidences. This man keeps turning up.'

Matthews smiled as he regained control of his temper. 'And sometimes a coincidence is just a coincidence.'

'Touché. All the same I think we should look into this man. In any case, we don't have any other persons of interest, do we?'

The DCS considered the matter. 'You're right. As it stands we've no other leads. Take Grimshaw with you. He knows the lay of the land.'

Philippa West spoke up. 'Shall I go with them, sir?'

Matthews steepled his fingers and gave the matter some thought. 'I think not. The Travellers are a funny bunch. Very traditional in their ways, for all their differences with ours. Don't quote me, but they're not as enlightened as we are when it comes to the role of women. I think two male officers are likely to have more luck. And Grimshaw, being a Yorkshire lad born and bred, will soon know the lay of the land.'

West's face said it all. 'So I'm to twiddle my thumbs here because a tribe of itinerant tinkerers are still stuck in the Dark Ages?'

Matthews shot her a look that was half smile, half warning. 'Careful, Philippa. You don't want to be accused of being non-PC!'

She scowled, clearly unhappy with his response.

GRIMSHAW MADE A PHONE CALL, and before ten minutes had passed he put down the phone, a smile on his face. 'The garage mechanic says the gypsies are still camped just north of the village, in a field next to the River Calder. I reckon I know where it is. Ready?' He looked at McDermott. They climbed into an unmarked police SUV and set out for the gypsy encampment.

'Be a new experience for you, I expect,' Grimshaw said.

'Wouldn't miss it for the world,' McDermott replied. 'On the way you can fill me in on this lot.' As they pulled out he noticed Philippa West observing them from a window in the CID suite. Dark storm clouds.

'Easy enough.' Grimshaw adopted the know-it-all tone of a tour bus guide. With West left behind, McDermott noticed that his earlier editorial comments about 'gyppos' had disappeared. 'Yorkshire is dotted with Travellers, or Roma, as they prefer to be called. Despite their reputation, they're mostly law-abiding folk. They usually travel in groups of extended families. Live off the land, mostly, eating fish, hedgehogs, hare, other small game. Sometimes they live in tents, but more often in caravans. A few of the better-off ones even have motor homes. Generally they don't have much to do with local folk, except to sell things or do odd jobs. They're into a number of trades: shoeing horses, selling pots and pans, sharpening knives. But whenever something goes missing, or there's a barn fire, or a bus shelter gets defaced, they're the first ones questioned. Even get accused of devil worship. The Caravan Sites Act of 1968 established their right to camp on unused lands, but most folk don't see it that way. I feel sorry for them, really. No place to put down roots, not welcome in most places. And it must be hard on the little 'uns, changing schools whenever they pull up stakes.'

'This chap Hearn. You said he has form?'

Grimshaw smiled. 'Don't put too much in that. Truth is, I was just trying to get up Her Nib's nose.'

McDermott's eyebrows rose, and he looked over at the man. 'Have a death wish, do you?'

'Man's gotta have a hobby,' he said, still grinning.

When they arrived in Kirk Warham they took the first turning and passed the Blue Bull where McDermott and Ridley were staying. It was on a minor side road flanked by a few council houses that dated from the early 1960s. Before long the village petered out into smallholdings marked by vegetable gardens and a few livestock. They crossed an ancient stone bridge and Grimshaw took a turning to the right. The farms here were more substantial, though hardly prosperous. They drove parallel to the river, though increasingly distant from it. Eventually they came to a field that sloped off to the right, toward a river in the distance. Nestled at the edge of the woods they could just make out a small encampment of caravans, a tent or two, several horses, and half a dozen vehicles. McDermott noticed with interest there was a Land Rover nearby, and although it was dark blue it had, rather incongruously, a white racing stripe running over the bonnet and across the roof. There was a bright yellow daisy painted on the front left wing as well. Not the vehicle that had forced him off the road, he decided. Another theory gone south.

They turned in at a pasture gate and drove down a muddy track that ended near the gypsy camp. A light rain was falling, but it didn't appear to bother anyone much. A few children of various ages were playing with some dogs nearby. They looked up as the SUV approached, as did several grizzled older men sitting around a smouldering campfire, smoking and drinking from metal cups. They were wearing oilskin jackets and flat caps, and except for a few oddments in the scene could have stepped out of a novel by Thomas Hardy.

Grimshaw and McDermott stepped out of their SUV and looked at the ground beneath their feet. It had been well trodden by horses, and there was no way to avoid the mud. There were wellies in the rear of the vehicle, but neither man had thought to put them on. It wasn't far, so the Sergeant sighed and set out for the cluster of men with McDermott close behind.

'Good day,' Grimshaw said as they approached. 'Wonder if we could have a word?'

One of the men touched the brim of his hat. 'Reckon you be the Garda, then.' It was not a question.

The sergeant winced, then smiled.. 'Is it that obvious?'

'We don't get many folk up here. But now as you mention it, aye.' One of the men sitting at the campfire couldn't resist a smirk.

'Well, we'll try and make it short, then. We're looking for a lad name of Noah Hearn. He hasn't done anything,' Grimshaw added. 'We just think he might be able to help us with our inquiries.'

The man with a smirk broke into a grin. 'Aye, right. We all knows what that means.'

'No, really,' McDermott intervened. 'We think he might help us to verify someone else's whereabouts, a local man.'

One of the men sitting by the fire turned toward a nearby caravan and shouted. 'Samuel, you in there? You know where your *chavo* is? Only there's a couple of *Shanglo* here that want to talk to him.'

'*Shanglo* is the Romany term for coppers,' Grimshaw whispered. Seeing McDermott's face he added, 'We get more than a few chances to talk to these folk. As I said, anything round here goes missing, the gypsies get blamed for it.'

A moment later a grizzled face emerged from the door of the caravan. 'What do the *gaudje* want with my boy?'

'They say he might 'a seen somethin,' the man near the campfire offered.

As Samuel Hearn stepped down from the caravan and came closer, McDermott could see that he was younger than he'd first appeared. True, his stubble was mostly white, and his hair heavily flecked with grey, and his face was deeply lined, and tanned from many years in the sun. But his eyes were bright, and his step was lively. McDermott put him at no more than fifty, perhaps younger.

'So, what do you want with my boy?' he asked as he grew nearer. 'Someone been tellin' lies? He's a good lad, and a father too.' As if on cue, a young boy emerged from the caravan. Not more than five or six, McDermott guessed. Blonde hair, large eyes, and a wary expression. Already he had learned to fear the police.

'No trouble,' Grimshaw assured the man. 'Like we said, he might be able to help us with some information.'

'Oh aye? And why would he want to do that?'

Grimshaw studied the man's face for a moment before answering him. 'Because you're all law-abiding folk here, and you don't want any trouble, right? Not like some other Romas, *Ziganis*. And because the sooner we get what we want, the sooner we'll leave, and you can go back to your pipes and your lies about the *Gaujes*.'

For a moment the encounter could have gone either way. Then the man's expression softened. 'Fair enough. Well, he's gone into yon woods to fetch tonight's supper. Can't say just when he'll be back, but he shouldn't be long.'

One of the men at the fire looked up. 'You want some *mesti*, some tea?' Grimshaw smiled and they moved closer to the fire; although the light rain was beginning to let up, there was still a chill in the air. McDermott noticed a few womenfolk peering out of the window in a nearby caravan. Their arrival hadn't gone unnoticed.

Their tea was still warm when McDermott saw a figure emerging from the woods in the distance. Wearing an oilskin and carrying some kindling and a small burlap sack, he seemed to be in his early thirties, and had dark hair and eyes, and a muscular build. He moved easily, unhurriedly, as if he'd lived on the land all of his life. If he was bothered by the presence of strangers in the camp he didn't show it; he didn't break his stride or look away, but changed direction slightly to join the group at the campfire.

'Here, Dad,' he said, handing Samuel Hearn the sack. 'Nice bit o' hare. Who's this, then?' he asked.

'West Yorks Police.' Grimshaw didn't bother showing his warrant card. He didn't want to put the man off by being too formal. 'Nothing serious. We think you might be able to help us with some information.'

Unlike his father, Noah Hearn didn't ask why he should care. Younger generation, McDermott decided. Perhaps in thirty years he, too, would be more confrontational, less trusting. Or maybe he simply had nothing to hide.

'You've been camped here awhile, Mr Hearn?' McDermott asked.

The man took his father's cup and drank from it before replying. 'Noah,' he smiled. 'My dad's Mr Hearn. Depends on what you mean by awhile. It's been what—three weeks or a month—since we stopped here?' The other men around the fire nodded.

'So you were in the area about two weeks ago?'

'*Va*. Yeh. Why?'

Grimshaw stepped into the discussion. 'Did you make the rounds of the local pubs?'

'Might 'a done,' Hearn replied, his eyes growing more wary. 'Why do you ask?' The other men were also becoming suspicious.

'As we said, nowt serious,' Grimshaw replied, trying to take the tension out of things. 'Just wondered if you could confirm that a person we're interested in was at a certain pub on a specific date.' This, of course, wasn't strictly true; they could confirm Julian Baker-Simms' presence by talking to any number of people, including the publican. But it deflected the focus of the discussion from Hearn himself.

'So what pub was it, and when?' Noah Hearn asked.

'It would have been a Monday night, two weeks back,' McDermott offered. 'The pub was the Grouse and Claret, just outside Kirk Warham, heading east.'

The man rubbed his chin. 'Aye, I know the place. Right twee, it is. I stopped by to see if they had any knives wanted sharpenin'.'

'Right. Do you remember any of the other patrons?'

Hearn allowed a slight smile. 'Patrons, eh. Is that what we are?' The other men around the campfire grinned, sharing his joke. After a bit he said, 'Oh, I remember some of them, right enough. A girl, could 'a been a Roma with her black hair and dark eyes, only it were all out of a bottle.' The other men laughed again.

Grimshaw and McDermott exchanged brief glances. So far, at least, Hearn was being honest with them. 'Was she alone, then?' he asked.

'No. She had a toff with her, lad with blond hair and an arrogant way about him.'

'You didn't get on with them, then?' McDermott asked.

Hearn smiled. 'Not likely. She were all right. Gave me a look when I went to the bar. You know, a *come up and see me some time* kinda look. I smiled back. Her man saw that and wanted to make somethin' of it.'

'What happened then?'

'Not much,' he shrugged. 'He were up in a flash and in my face, but 'afore I could do anything the bloke behind the bar said he'd have none of it in his place, and chucked me out. And me, I hadn't done nothin'.' He looked aggrieved.

'You mean the landlord?' Grimshaw pressed.

'That's right. Typical. Anything happens, bloody gyppo's to blame.' The other men around the campfire murmured their agreement.

'And just when did this happen?' Grimshaw asked.

'Lemme see. Must 'a been round eight or nine at night. I'd had supper here before settin' out looking for some trade.'

'And afterwards, where did you go?'

'I headed straight back here. Too late to stop anywhere else.' His expression sharpened. 'Here, now, is that what this is about? Something happen to that *Gaujo*? Has he been tellin' lies?'

'No, he's fine,' McDermott said. 'We just wanted to confirm his movements on the evening in question. You're certain about the time?'

Noah Hearn relaxed. 'Aye, sure enough. It was well after dark, and I had to cut through woods, then follow yon river to a place to cross. Must 'a been better part o' two miles.'

McDermott decided to go to the crux of the issue. 'And once here, you stayed put the rest of the evening?' McDermott asked.

Noah Hearn laughed. 'Aye. Not much else t' do that time a night. Not like we have a lot o' mates round here.' The others murmured their agreement.

'What did you do at that point?'

The young man looked at McDermott as though he was slow-witted. 'We drank a bit and played some cards. Then the sky opened up and we called it a night 'bout eleven.' He drained his cup and handed it back to his father. 'Anything else? Only some of us have better things t' do.' He looked pointedly at his burlap sack.

'Just one other thing, Mr Hearn,' Grimshaw said. 'Have you ever had any problems with the law?'

Hearn's expression hardened just fractionally. 'You know I do, or you wouldn't be askin'. Got fitted up for thievin', I did, about six months back. Near Thirsk, north o' York. A load o' bollocks. Farmer had some stock go missin', and blamed me 'cause I'd been round earlier that day, askin' after trade. Police found us roastin' a lamb that night, decided we'd nicked it. Magistrate saw no reason to doubt it.' He didn't mention where he'd got the lamb.

'What happened?'

Noah Hearn sneered. 'Reckon you know the answer to that, too. Got fined a hundred quid and costs, I did, and told to clear off. Just as well. Some folk just ain't neighbourly. Now if you're done…'

Grimshaw glanced at McDermott. It seemed like they had their answers, at least all the answers they were likely to get at the moment. 'Yes, that's all for now, Mr Hearn.' Then as an afterthought he asked, 'You plan on stopping here or moving on?'

The men by the campfire exchanged glances. Samuel Hearn said, 'This place suits us well enough. In a few months winter'll be settin' in. No time to be on the move.'

'Right enough,' Grimshaw replied. 'Can't be easy, living off the land. Well, thanks for your time. And good luck to you.' They turned and made their way back to their SUV in silence.

As they entered the road Grimshaw said, 'What do you think? Reckon young Hearn there could be the man who attacked Bert Ridley?'

McDermott frowned. 'I doubt it. First of all, the Blue Bull is at the far end of the village from his camp. Unlikely he'd have gone out of his way at that time of night without a reason. And no one at the Bull mentioned seeing him. Unless he hung about in the rain he'd have stood out.'

'True enough. And he knows his way around the law. If he'd mugged poor Bert, he'd not have lost any time getting rid of the watch. The last thing he'd want to do is keep it nearby. But so far it's not turned up. No, for my money the Baker-Simms lad was just winding us up, trying to deflect attention from himself.'

'Well, he did have an alibi,' McDermott said wryly.

'Right. Bedding his step-mum. Not that I would pass her up, mind you. But not much of an alibi, is it?'

'There was the matter of the housekeeper,' McDermott reminded him. 'I don't see her being quick enough, or having the guile, never mind the inclination, to lie for that family.'

Grimshaw thought that over. 'No, I think you're right. Did you notice the Land Rover?'

'Yes. Not the one. Paint's all wrong.'

'So where does all this leave us on Bert's killer?'

McDermott's jaw hardened. 'Back at square one.'

TWENTY-NINE

It wasn't a long ride back to Kirk Warham, but it was made in silence. All the while McDermott was thinking about his old friend, and he felt he'd let him down. He was the senior officer, but in many ways Ridley had taught him the ropes from his earliest days with the Met, even saving his life once. And now George needed him, needed to find his father's killer, needed to get some closure. But as far as he could see they were no closer to solving the case than they were that first day at Wakefield. Worse, he had no idea how to proceed. McDermott wrestled with the problem and his own sense of guilt; somehow, he knew, he would have to do better. He owed that to George.

By the time they arrived at the car park of the Blue Bull it was dusk, and Ridley was waiting for them in the doorway. He came over to the car. 'Find our man?'

'Not really,' McDermott said, climbing out. He turned to Grimshaw. 'Thanks for the lift, Joe. Up for a pint?'

'Thanks, but no. Wife will have dinner on the hob. But I'll take you up on it when you're doing the driving.'

'Right, then. We'll see you back in Wakefield tomorrow.' Grimshaw drove away, leaving the two men standing there. McDermott noticed an enigmatic smile on Ridley's face. 'Something on your mind, George?'

'Aye. Been waitin' for you to check it out. Might be summat, maybe nowt. Spare a moment?'

'Always,' McDermott replied. Ridley nodded toward the village church, which lay just down the road. He set off without saying a word, and McDermott fell in alongside him.

'Didn't know you were a churchgoer, George,' McDermott grinned, earning him a caustic look.

'Everything 'as its uses,' Ridley replied cryptically.

As they approached the church they noticed the vicar down on her knees, aided by a hand torch in the failing light, and pulling some weeds from amongst the flowers that bordered the path.

When they got closer McDermott said, 'Hello, vicar. I see you're hard at work. Is gardening part of the training for the clergy these days?'

She smiled, brushing a wisp of hair from her face, and adding some dirt in the process. 'God works in mysterious ways. The verger's wife usually looks after this, but she's feeling poorly. You're the police officers who were at Coniston Hall, aren't you?'

'That's right. Do you have a large congregation here in the village?'

The vicar rose and took off her gardening gloves. 'Not as large as we'd like. Mostly the older folks. The young ones seem to have better things to do.' McDermott was reminded of his recent visit to Italy, and the strong turnout at the church in Santa Cristina. A different culture, he realized, and wondered how long it would be before his own changed as well.

He turned toward George. 'My friend here would like a word with you, I think.' He was still at a loss for why they were there.

'Adrienne Whitechapel,' she said, extending her hand. 'Please, no jokes. How can I help you? No trouble with the Baker-Simms, I hope?' Her face clouded.

Ridley took the lead. 'Nowt t' do wi' them. Leastways Ah don't think so. Nice church you got 'ere. Bothered by vandals, are you?'

She smiled ruefully. 'Nothing big, actually. Donations box broken into, the odd window broken. We had to put up some grilles.' She looked at the stained-glass windows on the nave. 'No problems recently, though. Why do you ask?'

'Only Ah were walkin' by after lunchtime today, and Ah noticed you'd put up CCTV camera over main door,' Ridley said.

'Yes. As a matter of fact the insurance company suggested it—insisted actually—after we'd made a string of claims. Seems to have done the trick. At least we haven't had any break-ins since then. A shame that young people seem to be losing respect for their institutions.'

'So it's in proper workin' order?' George asked.

'Oh, yes.' She was clearly intrigued by his questions.

''Ow often you change the tapes, then?'

The vicar smiled. 'Actually, it's state-of-the-art, Sergeant. No tapes. What they call a hard drive. Doesn't need erasing for weeks, since it's on a timer for nighttime only, and set to take pictures only when someone or something comes within range of the motion detector.'

Ridley looked at McDermott. Maybe they'd finally caught a break. 'Only, Ah wonder if we could have a look at them pictures.'

'Of course.' She picked up her basket of gardening tools and led the way into the church. McDermott looked at the camera as they passed through the doorway. It was flanked by two small floodlights angled to illuminate the path and the doorway immediately below. He noticed they had already come on, triggered by the fading light. But because of the height and the angle at which the camera was positioned, it was unlikely to reveal much of the face on anyone standing just below it. He tried not to get his hopes up.

Once inside, the vicar flicked on the lights and led them to the vestry. She unlocked the door, and when they had joined her inside she unlocked a cabinet set against one wall. There, resting on a shelf, was a digital video recorder and a small monitor. She pressed a couple of buttons and the screen lit up. 'When are we talking about, Sergeant?'

'Would a been Tuesday night, two weeks ago, between, say, half eleven and one in the mornin',' George said brusquely.

She noticed the tone of his voice and glanced at McDermott. 'Let's see. That would make it the sixth, then, right?'

'That's right.' Ridley moved closer to the screen.

'Shouldn't be difficult.' She pushed some stay strands of hair from her eyes. 'The recordings are all date and time-stamped.' She pushed a button and scanned the images, watching a counter on the screen. When she got to the date and time in question she backed it up a bit further, then pressed Play.

For several minutes there was nothing but a record of the camera's perspective, the path leading into the darkness beyond, the only movement being the reflection of rain forming puddles and the odd branch blowing across the scene. The vicar fast-forwarded the machine. Then, at 11:37 it got more interesting. A young couple dressed in what appeared to be denim pants and windbreakers approached the doorway. McDermott made them out to be in their mid-teens or thereabouts. When they got nearer they huddled against the wall, and drew closer together. They began kissing and groping one another, the light revealing that one had long blonde hair, and the other had a wispy beard. Eventually the girl noticed the camera, and pointed it out to the boy, who made a face at it and began unbuttoning her blouse. She pushed him away and they set off, but not before she gave two fingers to the camera. They both laughed.

Another fifteen minutes of nothing but wind-blown branches moving back and forth at the edge of the image, then two more people came down the path. Like the earlier couple, they were wearing denim pants and trainers, but they were heavier, and, it seemed, older. They had hoodies pulled over their heads that were beaded with rain. Oblivious to the camera, they were gesturing and talking, and the taller of them of them pulled something from the pocket of his hoodie and examined it. It was small and might have been a wristwatch; McDermott wasn't sure. They seemed to laugh, and after a few moments he shoved it back into his pocket and they walked off together. The time stamp showed 12:15.

They watched another forty minutes of pictures, but nothing of interest showed up. 'Where does this path lead?' McDermott asked, pointing to the image on the video.

'Not many options, I'm afraid,' the vicar replied. 'Runs along the cemetery on one side, with the village common on the other. Then through a gate toward some council houses at the top of the hill. Eventually it turns back down the hill toward the village primary school, and ends up at the main road at the far end of the village.'

'So someone going that way would likely live in one of the council houses?' McDermott asked.

'Unless they were just out for a stroll on a rainy night,' she replied.

They reran the images several times. When they had finished, McDermott asked to borrow her recorder so the technicians at Wakefield could download the images. She agreed readily enough, and when he asked her not to discuss what they had seen with anyone she was, he thought, bemused. As a vicar she was used to keeping confidences.

As they emerged into the evening, the vicar said, 'I hope the Baker-Simms aren't in any difficulty?'

'I'm afraid I can't comment on that,' McDermott replied. 'Why do you ask? Do you think they might be?'

She frowned. 'No. They've been very generous in the past. Paid for that CCTV system, for example. *Noblesse Oblige* and all that.'

McDermott turned toward the path by which they had come. 'We really must be going. Thanks for your help.' He couldn't help thinking it would be a nice bit of irony if something recorded on the CCTV incriminated Julian. What did they call it? *Poetic justice.*

THIRTY

The next morning McDermott and Ridley arrived at Wakefield just as Philippa West made an appearance. Grimshaw was already there, and had brought freshly-brewed coffee and pastries, much to everyone's approval. *He might like to bait his boss,* McDermott reflected, *but he also knows when to butter her bread.* After settling in, and following the arrival of the other members of the CID team, McDermott described what they had seen the previous night.

West was pleased. 'Well done, George! Let's hope this is the break we've been waiting for.' She connected the video recorder to a nearby monitor and they all looked at the screen. But by the time they had finished she was more subdued. 'Well, it's certainly something for our forensics people to work on. Maybe they can enhance the image.' She looked at her watch and picked up the phone. 'They should be in their cubbyholes by now.'

Before long a white-coated technician arrived to collect the video recorder. After a certain amount of badgering by DCI West, he looked offended and said it was likely that he'd have something for them by the end of the day. Not for the first time McDermott reflected that although Yorkshire had its charms, London wasn't looking so bad.

Because the images were on a hard drive rather than on tape, it took only a couple of hours for the forensic technicians to transfer and enhance the video images. The wait was worth it. As they sat huddled around a table the incident team ran and reran the images several times, pausing to note some detail and to speculate on its meaning.

'Not much to go on,' Philippa West said, stretching her back. 'The hoodies pretty well obscure their faces. You'd think we were due to catch a break.'

'We may have done,' Grimshaw replied, scrolling back through the images. 'Here, have a look.' He zeroed in on one particular scene. 'See the taller of the two blokes, the one bending over? You can just about make out the logo on his back. Looks like the top bit of a football to me, with words around it. Anyone make them out?'

They strained to see the image. West said, 'Some of it's clear enough. There's *o-r-h* toward the top, followed by something, then *S-f-o*, then a wrinkle, or maybe a shadow. Can't tell which.'

'No, ma'am. That's a *k*, not an *h*. And I think the *f* is a *p*. You can see where it's folded over, just there.' Grimshaw pointed to the screen.

'So what do we have?' McDermott asked, grabbing a pencil and pad from a nearby desk. 'Something-*o-r-k*-something, then *S-p*-something. The rest is in shadow. Make sense to anyone?'

Joe Grimshaw thought a moment. 'Could be a local youth group. The West Yorks Sports Club used to be big hereabouts, up until maybe three, four years back. Fell victim to council budget cuts when the local lads became more interested in textin' one another on their mobiles than gettin' together for games and such. See? That bit there could be *Yorks*, followed by *Sports*. That would explain the football.'

Philippa West beamed. 'I think you're right, Joe. You mentioned it folded a few years back. Any chance of finding a list of boys who were members?'

'Council must have one.' Grimshaw reached for the phone. 'And I just happen to know the councillor who has the Youth dossier.'

A few minutes later he put down the phone. 'We're in luck. Toward the end there were only a few lads belonged, and not all of them could afford the jackets. Here's a list of the ones he knows about. Most were from Wakefield. Now, it only makes sense that the attack on Bert Ridley was a crime of opportunity. No one knew he would be outside the pub, and no offense, George, but if you were going to rob someone, you'd hardly pick an elderly man in a small, out-of-the-way village. So it stands to reason that it were local lads who did it.' He poured over the notes he had taken on the phone. 'There were four boys from Kirk Warham who were still in the sports club when it disbanded. One I know was killed a year or two later in a road accident. A second is a bright lad. He's away in Leeds, at university now. A long shot, at best. That leaves two: Lenny Bodger and Ian Richards.' He looked up, a smirk on his face.

Philippa West said, 'Obviously you know something, Joe. How about putting the rest of us in the picture?'

'Ah well, you wouldn't know this pair. Our paths crossed when I were a green DC. Mostly small beer, really. Shopliftin', things like that.' Grimshaw was busy entering something on his computer. 'Seem to recall they were suspected in a string of B&Es. Yes, here it is.' He peered at the screen. 'Two cases of Taking and Driving Away were also put down to them, but the cars had been torched, so no fingerprints. One charge of Affray, but dropped before it came to court. A case of Robbery with Menaces came to nowt when the victim refused to testify. It's a small village, after all.' Something clicked and Grimshaw cued up the video for what seemed like the fortieth time. He ran through the image of the pair in the hoodies a couple of times and finally backed it up and ran it again, freezing the motion when he reached the image he'd been searching for.

'Here, look at this,' he said. 'See that dark line down the side of this one's neck?' He pointed to the screen.

DCI West squinted. 'You mean the shadow?' she asked.

'I don't think it's a shadow.' He zoomed in on the image, then toggled back and forth frame by frame, until he had a clearer view. 'Notice how the image doesn't move with the light? Unless my mind is goin', that's the edge of a tattoo. See here?' He pointed to a curving line that kept its form even though the man was moving under the light. 'Tell me that's not the outline of a dragon's head,' he said, grinning.

West peered at it even more closely. 'You may be right. Where does that get us?'

'Let's pull up the records for one Ian Richards.' His fingers flew over the keyboard. After a few seconds he had retrieved a mugshot of Richards and found what he was looking for. 'See there? The Richards lad has a tattoo on his neck. In fact, one and the same, unless my mother raised an eejit.'

Philippa West looked at him as though she was prepared to give that possibility serious consideration, but on closer inspection she realised he might be onto something.

McDermott looked over her shoulder, and he too was convinced that the image in the police database was eerily similar to that in the CCTV video. 'Richards, you say. Any relation to the landlord at the Blue Bull?'

Grimshaw grinned. 'The very same. His son.'

'Now that's interesting,' McDermott said. 'It was the CCTV camera just outside the Bull that was malfunctioning the night George's father was attacked, according to Ben Richards. Because of that we had no visual record of the crime scene. And I seem to recall noticing during the reunion that a lad behind the bar there has a tattoo. What's the betting it's Richards' son? Who's the other man?'

'The image sucks,' Grimshaw admitted, still scrolling through Ian Richards' file. 'But…aha! Here we are. Under Known Associates we have one Lenny Bodger. Lives in—surprise—Kirk Warham. Small world.'

He had McDermott's attention. 'What do you mean, Joe?'

'Lenny's a bit slow, and looks up to the Richards lad, who's a year or two older, if memory serves. Richards is the alpha dog: Lenny pretty well does what he's told. I reckon the pair is worth talkin' to.'

BY MID-MORNING THEY HAD ADDRESSES for both suspects and were making plans to pick them up for questioning. The elder of the two, Ian Richards, still lived with his parents over the Blue Bull.

His mate, Lenny Bodger, lived with his mum in a Council house. It was, they noted, just up the path from the church where the surveillance camera was located.

They decided to approach them separately. The feeling was that Lenny was the weak link in the chain, and if Ian Richards wasn't around, he'd be more likely to talk freely. If they'd been involved, then with the passage of time the two had likely let down their guard; they wouldn't be expecting the police nearly two weeks later. It was nearly noon when the team set out in two unmarked cars for the village. It was agreed that Grimshaw and Ridley would pay a visit to Lenny Bodger's digs. If he wasn't there, they'd put the house under observation. Then McDermott and DCI West would run the Richards lad to ground.

As it turned out, Lenny was home having lunch—or rather a very late breakfast, as he had been playing video games since he woke up that morning. His mother answered the door, and when they identified themselves as police officers a look of concern came over her face. She led them through to the kitchen, where Lenny was just finishing a bowl of muesli. The young man was unprepossessing, to say the least: he was running to fat and had dull eyes and lank hair, and when he spoke it was with a mousy, high-pitched voice, in short sentences. Grimshaw did all the talking. 'It's nearly noon, Lenny. Don't you have a job to go to?'

Lenny was wary. 'I'm on benefits, you see. Unable to work 'cordin' to Social Services.'

'Ah. Well, we can't all be rocket scientists, can we? So what do you do to keep out of mischief?'

The lad glared at him suspiciously. 'Bit o' this and that. Helpin' people with their yard work. Deliverin' their groceries. Mostly older folk.'

Grimshaw managed to look impressed. 'Well that's real nice, Lenny. Not enough young 'uns treat retired folk with respect. Glad to see you've got a proper attitude.'

Lenny looked at him, unable to decide whether he was being made fun of. Then he went back to his breakfast.

As he mopped up the last of his cereal with a crust of toast, Grimshaw said, 'Don't you wonder why we're here, Lenny?'

He pushed his spoon around in his cereal bowl, picking up the last bits of muesli. 'Figured you'd tell me when the time was right.'

'Actually we're looking into the mugging of an elderly man couple of weeks back. He died from head wounds after the assault.'

That got Lenny's attention. He pushed his bowl away and looked up. 'Nothing to do with me.' His mother, though, couldn't conceal her apprehension.

'Likely not, Lenny. But the thing is, we've got CCTV footage of someone who looks a lot like you, shortly after the incident, and we'd like to eliminate you from our enquiries.'

Lenny tried to work things out for himself. 'What's that mean, then?'

Grimshaw shrugged. 'Not that much, really. We'd like to look at your clothing, see how it compares with what we have on video. Shouldn't take much of your time.'

'I dunno. You lot only care about makin' arrest. Seen some o' my mates fitted up for things they didn't do.'

'It'll look a lot worse if you don't cooperate, Lenny. We have to figure you've got something to hide. And if it comes out later that you are involved, it won't go down well.'

Lenny saw the writing on the wall, and Grimshaw took the next step, asking the lad to show them his room. He finally agreed, and they returned a few minutes later with a bag containing several pairs of trainers and a hoodie.

Lenny agreed to accompany them back to Wakefield to answer further questions. Grimshaw instructed his mother not to reveal their visit if Ian Richards turned up; she was told simply to say she had no idea where Lenny was, or when he'd return. As they moved toward their car she stood in the doorway, tugging at her cardigan and trying to hold herself together. 'He's a good boy!' she shouted as they drove off.

As Grimshaw and Ridley radioed in that they'd left with Lenny Bodger, Philippa West and McDermott set out for the Blue Bull. As they drove along the main road that bisected the village, McDermott made a mental note of one or two B&Bs; if their hunch about the landlord's son was correct, he and George would likely be looking for new accommodation by the evening.

When they arrived the pub was in full swing, catering to the lunchtime crowd. Ben Richards was nowhere to be seen, but his wife was tending bar and their daughter Miranda was waiting tables. She glowered at McDermott when she recognized him. *Still smarting over Julian's hanky-panky with his stepmother,* McDermott figured. They walked over to the bar where the landlord's wife looked up from pulling a pint and smiled. 'Hello Mr McDermott. Haven't seen much of you lately. In for lunch, then?'

McDermott smiled. 'Not at the moment, Mrs Richards. Is Ian around?'

Immediately her smiled morphed into a frown. 'I'm not sure. It's been that busy behind the bar. Why do you ask?'

Before McDermott could reply, the woman's eyes betrayed her. He turned around to see a young man in his early twenties just coming down the stairs. 'Ian Richards?' he called. 'Wonder if we could have a word.'

The man looked his way and his eyes narrowed. 'Who's askin'?'

McDermott produced his warrant card. 'My name's McDermott. This is DCI West, of the Wakefield Police. We'd like to ask you a few questions.'

The young man looked around, checking his options. In the end he decided to cooperate, at least for the moment. 'Wodja want?'

'We think you might be able to help us with our enquiries,' West said, coming forward. 'I understand you used to belong to the West Yorks Sports Club.'

Ian relaxed perceptibly. 'What if I did? Whole thing went belly up years ago.'

'Right. You still have the jacket, though? The one with the logo on the back?'

His face clouded over again as he tried to work out why they were asking. 'Might be. Might a' lost it a few weeks back.'

His mother chose that moment to intervene. 'Oh no, dear. I saw it in your room just the other day.' Ian gave her a murderous look.

'Said I might 'a done, din't I? Any road, what's it to do with you lot?'

DCI West adopted a placatory tone. 'Well, if it's here, we can clear that up easily, can't we? Let's just have a look, shall we? No harm in that. Why don't you lead the way?'

Ian spared a moment to glower again at his mother, then turned and led them upstairs. When they returned a few moments later they had a large carrier bag. Ian's father Ben Richards had just emerged from the cellar, struggling with two cases of ale. 'Don't know why folk have to have this imported stuff,' he grunted.

Then, seeing his son in the company of McDermott and a stranger, he set down his load on the floor. 'What all this, then?'

DCI West moved to defuse the situation. She didn't want either man getting belligerent. 'Police, Mr Richards. Just a couple of questions we have for your son. We think he might be able to help us with something we're working on.'

'Oh, aye.' The publican was wary. 'What's that, then?' He was looking straight at McDermott, ignoring the woman in their midst.

'All in good time, sir,' McDermott said evenly. 'We'd like Ian to look at a video recording with us, see if he can help us identify a couple of people we'd like to talk to.' West was impressed. Clearly McDermott was no stranger to putting people off their guard.

'Damned inconvenient,' Ben Richards complained. 'Lunchtime crowd, glasses and plates need clearin' and bar stock wants refillin'. I need 'im here.'

Philippas West said 'We shouldn't be long, Mr Richards. With any luck he should be back in time for the supper crowd.' *In your dreams,* she thought to herself.

'Here now, son, you goin' voluntarily?'

Ian scowled. 'Said I'd be back. Miranda can earn her keep for a change.'

As they led Ian toward the door McDermott paused. 'By the way, Mr Richards, ever get that camera fixed?'

Richards gave him a blank look. 'What are you on about?'

'You know, the CCTV camera near the side exit, the one that covers the road, near the car park. It wasn't working a couple of weeks back. Just wondered if you'd got it fixed yet. I'd have thought your insurers would have been onto you about that.'

The man wiped his hands with a bar towel and glared at him. 'Aye, it's fixed all right. Hasn't given me any more trouble.'

'Odd, isn't it?' McDermott said as he turned toward the door. 'Picked that one time to malfunction, when Bert Ridley was attacked outside. Just when we could have used it.' He held the door open for Ian and Philippa West, and caught Ben Richard's reflection in the glass. He looked worried.

THIRTY-ONE

It was early afternoon when the group arrived back at Wakefield Police HQ. They took Ian Richards directly to the CID Suite, where Ridley and Grimshaw were already waiting for them. Lenny Bodger was nowhere to be seen, but Grimshaw nodded toward one of the interview rooms just down the hall.

As they walked down the hallway it was clear that Philippa West was determined to reassert her role as Senior Investigating Officer in the case, and McDermott had no issue with that. He was, after all, on loan to Wakefield and had no official standing. In any event, he was confident that West would want to prove herself, and that meant she would be conducting a strong interview.

When they entered the room West poured the contents of the carrier bag onto a nearby desk. There was a grey hoodie and several pairs of trainers. All business, she said, 'Before we begin, Ian, can you slip off the trainers you're wearing and pass them over?'

'What for?' Richards asked, his tone somewhere between wariness and insolence.

'Purely for elimination purposes. We have some shoe prints of interest, and we don't want to get them confused with yours.'

Richards hesitated a moment, then bent forward and removed his trainers. West was amused to see that his big toe was sticking out of one sock and the other had a large hole in the heel.

'Thank you, Ian.' She placed them with the others on the desk. McDermott noted with approval that West had used Richards' given name. That was a good move, establishing some rapport with him, and suggesting that they were not adversaries. Of course, that could all change in an instant. Without a word Grimshaw placed the trainers in evidence bags and left the room with them. She motioned for McDermott to keep an eye on Richards and followed Grimshaw out. When she returned a few minutes later she whispered a few words in McDermott's ear, then turned to Ian.

'Now then, come this way please.' She led him to a vacant interview room where a uniformed officer was waiting. A video camera was positioned high in one corner of the room, focussed on the table. There was also a video monitor on a wheeled cart at the end of the table. Motioning Richards to have a seat, Philippa West took a chair opposite him, and McDermott did likewise. She switched on the audio recorder, waited momentarily for a light to confirm that it was running, and looked at a clock on the wall, noting the date and the time for the record. Then she said, 'Present are PC Robert Allingham, DI Colin McDermott of the London Metropolitan Police, and myself, DCI Philippa West of the West Yorkshire Police, and SIO in this case.' Then she turned to Richards. 'For the record please state your full name and address.'

For the first time McDermott saw fear replace the arrogance in the young man's eyes. Richards was coming to realise that events were rapidly moving beyond his control, and headed in a direction he did not fully understand. He was struggling to figure out what to admit to and what to deny.

'Come along, Ian.' West was drumming her fingers on the table.

'My name is Ian Richards. No middle name. I live at the Blue Bull in Kirk Warham.'

'Thank you, Ian. This is a preliminary inquiry, and for the record you are here freely and of your own consent, and have not been charged with any crime. Nor have you asked for legal counsel. Is that right?'

He nodded.

'You'll have to speak up, for the benefit of the audio record, Ian.'

'Tha's right,' he said sullenly.

At that point a uniformed officer entered the room and handed West a note. She opened it and read it carefully, then placed it in a manila folder on the table in front of her. Then she turned her attention back to Ian Richards.

'Very good. Now I'd like you to look at the video monitor please, Ian. This is a recording from a CCTV camera at the church in Kirk Warham, just across from the Blue Bull. We'd like you to see if you can help us identify some of the people pictured there.' Philippa West reached for the remote and switched the machine on. After a few moments the image resolved itself: it was the scene just outside the church door in Kirk Warham, the same scene that the officers had run and rerun that morning.

The first images were of the two young people snogging near the church entrance. Richards visibly relaxed. He smirked as the couple fondled each other, then noticed the camera and moved off. 'Too bad,' he joked. 'They might 'a got good brass for that on the internet.'

When the video was advanced to the part with the two figures in hoodies Richards' attitude changed. He stiffened at first, then became restive, watching the recording but feigning disinterest. When they came to the scene where one figure leaned forward, exposing his back, Philippa West paused the recorder, using the zoom and pan features to zero in on the logo on one of the hoodies.

'Any idea who that is, Ian?'

'Could be anybody,' he said guardedly. 'I mean, it's dark, innit?'

'Come on, Ian, look at the jacket. It's from the West Yorks Sports Club, isn't it?'

'Might be,' he replied guardedly. 'Lots o' them about. Club got rid of 'em cheap when it folded a few years back.'

'Very good, Ian. Full marks for quick thinking. But we've checked, and there were only four lads in the village that splashed out for the jackets. One of those is dead, and another is away at uni. That only leaves you and Lenny.'

'Lenny? What's he got to do with this?' His bravado was waning rapidly.

'Oh, sorry. Didn't I tell you? Lenny's in another room as we speak. He's talking to a couple of other officers. One of them is the son of the man who was attacked outside the Bull that night.'

Richards fidgeted in his chair. 'What night?'

Philippa West tried not to let her impatience show. 'You'll have to do better than that, Ian. Have a closer look at the image of the taller of the two persons in the video.' She rewound it, and this time she paused it when the image of the tattoo appeared.

Richards wasn't going to give anything away. 'So?'

West pointed to the tattoo. 'That looks very much like yours, doesn't it, Ian?'

He stalled for time, looking for options. 'Maybe. Maybe not. Lots o' blokes have tats these days.' Then an idea occurred to him. 'Any road, even if it were me, it proves nothing. I lives in the village, don't I? Could 'a been taken anytime.'

'Take a look at the date-and-time stamp in the lower corner of the image.'

Richards tried to put on a brave face, but the image revealed all too clearly that it had been recorded just minutes after the assault outside the pub. He tried changing tacks. 'You got squat. I wasn't even in the village that night. Went into Wakefield for a few laughs. Got lucky with some bird at a club and spent the night at her place. Didn't get back until next day.'

'That's very interesting, Ian. I don't suppose you can give us the name of the, ah, young lady?'

'What, after almost three weeks? You're joking.' He shuffled in his chair and gave her a smug look.

West's expression suggested she wasn't buying it. 'The address of her flat, then?'

'Couldn't say. I'd 'ad a bit to drink, hadn't I?' His confidence was growing by the moment.

'I see,' she replied. 'Then in fact, you have no alibi at all for the night in question. How unfortunate. It seems we'll have to talk to Lenny then.'

Ian's smugness disappeared in an instant.

'You oughtn't to be havin' a go at poor Lenny. He's a bit slow like. He doesn't always understand what someone is sayin' to him. He's liable to say anything.'

Philippa West smiled. 'Indeed he is, Ian. I've just had a note from the officers questioning Lenny. Seems he's admitted that it was the two of you who mugged Bert Ridley that night.'

'Bollocks! We never did no such thing, and if he said we did, it was because you lot confused him. I told you he ain't right in the head!' Fueled by desperation, Richards' arrogance was returning.

'Calm down, Ian. Have a look at this.' She advanced the video several seconds' worth, and froze it on the image of the hooded figure holding an object. She zoomed in until the object could be identified. At this magnification the image was pixilated, but the object was clearly recognizable as a pocket watch.

Ian glanced at the monitor, then looked at the pair of officers. 'It's a watch, right? What of it?'

'The man who was mugged, and later died, lost his wallet and watch, Ian,' West said patiently.

'So what's it to do wi' me?' he retorted. 'Can't even tell what kind it is from that, can you?' But his swagger was eroding: his voice had lost some of its combativeness, and he looked from one officer to the other, trying to gauge his chances.

West stuck her boot in once again. 'And an old man's medal from the war went south as well, Ian. Must have made you feel right proud.'

Ian Richards was in full denial. 'Dunno what you mean.'

DCI West shrugged and rose from her chair. 'Ok, Ian, if that's how you want to play it. But remember, we have Lenny's statement, and even as we speak the lab technicians are going over your trainers and his, trying to match them to the prints from the crime scene and the images from that CCTV. Once we've got the physical evidence, it will be too late to do a deal.'

'Here, now, if you're meaning to charge me for summat I want a lawyer, and I'm sayin' nowt 'til I have a chance to talk with one.'

West concealed her irritation with herself. She'd pushed him too far, and now that he'd asked for counsel, they'd have to provide it before continuing. 'Certainly. I'll have a look at who's on duty today. I'm sure he or she will be able to see you later today.'

'She? I don't want no bird! You get me a proper brief, see?'

As they left the room her expression was smug. 'More fool him. He doesn't realize that juries tend to be more sympathetic to men represented by female counsellors than by men.'

'Good job, just the same,' McDermott said. 'You put the wind up him. I suspect it won't be long before he coughs.'

Philippa West actually smiled. It seemed she wasn't used to being praised.

After arranging for Richards to be returned to a holding cell West and McDermott made their way to the interview room at the end of the corridor, where Grimshaw was questioning Lenny. They knocked, and Ridley answered the door. West said, 'Can we have a word, George?'

He stepped into the corridor and pulled the door closed. 'Lad's been singin' like 'e's in church choir. At first 'e denied owt, but your man Grimshaw told him we 'ad evidence of 'im and Richards stoppin' at church to examine their takin's. He knew right away we 'ad 'im.'

'Brilliant! Did he offer you any corroborating evidence?'

'Oh, aye. Said they'd kept watch, figurin' it were too hot to flog 'round 'ere. Thought they might do summat with it elsewhere. Also kept wallet wi' bank card. Knew they couldn't use it themselves, but figured they could flog it to some poor sap in Leeds or Manchester later on.'

Philippa West actually gloated. 'So we've got them cold. Bloody marvelous!' Then, seeing George's face, she reigned in her enthusiasm. 'You must be very pleased, George, after all this time.'

Ridley gave her a look. 'Aye, right enough. But doesn't bring my dad back, does it?'

After preparing a written statement and having Lenny Bodger sign it, the team moved Bodger and Richards to separate holding cells. Richards complained that he hadn't seen a solicitor yet, and was asked if he wanted a cup of tea whilst he waited. He'd replied that it wasn't tea that he bloody wanted, and told the duty sergeant where he could put it. The officer was impassive; he'd heard it all before.

When the Duty Solicitor finally arrived and spoke with Richards the team reviewed their progress. Lenny Bodger had been cautioned before he'd admitted anything, and had declined a lawyer. When faced with the evidence and the prospect that he'd go down for the assault and robbery alone, he soon admitted that it had been Richards' idea. That came as no surprise.

Lenny described in detail what had happened that night. The pair of them had been walking toward the Blue Bull, Ian complaining that they had no money to go drinking in Wakefield, when Bert Ridley emerged. Ian saw an easy mark, and they went over to Ridley and asked for a light. When Ridley reached into his pocket for a match Ian grabbed him from behind, wrapping his arms around him. He told Lenny to snatch the old man's wallet, but Lenny had fumbled it, dropping it in the mud. When he bent over to retrieve it, Bert had lashed out with his boot, catching Lenny on the side of his head. Enraged, Ian had shoved him into the construction hole where he hit his head on a partially excavated drainage pipe. He didn't move, and they could see that he was in a bad way. Richards picked Lenny up, retrieved the wallet, and grabbed his pocket watch and chain. When they went through his pockets they discovered the medal. The two of them looked round to make certain no one had seen them and started to leave. They'd gone only a few steps when Ian remembered the CCTV camera outside the pub. Richards told Lenny to wait in the shadows while he went inside. A few minutes later he returned with a video cassette in his hand.

The pair were excited about their score, and talked about what to do next. They crossed the road and headed for Lenny's mum's house, but before they got there they paused under the light at the church to see how much money the wallet contained, and to examine the watch. They spent only a few moments there before setting off again, changing their course for a wooded area just behind the village. The CCTV coverage ended there, but the evidence was clear enough.

The team was jubilant: they had Lenny's statement and by the next morning they would have the physical evidence as well. They planned to take Lenny along and have him point out the stash, all recorded on video for use later at the trial. But they had one more surprise when the forensics lab telephoned to say they'd compared the trainers collected from Ian and Lenny with shoe prints taken at the crime scene. Although the trainers were fairly common, one print was a perfect match, owing to a deep gash across the instep. The trainer belonged to Ian Richards.

They decided they had everything they needed, and more. Tomorrow they would discuss with a Crown Prosecutor the handling of the interviews and the collection of the evidence, but as nearly as they could tell they had gone by the book. True, they'd had no search warrant, but both Lenny and Ian had cooperated at that point, handing over their trainers and clothing voluntarily. And although Lenny had made his confession in the absence of a solicitor, he'd been cautioned and had waived his rights. They agreed that given his mental capacity Lenny probably wouldn't be tried as the principal defendant in the case, but as a minor accomplice. The burden would fall on Ian Richards, where it belonged.

As they broke up for the evening Colin McDermott turned to Ridley. 'You and I had better return to the village, George. We need to go to the Bull and pack our bags. Somehow I think we'll have worn out our welcome.'

IT WAS NOT YET DARK when they reached the village. They stopped at two B&Bs on the way to the pub. The first was full, but the second had a twin room going, and the owners seemed pleasant enough. After saying they'd be back shortly McDermott and Ridley made their way to the Blue Bull for what they suspected would be the last time. When they entered the lounge it was deserted, and they went directly to their room. After packing they returned downstairs. Mrs Richards was handling the bar. Her husband was in the lounge, collecting glasses from the empty tables and wiping them down. The evening crowd would be arriving soon.

She looked up from her duties and was surprised to see their bags. 'Not leaving us, already, are you?'

'Afraid so, Mrs Richards. If you can prepare our bill?'

'Mrs Richards? My, that's grand. I thought we were on a first name basis.' Then she recalled the events of earlier that day, and her face clouded. 'What's happened to our Ian, then?' she asked. 'We've not seen him since he went away with you earlier.'

'Perhaps you might like to call your husband over, Mrs Richards. It might save some time.'

She looked as though someone had driven a knife through her heart. 'Ben,' she called out. 'Can you come here a moment?'

Ben Richards looked up from the table he was clearing and saw McDermott. His glance took in the bags at their feet and he tucked the bar towel into his belt and approached the pair. 'So where's Ian, then? You promised he'd be back to help with the supper crowd.'

'There have been some new developments, Mr Richards. He's being detained overnight, and I'm afraid he won't be coming home anytime soon.'

The colour rose in the man's face and he stepped closer to McDermott. 'What are you on about? You said he was helping you to identify someone. That's all!' The man was right in his face now. He wondered briefly how Mrs Richards handled her husband when he lost his temper.

'It turns out the person he helped us to identify was himself, Mr Richards. Not to put too fine a point on it, it seems your Ian, with a little help from his friend Lenny Bodger, was responsible for the robbery and assault on George Ridley's father a few weeks back.'

'Oh my God!' Mrs Richards cried, causing several heads at the far end of the bar to turn in her direction. 'It can't be true. It must be some terrible mistake! That Bodger boy, he's not—well,

I mean, he's not really all there, is he? You can't rely on what he says. Surely you're not—'

'No, Mrs Richards, we're not as gullible as all that. In addition to a confession from Lenny we have a video recording of Ian with incriminating evidence, and shortly we'll have the physical evidence as well. I can't go into the details right now, but I assure you that we have, or will have very soon, everything we need to go to trial.'

Ben Richards intervened. 'Bollocks. Where's he being held, then? I'll get the best—'

'That's your prerogative, of course, McDermott interrupted. 'He's being held at the West Yorkshire Police Headquarters in Wakefield.' In the silence that followed Ridley and McDermott settled their account and left the Blue Bull for the last time.

THIRTY-TWO

A trip to the abandoned scout hut in the woods the next day turned up Bert Ridley's wallet, pocket watch, and war medal, which sealed the men's fates. By noon the McDermott and Grimshaw had returned to Wakefield and turned the evidence over to Forensics, then they resumed their questioning, building their argument for the Crown.

By now Richards' solicitor had showed, an otherwise capable-looking man in his early thirties who seemed to be content with taking his cues from his client. When Richards was confronted with Ridley's personal effects, at first he denied all knowledge of the objects. But when he learned of Lenny's confession he threw his mate under the bus, alleging that Lenny had mugged the old man, but he hadn't been involved.

It wasn't long before Forensics got back to McDermott. The wallet, the bank card, and the pocket watch contained both men's prints. McDermott returned to the interview room where Ian Richards, Philippa West, and George Ridley were seated.

'Well, that's you done,' McDermott said breezily. 'We just heard from Forensics. Your prints are all over the victim's personal effects. Anything you want to say before we book you?'

Richards had been combative, but now he turned silent. Grasping for anything that would justify his presence his solicitor said simply, 'I'll need to see the statement by this Bodger chap.'

McDermott assured him that would be no problem. He'd be provided with a copy in due course.

After reviewing the dossier the Crown Prosecutor agreed that Richards had almost certainly been the instigator as well as the assailant, and charged him accordingly. Lenny Bodger pleaded guilty to being an accomplice, which sped things up considerably. Months later when it got to court Richards tried to keep up the pretence that Lenny had planned the attempted robbery and that it was he who had struck Bert Ridley, sending him into the roadworks ditch. That defense proved to be a mistake: the members of the jury were unimpressed with Richards' demeanour from the outset, and when Lenny took the stand and they could see how he could be used, Richards' fate was sealed. His parents asked that he be allowed to serve his sentence nearby, and they got their wish: Richards was remanded to Her Majesty's Prison at Wakefield. It proved to be a mixed blessing: the largest maximum-security prison in the UK, HMP Wakefield housed nearly six hundred of the nation's most dangerous offenders, and was known by its inmates as the Monster Mansion. It was a source of grim satisfaction to Ridley that Ian Richards would find himself tested by the other inmates on a daily basis. For his part in the crime Lenny Bodger was remanded to a mental health unit indefinitely. Even though he would be confined, perhaps for the rest of his life, at least he would not become caught up in the criminal actions of others.

THE MATTER OF THE MISSING ARTIFACTS proved to be more challenging. After consulting with the Home Office, the local Crown Prosecutor found himself on the horns of a dilemma: filing formal charges for the illegal possession of the artifacts found in Baker-Simms' possession meant raising the issue of the deaths at the villa during the war, and the Home Office had no appetite for that. Apart from the difficulty inherent in prosecuting a charge of murder based on events that had occurred six decades earlier, there was a feeling that such a case was bound to generate significant publicity, even at the national level. It was felt that this would inevitably damage the public's perception of an honourable and decorated regiment, and in the tabloid press the issue might even bring the British military in general into disrepute. The mandarins in Whitehall firmly forbade even raising the issue with outside agencies, pointedly including Interpol and the Italian Carabinieri.

McDermott was frustrated, and Matthews threw his hands up in despair, realising that matters were clearly out of their hands.

Not one to give up easily, McDermott formed a plan. He floated it to the DCS, who agreed to place it before the Crown Prosecutor. A few days later they had their answer: the Crown Prosecution Service and the Home Office agreed, reluctantly, to let him have a go, but with the proviso that if he failed the matter ended there.

McDermott had to accept that risk, and two days' time found them back at Coniston Hall. This time the team from Wakefield included DCS Gareth Matthews, DCI West, McDermott, and a senior lawyer from the Crown Prosecution Service sent especially from London. The family was represented by the Brigadier, his son Gordon, and the family solicitor, Alistair Summerfield. Both Fiona and Julian were conspicuous by their absence. McDermott wondered, not for the first time, whether the family itself would survive the revelations that had already come, or were about to come.

As they gathered around the dining table it was clear that the Brigadier had regained some of his earlier self-confidence. He was smug, even condescending. 'So you're back, are you? I should have thought you'd want to stay well clear of this house!'

As the strategy for the meeting was his idea, McDermott had been given the lead. 'Considering that the events in question took place over half a century ago, and we've only been looking into this matter for the past few weeks, I think we're doing rather well, actually.' He focused on Reginald Baker-Simms, looking him directly in the eye. 'Let me begin on a positive note. You should know that we no longer consider anyone in the family a person of interest in the death of Albert Ridley. We now have two suspects in custody, and they have confessed.'

'Have you really? About time, I should say!' Baker-Simms sensed victory in the air.

McDermott spread his hands on the polished mahogany table. 'I'm afraid that still leaves the matters of the death of the two individuals in Italy in 1943, and the disappearance of a number of significant items of cultural heritage from their villa a few days later.'

'Really? I've already answered those questions on at least two different occasions. How many times must we go over the same ground?' He looked to his solicitor for support, but the man's expression was impassive. He knew that more was coming.

'So you did,' McDermott said. 'But since then we've come into additional information relevant to the investigation.'

The Brigadier was wary now. 'Indeed. What information is that?' Summerfield winced; he knew better than to give an adversary an opening like that.

'Well, for starters, there's the matter of the pistol found by the bodies.' When Baker-Simms said nothing, McDermott continued. 'The thing about the Nazis is that they were very methodical. Everything had to be planned in advance, and every detail accounted for. I suspect that explains their extraordinary success in the early days of the war. Poland, and all that.'

The Brigadier looked at him impatiently. 'I suppose so. But what's this to do with anything?'

'Just this. I checked the serial number of the Luger pistol recorded at the shooting inquiry against German war records. It seems it was originally issued in Munich on July 1, 1940 to a young tank commander, one Oberleutnant Helmut Schmidt, who later became part of Rommel's lot in North Africa. When they were captured by a unit of the Eighth Army in the desert, *by troops under your command,* he surrendered his gun to a member of your regiment, who turned it over to you on the twenty-third of February, 1943. That much is a matter of record. But perhaps you can explain how *the very same weapon* was found in the possession of the elderly couple in the villa in Santa Cristina nearly seven months later, on the fourth of September, 1943, when you shot and killed them.'

Baker-Simms stared at McDermott for some moments, then decide to brazen it out. 'How should I know? One of the quirks of war, I should imagine. It's not for me to chase down all your allegations and speculations and refute them. Presumption of innocence, you know. You'll have to do better than that!' But the expression on Summerfield's face told McDermott that he had got to the man.

'Well, Brigadier, that would be for a jury to sort out. But you'll be relieved to know that we have no plans to proceed with charges of causing an unlawful death—or even more seriously, of war crimes—at this time.'

Baker-Simms sat back in his wheelchair, clearly relieved. Once again McDermott noted that Summerfield was watching him intently, his expression giving nothing away, waiting for the other shoe to drop.

'So again, why are we here, Inspector?' This time it was the Brigadier's son, Gordon, who was talking. He, too, was being wary, impatient to know where McDermott was heading, but apprehensive lest it lead in a direction he wasn't prepared for.

'I'll be glad to tell you, sir. Although at this time we are not prepared to proceed with charges centering on the deaths of the two elderly people at the villa, we have built a substantial case against your father for art theft, a criminal act in itself, and for violating Italian law for the illicit removal of works of cultural patrimony from the country for personal gain.'

The atmosphere around the table had become charged with tension. McDermott was aware that every eye was on him, not least his colleagues from Wakefield and the Crown Prosecutor from London. It was very much like playing a game of high-stakes poker, and the next few minutes would reveal whether McDermott had a winning hand or would leave the room empty-handed and humiliated.

Alistair Summerfield stepped in to fill the void. 'Forgive me, Inspector, but legally speaking this issue must be fraught with difficulty. First, there is the matter of establishing that the artworks in my client's possession are indeed the same artifacts in the house in Italy. As I mentioned when we last met there must be many similar works extant, and almost certainly no one alive who can recall, with clarity and beyond all doubt, that a specific object is or is not the same object in the villa sixty-plus years ago. Second, even if that could be shown to be true, it doesn't follow that my client is responsible for having them in his possession. The family has a history of acquiring works of art for the past two centuries at least. They might have come across a specific work quite innocently and perfectly legally.' He leaned back in his chair, resting one arm of his very expensive suit on the edge of the table, and tugging almost imperceptibly at one cuff of his immaculately-ironed dress shirt.

The family members in the room looked at Summerfield approvingly, certain they'd got the right man for the job. McDermott was aware that even his own colleagues were watching him intently.

'You are quite right, Mr Summerfield. There is certainly room to go wrong, especially when a great deal of time has passed. But you should know that we've vetted the pieces, as well as those making the claims, very carefully. We have photographs in our possession showing some of the works in the villa before their disappearance, and identifying marks on some objects correspond to damage known to have been caused whilst the objects were in the villa.' He paused to retrieve a photograph from a folder and passed it over to the lawyer. 'Finally, one of the objects we found at Coniston Hall is rather distinctive: a *cassoni*, or Florentine wedding chest. Are you familiar with those?'

Summerfield's expression told him that even if he was familiar with the objects in question, he wasn't about to admit it, so McDermott continued. '*Cassoni* were objects of some considerable importance amongst prominent Italian families during the late Middle Ages. They were more than simply objects containing a bride's trousseau, or forming part of a dowry. Their history has been well documented in the art world; in fact, there is an impressive collection of cassoni here in England, housed in the Courtauld Gallery in London. They are often described as Florentine, but their creation was not confined to Florence, or even to a single region of Italy. The most impressive of these chests were referred to as *forziere*; they were ornately carved and painted, often depicting some especially important aspect of a family's history.' He paused and noted that the Brigadier and his son were struggling, not entirely successfully, to conceal their impatience. Summerfield, on the other hand, had his full attention fixed on McDermott.

He went on. 'As they represented in material form the union of two important families, the artists who created these chests often incorporated symbols of those unions, such as family crests and coats of arms.' He passed a photograph over to the lawyer. 'Here you can see quite clearly the painted image of two shields, each bearing a family crest intertwined with that of the other family.' Summerfield made a pretense of examining the photo closely, doubtless thinking through his options. When he didn't comment, McDermott pressed on.

'I think you will agree these objects are quite unique. And it passes the bounds of coincidence that this family should come into the possession of one such chest from the very same family living in the villa in Italy.' He passed another photograph over to the solicitor, making certain that Brigadier Baker-Simms had a good view of it. 'In fact,' he said, turning to look at an object just behind the family, 'it beggars the imagination that we should find the exact same *cassoni* in this very room, and I should think a court would find it similarly incredulous.'

The elderly man looked startled, his son still struggling to take in the implication of this latest revelation. McDermott rose from his chair and walked to the bay window behind the Brigadier. At the base of the window was an oversized piece of furniture, with cushions at either end, that apparently served as a window seat. He took a second copy of the photograph with him, identical except for several details that had been circled with a red marker.

'As you can see, this chest is not only similar to the one in the photograph, it is identical. There are two coats of arms illustrated on the main panel at the front. They represent the union of two important families in marriage. One represents the Grimaldi family, and is quite distinctive. The shield is divided into four quadrants, with designs repeated in opposite corners. One features a repeated diamond-shaped motif rendered in red and white, the other corners are designed in a sort of checkerboard fashion, intersected by a single stripe cutting across the shield from upper left to lower right.' He paused to let them take this in. 'The Montefiori coat of arms is even more intricate. It consists of a lion rampant on the left, balanced by a stag on the right, with a rather elaborate shield in the centre. Rather resembles the British Royal Standard, don't you think?'

The Brigadier's patience was wearing thin. 'Most interesting, Inspector. Perhaps you would be so good as to explain the relevance of all this?' Alistair Summerfield looked to the ceiling, less anxious to have that information.

'Of course, Brigadier. I've been researching the family who lived in the villa. It seems the union of families depicted on this wedding chest dates all the way back to 1349, when Allesandro di Montefiori of Parma married Francesca Grimaldi, who came from Florence. Fast forward several generations and you have two of their descendants, the elderly couple who lived in the villa outside Santa Cristina, very near where the Brigadier's company was positioned. This *cassoni* belonged to the couple; it was an important part of their family patrimony, more important than any mere wedding certificate would be today. And critically, for our purposes, the benefactor had commissioned identical chests, one for each side of the family. The sister to this one is presently housed in a collection at the Uffizi Gallery in Florence, where it can be admired by all.'

McDermott handed them a photocopy of a museum pamphlet clearly depicting the chest, along with other artifacts of the Grimaldi family. 'And it proves, beyond any reasonable doubt, that this *cassoni* was taken from the home of the elderly couple killed in Santa Cristina.'

The silence in the room was palpable. Finally, Summerfield spoke, and his tone was conciliatory. 'You'll have to pardon me, Inspector. This is quite a bit to take on board. Perhaps you and your colleagues would care to wait in the drawing room whilst we discuss these…revelations. I don't expect we'll be long.'

McDermott looked at the others. 'I don't see why not.' They collected their file folders and left the room.

Once they'd gathered in the drawing room, the crown prosecutor from London spoke up. 'I hope you know what you're doing, Inspector.'

Gareth Matthews also looked concerned. 'What's to stop them from simply staying stumpf? Then the ball would be back in our court, and the Home Office has been quite clear: if that happens the matter is closed.'

McDermott made no effort to mask his own concern. 'You're quite right, of course, but I'm gambling they cannot know that, and I doubt very much they're willing to risk a trial and the attendant publicity. At any rate, what else have we got?'

Twenty minutes later there was a knock at the door and Gordon Baker-Simms looked in. He was clearly unhappy, and angry as well; but he'd been raised a gentleman, and he kept his composure. 'We are ready for you now.'

THIRTY-THREE

As they returned to the dining room McDermott couldn't help noticing that the elder Baker-Simms had lost a great deal of his combativeness. His son glared at McDermott, and Summerfield was busy shuffling his notes. There was a decanter of brandy in front of the Brigadier, and a single glass, largely empty. *Dutch courage*, McDermott decided.

After they were seated Summerfield took up the banner. 'You've raised some serious concerns, Inspector. But frankly, we're at a loss to know what to make of them. Is it your intention to take these issues to court? Because if it is—'

McDermott cut him off. 'We're reasonable people here, Mr Summerfield, regardless of what your clients may believe. Brigadier Baker-Simms is an elderly man, and I'm sure that during the war he acquitted himself honourably, on the whole.' The qualification earned him a scowl from the former officer.

'Then what, exactly, is it that you want?' Summerfield asked.

McDermott glanced at the lawyer from London. He nodded, just perceptibly, and McDermott rested his elbows on the edge of the table and steepled his fingers. 'The owners of the villa are dead. No court case, regardless of the verdict, will bring them back. And their descendants were not alive when these events took place. They can get no sense of satisfaction, no closure, on something which happened so long ago.'

Everyone on the other side of the table relaxed perceptibly. But if McDermott was right, their satisfaction would be short-lived.

'The thing is, it remains true that this family has benefitted improperly from artworks which disappeared during the war, and somehow found their way to England, and to this very house. The Italian state police—the Carabinieri—are quite adamant about stolen artifacts being returned to their rightful owners. They even have a specific department—the Command for the Protection of Cultural Heritage—for investigating such matters. It is a matter of national pride to Italians that the patrimony of their nation be recovered. They are already aware that some of these objects may be in British hands, and they will move heaven and earth to get them back. The impact on the reputations of British soldiers, even high-ranking ex-officers, is of no concern to them.'

He paused to allow his words to fully sink in. 'Based on the list of objects provided by a person familiar with the villa in Italy, together with research conducted by art historians here in England, we have prepared a list of those objects still in your possession which we believe were taken from the villa. I should stress that it is a fraction of the objects that disappeared. Nonetheless, we are prepared to drop all charges relating to the deaths of the couple at the villa, together with any charges relating to the theft of these artworks, *provided that* the objects on this list are returned to their owners intact and restitution is made for those works that cannot be located. Our experts have placed the financial value of the missing objects at a very conservative 550,000 pounds.' He passed the list over to Summerfield, where both father and son examined it carefully.

'That's blackmail!' the Brigadier said. His face was livid.

But McDermott was prepared. 'Not at all, Brigadier. In legal circles it's known as plea bargaining, and very generous, too. In return for giving up things you never had a right to in the first place you avoid the indignity of a trial, the humiliation of public censure, and the risk of seeing the inside of one of Her Majesty's Prisons.'

The elderly man stared at McDermott. There was contempt in his eyes that reached across the years that separated them. 'You think you know it all, don't you? Sitting there smug in your own little world. You've no idea what it's like to be in a foreign land, surrounded by hundreds of men and *boys*—too many boys—who depend on you to tell them what to do in life-and-death situations. You've never had to plan a battle knowing that some, perhaps many of your men, men you know well, will be going to their deaths. You've never had to lead men into battle, to be first over the top, to face machine guns and tanks.' He paused, and his voice grew hoarse. 'And you've never had to write letters to mothers, telling them their sons wouldn't be coming home, ever.' He sat back in his wheelchair. He was trembling now, haunted by the very memories he himself had called up.

Everyone in the room was silent. It seemed likely that Baker-Simms had never shared his thoughts in such intimate detail, even with his son, before this moment. Finally McDermott found his voice, and there was humility in his words. 'You're quite right,

Brigadier. I'm not a military man. I have no experience of what it's like to fight in war, thank God. But we each have our roles in life. As a copper, and as a human being, I do know something of the difference between right and wrong. You may have panicked that day in the villa; so might I well have done, come to that. But it wasn't dark, and there was no one pointing a gun at you, when you decided to switch the cargo manifest on the lorry that Albert Ridley had been riding in, the one that remained on the road. The one that contained the works of art removed from the villa. That decision wasn't made out of fear. It came from greed. And at that point you crossed the line and became no better than a common thief.'

The Brigadier snorted. 'Who's to say they'd even exist today if they'd been left there? They could well have been casualties of the fighting.'

McDermott's expression hardened. 'These are not the Elgin Marbles, and you weren't removing them for their safekeeping. This was a case of looting, pure and simple. You were lining your own pockets. As I said: a common thief.'

His words drained the Brigadier's face of all colour, and the elderly man lowered his eyes to the table and said nothing. Summerfield moved to fill the void. 'You've made an interesting proposal, Inspector—'

The Brigadier turned and interrupted him. 'Alistair, you're going beyond your remit. This is a family decision, and I'm still head of the family—and the business! I'll decide our course of action, and you'll be informed.'

Before Summerfield could respond Gordon Baker-Simms stepped in. 'It seems to me you've done quite enough, Father! I'm not about to see the brewery destroyed, and the family subjected to damning publicity, in an ill-fated attempt to salvage your reputation. You might still sit in on board meetings, but the decision will be mine, and the board will back me.' For a moment the Brigadier was stunned by his son's remarks. He glowered at his son, then sat back in his chair, the wind finally taken out of him.

Gordon Baker-Simms turned to McDermott, straining to control his emotions. 'I doubt you understand the position we're in, Inspector. The business isn't what it used to be. Not like the old days, when people couldn't get enough of Best Bitter and IPA. Nowadays the younger crowd has all the brass, and they can't get enough of fancy foreign stuff: German, Danish, the Belgians—even watered-down American canary piss, the lot of it. This could spell the death of the firm.'

McDermott looked at the man, unable to believe what he'd heard, and his voice was hard. 'If your brewery has been doing well over the years, it's been on the backs of others, whose money you had no right to in the first place.'

Gordon Barker-Simms stared at him for several moments, then had the grace to look away. He turned to the lawyer. 'Arthur, you were about to say?'

Summerfield turned to the Crown Prosecutor, one lawyer looking at another, searching for some common ground. He alone seemed to grasp the magnitude of the dilemma facing them. 'Am I to understand that the Home Office is in agreement with this offer?'

The lawyer nodded. McDermott thought he was being extremely cagey. By saying nothing, there was nothing on the record, so to speak. He could deny his agreement later, claim he'd been misunderstood, if need be.

'We will need time to consider matters,' Summerfield continued. 'As Gordon has pointed out, there is not only my client's legal status to consider, but also the impact of this proposal on the family, and on the business itself. At the very least, the firm's accountants will need to see what is financially possible. We should be able to get back to you in, say, a week's time.'

'Three days,' McDermott said, taking those on his side of the table by surprise. 'Remember, the Carabinieri are already aware of things, and they are not a people known for their patience. I cannot guarantee the consequences if we delay longer than that. But if they do become involved I can guarantee you that any chance for plea bargaining, or keeping the matter quiet, will have sailed with the tide.'

Summerfield looked at him, stone-faced. 'Very well, Inspector. Three days. My office will contact you once a decision has been taken.'

THIRTY-FOUR

Once they were back in Wakefield Gareth Matthews settled into a chair and gave McDermott a hard look. 'You were a bit hard on the Brigadier back there, weren't you?'

But McDermott was unfazed. 'Do you think so? He made a lot of high-sounding noises about the glorious history of the regiment down through the centuries, but during the war when he saw an opportunity to line his own pockets he was quick enough to take advantage of it.' The more he thought about it, the more McDermott's anger grew. 'No, Baker-Simms has a great deal to answer for. It's just a pity that it won't be in this world.'

The others were stunned by the depth of his anger, and no one in the room said anything for a bit. Then DCS Matthews spoke up. 'Explains your ultimatum. What's the reasoning behind the strict deadline, though?'

'It's simple, really. So long as they can set the agenda, including the schedule, they have to think they're in control. We need to press them a bit, make the Brigadier face reality.'

Matthews raised an eyebrow. 'Which is?'

'That this is not simply going to go away. A decorated veteran officer, member of the landed gentry notwithstanding, Baker-Simms has harmed no shortage of people during his lifetime. Confining ourselves to just what we already know, he's killed two elderly civilians and looted their home. I haven't mentioned this before, but I met their great-grandson during my trip to Calabria, and he and his wife are struggling to make a going concern of a fledgling winery. If they had the wealth those stolen artifacts represent they could realise their plans in a heartbeat.'

Even now McDermott didn't mention the fact that the Brigadier had also taken advantage of the grieving granddaughter of the couple at the villa, making her pregnant and arguably being responsible for her death as well. It occurred to him that fathering Giancarlo Montefiori was, perhaps, the finest thing Baker-Simms had done in life, though he would never know that.

Gareth Matthews sat back, partly persuaded by McDermott's words. His telephone rang, and he picked up. 'Yes? Oh, hello, Galbraith.' He shot McDermott a look. 'Yes? Really? No, it's no bed of roses up here, either. Well, to be honest we're at a crucial point here at the moment. Yes, we should have a result before the week is out. Right, I'll tell him. Cheers.'

The DCS put down the phone. 'That was your guv in London, Colin. Wanted to know when you'll be finished here. Seems they can't get along without you. I told him we'd know better in a few days. Ok with you?'

'Thanks,' McDermott said. 'What was his mood?'

Matthews smiled. 'Somewhere between a bear with a thorn in his paw and a nutter who's gone off his meds.'

'Care to go on the record?'

'Let's hope Summerfield gets back to us before the weekend, so we don't have to,' Matthews said.

AS IT TURNED OUT, THEY HAD THEIR ANSWER LATE THE FOLLOWING DAY. The family's lawyer called to say they accepted the terms, in no small part to spare the Brigadier the stress of what they saw as a protracted and contentious trial. Summerfield managed to convey the feeling that he'd been opposed to a settlement, which McDermott took with the proverbial grain of salt. As a lawyer he would have benefitted significantly from the case going to court, always assuming there would be anything left for him after the dust had settled.

The family's acceptance of McDermott's terms, together with the court proceedings against Ian Richards for Bert's death, meant that Ridley and McDermott could finally return to London. After the team enjoyed a slap-up supper at a local restaurant the pair thanked their hosts and made their goodbyes. Joe Grimshaw was sorry to see them go; he'd confided in the gents' that he found it a lot easier to work with McDermott than with, as he put it, Her Nibs. Gareth Matthews said he too was sorry to see them leave, and hinted that if McDermott ever tired of London he'd do his best to find him a spot in Wakefield. On their way to the train station Philippa West said she'd learned a lot from watching McDermott work, though it wasn't clear from her tone whether she meant things to emulate or things to avoid. But just before they boarded the train she gave him a hug that seemed heartfelt.

GEORGE WAS SILENT DURING THE TRIP BACK TO LONDON, and it wasn't difficult to guess the reason. With no family left in Yorkshire, nor any close friends there, it might be the last time he would see the Dales. He was looking out the window, and McDermott knew he was thinking about his father and the life they had shared. But as tragic and unnecessary as Bert's death was, it had led to the discovery of a crime committed decades earlier, and ultimately to some small measure of justice. *Out of evil some good may come.*

THIRTY-FIVE

By the time they reached King's Cross it was late at night, and McDermott asked George if he wanted to share a taxi, but Ridley said they weren't going the same way. They agreed to meet at the Charing Cross Police Station early the next morning to brief Galbraith before settling in to whatever duties awaited them.

McDermott made his way home and surprised Anna. Their daughter Megan had gone to bed for the night, but after a joyful reunion the following morning Anna treated them to one of her special breakfasts, and they made plans for lunch together.

When McDermott and Ridley met in Galbraith's office they could see he was clearly glad to have them back as well, though he couldn't resist a bit of fun. 'I was about to ask you if you wanted to transfer up there permanently. Got to like the place, did you?' he asked.

'Please!' said McDermott. 'Fair play: the countryside is beautiful, and you can drive down a road without having an impatient taxi driver cutting you off or a builder's van blocking the road,' he admitted. 'But on the other hand, it's no fun being stuck behind a farm tractor pulling a manure-spreader with no place to pass because of the hedgerows. And I won't get started on the pubs!'

Galbraith grinned. 'Curious. A little bird told me you'd made a friend whilst you were there. Very taken by you, she was.' He winked at Ridley, who was clearly enjoying watching McDermott being on the sharp end for once.

'Very funny. I suppose that was Gareth Matthews taking the piss.'

'My lips are sealed,' Galbraith was still smiling. 'Got on well, did you?'

'As a matter of fact she—that is, DCI West—wasn't best pleased when a couple of big-city folk waltzed in and took over what was rightly her case. Can't say I blame her. But that said, she was brittle and more than a little insecure. I won't cry if I never see her again.'

'Just as well, then.' He turned to a file folder on his desk. 'I suppose you're still expecting to be reimbursed for skiving off to the Continent,' he said, his expression not giving anything away.

McDermott had expected this. 'Well, it seems straightforward to me. I admit that in the end Bert Ridley's death had nothing to do with stolen art. In fact, it had nothing to do with Italy, or the war. But we agreed I had to get a result, and I have. We have the pair responsible for Ridley's death, and in the process we've solved not one, but two crimes dating from sixty years ago. The Home Office even sent a Crown Prosecutor from London to make certain we dotted our i's and crossed our t's. We confronted

Brigadier Baker-Simms, who'd killed the couple at the villa and then looted their artworks.'

'But it's not going to court, is it?' Galbraith was playing hard-ball—either that, or having him on.

'Not up to me. But we struck a deal to return all the Italian art-works the Baker-Simms have in their possession, *and*,' he emphasized, 'to compensate the family in Italy for those we could document but couldn't locate.' He sat back, still unsure whether Galbraith was winding him up.

The DCI drummed his pencil on the top of his desk. 'Quite right,' he said at last. 'I'll have the lads in accounting draw up a cheque covering your expenses in full. And I've had a word with HR. Since you were on the job during your little jaunt you won't have to eat the time as a personal holiday. It seems Christmas came early for some, this year.' He smiled and looked over to George. 'I'm sorry about your dad, George, but at least we collared the scum who were responsible.' Ridley nodded his agreement.

'Now get out of here, you two,' he continued. 'You'll find a backlog of cases on your desks. Time you pulled your weight around here for a change!'

McDermott couldn't resist the last word on his way out. 'Nice to be back, sir.'

HE WAS GLAD TO BE BACK, but as he looked at the pile of telephone messages, emails, and dossiers on his desk McDermott allowed himself to reflect on his time in the Yorkshire countryside. He had to admit he was not a country lad. He'd ceased to define himself by rural pursuits decades earlier, when he'd left Ireland as a boy with his family. The price to be paid for that move, he reflected, was having to deal with a constant stream of urban misadventures: the minor ones like petty theft and pub brawls could be delegated to junior officers, but that still left domestic disputes which resulted in violence and sometimes death, the drug scene, with its depressingly tragic consequences that extended far beyond single users to engulf entire families and even total strangers, and the more challenging cases of organized crime, which were constantly morphing to involve complex technology and extend across national borders.

McDermott looked over to Ridley, who was facing a similar mountain of backed-up cases, trying to sort out those that had moved on from those that had stalled, and prioritising the latter. It was nearly lunchtime, and McDermott was looking forward to it. He'd arranged for Anna and Megan to join him at a favourite restaurant nearby. His time in the North had reminded him, if it had been necessary, that his family was the centre of his universe, and made it possible for him to cope with the litany of misery that often made up his job.

He was about to reach for his jacket when an email came through. Capitano Russo confirmed that an itemized list of recovered artworks had been received from the Wakefield Constabulary, and the objects in question were being prepared for shipment back to Italy, along with a certified bank draft for £550,000. He thanked McDermott profusely for his help and assured him that when he next visited Calabria he would be warmly received. Russo's gratitude went some distance toward assuaging McDermott's funk about the current backlog of cases on his desk.

He was at the door when another email came in. He checked the time: still fifteen minutes for what was a ten-minute walk.

The email was from Gareth Matthews, and contained an attachment. He read it over quickly, then clicked on the document. It was a recent article from a regional weekly newspaper in Wakefield, the sort that deals mostly in local and social news rather than world events. There was a photograph, clearly taken some decades earlier, of Brigadier Reginald Baker-Simms in full dress uniform. McDermott read the article carefully:

DISTINGUISHED WAR HERO DIES

The list of living British veterans who fought bravely in the Second World War is shorter by one today, as the WEST YORKSHIRE COURIER has learned that Brigadier General Reginald Baker-Simms, formerly Regimental Commanding Officer of the King George's Yorkshire Light Infantry, has died suddenly at his home near Wakefield. His death came on the heels of a recent announcement that the family brewery was being sold to an unnamed rival firm based in Japan. The Managing Director, Mr Gordon Baker-Simms, hailed the move as a way to achieve a much-needed cash infusion whilst opening up new markets in Asia at the same time. He gave assurances that the present workforce would be retained. Reginald Baker-Simms followed both his father and grandfather in commanding the regiment, rising from Lieutenant at the outbreak of hostilities in WW II to Lieutenant Colonel of the regiment on the retirement of his father from that position in 1964. During his time with the regiment Baker-Simms served with

> distinction in North Africa, Sicily, Italy, and following the Normandy Invasions, in France and Germany. He returned home following the war to lead the rebuilding of the family brewery, known for its fine line of regional ales. He also played an active role in local politics, serving for several years as Chairman of the West Yorkshire County Council until its dissolution in 1974. The Brigadier is survived by his son Gordon and daughter-in-law Fiona, and his grandson Julian. A remembrance ceremony will take place at Regimental Headquarters later this week.

Died suddenly. It covered a multitude of possibilities. Stroke. Heart attack. An accident. Suicide. Even murder. But McDermott didn't think that was the situation here. Did it really matter? To the family, of course, the answer was yes. But from a larger perspective it meant that any further inquiries into the events that had taken place in Italy all those years ago would now be closed.

McDermott read the article for a second time, then printed it out and put it in the folder dealing with the events in Wakefield. He thought a moment, and forwarded a copy to the CPS lawyer who'd been present during the meeting with the Baker-Simms. He likely had the news already, but it didn't hurt to be thorough. He looked over to Ridley's desk and saw that his friend had left for lunch. He'd fill George and Galbraith in when he returned. Then he left to meet Anna and Megan.

THEIR LUNCH TOGETHER HAD BEEN TIME WELL SPENT. Anna was pleased that Colin had managed to carve some time out of the middle of his day for them, and Megan was clearly delighted to have her father back after so many weeks' absence. He promised her that he wouldn't be going away again anytime soon. After a leisurely meal they made their way along the Embankment, Megan peering over the railing at the boats going up and down the river. By the time he'd seen them off McDermott was a contented man. He took satisfaction from the fact that his university training in art history had stood him in good stead, and his mind went back to Franz Decker, and their meeting at Interpol weeks earlier. He, too, would be pleased. After seeing them off McDermott turned toward the Charing Cross Police Station, his thoughts focussed on his wife and daughter. He had no way of knowing that in a few brief months their lives, and his, would be shattered forever.

Acknowledgments

If it takes a village to raise a child, it must require nearly as many to see a book through from first unformed idea to final completion. My thanks to the many people who, directly or indirectly, have helped *Ridley's War* to see the light of day, including Roya Abouzia, Bob Barclay, Gail Bowen, Jillian Dore, Martin Edwards, Andrew Fletcher, DS Claire Hutchinson of the Metropolitan Police's Art & Antiques Unit, Maureen Jennings, Dr Stuart McKelvie, Michael Murphy, Bruce Redwine, Michael J. Rose, formerly of INTERPOL, Mike Ripley, Ian Thomas Shaw, Ann Shortell, James Wilson, Melissa Yuan-Innes, and the dedicated team at Friesen Press. I also want to give a shout-out to those bookshops, independent and otherwise, which have helped spread the word, either by hosting author events or stocking my earlier novel, *Legacy*, and introducing my work to new readers. A partial list includes The Black Cat Bookstore, Books on Beechwood, Brome Lake Books, Chapters Indigo branches in Ottawa, Montreal, and Pointe Claire, Librarie Clio in Pointe-Claire, Perfect Books, The Townshipper's Association, and public libraries in Coté St-Luc, Cowansville, Knowlton, Lennoxville, Montreal, and Ottawa. (One nice lady bought two copies of *Legacy*: one for her book club and one to donate to a public library in the Caribbean, where she's a volunteer. It's great to have such thoughtful readers!)

Sources

Unless they are flights of the purest fantasy, all works of fiction inevitably include matters of fact. But novelists who build their stories around actual and historical events must tread carefully, lest they blur distinctions of interest to their readers. The turbulence and tragedy of World War II provided the necessary backdrop for the plot of this book. That said, excluding well-known military engagements, the dramatic events depicted here are entirely of my own making. There is not (nor ever was) a regiment known as King George's Yorkshire Light Infantry; indeed, since 2007 traditionally country-based regiments have been largely consolidated into larger and more anonymous units.

The same can be said of the characters in *Ridley's War*. All of them, not least those responsible for the criminous actions described in these pages, are figments of the author's imagination. It follows that no events described in these pages can or should be attributed to any actual person, living or dead.

Those familiar with the war in the Mediterranean may find that the lyrics of the song "D-Day Dodgers" differ from the versions they know. The original version is attributed to Lance-Sergeant Harry Pynn of the 78th Infantry Division, who wrote it in 1944; there are many variations, differing in part in their use of profanity, especially when it comes to the remarks of (the American-born) Lady Astor, who criticized the troops for not taking part in the Normandy invasions. I have chosen lyrics that I believe convey the attitude of the fighting men, and have shortened it for creative purposes. More complete versions can be found on *YouTube/D-Day Dodgers.*

Finally, despite the many literary liberties I have taken, I have also endeavoured to remain faithful to the facts in describing the events of the war, especially as it pertains to actions that occurred in the Mediterranean theatre during 1942 and '43. To that end I have relied heavily on the works of others. I would like both to acknowledge their efforts and thank them for the many insights and historical details that they provided, and which figure prominently in my narrative. Of the more than fifty books and countless other sources I consulted during my research, the following were especially helpful:

Books

Adams, Lauri Schneider, *Italian Renaissance Art,* Boulder, CO: Westview Press/Perseus Books, 2001

Aldrich, Richard J., *Witness to War: Diaries of the Second World War in Europe and the Middle East,* London: Corgi Books, 2005

Atkinson, Rick, *The Day of Battle: the War in Sicily and Italy, 1943-44,*
vol. 2, New York: Henry Holt and Co., 2007

Brayley, Martin J., *The British Army 1939-45 (2): Middle East & Mediterranean,* Oxford, Osprey Publishing, 2002

Campbell, Caroline, *Love and Marriage in Renaissance Florence: The Courtauld Wedding Chests,* London: The Courtauld Gallery, 2009

Dear, I. C. B., and M. R. D. Foot, editors, *The Oxford Companion to World War II,* Oxford: Oxford University Press, 2005

Edsel, Robert M., and B. Witter, *The Monuments Men: Allied Heroes, Nazi Thieves, and the Greatest Treasure Hunt in History,* Nashville, TN: Center Street, 2010

Follain, John, *Mussolini's Island: the Battle for Sicily 1943 by the People Who Were There,* London: Hodder & Stoughton, 2005

Ford, Ken, *Battleaxe Division: From Africa to Italy with the 78th Division 1942-45,* Phoenix Mill, UK: 2003

Genelin, Michael, *Requiem for a Gypsy,* New York: Soho Press, 2011

Graham, Dominick, and S. Bidwell, *Tug of War: The Battle for Italy 1943-45,* Barnsely: Pen & Sword Books, 2004

Holland, James, *Italy's Sorrow: A Year of War, 1944-1945,* New York: St. Martin's Press, 2008

Houpt, Simon, *Museum of the Missing: the High Stakes of Art Crime,* Toronto: Key Porter Books, 2006

Hunt, J. L., and A. G. Pringle, *Service Slang,* London: Faber and Faber, 2008

Ireland, Bernard, *The War in the Mediterranean,* Barnsley: Pen & Sword Books, 2004

Jurado, Carlos Caballero, *Resistance Warfare, 1940-45,* Oxford: Osprey Publishing, 1985

Lewin, Ronald, *Rommel as Military Commander,* New York: Barnes & Noble, 1998

Mitcham, Samuel W., Jr., and F. von Stauffenberg, *The Battle of Sicily,* Mechanicsburg, PA: Stackpole Books, 2007

Nicholas, Lynn H., *The Rape of Europa: the Fate of Europe's Treasures in the Third Reich and the Second World War,* New York: Vintage Reprint, 1995

Severgnini, Beppe, *La Bella Figura: A field Guide to the Italian Mind,* New York: Broadway Books, 2006

Strawson, John, *The Italian Campaign,* New York: Carroll & Graf Publishers, 1988

Swift, Michael, and M. Sharpe, *Historical Maps of World War II: Europe,* London: PRC Publishing, 2000

Walsh, Mikey, *Gypsy Boy,* London: Hodder & Stoughton, 2009

Williams, Patrick, *Gypsy World: The Silence of the Living and the Voices of the Dead,* Chicago: University of Chicago Press, 2003

Willmott, H. P., and Charles Messenger and Robin Cross, *World War II,* New York: DK Books, 2004

Websites

British Army Officer Ranks and Command Duties
https://en.wikipedia.org/wiki/
British_Army_officer_rank_insignia

British Light Infantry Regiments, Yorkshire
http://www.lightinfantry.org.uk/regiments/koyli/kingyork_
index.htm

Calculating time and distance between Liverpool, UK, and Alexandria, Egypt by sea
http://ports.com/sea-route/#/?a=0&b=3687&c=Port%20of%20
Liverpool%20&d=Port%20of%20Alexandria,%20Egypt

Commanding Officers, British Light Infantry Regiments, Yorkshire
http://www.lightinfantry.org.uk/regiments/koyli/kingyork_colo-
nels.htm

D-Day Dodgers
https://en.wikipedia.org/wiki/D-Day_Dodgers

German Air Force, 1918-1945
https://www.feldgrau.com/WW2-German-Luftwaffe-Airforce

Interpol site for stolen works of art
https://www.interpol.int/Crime-areas/Works-of-art/Works-of-art

Italian Nobility during the Renaissance
www.italian-family-history.com.html

Italian Titles of Nobility
http://www.regalis.com/nobletitles.htm

Italians in World War II
https://www.lifeinitaly.com/history/ww2.asp

Regiments, British Army
https://en.wikipedia.org/wiki/regiment/British Army

The Art Loss Register
http://www.artloss.com/en

The British Home Office
https://www.gov.uk/government/organisations/home-office

The Imperial War Museum
https://www.iwm.org.uk

The Italian Carabinieri
http://www.carabinieri.it/Internet/

The Metropolitan Police Service, UK
https://www.met.police.uk

The Monuments Men
https://britisharmy.wordpress.com/2016/10/21/monuments-men-part-one/

The Monuments Men
http://www.historynet.com/?s=Monuments+Men

The UK Ministry of Defense
https://www.gov.uk/government/organisations/ministry-of-defence

Don't miss the third novel in the Colin McDermott Mystery Series

Family Matters

While Colin McDermott struggles to rebuild his life after a staggering personal loss, he encounters a man bent on personal revenge. Meanwhile, changes at the Met poses challenges for George Ridley, and Wilhemina Quinn struggles to mentor a headstrong new member of the team.

ABOUT THE AUTHOR

An **unapologetic Anglophile, Jim Napier** has spent considerable time in the UK, dating from 1987. After a successful academic career that included teaching crime fiction and creative writing, he turned to writing full time. Since then he has published over six hundred reviews, interviews and articles about crime writers, both in print and on multiple internet sites, and has participated in writing workshops and served on crime-writing panels in Britain and Canada, including Montreal's Bleu Metropolis, the Knowlton Literary Festival, and the former Canadian crime writing festival, Bloody Words. He twice served on juries for the Arthur Ellis Awards for Canadian Crime Writing, and in 2009 he chaired the awards. Along with such notable authors as Louise Penny, Peter James, Sophie Hannah, Simon Brett, Marcia Talley and Rhys Bowen, he contributed to an anthology on the craft of crime writing titled *Now Write! Mysteries* published by Tarcher/Penguin. Beginning in 2012 he was commissioned to write biographies for several Canadian crime writers for the Canadian Encyclopedia, and also joined Louise Penny in co-chairing a fiction-writing workshop at the Knowlton LitFest. *Legacy*, the first novel in the Colin McDermott Mysteries series, was published in 2017; *Ridley's War* is the second novel in the series. The third is underway and is slated for release in 2022.

Ridley's War is published by Friesen Press and distributed by Ingram, and is available at over 50,000 booksellers worldwide, including the Friesen Press Bookstore, Amazon, Barnes & Noble, and Chapters Indigo. E-books are distributed through the Apple iBookstore, Amazon Kindle store, Google Play Bookstore, Nook Store and the Kobo store.

If you enjoyed this book please consider posting a review on Amazon.com and/or Goodreads. It needn't be long or detailed, simply your honest reaction. It's quite easy to do – and thank you for your time!

Further:

For more on the Colin McDermott series, or to contact the author, go to https://www.jimnapiermysteries.com

For the author's reviews of other crime fiction novels, interviews with leading crime writers, and more, see his review site: https://DeadlyDiversions.com

CPSIA information can be obtained
at www.ICGtesting.com
Printed in the USA
BVHW070410160222
629080BV00004B/773